I0564597

THREE AND A HALF WEEKS

LULU ASTOR

I, Sisyphus Publications

FIRST EDITION
Designed by Indianboy Art

ISBN 13: 978-0692204672
10: 0692204679

This book would not have been remotely possible without all of my faithful online followers of *One Shady Character*. Over seven hundred of you were there for every chapter and we had well over 300,000 visits to the story site. Thanks to your enthusiastic support, sharp insight, pep talks, and loyalty, a silly spoof on a popular novel became a book all its own. A thousand cyber hugs to y'all.

I also have to give a nod to the authors who inspired me while writing this work. First, and obviously, E.L. James. I'd like to think I inspired her, too. For the wicked pulley idea, thanks to Cherise Sinclair and her book, *My Liege of Dark Haven*. I had C.J. Roberts' *Captive in the Dark* on my brain when deciding Natasha's fate. Finally, my new best friends, the irresistible (and fantastic author) Nicole Reed, and the fabulous Ena Burnette she introduced me to, who helped launch this book into the blogosphere.

Other titles by Lulu Astor:

Complements, Book I

Complements, Book II: A Force of Nature

Complements, Backstory: Between Us

Prologue

His instructions begin in the hotel room.

"Do you have a garter belt?"

"No. But I do have silk stockings that stay up without a garter. Do you want me to wear those?"

He nods. "And your black stilettos, please."

It's not until we get in the taxi that he makes his next request. Once he gives the driver an address, he leans in to whisper in my ear. "Take off your panties."

I look at him as if he's lost his mind. "What?"

His face is unyielding. "You heard me. Do it."

"In here?" I screech, thinking about all the people and... *stuff*... that's been on these car seats. "It's not hygienic."

He shakes his head, a gesture he uses when he is dismissive of my concerns.

I am sitting in a taxi in New York City with Ian Blackmon. *The* Ian Blackmon of Wall Street and the *WSJ*, *Forbes,* and *People* magazine renown. That list actually goes on *ad infinitum*. Before our chance encounter, I'd never heard of him. Now I see his name and likeness everywhere I look. Before Ian, I'd never even dreamed of meeting a man like him. Now I share intimate moments with him and revel in his possession. Before, I'd never been tied up, dominated, and ravished.

Now I am... *frequently*.

My name is Ella Strong. Welcome to my brand-new world.

Chapter 1

The whole thing was meant to be a joke.

I wrote the book as a Christmas gift for my closest friends: it was way too dirty to send to anyone else. My best buds believed it to be pure fiction (and why wouldn't they?) and that was exactly how I planned it. How many of them would believe that the kinky man in my book was someone I had actually met, the man who took my virginity, who made me an indecent proposition, who wouldn't get out of my head no matter how hard I tried to kick him to the curb?

I had met Ian Blackmon, gorgeous CEO-extraordinaire, by pure and accidental chance. At the time, I was in my last year of college, and my friend Mariah had helped me snag an excellent part-time job in an upscale boutique. Trying to get me ready for the job interview—me, the girl who shops at Target (pronouncing it Tar-zhay to give it panache)—was a comedy of errors in and of itself.

"Okay," Mariah said, holding up a pair of platform patent-leather high heels, "what designer?"

"Jimmy Chow?"

"Choo. Jimmy Choo—Jimmy Chow's is a restaurant—and, *no*. They're Louboutins! For God's sake, Ella, pay attention. What about these?" She held up a pair of low, very pointy slingbacks.

"I know this," I yelled, snapping my fingers. "Those are Manolo Blahniks!"

"Right! There's hope for you yet. Okay, let's move on. What about this skirt?"

And it went on all evening long, with one break for

yummy thin-crust pizza. By the end of the night, I had my upscale designers down pat. Then it was time to score some pricey clothes on eBay. For the interview itself, Mariah lent me her red Stella McCartney suit and I somehow managed to dupe the owner and snare the job. Woohoo.

It was on a Friday night, just before closing, when he walked in, commanding the small shop without even trying. I was at the register, collating the cash receipts and filling out my timesheet, when the door tinkled open and in strode the most beautiful man I'd ever seen. I had never heard of Ian Blackmon, new to Portland as I was, so when he handed over his credit card to pay for the pricey necklace he hastily selected, I had no idea who he was. Didn't matter anyway.

He'd come in with purpose, as if on a strict time schedule.

"Good evening, I'm shopping for a gift. Jewelry, perhaps."

My knees were shaking so much they were bruising one another. I cobbled together as much courage as I could. "Please step this way," I managed, leading him to the corner glass display where we kept our mostly costume jewelry. He peered carefully at the selection and quickly zeroed in on one he favored.

He never asked the price on anything but then, so many of our customers don't. Asking the price of items is *gauche* when you have money to fritter away. The cost of this particular necklace was astonishingly stratospheric at three thousand dollars for costume jewelry, but it was a designer piece.

"May I see those two as well, please?" He gazed at me when he addressed me and I couldn't help but be affected by his overall beauty and focus.

Working in the pricey shop for the past two months, I'd managed to acquire some small amount of grace while in the company of affluent, important people... so why my knees were knocking together just because I was standing in front of this man was an enduring mystery.

One would think that I'd never set eyes on a perfect human being before.

He was wearing an espresso-brown suit, elegantly tailored and so dark it was almost black, brown wingtips, crisp white shirt, and a silver tie. Mmm, edible was the first word that sprang to an inquiring mind.

"Yes, of course." I carefully removed each piece from its display, willing my fingers not to visibly tremble, and set them, side by side, on a black velvet tray. One was sterling set with onyx and the other two had amethyst stones. All three were very pretty and very expensive.

"Hmm. Which one do *you* like?" he asked me, looking up from the jewelry to my face. Wow, his eyes were light and beautiful, fringed as they were by his lush, dark lashes. Would he think me rude if I gripped him by the ears, dragged his face to mine, and made out with him over the counter? Shaking my head to dispel the image, I tried to answer his question intelligently, all the while staring at his lips.

"All three are quite stunning," I said, wondering if he could hear my pounding heartbeat. "What color does your wife favor?"

"It's for my sister and she wears a lot of bright colors, pinks and purples, in the main; I guess the amethyst then?"

"Probably a sure bet if purple's a favorite color."

"Yes, I think this one," he pointed to the nicer of the two. "Please giftwrap it; I'm running late and I almost forgot her birthday," he said as he handed me his credit card.

"Of course," I said, keeping my voice neutral when my body was imploding inward like a controlled demolition. I rang up the sale and he signed the slip quickly. I watched him closely: this guy was too damned gorgeous and he was near enough to me that I could smell him—his cologne or aftershave or whatever, and it was, like, sublime. He was tall too, with thick, dark hair that contrasted with those light eyes. But never mind what he had; what he didn't have was a wedding band on his finger. Another woohoo.

Yeah, right. Why would a man who looked like he did and could spend three grand without batting an eye have any interest in a mousy shop girl? I went to the other counter to wrap the box, selecting the store's signature silver and white paper and finishing it with a purple ribbon.

"Sir? Here you are. I hope your sister enjoys the necklace."

He looked at me long and hard. Did I say something wrong?

"Thank you," he said, his voice smooth as silk. "I'm sure my sister will love it. I appreciate your assistance, Miss...?"

My face got hot so I knew I was blushing to my hair follicles. "Ella... well, Ariel, actually. Ariel Strong."

"Very pretty name—*unusual* name. Thank you again, Ms. Strong," he said, smiling for the first time and he sauntered off.

Wow. That smile could effectively compete with the Caribbean sun.

The next day, I asked Mariah if she'd ever heard of him. I'd Googled him and reams of information and images flashed brightly on my computer screen.

"Ian Blackmon? Of course I've heard of him. Haven't you?"

"Uh, no? Or I wouldn't ask you, right?"

"Well, it's true he's Portland royalty and you haven't lived here very long at all. Okay, how would I describe Ian Blackmon?" She tapped her finger on her upper lip. "Combine the mind and personality of Steve Jobs, the looks of, oh, I don't know, the most terrifically gorgeous man in Hollywood, for example, the philanthropy and bank account of Bill Gates, Warren Buffett, hell, even Angelina Jolie—and you've got Ian Blackmon."

I naturally assumed Mariah was grossly exaggerating about him, as she was wont to do. "Really? Well, I met him last night at the shop. I can attest to the gorgeous and rich part. I felt like a giggly schoolgirl crushing on her teacher or something."

"I'll bet. Well, he's a notorious bachelor who's never seen with the same woman twice. God, I hope he's not gay—that would be so unjust. The gays have more than their fair share of good lookers playing on their team, don't you think?"

"Hmmm," I replied, my mind back in the company of the man in a dark brown suit. I hoped he'd come back into the shop sometime soon.

Or did I?

I wrote the book because it was fun; I wrote the book to exorcise him from my system; I wrote the book because I had no extra money for Christmas gifts for my friends. I didn't consider it a violation of the legal contract he had me sign, first, because the book was presented as fiction with no real names used, and second, the book was supposed to be read only by my friends, with no wider circulation than that one small circle of women.

What ended up happening was something I could never in a million years have predicted nor anticipated. I mean, come on: how could he hold that against me? But he very much was holding it against me and though I doubted he'd really drag me through court over it, he was planning on making me pay, one way or another.

He was the man who took my virginity. From the first moment I saw him in the shop—Archipelago—I wanted him.

Badly.

Still, I didn't believe I'd have a ghost of a chance. The man was perfection in every way: looks, grooming, voice, and wallet. I was vastly inferior with my untamed hair, my designer knock-offs (for the most part), and my pathetic bank account. He had it all over me—just call me Cinderella.

Something about me must have appealed to him, though, because before too long, I found myself in his mansion on the mountain, hoping he'd try to seduce me.

To say it didn't go as swimmingly as it did in my feverish imagination would be vastly understating the situation.

I guess the fact that he had me sign a confidentiality agreement the day he summoned me to his office should have clued me in to the fact that he had something to hide. But I was too much in awe over him to notice any imperfection—the man could have had human taxidermy propped up on his desk and I might have overlooked it. It's not everyday that one meets a man like Ian Blackmon.

Besides, he also had me sign a liability disclaimer. I just figured these kinds of waivers or contracts were standard issue for someone of his position and wealth. You know, no biggie.

In addition to being gaga over him, I remember being somewhat terrified by him that day in his office. He's an important man for a reason: he oozes competence, grace, and confidence. It's ridiculously intimidating to us mortals.

Truthfully, I was feeling intimidated before I even stepped foot into his office. The platinum-frosted blonde who manned the reception desk tried her level best not to stare at me as I sat fidgeting in reception. She clearly couldn't figure out why someone who looked and dressed like me would have business here in Blackmon's universe.

"Miss?"

I sidled up and stepped nearer to the desk. "Yes?"

"May I offer you a beverage? Coffee, tea, or perhaps iced water?"

"No, thank you," I answered, feeling at a disadvantage, a fish out of water.

The woman's eyes skidded over my outfit and frowned, barely hiding her disdain.

For my part, I didn't much care about Frosty's attitude. I just wanted to do whatever was necessary to take my leave in short order. Uncomfortable was how I felt in the manufactured air of Excalibur's luxurious corporate offices. But first I needed to satisfy my curiosity—my mother always warned me that my intense curiosity would prove to be my undoing. When his driver deposited me at the front entrance of the building a few minutes before, I looked up and saw the name Blackmon—*his* name—carved indelibly into the imposing limestone edifice of the tall building. Was the whole gigantic building owned by his father? I decided to ask Frosty.

"Excuse me, does Mr. Blackmon's father own this entire building?"

The blonde stared at me in consternation. "Mr. Blackmon's father?" she repeated like an idiot.

"Yes," I elaborated, unable to resist, "you know, the man whose wife gave birth to Ian Blackmon and who then raised him into adulthood?"

"I'm sorry I don't understand. Mr. Blackmon's father has nothing to do with the corporation."

Though the frosted blonde behaved very politely, her tone was dismissive, putting me in my place. "Are you here to interview for a job?"

"Job?" I repeated, perplexed. "Uh, no. I'm here because Mr. Blackmon summoned me."

Now Frosty looked taken aback. "Oh. Please accept my apology, Ms. Strong. I thought you might be one of the candidates for the open positions for which we're interviewing. I was wondering why you were on this floor, rather than 23 where HR is located.

I didn't much care about the slight. I was too worried about whether my extreme agitation was plainly visible to everyone in this plush corporate bubble. Could they see me perspiring excessively? Was my face shiny with sweat, my eyes bulging in terror like the fish out of water? Or were they all too distracted by my wrinkled clothes and messy hair to take note of anything else?

Just then the massive mahogany doors opened and a tall, wickedly handsome man emerged with two people in tow, an older, silver-haired man and a stern-looking, fiftyish woman. I looked up and everyone else disappeared. There he stood, the man in the brown suit in all of his Armani glory. Today, though, he wore navy, with a pearl gray shirt, and *aubergine* tie. His light eyes swiveled toward me, dazzling me with his peppermint smile—all red and white and delicious.

"Ms. Strong," a silky baritone voice slid through the air and into my ears where it diffused into all the pertinent body parts. "Thank you for agreeing to see me on such short notice. Please come into my office." He turned to Frosty and said, "No calls, please, Janine. You might also have to reschedule my five o'clock. If you don't hear from me by 4:30, cancel... but check with Claudia for conflicts before rescheduling."

Frosty, a.k.a. Janine, nodded deferentially, jumping to puppy-like attention. "Yes, Mr. Blackmon."

Mr. Blackmon seemed annoyed by her slavish obedience, frowning at her before turning his attention to me.

After leaving Frosty sitting there bewildered, he escorted me into his spacious office and told me to take a seat. *Told*, not *asked*. Imperious was an adjective I'd definitely use to describe Mr. Blackmon. I looked around for the most uncomfortable chair to sit on, so I could keep my guard up... but there were none. Every piece of seating furniture looked stupidly comfy, inviting one to sink into the lap of luxury and stare up in awe at the exalted assets of the man inhabiting the office. Fine, I'd take the one closest to the door. All of this rumination transpired in about five seconds.

"I suppose you're wondering why I asked you here, Ms. Strong."

Did he know his voice was like liquid sex? Merely hearing my name spill from his throat did things to me, deep inside. Why *was* I here? I cleared my own throat. "Yes, I am actually at somewhat of a loss..."

His expression was stern. "You do recall our last meeting, I hope?"

"Yes, of course. You came into the shop where I work, looking for a gift for your sister. How'd it work out, by the way?"

"She loved it, thank you. However, Ms. Strong—and I have to be honest—ever since that evening, I've had trouble getting you out of my mind..." he perched on the corner of his desk and crossed his arms, "so I asked you here today to consider a proposition I'd like to put forward."

"Pro...*p-position*?" I stammered, and it sounded like *proper position*, turning my cheeks even redder at the sexual allusion. God, I wanted to kick myself.

He acted as if he didn't notice, continuing smoothly. "Yes. Before I do, however, I must ask you to sign some paperwork, specifically, a confidentiality agreement and a liability waiver. Is that acceptable?"

"A what?"

"A legally binding agreement not to divulge any information you may learn about me, and a disclaimer, waiving rights to litigation should any accidental injuries be sustained on my property. I ask everyone who enters my private realm, either personally or professionally, to sign this type of contract. It's to protect myself to some extent, of course. Do you object?"

"What kind of accidental injuries?"

Smirking wickedly, he answers, "Accidents, Ariel. A trip over something, a fall down the steps. I don't intend to harm you, if that's what you're thinking. People attempt all manner of things to enable a lawsuit against people of wealth. My attorney insists I protect myself to the extent possible. That's all. Do you object to signing?"

"No, I don't, not at all. I was just curious. Yes, I'll sign it."

"Very good." He went around his desk and removed a manila envelope, bringing it over to where I sat. He pulled out a thick wad of paper and handed it to me, along with a pen. "Look through it and sign the last page. You'll also need to initial each and every page in the upper right-hand corner."

I skimmed through it quickly, signing and initialing as requested before handing it back to him. He perused it and then nodded, bringing it back to his desk.

Returning, I saw him surreptitiously adjust his trousers and I wondered if Mr. Blackmon might feel a bit for me as I felt for him. Was it even within the realm of possibility? I was so tempted to open the top two buttons of my shirt to see if it made a difference.

Watching him, I estimated him to be about 6'3" and though muscular, he was on the lean side. His clothes fit him just so well; it's difficult to describe but when you see it, it's poetry in motion. He wore no jewelry apart from a high-tech looking watch, perhaps a TAG Heuer? (Mariah would be so proud I knew that!) I loved everything about Ian Blackmon that I'd so far been exposed to.

Crossing his long legs after he sat down across from me, he took a minute or two to do nothing but gaze at me speculatively while I squirmed beneath his scrutiny.

I remember my mouth was as dry as the Sahara and my legs were trembling like the San Andreas fault or perhaps even the Cascadia subduction zone. Okay, yes, I worry about earthquakes and tsunamis.

First, it was his turn. He told me all about his privately held beliefs about relationships and the laws of attraction... oh, yeah, and about practicing BDSM and some of the things it involved. The whole time I watched the shining animation in his pretty light eyes as he spoke.

BDSM is something I've heard about before, and even read about in juicy parts of Mariah's naughty books. It's something I'd always figured might be darkly exciting but never entertained the idea of trying it myself. I did know, though, that Mariah had a boyfriend last year who liked to tie her up and gag her before they had sex. Gagging Mariah made perfect sense to me... but tying her down? It seemed strange but I'm always willing to try things once. First, though, I'd like to lose my virginity in a more traditional manner.

He made the notion of physical attraction and ensuing romance slash sex sound so clinical. "Don't you believe in love?" I was cheeky enough to ask him.

"Love?" he repeated. "Yes, of course I believe in love... mainly familial love. I love my mother, my father, my siblings... and my dog. Next question?"

Oh, so he was done answering that one? And he'd given me that pat response without even a hint of a smile. My but he was cynical. So in his orderly mind, he kept love and sex as two separate, discrete things. Pity. I wholeheartedly believed in romance and love preceding anything sexual—hence my untried womanly status.

"Do you understand now?" He prodded me, not allowing me to sink into my own reveries. "I'd like to enter into an arrangement with you, Ms. Strong."

I gulped and nodded. Since he'd shared such intimate details of his life, I had to 'fess up about my being a complete sexual neophyte—a virgin, in more simple vernacular. It might have ended there... but it didn't. I think he saw it as a challenge. Or perhaps he saw me as one?

"I'm really not sure I'm up for this kind of thing, Mr. Blackmon."

Now a smirk danced on those luscious red lips as I stared at his face, knowing the moment of truth had arrived. "What gives you pause... specifically?"

I didn't answer right away, mulling over how to proceed.

"I asked you a question, Ariel," his satin voice broke into my self-distraction.

"Oh... um, I, uh, I'm new to all of it. Not to BDSM," I quickly added. "I mean, I *am* new to BDSM, too, brand new, in fact... but I'm also new to sex." I became a blithering idiot.

"You're new..." His words dropped off and the look of first confusion and then astonishment that descended over his face was priceless and nearly comical. "How new?"

Cheeks flaming, I nonetheless grinned, trying to keep the moment light. "Very?"

He was incredulous. "To clarify: are you actually

telling me you're a virgin?"

I nodded. "I think so."

Poker face. He tapped his lips in thought, keeping his cards close to the vest. Seriously close: I couldn't read his expression. He began to speak again after a minute or so. "At twenty-one, nearly twenty-two..." a look of horror hijacked his face and his voice dropped in volume, "...you are twenty-one or so, right?"

"Oh, yes. I'm nearly twenty-two."

Relief eased his tense features. "And you're still a virgin?"

"Is it a problem?"

"No, no problem, but..."

And now I saw the fire in his eyes.

"...you didn't see fit to mention it *before* I invited you to join me in my chamber of sin?"

"You didn't see fit to tell me your real name is Dorian," I countered, trying to make him smile. His birth name was on the contract I'd signed. Right now, though, he didn't have names on his mind—or humor. His light eyes pierced through any armor I might have worn and I couldn't identify what was going on in his head.

He was genuinely freaking me out. Was this really all about sex or was there more to it? I felt drops of perspiration sliding down the back of my neck. I'd be willing to bet folding money that Frosty didn't sweat buckets like I was doing right now and certainly Ian didn't either. Clearly I was out of my element. "'Mr. Blackmon," I said, my hands reaching for my hair and, twisting it up, secured it with a pencil I'd filched from the low table between us, "I think it's time I took my leave. It's been an... *interesting*... afternoon." I stood up.

"Women?"

"What?" I frowned in confusion.

"Do you prefer women?"

"Oh... no."

His eerie eyes held me captive—they looked as if they were backlit from inside his skull. They were trained on me as if I were an exotic specimen of something, or maybe even that fish out of water, with the bulging eyes. Without responding to my intended farewell, he stood up lightning fast, strode over to me, and grasped my shoulders, peering into my eyes and possibly my soul. "Beautiful Ariel, was there no one who ever made you hot and bothered enough to pull up your dress?"

There was *now*, I wanted to tell him. Was it the insanely personal topic of conversation between strangers or his close proximity that was like a heady drug? I felt myself swoon a bit. "No. I'm always more annoyed than hot and bothered." I gasped the words out since I had very recently run out of breath. He was so close I could hardly draw in oxygen.

His eyelids dropped to half-mast. "Perhaps you'll allow me to introduce you to the pleasures of the flesh, then?"

"Perhaps," my word huffed out on a current of hoarded breath.

"Tonight?"

I could see the glint of excitement in his eyes at the prospect. It made me excited, too. "Tonight," I agreed and immediately began to question my sanity.

Our so-called date that evening had begun with a very romantic ride in his catamaran at dusk. I watched him at the helm, the briny breeze blowing through his dark hair while his eyes remained focused on the horizon ahead and the task at hand. While I gaped at his perfect profile, his lips curved into a small smile as he rode the waves. I suspected he liked the thrill of speed and wondered if he was an adrenaline junkie in disguise as a suit.

After, we drove to his house in his very fast, very sleek sports car.

"Ella, allow me to show you around," he said, and while taking my jacket his fingers grazed skin and whoosh. It felt as if an electric spark snapped and crackled up my arm.

As I walked around the palatial estate, gaping at and running my fingertips over surfaces and fabrics, my attention was diverted from Mr. Blackmon for a few moments. Turning around suddenly to ask him a question, I caught him staring intently at me. He was leaning against a wall on one hip, showing off those long, luscious legs, and he had his middle finger through his heavy sterling key ring. He was rhythmically swinging his hand, so the keys would spin around his finger. For some weird reason, I couldn't tear my eyes away from that masculine yet elegant hand and its perfect, sinuous rhythm... until he laughed, a deep-throated, sexy chuckle that liquefied my insides. It broke the spell.

"Do you approve?"

Do I approve of what? "Of?" I squeaked.

"My home, of course."

Glancing around at the cavernous room, I nodded slightly. "It's amazing." And, naturally, it was. Gleaming mahogany-colored hardwood flooring stretched across the expanse of the great room, whose walls were in very masculine tones of pearl gray, taupe, and chocolate. Beautiful pieces of sculpture dotted the room, as well as a few impressively large-scaled paintings. Expensive Persian rugs were spaced precisely on the floors, and the sofas and chairs had clean lines and simple but luxuriant fabrics.

Finishing my tour of the place, he happily (and even proudly!) boasted that it sat on land that originally hosted an insane asylum. The asylum was later converted into condominiums and houses were built around it to form the gated community, in which he bought the largest one with the highest elevation of the whole campus. Naturally.

I looked out the conservatory window and marveled at what lay before me. The view alone was worth millions and I wondered why an insane asylum was ever sited at such a place. The palatial house sat high in the sky overlooking Portland, like a snow globe hovering in the clouds, looking down in judgment on the city skyline.

Well into my second glass of vino, I was already significantly tipsy—but it was all good, since he'd very recently trampled on my fantasy with aplomb, a feat akin to delicate daisies being crushed under the biggest steel-toe boots possible. This, what I considered to be our second date (my visit to his office sort of being the debut), but actually our first, was when he gamely introduced me to his medieval torture chamber that he charmingly called his *dungeon*.

Pushing himself off the wall, he strode over to where I was standing. "Come, Ella, let's have a drink in the library."

I took his hand and he led me down a long hall to double doors. Just beyond those doors was his library.

"Oh my God, this room is beautiful," I exclaimed, for it took my breath away. Rich mahogany wainscoting lined the walls from floor to ceiling. A Mission-style mantel framed a stone hearth, currently hosting a cozy fire. On the two far walls, there were books lining shelves from floor to ceiling and a sliding ladder attached to handily reach the books on the upper reaches. The furniture, rugs, desk—everything was meticulously perfect.

"Sit," he ordered me and I complied. It did strike me as odd how he didn't ask but rather told, but I instinctively kept kowtowing to his superior rank.

"Would you like a drink?"

"Um, sure, if you're having one."

He nodded and walked over to a cabinet. When he opened it I could see there were numerous bottles of wine, stemware, and probably every bar *accouterment* available at Williams-Sonoma.

"So, Ariel Strong, since this afternoon, you've learned much more about me. I think I've given you fair warning. Even so, you're here with me tonight. Might I consider it your capitulation?"

"Capitulation?" There goes my cat-in-heat voice

again.

He smirked. "Are you not fond of the word? Perhaps you would prefer acceptance?"

I gulped my wine. Things weren't going as I'd envisioned in my fevered imagination. In my original version of the play script, this is when he'd begin to seduce me and we'd end up in bed, having the most incredible, mindbending sex ever. He'd peer into my eyes longingly and swear he'd never met anyone like me before. Afterward, I'd officially be dating the most eligible bachelor, possibly on planet Earth. Alas, I had to make major revisions in the plotline. Instead, we once again dissected our potential relationship in terms too clinical to suit me—me or any other woman in the world.

"Acceptance? Of your terms?"

I couldn't read the look in his eyes but I knew there was some volatile emotion swirling about in the depths of those silvery blue orbs. He strode forcefully to the large mahogany desk and removed some papers from a locked drawer.

"Here," he said, handing them to me and sitting back down. "These will afford you a deeper understanding and then I'll show you my little dungeon."

"Your what?" The words were out of my mouth before I could do any neural filtering. Dungeon? Had I landed in some kind of twisted fairy tale?

"Relax," he drawled, "it's just a word. I'm aware of your innocence and I'm not trying to frighten you, Ariel."

Could have fooled me. He'd drawn up paperwork with forms attesting to health, hygiene, and the multitude of sexual acts that might be involved. Some of the options were utterly horrifying. Fisting?

I looked down at my hand, envisioning a fist and what one might do with it. Shit. Was it truly the way it sounded?

The terminology creeped me out, too. I know sexual slang is crude but somehow it seems more honest and less creepy. The technical terms seem to me as if one is cloaking a base act in a civilized robe... but it remains base: blowjob is honestly descriptive; fellatio is just creepy, even if its literal meaning, *to suck*, is more direct. I won't even mention the female equivalent.

I looked up briefly to see Ian smiling in a smug fashion as he watched me reading the various papers. The thought occurred to me that he'd been here already, probably many times over, and suddenly I had to know.

"How many women have you done this with before?"

He leaned forward, elbows on knees, eyes inscrutable. "Too many to count. Next question?"

I hated that answer. "Any men?"

"No."

"Do you find partners wherever you can?"

"Not generally, no. Usually in one place."

To my questioning look, he responded. "A club where likeminded people gather."

"Not high-priced boutiques then?"

Broadly smiling now, he shook his head. "Never before."

"Then... why this time?" I was truly puzzled as to why he'd proposition me. Do I send out some subliminal message that I want to be beaten and dominated?" If so, I needed to know.

"I can't answer that question, Ariel."

"Why not?"

"Primarily because I'm uncertain as to the answer. Any other questions?"

Oh. Or was it an *aha* moment? He didn't know. I wasn't sure if I should take that as a victory of some sort... or be insulted. Rubbing my lips together in nervousness, I put it aside for the moment.

I looked at the paperwork again and began to wonder about all those women who'd sat here before me. The world was a strange, frightening place if one chanced to look into dark corners.

"Why are you like this? Is it to keep yourself at an emotional remove?" I finally got up the gumption to ask.

He reared back, as if I'd slapped him. Then he closed

24

his eyes briefly and when he opened them, his face was impassive again. "Once burned, twice shy."

"Who burned you?" I whispered the question, afraid to ask it, and afraid he'd answer it.

"A girl."

"A girl?"

"A girl... I loved... or thought I did anyway."

Aha. "So this type of sexual relationship is your way of keeping emotionally detached?"

"In a manner of speaking."

"A manner of speaking, i.e. you don't want to fall in love again?"

"I'm not even sure I ever was in love to begin with... but to answer your question, no, Ariel, I do not."

Later that night, he made up for all of the weirdness by being sort of romantic—definitely seductive. If nothing else, Ian was not letting me escape his clutches until I'd at the very least surrendered my chastity. He must have seen it as a conquest—and he was all about conquests. So I finally lost my charter membership in the virgin forever club. If not for the conversations that preceded it in his office earlier that day and then just an hour before in his library, I would have felt my fantasy fulfilled. He was gentle, sweet, and achingly sexy. I was thrilled to have Ian as my first.

I spent the night and the next day with him. The following evening he drove me home himself, kissed me chastely on the cheek, and wished me goodnight. That night, instead of sleeping, my mind endlessly rehashed all of the requirements of the position that Ian was offering me: no emotional intimacy, slavish obedience of his rules, no looking at him without permission, kneeling at his feet during scenes, no public relationship, and strict adherence to monogamy—I wasn't even allowed to cheat on him with myself, if you get what I mean. I'd belong to him... but he wouldn't belong to me.

I tried picturing myself in the role. I couldn't. How could I be around this handsome, thrilling man and have no rights of claim to him? He wasn't looking for a girlfriend, didn't *want* one. He was seeking a sexual partner, the latest one in a long line of them. I wanted a lover, a confidant—if I got lucky, maybe even a soulmate.

I was forced to make a painful decision. Even though I barely knew him, it was truly difficult to make and it hurt my heart, knowing I was shutting the door to ever seeing that glorious man again: his endearing grin, his beguiling eyes, the way his ass looked so bitable in well-fitting suit trousers.

The next day handmade chocolates arrived in a sterling silver box with an invitation to again join him for dinner.

Instead of accepting, I forced myself to send him a text message, begging off. Even if he weren't so mesmerizing, it would be dangerous. I have a bad habit of being able to be talked into just about anything by just about anyone. I always expected to one day find myself on the six o'clock news as the stupid friend who leaped off a bridge, sat on a train track, bungee jumped into a cliff, or whatever, because her friends told her to do it. I could just see myself, in traction in the hospital, both eyes black and blue, the television news camera right in my purple, pulpy face, whining, "My friends told me it would be fun!"

I knew I needed to walk away from Ian Blackmon. He didn't want what I wanted and he never would. I wanted a mate, someone with whom to grow intimate, share secrets, and enjoy simple things together, like good music or wine or a fat, cuddly puppy. Someone with whom to laugh and cry, have important discussions about current events, curl up and spoon in the cold, dark night. A boyfriend to introduce to my friends and family, to be seen out in public with, and to have the right to drape my arm around his waist whenever the urge took me.

He wanted a sex slave, an unequal partner to submit to him in every way possible, a woman who wanted nothing more out of her life than to please him.

I wouldn't mind pleasing him; in fact, I would damn well love to make him happy, in every way possible. I'd gladly give myself to him, body and soul. But I wanted him to offer me the same. And therein lies the rub.

Ian Blackmon was dangerous—to me, my tender heart, my mental wellbeing, especially. I'd known him for ten minutes and I already felt attached to him. What would happen to me in a month? A year? He could destroy me, break me into a million little pieces, kill me with a thousand cuts.

Saying goodbye by text was shitty, I concede, but I knew I wouldn't be able to do it in person. Simply stated, staring into those penetrating eyes of his would preclude me from saying no to anything he suggested and, really, that wasn't good for my health.

The message itself was short and simple:

Ian,
Thanks for a great time. I enjoyed getting to know you further (much further actually) and the tour of your lovely home as well as the exhilarating evening sail. I enjoyed other aspects of our time together, too.

I don't think we'll be seeing one another again but I do want you to know that I very much appreciated all the attention you showed me. I'd wish you good luck in your life but it seems you already have plenty of it. I don't know what else to say.
Ella

I cried when I wrote it, knowing I was doing something irrevocable when I hit *send.* When would I ever meet another powerful, enigmatic man like Ian? Probably never. I drew my knees up to my chest, hugging them to me in a sorry facsimile of affection, and waited for his response.

When he didn't reply to my text, I thought a.) he wasn't near his phone and he'd see it later, or b.) he readily accepted my farewell and was moving on, casting his eye about for the next sex slave candidate. What did I expect anyway? I couldn't be important to him, not this early in the game. If ever.

Less than an hour later, the doorbell rang. There he was standing at the door to my apartment, looking as delectable as ever, his hair windblown, his shirt unbuttoned at the throat, with his tie in his hand. He smelled like fresh laundry.

"Come for a drive with me," he said, his deep voice like endorphins to my brain, but his pretty eyes held uncertainty.

"Um, I'm not dressed," I looked down at the yoga pants and ripped tee I was wearing. "I wasn't planning on going out again today."

"May I come in, then?"

"Sure." I backed up a few feet to allow him entrance. It was strange having the larger-than-life Ian Blackmon, a man recognized in public, in our small, humble apartment. Now I felt happy that Mariah had replaced the old laminate countertops with a beautiful slab of black granite only two months ago. Gesturing to the stools at the kitchen counter, I said, "Have a seat: I'll go throw some clothes on and we could go for that drive." I then scurried out of the room, padding barefoot down the hall, in a rush to get to my bedroom. I wanted to hurry him out of the condo before he could work his magic on me again.

But when I turned around to close the bedroom door, he was right there—so close I could smell his aftershave and his own beautiful Ian scent—and without another word, he kicked the door shut behind him and pushed me up against the nearest wall. Pinned by his hips, I could feel his rock-hard erection on my belly.

I went on the offensive. "Ian. I want you to know that I don't think this Dominant/submissive thing will work for me," I said breathlessly. "I'm just a very disobedient type—ask my mother—and I have a willful personality. Both of those traits will serve to undermine my value as a sex slave. Plus, I've never aspired to be one, but...

listen... if I *were* the type to want to be a slave, I swear you'd totally be my idea of a very fine master or sire or liege... or whatever they call you. I just..."

He never allowed me to finish my rambling. He kissed me until I was seriously depleted of oxygen and would agree to anything. His voice, both soft and menacing, spoke directly into my ear.

"Did you expect me to just accept your rejection, my sweet Ariel? If so, you have no idea with whom you are dealing. I always get what I want—and make no mistake, darling girl, I want you. You want me, too."

True that.

His hand curved around my face, lifting it to get my undivided attention. His eyes were blazing with some kind of volatile emotion when he looked into mine. "You feel it too, don't you, Ariel?"

I couldn't deny it. The *it* he referred to was the palpable electricity that snapped and crackled around us whenever we were together in the same room. But I was scared of *it* too. And of him.

"Yes," I whispered, "I feel it, too."

"Now wouldn't it be foolish to cast aside such a gift without further exploration?"

I nodded, wanting nothing more than to throw my arms around him and snuggle into that delicious-smelling chest.

"Then don't," he growled, "it's really quite simple."

Then he tore off my clothes, throwing me on the bed to ravish me and lay waste to my objections. It's amazing how agreeable I am after two consecutive orgasms. So, yes, I agreed to dinner and more discussion. I wanted to meet at a neutral place, say a restaurant; he wanted me to come over to his house. We compromised and I went over to his house—I didn't say it was a *good* compromise.

Again I sat in his palace of a home, requisite wine glass in hand and a tad intoxicated, queasy even, still trying to digest the whole thing—that which he'd hoped to induct me into that very night. The delicious dinner I'd just consumed was being curdled by more detailed information about his... implements. During my last visit, when I'd endured his eye-opening lecture on the delights of BDSM and a guided tour of his dungeon, he'd mentioned a virtual cornucopia of deviant sex acts associated with each piece of equipment. Now he was telling me what he expected to use on me right away and what would come later, as I became more experienced.

And, honest, he looks so damn normal!

This was our third discussion on the subject. But familiarity was not breeding comfort here. Not in the least.

"I think I now understand why you had me sign those papers. Protection from sexual exposure?"

"It could be," he answered cryptically. Probably seeing my confusion, he elaborated. "I don't like the press, Ariel. I try to keep my life private and they do their utmost to thwart me—apparently I make good tabloid fodder." He shrugged. "It's a game: sometimes I win and sometimes I don't, but I try to never make it easy. Let's leave it at that."

"If I agreed... *if*... am I allowed to change my mind mid-game?"

Exasperated, he'd snapped, "You're not going to be imprisoned, Ariel." His face then split into a disarming smile. "Well, perhaps I should amend that to, you won't be imprisoned *all* of the time."

Oddly, those words didn't go far in reassuring me. "I'm not a brave individual, you know. I've never even gone bungee jumping due to trust issues."

He shook his head in dismissal of my feeble attempt at humor. "This is just sex on steroids, Ariel. What's more, based on the little I know I about you, I can almost guarantee you'll like it."

Though I offered him my most suspicious look, his smile continued to widen. Uh-oh.

It happened that very night; patience wasn't among Mr. Blackmon's many virtues, I concluded. He took me into the dungeon for the first time and I had to admit... *I did like it.* Or at least my body did.

On our first night together, he'd made love to me—no question about it. He'd taken his time, tried to make me feel comfortable, and was exceedingly gentle. Seeing him without clothes made me pant so enthusiastically I nearly hyperventilated. The man was an exquisite specimen of the human male, from his luxuriant head of hair down to his beautiful, masculine feet. Believe me, I searched for at least one imperfection, scouring him with enthusiastic eyes, but there was nothing to mar Mr. Gorgeous, just a big, fat zero.

And I? Instead of being nervous, I found myself eager to get things going, but he took his sweet time, slowly removing my clothes first and only later his own. In fact, he left his jeans on until the very last minute, a subtle reminder to me of the power exchange underway here, and where I was going to fit into his life—under him in more ways than one. By the time he was actually where I needed him to be—between my legs, ready to take my long-held virginity—I was beyond coherence and I'm pretty damn sure he knew it. I begged him to sully my virtue—and quickly. He finally did but though he was gentle, there was nothing quick about it. The next day, walking was a challenge for me.

I wrote the book because it ended far too soon, when I refused to agree to his terms, to become essentially a slave to his every whim. I wanted him on my terms; he wanted me on his—and never the twain shall meet.

My book was jokingly called *Three and a Half Weeks*, after the movie *Nine and a Half Weeks*, but modified since that's how long our relationship limped along, propelled by nothing more than unadulterated lust. I briefly considered calling it *The Story of A* but that would have been too obvious, I think.

Chapter 2

Even though he was always so supremely confident of himself, when I agreed to try doing this thing with him, he looked somewhat taken aback, as if he weren't expecting it. Why not? He'd told me he wouldn't give up on me easily.

"You're agreeing?"

"Yes," I replied, my voice sounding hoarse and alien to me.

He stood up and extended his hand toward me. "Well, then. No time like the present. Come."

I gave him my hand and he pulled me to my feet. Walking ahead of me, he held onto my hand, nearly dragging me behind him. I thought it was a fitting metaphor for the whole experience. Too soon, we reached the door of the dungeon. Naturally, it was in the basement of the house, next to the wine cellar.

"Ian," I croaked out, "just in case you're a serial killer, I should tell you that both Mariah and my mother know I'm here with you."

He turned around and gifted me with the most delighted grin. "I'll bear that in mind, Ariel. Ready?"

"As much as I'll ever be."

"Good." He opened the door and urged me inside with his hand on my back.

I stepped in as if walking to my own doom. Sort of octagonal in shape, the room was dim and cool and smelled like cinnamon or something similar. As soon as we were inside, he closed the door.

"Ariel?" His voice was so soft.

I turned to peek at him and as soon as I caught his

eye he issued a terse command.

"Strip."

What? I paused for, like, a millisecond and it annoyed him. Talk about impatient!

"I resent having to repeat myself, Ariel."

I was wearing fitted trousers with a silk tee. I started with my top, quickly lifting the hem up and over my head. He watched, his lips tight with impatience, I think. I hurried to unzip my pants and shimmy out of them, kicking off my shoes when my pants dropped to my ankles. Now I was in only my lingerie and I assumed it would be enough, at least for a few minutes. It wasn't.

He strode over to where I stood and pulled something out of his pocket. Before I knew it, he'd cut off my bra and panties with a utility tool. I gasped in horror.

"Why did you do that?"

His face softened slightly, probably because of the appalled expression on mine. "One of the most basic but important lessons for you to learn is that actions or inactions have consequences, Ariel. I issued a simple command. First, you hesitated—transgression number one. Then you complied but only partially, a more serious misstep. As a result you lost your drawers. Next time I tell you to strip, I do believe you will divest yourself of everything you don't want to lose. Am I correct?"

I quickly realized that the man in this room was decidedly different than the civilized man in the library. In here, all of his potency and character traits (both dubious and admirable) were magnified tenfold: his bearing, his facial expression—everything announced his unquestionable dominance.

I nodded, desperately wanting to stick out my tongue at him but repressing the urge.

"Good." He lightly grasped my wrist and led me to a dark corner. "Whenever you enter this room, you will kneel in this corner, face cast down, your hands palm up on your thighs. Is that clear, Ariel?"

"Please, call me Ella. People call me Ariel when

they're angry with me."

"All the better in here. When you agree to enter this room with me, you are relinquishing your autonomy and giving me full authority over you. Formality will help put you into the correct frame of mind." He paused for a long moment. "I don't want to overwhelm you with too much at once but you really should be addressing me as Master within these walls."

"Master?" I sputtered. "I don't think I can do that."

He smiled tightly. "Very well. You may use Sir, if you find that easier."

"That's just as creepy. If formality is what you desire, may I call you Mr. Blackmon?"

He nodded curtly. "For now it will suffice." He pointed toward the floor. "Kneel."

Feeling like a German shepherd, I dropped to my knees. He bent down and went about repositioning me. His body was so close that I could smell his cologne and it made me want to fling myself on him. I've never had an overactive libido—just the opposite, hence my long-held virtue—but Mr. Blackmon seemed to bring out the wild child in me. Hmm. And all it took was a ridiculously handsome, young billionaire to do it. That thought hit me sideways and led to hysterical giggles bubbling up in my chest and I knew instinctively it would be a very bad thing to let loose in here. Immediately, I conjured up a vision of a natural disaster and rescue dogs poring through rubble in search of survivors, to push it away.

"I've explained to you about reward and punishment. I believe you understand that punishment will usually be corporal. I do have other methods, however, that I will employ from time to time."

Corporal punishment meant physical pain, right? So what other kind of punishments could he mete out? Psychological torture? Sleep deprivation? Extreme tickling? *What?* I couldn't imagine so I had to ask. "Might I know what those are?"

"Oh, Ariel, you will find out soon enough. Being new, you're bound to make mistakes."

I was too terrified to appreciate word play but I asked anyway, "Was that pun intended?"

"No. Remember, whenever you address me, you must use a term of deference to rank. As I stated a few moments ago, I would prefer Master but for now I will settle for Mr. Blackmon. If you forget to use it, you'll be reminded."

"Behavior modification?"

The modification came instantly. I didn't see what he used to slap me but it wasn't his hand and it stung so much that I squealed.

"Excuse me?" his voice was thunderous.

"I'm sorry, Mr. Blackmon." And I *was* sorry—truly—for my butt was burning.

He stood up. "Remain in position until I instruct you otherwise," he said sternly, and left the room.

I couldn't tell how long he was gone. Time is elastic and can stretch or contract, depending on one's state of mind. Heightened anticipation makes time stretch into oblivion so it seemed an eternity before he came back. By then I was intensely anxious but also brimming with excitement. I wondered about my sexuality, then: why was this so damn exciting? Was I some kind of pervert?

He walked over to me. I remembered to keep my eyes down so I could see only his lower legs and feet. He lifted me up by my elbow. I let myself go limp so I could allow him to guide me. He brought me to a wooden thing, about hip high and covered in leather.

"I'm mindful that this time will be only your third time out, sexually speaking, so I don't want to go too far in this room tonight. We'll take things slowly. But I'd like you to become familiar and relatively comfortable with the equipment. This," he patted the leather-covered wood thing, "is a sawhorse. Normally you'd lie on this bench, face down and straddle the end with your legs, your bottom hanging over the edge by a few inches. However, because you're so green, I'm going to put you on it on your back."

I didn't respond so as to avoid using any of those

terms of address that made me squeamish. Placing his large hands around my waist, he lifted me onto the horse.

"Lay down and draw your knees up," his instructions were swift and terse, as if we weren't in this compromising position together—clinical, I suppose would be an apt description for his attitude. Where was the charming man I met in my shop?

It's not that I didn't appreciate this dark, exotic male in front of me. I was just confused by him.

He buckled cuffs on my wrists and ankles and chained each wrist to the corresponding ankle so that I was on my back, all fours in the air, in a fetal position. Then he reached for a strap on the side of the horse, pulling it over my abdomen and securing it on the other side so I was held tightly in place.

He was wearing black: a black silk shirt and black trousers. Shit, that's where he went—to change into his Satan outfit. Without removing a single article of his own clothing while I was stark naked, he calmly unzipped his fly and unfurled a condom over his impressive erection. There wasn't even a trace of good humor on his face; his countenance was sternly arrogant. I couldn't take my eyes off the transformation in him.

"Do you recall, Ariel, that I instructed you not to look at me while we assume these roles?"

Oops, I forgot. I quickly averted my eyes but I heard a bitter chuckle. "Too little, too late, I'm afraid. You've already seen too much."

Nervously I glanced back, just in time to see his hands reach toward my face and slide a blindfold over my eyes. As soon as I lost my sight, everything else became instantly more intense: the music playing, the sounds of him moving and breathing, and even the cinnamony scent of the room. In that moment I knew that when he began to touch me, that sense would be magnified too. My innards instantly contracted sharply in anticipation.

I swear I almost came the moment his warm hands

touched my legs. He pulled my knees apart so that I was in a most unladylike position. Almost simultaneously the music became louder, with the booming bass resonating through my body, pumping through and with my heart.

His hands skimmed over my skin lightly, giving me goose bumps, and then landed on my breasts. I felt his fingers circling my nips and in response they began to tingle and burn. What the hell? He must have put something on them. The sensation grew more intense—almost uncomfortable. Next, his hands moved lower and other things began to tingle and burn. I squirmed, trying to evade the sensation but I couldn't move much: not only was the strap pinning me down but he was now holding both my knees and my limbs were chained together. With no warning, he thrust himself fully into me, while at the same time sliding a hand down to pinch my backside: pain and pleasure merged, hot and instant, and I climaxed immediately. I heard his deep-throated laughter then but he was just beginning the ride. By the time he was through with me, I couldn't easily close my legs nor could I walk very gracefully.

Good times.

Afterward, as we lay in his understated but still sumptuously comfortable bedroom, I asked him about his past.

"Have you ever had a normal relationship?"

He was back to his charming self and kissed the tip of my nose. "This kind of relationship *is* normal to me."

"You know what I mean."

He reared his head back in irritation. "Ella, I'm nearing thirty years old. Of course I've had relationships. It's just that I prefer this type of one. Let's move on." He looked at me from down his nose and I quickly averted my eyes. His hand reached over and grasped my chin, turning it toward him. "I'm uncomfortable speaking of other women to you, Ariel, but if you must know, I had a bad experience when I was young. I prefer relationships with some emotional distance, but I'm not willing to give up the physical intimacy. Does that answer your question?"

I nodded, now more addled than ever. What kind of bad experience did he have?

"For what it's worth, I will admit to one little concession: *you* are special. I've never had to pursue a woman as I've pursued you, but I think you're very much worth it." He rubbed the end of my nose with his and kissed me again.

Those few sweet words of his proved stowaways on my eventual flight to the UK, staying with me for weeks afterward as I tried to muddle through the motivations and feelings of this most frustrating man.

On the second visit to his dungeon, we had more fun. At least *he* thought it was fun. That time, he used toys: a vibrator he called a butterfly—I was rather fond of that one and I wouldn't mind getting one for my very own—a type of fluffy feather, a vibrating thing that looked like a massager, and tiny metal balls that are strung together and are inserted into various orifices and pulled out slowly during climax. He also used a flogger on me. Over our last two encounters, he gifted me with multiple orgasms. This time he denied me even one.

I was so frustrated, I was whimpering. Ian just watched me closely, occasionally offering me a wicked grin. I couldn't believe he was being so mean. Sexual frustration is cruel and it had been going on for what seemed like hours. I was about to really lose it when he finally gave in.

My wrists were restrained to a chain that dangled from the headboard on the dungeon bed. He flipped me over onto my stomach so suddenly that I screamed out loud but the loss of balance caused my face to smush into the pillow, muffling it. He didn't stop there: he slid both of my knees up the bed until my backside was up in the air and then he slapped me so hard, once, twice, and then a third time, pinching my nip before slamming himself into me. I came so hard and so instantly (and so amazingly) that I managed to scrounge up enough humanity to forgive him the previous torment. But he kept pounding into me, right through my orgasm, and, exhausted, I realized he wanted me to come again.

"I can't," I whined.

"You can," he snarled, "and you will, Ariel. I want you to give me more...now!" He leaned over, pulled my head back by my hair, and bit my neck as he hammered at me and his fingers did a reach around.

So I did. Come. Bombarded by sensations everywhere at once, I caved to his dominance and fell before the altar of his alpha-maleness. My body was in control, relegating my mind to the backseat—my body was proving to be such a slut. The idea unsettled me but I tried not to dwell on it.

After he hit his orgasm, he stilled, remaining on his knees, and looked down at me, while I peered up at him from the corner of my eye.

"How was that, baby?" His eyes were shining with triumph.

I sighed heavily. If I had to die young, this was as good a way to go as any I could think of.

Then there was the third visit. On my third and last trip into that room, he whipped me.

He *whipped* me. With an actual whip.

He used what he called a single-tail and it left hot-pink stripes up and down my thighs, and rear end. He'd promised me he'd only do as much as he thought I could take, that he wouldn't exceed a tolerable threshold, but he breached that boundary and then some. Under the haze of shocking pain, I finally remembered to use my safe word, shouting it at the top of my lungs. When I said the word, he stopped instantly and cast the whip on the floor. Yet I still have nightmares where I scream out the safe word but it falls on deaf ears and the forceful blows keep raining down on me.

Afterward, he was apologetic and so very solicitous—and out of breath. We were both panting but for very different reasons. But no matter how deep or heartfelt his apology, the line was most definitely crossed and I was done. Why did I ever even entertain the thought that I was up for it? When I got home that night, I swallowed some ibuprofen and went straight to bed, sore, shocked, and mourning the loss of what never would be—my fabulous fairytale romance with the dashing Dorian Blackmon. Like his namesake Dorian Gray, his beautiful face hid something ugly underneath.

Arriving like a gift from the universe, the next morning a letter came in the mail: I had been awarded a fellowship to Cambridge University to study under the renowned historian Charles Norwood-Finch. I would continue my studies in art history, specifically the Protestant Reformation's impact on art in 16th century England. I had exactly two weeks to pack and get there. I only needed two days.

I never saw Ian Blackmon again.

I was in Cambridge when Christmas rolled around. Britain is so very charming during the holidays but I felt desolate. I began to write my book on Thanksgiving Day, only it wasn't Thanksgiving in the UK, so that led me to have a one-woman pity party before sitting down, pen in hand, to the real tears. I thought perhaps I could exorcise the memories that tormented me by writing them down, seeing the man in brown in black and white.

Now, I'm no writer: my interests and strengths lie in history—its details and facts, its fascinating evolution. But I had read enough literature in my life to fake it. I tried to channel the bleak despair of Dostoevsky, the witty repartee of Noel Coward, the happily-ever-after of Cinderella. Granted, I knew nothing about pacing, character development, point of view, omniscience—I mean, people who aren't professional writers have no idea how complicated writing a good book can be.

Still, the one thing I had going for me was that I was, in fact, recording history, not writing fiction. And it was *my* history—who better to write it? So I knew it would be in first-person. And I knew it would be a character-driven story. Finally, I knew how it began and ended. Plus, only a handful of people would ever see the book, so I was safe.

I went to one of those print-on-demand publishers and had my book bound, printing up a batch of 25 copies, though I only needed eleven. I wrote a pithy dedication to all my girls—the gift recipients—and patted myself on the back for coming up with the best inexpensive gift ever.

But the morning after I finished my book, I woke from my dreams to discover I still had my friendly demon yoked around my neck for constant company. I couldn't rid my soul of Ian Blackmon, no matter what I did to try to banish him.

I know it sounds stupid because intimate though we were, I only knew him for a few weeks... but I missed him... so, so much. Like any despair-inducing loss, the pain penetrated to the center of my soul. I wanted to run back to him but I forced myself to be strong, to do anything but dwell on him: crochet, run, study, take up synchronized swimming—anything. But in any and every quiet moment, scenes from our brief time together would suddenly drop in to revisit me, causing me anguish. Like the time he almost got me fired...

After our second night together, he dropped by the store unexpectedly while I was working. I just so happened to be waiting on a young male customer who was hitting on me big time. Ian strolled in through the door just in time for the grand finale. That's when I learned how jealous and possessive he was. I'd been showing the guy possible gifts for his mother: scarves, bracelets, and wallets, I think. The customer, a mid-twentyish, blond athletic type in a tight tee-shirt, jeans, and leather coat had finally selected a sterling bracelet, I believe. That's when the fun started.

"Would you like it giftwrapped, sir?"

"Absolutely. But before you ring it up, I'd like to

make another purchase."

"Yes?" I asked politely, happy for another commission.

"My girlfriend is just about the same size as you and I'd like to buy her some lingerie. Would you mind trying on a few pieces for me?"

I was stunned by the man's audacity. "You want me to try on lingerie?"

"Would you, please? I wouldn't want to misjudge her size—that could get me into all kinds of trouble," he laughed, flashing a row of straight, white teeth with sharpened incisors. Predator teeth.

I had seen Ian walk in a few seconds before but he'd begun to browse while I finished with the customer. Just his exalted presence in the small shop made me nervous but now that the man was flirting with me—beyond flirting, really—I could feel Ian's eyes boring into me as he watched the scene unfold. I wondered if he'd take any action or not.

I forced a laugh. "I don't think that's possible. Sorry."

"Oh, come on, be a good sport. You work on commission, don't you? This sale is going to go over five hundred if you're a good girl and help sell me the sexy lingerie."

He was there in a flash, a collage of dark suit, white teeth, and deadly aim. "Get the fuck away from her and out of the store if you value your miserable life, you piece of shit cretin." The words streamed out of his mouth like ammo from an AK-47.

The blond man got red in the face and whipped his head around to find a fuming Ian Blackmon towering over him. "Who the fuck are you?" he demanded, but his voice lacked conviction in the face of Ian's black fury.

"Who am I? That depends. If you don't disappear in five seconds, then I'm the worst thing that ever happened to you. Clear enough, douche bag?"

The man turned and stomped out of the shop letting the door bang behind him, his potential purchases forgotten. I studied Ian, watching him try to wrest control of his ugly temper. Well, now I knew the answer to the question, *was he jealous*?

"You just cost me a hefty commission, Mr. Blackmon. Plus, my boss lost a big sale."

"Really? Well, it's no problem since you're quitting your job today anyway. Right now in fact."

"Quitting? Are you nuts? I need this job; not all of us are obscenely wealthy dilettantes, you know."

"Dilettante? Either you don't know the meaning of the word or you have no idea of who I am, Ms. Strong. But you are quitting this job: I assure you."

I was flabbergasted. Who the hell did he think he was? "I am not quitting, Mr. Blackmon. Now that that's settled, what can I do for you?"

Transforming from angry, protective lover to smooth, powerful CEO, he smirked and pulled out his phone, watching me intently while he swiped in a number. "Claudia? I want you to contact the owner of Archipelago... yes, the boutique near the Barnes & Noble in the University district? I believe her surname is Vickers. Please inform her that I planned to make a very large purchase in her store today but was displeased with her salesperson, a young woman named Ariel Strong. Correct. Yes, thank you, Claudia."

The gasp that came out of my throat could have drowned out a fire engine's screaming siren. I could not believe he just got me fired. What a dick.

Smirking, he grabbed my hand and kissed it before I could snatch it away.

And snatch it away I did, so violently I nearly fell backward when he released me. "I never want to see you again, Mr. Blackmon. I can't believe you just did what you did. I happen to need my job to pay my bills!"

He was so cool, his eyes hard like chips of flint. "Not anymore. I'll see to all your needs, Ariel."

"I am not a prostitute, for your information." My voice was trembling with unspent rage. "Call her back and tell her not to do it. I'm serious."

He was stubborn but I could see his pigheaded

resolve crumbling. "You can work for me, Ariel. I'll pay you considerably more than you earn here in your best week and you'll be safer."

I stamped my foot in frustration. "I'm perfectly safe here. That guy was an idiot but I could handle him. Please call her." I couldn't help it: tears were pooling in my eyes. His audacity was without bounds.

Sighing, he made the call. "Claudia, disregard my last request. Sorry. Yes, I'll be back in the office shortly."

Ironically, that ended up being my last day at the shop anyway. The next day started my boss's three-week buying trip to Europe and Indonesia, a yearly tradition of hers when she closes up shop. Consequently, I had a forced vacation of three weeks and then all that darkness went down with Blackmon and I left the country.

Life in Cambridge dragged by as I studied diligently and missed my friends. Weeks passed. In early February, I finally heard from a couple of my girlfriends who had received the book. They loved it and said it was the best present ever. Jade even said she was inspired to buy a bigger vibrator after reading one of the steamier scenes and I laughed hard enough to earn myself a stomachache, picturing the petite Asian beauty at the sex shop browsing for naughty toys. Mariah had passed her copy around to other friends and so had Kayla. I had a moment of panic when I heard that.

"How well do you know these people?" I asked Mariah.

"What difference does it make? It's a great read, Ella. Just calm yourself and go have a cup of Earl Grey or something. I think I may come visit before your semester is over. Would that be a good idea?"

Kayla was just as *savoir faire* about the whole thing. "Oh, Ella, this novel is a surefire winner. I think you should try to have it published and—"

"No!" I screamed across the Atlantic into her eardrum. "Are you insane? I'm not a writer. Please, Kayla, don't lend it around or you'll embarrass me. I need my name to be respectable, after all, if I want to be taken seriously as a historian. The book is filled with kink, for God's sake. Damn, damn, damn, if I had known how inconsiderate you all would be, I would have used a pseudonym. Damn."

"Inconsiderate? I'm praising you to high heaven, silly."

"No, you just cannot pass it around, Kayla. Promise me."

"Okay, my bad, please forgive me for being a loyal friend. Listen, I've got to run. Keep me posted on that new man you met. What was his name? Simon, right?"

"Just a friend, Kayla. I like him because he never makes a pass at me."

"Really? What's there to like about that? Ella, don't you have any kind of libido?"

I laughed. If she only knew. Actually she did know but I can't ever let her realize it. For the first time since I patted myself on the back over my book, I was beginning to realize it might have been a gargantuan mistake. Shit.

In March, Mariah came to the UK to visit. I met her at Gatwick and took her to Earl's Court to have lunch—there's a little Pakistani restaurant tucked into a dead-end street and the food is to die for.

"So, catch me up," I said. "How is everything?"

Mariah's brown eyes gleamed. "Everything is super good. I have news, Ella. Good news. Big news."

"Really? What?"

"Well, you'll recall you wrote a book entitled *Three and a Half Weeks*? I loved it so much that I loaned it to a few friends." Before I could interrupt by strangling every last breath out of her, she rushed to continue. "My friend Tamara was in the middle of reading it when she started working as an intern for a hot literary agent, Mo Jackson. Anyway, long story short, Mo asked Tamara what she was reading and she told her about it. Mo asked to check it out, read it in one night and asked if she could represent it. Isn't that super?"

"Just fucking super, Mariah. I'm absolutely thrilled

that the whole world might learn that I like to write kink in my spare time."

"Well, you know what Sarah did with her copy, right? She scanned big parts of it and put it on a literary web site and it went viral in one week. Ella, you're a star. You're going to make mega bucks on this book. You have to get past this sense of embarrassment—the book is good."

I raked both of my hands through my hair as my frustration mounted. "It's not good; I'm not a writer. I mean, it may contain titillating prose but it's not well constructed and it's not something I could be proud of. Don't you understand?"

She shrugged casually, amusement lighting up her hazel eyes. "Well, I would say you could use a pseudonym but I think that ship has long since sailed."

Burying my face in my hands in the blackest despair, I mumbled, "I could really kill Sarah. Damn, I should have just bought you all a pair of fucking gloves."

And that's exactly how it happened. Before Mo Jackson even sold my book to a major publishing house, it had been read by over a hundred thousand people and counting. Mo worked out a seven-figure deal for me—let me say that again, seven figures. And that wasn't all. Hollywood came calling and before the beautiful people left my attorney's office, I had a second seven-figure deal in my hot, little hand. Shit. I was wealthy!

By July, I had finished my time at Cambridge, traveled Europe a little, and finally returned to the States. All told, I'd been gone a few weeks shy of a full year. While still in Britain, I decided to relocate from Portland to Los Angeles, so I went straight there and rented a cottage while I trolled for the perfect house. I was having lunch with a college friend in Los Feliz—the neighborhood I'd chosen for my real estate search, when my cell phone began to blare Aretha Franklin singing *Respect*. I looked at the number but didn't recognize it.

"Hello?"

"Am I speaking with Ariel Strong?" The voice was smooth, deep, and unfamiliar.

"You are. May I ask who is calling?"

"Yes. Ms. Strong, my name is Jackson Delacroix. I am an attorney with Delacroix, Steinem, and Tucker. I'm contacting you on behalf of a client, a Mr. Ian Blackmon. Ms. Strong, I'm afraid Mr. Blackmon is filing suit against you for breach of contract. I'll need to meet with you and your attorney as soon as possible.

"Ms. Strong, are you there?"

Chapter 3

Got her! Ian thinks. For a year now, he'd been trying to figure out a way to get Ella back into his life. He'd been rendered senseless at the desolation he felt when she disappeared: he didn't want to admit it, even to himself, but the girl had worked her way under his skin and so very quickly. He'd even been ready to give in to her, to agree to a traditional romantic alliance—just one ordinary relationship, hold the kink.

But then she up and disappeared.

He knew why, of course. He'd displayed an appalling lack of good judgment in using the single-tail on her—a girl who was brand new to any of it, reward or punishment. He should have waited, at the very least, bided his time, until she got more comfortable with the whole idea. But he'd been anxious. His last submissive had been banished for nearly six months when he met Ella and he needed some consistency back in his life. The club had not been doing it for him and he knew most of the regular subs there already. None of them tripped his trigger. So he'd gone too fast with the innocent Ella, overly eager to play with her, introduce her to the pleasure of erotic pain, and it ended up costing him. Big time. He was furious with himself when she went MIA.

He tried to move past it—no girl was worth such grief. But he found, much to his profound consternation, that no other woman interested him in the least anymore.

He fucking wanted Ariel.

At first, he couldn't find her. It was infuriating: he could make anything happen and here was this little slip of a girl running him ragged, both emotionally and literally, all over town searching for her. He tried everything he could think of to locate Ella himself and came up flat. Where was she? What stuck in his mind most about that time was his unabiding panic at not knowing where she was, his pretty girl. Losing her threw him into the blackest funk, a place where no sunlight managed to filter into the dark. He had to find her, get her back.

Finally, he resorted to hiring a private detective and the man ran her to ground in less than forty-eight hours. She was in the UK, studying at Cambridge, on a fellowship, he'd said. So Ms. Strong was as smart as she was beautiful. Somehow he wasn't at all surprised.

Ian was a man who knew his own mind, accepted his limitations, and made peace with his very real flaws. One thing he was not comfortable with was emotion. He loved his parents, his siblings, even the family dog: he did not, however, ever love his women.

No. Emotions clouded reasoned judgment, thus getting in the way of an otherwise harmonious relationship. Women made for excellent dining or party company and for sex. That's all. And that's exactly how he liked it.

Until he met Ariel Strong.

She'd fiddled with his sense of self, unknowingly or not. He found himself stalking her. He had a dossier compiled on her, as he did with business competitors, and the wretched girl invaded his thoughts without warning on a regular basis. All it took was one chance meeting in a shop and a girl with wild tresses of chestnut-colored hair, looking up at him with impossibly huge eyes and calling him sir. He shook his head in self-disgust. What a pathetic ass he'd become.

He'd been having lunch with his sister two weeks ago. Zoe had decided it was her mission in life to see him in a long-term relationship. Of course, she had no idea he usually had one, since he kept his romantic life quiet. They had just ordered their lunch when he stepped away to use the men's room. While he was gone, Zoe had pulled out her iPad and was engrossed in reading something on it.

"Well, that must be a good book since you're risking my displeasure at your display of bad manners to read it."

Zoe's face colored. "God, so pompous." she muttered.

At his sharp look, she rolled her eyes. "Sorry, Ian," she said, and then her eyes turned mischievous, "but it *is* good. Dirty, too," she whispered with glee.

"Dirty?" he raised his brow. "I'm shocked. What is it?"

"It's called *Three and a Half Weeks* and it's about this girl who meets this gorgeous guy who happens to have a taste for whips and handcuffs. It's a lot of fun."

Ingrained in him by years of business dealings, his poker face served him well, as he now kept it devoid of any expression. "Interesting. Who's the author?"

Zoe shrugged. "Someone named Ariel something or other. Oh, right. Ariel Strong."

He just managed to finish the swallow of Cabernet without aspirating it and muffled the choke to sound like a cough that hit at an inopportune moment. "Really? I think I've met the woman actually. I'd never have pegged her for a writer of kink, though."

"You know her? How?"

His sister's cheeks flushed even pinker—was it the wine or the conversation? Zoe had a pale complexion with dark brown hair and when flustered it was readily apparent on her face—like someone else he knew. Instantly he felt the familiar sharp ache in his chest.

"If it's the same woman, I met her one evening as I shopped for your birthday gift, as a matter of fact. She was the salesperson in the boutique. I took her out for dinner a couple of times."

"Well, well, aren't you just full of surprises." Her eyes narrowed. "You know, Ian, I suspect you have a secret life that you keep hidden from everyone. You probably have a whirlwind social life and binders full of women and then when any one of us, your family, I mean, comes over, you hide all evidence in your oversized closets and reach for a biography of FDR or something of that ilk. It's all a big charade, isn't it?"

He managed to laugh. If she only knew how close to the truth she actually was.

The next day he put in a call to his attorney. Delacroix was the soul of discretion and that's precisely why he was his attorney. He set up an appointment for that afternoon, told the man it was critically important. At two the next afternoon, Delacroix strolled into his office, perfectly punctual as always.

"Ian, good to see you. I hope all is relatively well?"

"Yes, Jackson. Relatively. Please," he gestured to the chair opposite his own, "have a seat. May I get you a drink?"

"No, thanks. I have to be in court at four—with a clear head. Tell me what's up."

Ian pressed his index fingers together, resting his chin on the point of them. "A bit of a dilemma, Jackson." He proceeded to recount to the middle-aged blond attorney the whole sordid story.

"You wouldn't want this thing to go through the courts."

"Of course not."

"Yet there's really no need for Ms. Strong to know that."

"No, none at all," he agreed pleasantly.

"Do you want to go after her money? She's got to have plenty from the book sales, plus I believe that I read she sold the movie rights in a seven-figure deal."

"I'm not interested in her money, either. I'd like to use her breach as leverage to convince her to return to me, Jackson. She cannot, however, be made aware of that fact."

Delacroix smiled wickedly. In addition to being the soul of discretion, he shared his client's penchant for kink and often played at the club Ian frequented. "My lips are as sealed and impenetrable as my ex-wife's asshole." He stood up, smiling as Ian chuckled at the comment, and extended his hand to shake. "I'll see what I can do. You'll be hearing from me soon, Ian."

"As always, thank you, Jackson, for your sage counsel. Will you be at the kickboxing exhibition at the dojo next weekend?"

"Wouldn't miss it for the world. I assume I'll see you there."

"I wouldn't pass up the opportunity to kick your ass, Delacroix." He gave his friend a two-finger salute.

"Bring it on, Blackmon." Delacroix exited the office laughing.

Delacroix called the very next afternoon.

"News, I presume?"

"Indeed. Turns out our dear Ms. Strong is back in the States and, as of this morning, a bit anxious. You need to decide how you want to play this, Ian. Do you want to lull her into a false sense of security by allowing her to think it's a simple matter of legal remedy and that the lawyers will handle the matter or do you want her to know from the start that the redress will require a... ahem... more personal approach?"

"Hmmm, conundrum." He rubbed his chin. "What do you suggest—since I pay you such a handsome hourly rate for your erudite counsel?"

"I think the best approach is a soft one, as long as you're not in a rush. I'll meet with her and her attorney and we'll discuss various outcomes. Perhaps I'll feel her out about actually meeting with you directly to see if there's a way all parties can walk away from the table feeling like winners. Sound acceptable?"

"Very. Keep me posted."

Chapter 4

"Normally, Ella, I'd say don't worry about it—it's just a simple matter of remedy but this is Ian Blackmon we're talking about. The man wields considerable influence."

My attorney doesn't sound optimistic.

"Stephen, that's not what I want to hear."

"Yes, Ella, I'm aware but it is what it is. Accordingly, we need to take a proactive approach."

She'd never seen Stephen look so defeated—a fact that didn't bode well for her. "Why isn't the disclaimer in the front matter of the book enough protection to defend against breach?"

Stephen sighs. "Normally it is, however, if a book is transparently disguised as fiction and actually about a real person... and that real person has the money, clout, and inclination to pursue a legal remedy..."

He must see the dejection on my face for he smiles and brightens his voice. "Look, Ella, let's not get ahead of ourselves here. Before I commit to any course of action, I'm planning to meet with Blackmon's attorney to get some clarity as to how far his client wants to take this suit."

"Give me an idea of what we're up against. My imagination is taking me to ugly places, Stephen."

"Well, it can go one of several ways. The worst-case scenario is that we have to pull the book off the shelves and remunerate Blackmon for copies already sold. I don't think it will ever get that far—especially considering that the book was marketed as fiction and no real harm to Blackmon can be measured, at least none that we know of.

"Or Blackmon might demand a percentage of all profits on a retroactive basis. That can become costly very quickly but it won't bankrupt you. You'll just be a lot less wealthy tomorrow than today. You'll still do well, Ella, and we might be able to shield the film profits from his reach.

"The third possibility—and this is the best outcome—is that you and Blackmon hash it out personally, as friends. If that's a viable option, it would be best, since you may be able to mollify him with a few simple assurances. After all, he certainly doesn't need your money. I can't imagine what's motivating him to do this since all it can garner him is negative publicity. Unless that's what he's looking for? Some notoriety?"

I snort. "I seriously doubt that, Stephen, or he wouldn't have everyone who comes in contact with him sign all sorts of legal contracts to protect him—from exposure and litigation. To my mind, that spells paranoid with a capital P."

"True, but it could be he's merely acting on his attorney's advice. You don't get where Blackmon is without making a few enemies along the way."

"How did he make his money? Do you know?"

"Yes, I know a lot more about Blackmon today than I ever did before. I do my homework, Ella. Let's see: he was some kind of financial *wunderkind* back in college. Began at MIT, switched to Yale, I believe, for graduate studies. Money can buy one's way into those schools but it can't buy the grades and Blackmon had them. Graduated *summa cum laude*— Greek, of course, *Delta Kappa Epsilon*. So he's not just a pretty face.

"Apparently, though his parents are wealthy, they're not big proponents of inherited wealth so their kids were encouraged and expected to succeed on their own merits, which undoubtedly he would have regardless but Ian had a friendly hand assist him. As a teen, he befriended an elderly lady in his neighborhood—you know, mowed her lawn, took out her dog, picked up groceries for her—and when the woman died, she left our Mr. Blackmon a bundle. He was not even twenty.

"He must be a poker player because he went all in. Bet on a few friends' Web start-ups and parlayed his original principal—I think it was a few grand shy of a million—into a fortune. From there, he began to diversify, investing in commercial real estate, green-energy initiatives, and hydro technology. He has keen business acumen and he made the Forbes list by his second or third year in business."

"Hmmm." I'm not surprised so a verbalization is unnecessary. Stephen's eyes bore into mine. "What?" I inquire.

"Ella, I have to ask some uncomfortable questions of you. First, do you have any idea why Blackmon is coming after you?"

Blood rushes to my face. "Have you read my book, Stephen?"

Now he flushes. "I regret to say I have not. I have a general idea as to its contents, however."

"Well, I met Ian last year, right out of college, and we dated for a brief time." I know my eyes reflect my amusement as I train them on him—it's important to look a person in the eye when talking about really, really embarrassing things. "Three and a half weeks to be precise."

Confusion was reflected in my attorney's eyes. "Oh?"

"Yes. Blackmon had me sign the CA right from the get-go. I had no intention of violating it, by the way. None. Circumstances created a totally unpredictable problem. You see, Mr. Blackmon..." I stop, grossly discomfited by what I have to reveal. "Is this conversation protected? For in disclosing this information to you, I may be in further violation of the CA."

"Attorney-client privilege, Ella. It wouldn't be considered a violation. Go on, please."

"Ian Blackmon enjoys a certain... lifestyle. His desire was for me to join him in a particular type of relationship. I declined by leaving the country rather precipitously. I've been told that he made numerous attempts to contact me but was unsuccessful. After a few months, he stopped." I shrug my shoulders. "That's about it."

"Hmmm, so do you think this suit is retaliatory?"

Giving it a minute for serious consideration, I wait, framing my answer carefully. "I tend to doubt it. He never struck me as the vindictive type. I think he's probably genuinely distressed, believing I am truly in violation of the legal agreement."

"Can it be a ploy to get you back into the relationship?"

I snort. "I seriously doubt it. Why would he? I mean, we haven't had any contact at all between us in a year. I'm sure he's moved on... socially."

"So then, you have no idea as to his impetus?"

"Well, he may be embarrassed by the book and possibly desire to embarrass me also. I'm just not sure."

"How much of the book is true?"

Damn. I do not want to answer this question but everything hinges on it, doesn't it? "All," I say quickly, under my breath.

"Excuse me?"

I clear my throat. "All of it... but no names were used and locations were changed. Someone would have to be clairvoyant as well as totally malevolent to try to narrow in on identity. Plus, if it's presented as fiction, why would anyone doubt it?"

"You'd be surprised at how easy it can be to do so. You may not realize it but there very well may be some identifying details contained in the book of which you're not even cognizant. If, say, one of your friends figured it out and casually mentioned it to someone else, the information can spread like wildfire in the public realm. Especially online. It could very well be traced back to Blackmon... and his business reputation could suffer as a result."

Under his breath he muttered, "It's actually much easier to prove than when one author plagiarizes another writer's work—even though it can be blatant theft."

He begins to spin to and fro in his swivel chair, obviously thinking, so I sit quietly and wait.

Finally, he leans in, placing his elbows on the desk. "Okay. Let me meet with Delacroix this afternoon and then we'll talk again. If he suggests a meeting between you and Blackmon, would you agree to it?"

I close my eyes, frustrated. I'd spent so many sleepless nights missing him and crying over him—all from knowing him all of three weeks. *Three weeks*. I'd finally reached a point where I'd begun to slightly consider, maybe, possibly, in the near future, the perhaps unlikely possibility of dating another man. Seeing Ian would throw that all up in flux again. But, though, I didn't want to acknowledge it even in my own head, just the mere suggestion of seeing him up close and personal sets my pulse to racing.

"If you think it advisable, then, yes," I simply say. Heave the ball into Stephen's court.

"Okay. I'll let you know later this evening what we decide."

I rise from my chair. "Thank you, Stephen. I really appreciate your assistance in this matter. I know you don't normally handle this type of case."

"Not at all. It's a lot more interesting than copyright law... and I do handle this kind of thing, though admittedly they come few and far between."

Just as I reach the door, he calls to me. "Oh, and Ella? Please try not to worry yourself into a psychotic state. It will all work out just fine."

I nod and back out of the door, anxious to be free of this worry, even if only for a little while.

I have a salad for dinner and am lounging on the sofa with a glass of wine when Aretha starts singing her heart out. Squinting at the number on my cell, I don't recognize it right away but I answer it anyway. "Hello?"

"Ella, it's Stephen. I'm on my friend's phone because

mine is misbehaving. I wanted to update you so you wouldn't continue to angst over it. "Jackson and I had a protracted talk and we both think you and Mr. Blackmon should meet face to face and discuss how best to go forward. Since I already had your approval on this course of action and he had Mr. Blackmon's, we set up a dinner meeting for the two of you for tomorrow evening at eight. Is that doable?"

"So soon?" My throat begins to constrict.

"Ella, the sooner we reach a resolution, the sooner all this unpleasantness goes away. No?"

"Yes, of course. Where will we meet?"

"I've given your cell number to Jackson to give to Mr. Blackmon. Expect a call from him either tonight or tomorrow morning. Good luck, Ella, and please feel free to step away and call me if the need should arise. Also, don't agree to anything until you run it by me first. Are we clear?"

"Yes. Thank you, Stephen. Have a good night."

"You, too, Ella."

Chapter 5

He stares at the number Jackson had given him. How many times over the past year did he want to call her? And now? Now she is expecting his call, ready to set up a meeting with him, to discuss their little problem. Ian leans back in his leather chair, gazing up at the ceiling, allowing himself—finally—to reflect on the past year. It still stings.

He'd known he'd made a grave error the moment he saw Ella's face afterward. After he... lashed her... with a fucking single tail. God, but it was such a stupid decision on his part. He'd been trying to introduce her to his sensual way of life, attempting to show her how pleasure and pain can so easily overlap, mingle seamlessly even, providing they're delivered by an experienced Dominant—which he was. But he'd done it while in a poor frame of mind and he'd rushed it: she wasn't nearly ready for that level of pain and he succeeded only in terrifying her. She must have thought him a monster.

He'd decided to wait a few days before calling her again. It had cut him to the quick to let her run from him that night, but he dared not risk making any more mistakes with her. Cultivating relationships obviously wasn't his strong suit since he rarely had any involving deep affection—he was picking his way through the dark. Adding to this volatile mix was the fact that she had been entirely innocent when they met—virginal, for God's sake. So he let things lie, hoping she'd be able to process the experience and then come back to talk about it—at the very least.

Those three days were torturous for him. So many

times he began to punch in her number so he could hear her lyrical voice. Several days later, he could not tolerate waiting any longer and called her, but by then her cell phone had been disconnected. Panicked, he went by Mariah's condo and she told him that Ella had moved out of the country. In three days? Impossible, but obviously Mariah had no intention of telling him where Ella really was, so he had to try tracking her down himself. His efforts, however, proved fruitless.

Two weeks later he caved and hired a private detective. The man worked quickly and efficiently and his call came a day and a half later.

"Mr. Blackmon? This is Allan Larson. I tracked down Ms. Strong, sir. I'm putting the case file into a manila envelope and sending a messenger with it to your office tomorrow morning but I thought you might like an immediate report."

"Yes, Mr. Larson, please."

"Ariel Strong has indeed left the country, sir. She is presently residing in the United Kingdom where she will shortly be attending classes at Cambridge University. Apparently she was awarded a fellowship to study at the esteemed institution. She left Oregon state exactly one week before you initially contacted me, so she's been overseas only a little over a week. As far as I could ascertain, her stay is for a finite period of one year, however, she appears to have shut down her life in Portland before she left, closing bank accounts, disconnecting her cell phone service, and leaving no forwarding address for herself, though she did provide her mother's address for next of kin, so I was able to obtain that as well.

"I have secured for you her present location in Cambridge but I was unable to gain access to any telephone number in her name. It's all in the report, sir."

"Excellent work, Mr. Larson. I'm impressed. I'll look forward to receiving your report and I will certainly make use of your services in the future. Thank you."

So then he'd had her address but what good would it

do him? Should he visit her? Another two weeks elapsed before he was desperate enough to answer his own question in the affirmative and he got on his company jet and flew to Gatwick.

Once there, he vacillated between going home and dropping in on her. He waited outside her flat and the first time he caught sight of her, his lungs were robbed of all breath and his chest tightened painfully. Instinctively, he rose to his feet and followed her for a few blocks, just to see her beautiful face, watch her narrow hips sway gently as she walked, oblivious to her own charms. He missed her so much: how had she managed to do what no other woman had done before her?

In the past, every time one of his subs had begun to develop any strong feelings for him, he'd quickly and coldly terminate the relationship, always softening the blow with expensive parting gifts. Sometimes it was harder than others but it never felt impossible. With Ella, it did feel impossible yet he wasn't the one at the wheel—she was, damn it—and perhaps that burned his ass most of all. Losing control, and to a little slip of a girl? And she'd decided to lose *him*. He was going to have to accept it, bitter though it might taste. He flew home less than a week later, never having made his presence known to her, and resolved on putting the young woman behind him for good. His resolve lasted at least as long as the flight home.

Almost immediately upon returning to Portland, he began to inch inexorably toward swallowing the truth, consuming it in very small portions, for the whole taken in one sitting might choke him: he accepted the fact that despite knowing Ella for such a brief time span—what was it? Five, maybe six nights spent together, all told?— he had developed feelings for her. It infuriated him because he'd worked so hard to keep himself detached from romantic entanglements only to get ensnared while he wasn't paying attention. The pain of losing her was real, constricting his chest to the point where he thought he might be having a heart attack and actually went to the doctor for a check-up.

After, he began to slowly come to terms with the idea that he might possibly love her. Once he was comfortable wearing that on his sleeve, he began to let seep in the crazy notion that he might just be *in love* with her. That was the most difficult of all. How could it be true? What was so different about this girl that caused him to fall so hard and fast for her? All these years he'd been with women—happily—and yet was easily able to walk away at any time. Why now? Why her? Was it her innocence? Her witty repartee? Was it that she continually stood up to him despite how he intimidated her? Or was it merely her ethereal beauty, the kind that left his mouth dry and his eyes locked on her? Most likely it was the amalgamation of all of these things. The real question now was how was he to get her back?

The answer seemed to be as simple as it was awful: he wasn't. Someone had finally said no to Ian Blackmon and that was essentially that.

As the months went by, he became used to the separation, perhaps as one gets used to a missing limb, but he never could get over wanting her. Even more disturbing to him was his complete lack of interest in any other women. For the first time in his life, he experienced a protracted period of sexual dormancy… and he didn't like it. Not since he'd begun to be sexually active at fifteen had he gone even a month without sex and now many months had gone by. In the beginning, right after Ella left, he'd gone to the club and tried topping one of the regular submissives but ended up retreating before they could become intimate. It felt too much like cheating.

By the end of the year he'd embraced his new way of life: he directed his energy and efforts into exercise and work. His net worth had nearly doubled and he was in the best fighting shape of his life. He was battle ready.

Still, the problem was thorny—even if he could get her back long enough to have a chance, he just didn't see a clear path to get her past their fleeting history together.

And now that so much time hung between them, it only made matters more difficult. Sailing his catamaran west of Tillamook, he spent long hours mulling the situation and ultimately realized he would have to force her to listen, to give him a chance. The question remained how? The elusive answer came to him one afternoon when Zoe pulled out an iPad and showed him a book—the book that was like a gift that fell to earth. Now he had a situation that would coerce Ella into his company, impel her to listen to him, and the convincing was up to him.

But he had to be sneaky about it: he didn't want to show his full hand—not right away. He would first make her believe that he only wanted her as a submissive, as was his original offer to her, and only as reparation for the legal breach.

How would he find Ariel? The last time he saw her she was an innocent girl, fresh out of college. Now she had a year of life abroad under her belt, not to mention a few million in her bank account. Would she be changed? He hoped to hell not and didn't think so. He'd never met anyone less affected by wealth than Ella: she'd still be the same sweet girl—he'd bet money on it.

He punches in the number he'd jotted down on the piece of paper in front of him.

Chapter 6

Less than an hour later, he calls. I'm glad the call comes so soon because my entire body had begun to tremble somewhat violently as soon as Stephen told me I was meeting Ian tomorrow evening. Over the past twelve months, I'd spent so many hours trying to exile the man from my heart and mind; leaving him nearly broke me in two. I had never understood real grief before I left Ian; now I definitely do—I understand it with my chest, my throat, and my stomach, in addition to my heart and soul.

How could a person fall in love in three weeks? We were together exactly eight nights with a few days strewn about here and there. It seems impossible but I so did. I loved the bastard so much. It took a Herculean effort to leave him and break off all communication. But I did it. *I did it*, and proved to myself that I was made of tempered steel. Maybe my name is Strong for a reason.

Warrior I may be, but I definitely bear battle scars. I left him because he whipped me... but even I had to admit the pain from losing Ian made the whip's bite pale in comparison. Pale into utter insignificance, I should qualify. I also might have given him a chance to explain himself more fully. He'd been so sweet a lover the night he took my virginity, going slowly, deferring his own pleasure to ensure mine. The least that I could do was to allow him another chance to explain why he felt the irrepressible need to beat on women.

Here's why I didn't give him the opportunity: I knew whatever he said, whatever words he so eloquently flung in my direction, I'd accept as gospel and stay with him— not because I'm weak or because I'm gullible, but simply because I love him too fucking much and that love leaves me way too vulnerable to him and his dirty little proclivities. And if I already love him after knowing him for just a few weeks, what would become of me if I had to walk away from the man after a few months or even years? Total annihilation.

So, a clean break was made, the bloody wound healed— albeit covered over with lumpy scar tissue— and my life kept on trucking.

But now? Now it's going to start all over again and the only thing left for me to do is answer the phone.

I pick it up on the fourth ring. "Ian."

I can hear the tremor in my voice so clearly—can he?

There's a moment of... not silence but emptiness, as if the single word, his name, needs to travel across a great divide of emotional distance.

"Hello, Ariel. Is this a convenient time to for you to speak to me?"

Exhale. Inhale. Breathe, you idiot. "Yes, fine."

"Good. I trust that you are well?"

I try to laugh, keep things light but it sounds more like something's lodged in my esophagus. "As well as can be expected, considering the circumstances."

"Yes. My attorney provided me with your number, informing me that you and I are to meet to discuss the matter between the two of us. Is that plan agreeable to you?"

"It is."

"I was given to understand that you are no longer residing in Portland?"

"Correct. I'm currently in Los Angeles."

"Ah. Would it be terribly inconvenient for you to make a trip to Oregon? I could send my corporate jet to pick you up?"

"That will work. Yes, fine. Are we still on for tomorrow evening?"

"If that's acceptable to you, then yes."

So polite, agreeable even, but that's how he sucks his prey into his lair to ravage, isn't it? "Okay. So how do I...

where do I meet the plane?"

"I'll have the pilot text you with the flight information tomorrow morning. You should plan on leaving Los Angeles no later than two o'clock. It's about a three-hour flight, and you'll want time to check into a hotel and get changed, I presume... Unless you'd care to stay with me?"

"No," I say far too quickly, hearing him laugh quietly in the background. Damn him, he said that just to get my back up and I fell for it. I should have accepted—that would show him.

"Well, then, if you could text me with your hotel information, I will pick you up at 7:45 so we could make an 8:00 reservation. Agreed?"

"No, just text me the name and address of the restaurant. I'll meet you there."

"If you prefer. I'll have my driver pick you up at your hotel and deposit you at the restaurant."

Deposit me? As if I'm a check to be cashed? But I suppose in a way I am some kind of deferred payment for his trials over my silly, little book. "I'll check for the flight information first thing tomorrow."

"Very good. I'm looking forward ..."

I disconnect the call without saying goodbye. My heart is hammering in my chest, my hands are so sweaty that my phone is slipping out of my grasp, and I think I might regurgitate my salad any minute now. In just about twenty-four hours, I get to see him again. It should feel like an onerous burden—after all, the man is suing me. But all I can think of is how much I want to see him, kiss him, hold him... and my very next thought is—what the hell am I going to wear? I'll have to go shopping tomorrow morning."

Chapter 7

Pierre has a room ready for Ian when he arrives at the restaurant. What he really would have preferred was to host the dinner at his house but he knew Ella wouldn't feel comfortable with that arrangement. Not now. Still, their discussion required discretion and privacy so he selected the French restaurant for its private dining rooms.

"Is this acceptable, Mr. Blackmon?" the maître d' is annoyingly fawning.

"Yes," he answers tersely, "it will do nicely. When my companion arrives, please ensure she is directed to join me here. Her name is Ariel Strong."

"Very good, sir. I'll send a waiter up immediately to take your drink order."

Ian nods at the man and pretends to look at the menu, effectively dismissing him. *I'm nervous*, he realizes with some small amount of shock. *When was the last time I felt this out of control? Was it when she left me? I've never felt this way in the boardroom, never with any other female, never in a fight I couldn't win. This woman has me twisted in knots.* He laughs. If she only knew.

Checking his watch, he expects she'll be here in about five minutes. His driver called as soon as he picked her up at her hotel.

The door opens and he catches his breath. Not her. It's a young waiter in a black suit that appears a bit too large for him. "Would you care to order drinks, sir?"

"Yes. I'd like a bottle of the California *Malbec*. Also, some mineral water. Thank you."

"Yes, sir."

As the waiter opens the door to take his leave, she is suddenly there in the doorway, the light from the hall radiating around her like an aura, and deepening the impact of the moment. When Ian makes eye contact, it feels as if the air gets immediately sucked out of the room, leaving him desperate for oxygen. He takes a step back before even realizing what it will say about his frame of mind.

Ella. She looks ethereal, angelic even, if angels wore killer heels. Her hair has gotten much longer, the soft waves cascade well past her shoulder blades, nearly to her waist. She's wearing fitted black pants that highlight some of her best attributes, and a silver silk camisole, over which she has on a mesh silver sweater, open so it covers only her arms. A belt with a huge buckle sits low on her hips—as do the pants—matching her sterling jewelry that catches teasing glints from the lamplight, and her shoes are black patent leather fuck-me stilettos. The phrase *dressed to kill* springs to mind and he smiles slowly.

He forces himself to stand still and wait for her to come to him, all the while his eyes drinking in every ounce of her. Yes, she looks different: more confident, a bit older, even thinner. But she also looks the same: sweet, unpretentious, and possibly… terrified.

Good.

He holds out his hand as she approaches. "Ariel. I'm pleased to see you."

"Ian." She places her hand in his and pulls it back just as quickly.

"Please, have a seat." He holds out her chair as she sits and then returns to his own. "You look beautiful. I hope all is well with you… apart from our little situation?"

She nods, taking a few moments to appraise the man in front of her. He's as handsome as she remembered— more handsome than the picture stubbornly residing in her memory: the impossibly strong jaw, straight nose, mercurial eyes, long lashes, and gracefully arched brows.

Oh, and that illicitly sensual mouth. The things he could do with that mouth. Naturally, everything is in proportion and topped by a headful of lustrous hair. She wouldn't even think about the body underneath his custom-tailored clothing. For Ella, that was wading into treacherous waters since she could barely resist him physically without even going there.

There are some changes, though. He looks leaner now and his eyes aren't as bright as before; in fact, if Ella were pressed to say, she'd swear he looks haunted. But why? It couldn't have anything to do with the lawsuit, could it?

"Yes, thank you, Ian. You look good, as well. And... how are you?"

"Fine. Business is hectic, but that's par for the course. Other than that, life is fairly serene."

The waiter returns with the bottle, opens it, and pours a bit into his glass to taste. Ian does and nods his approval, anxious for the man to make himself scarce. "Very good, thank you." After pouring the wine and water, the server retreats quickly.

Ian turns his full attention back to the girl seated in front of him. "So, Ariel, I'm exceedingly pleased to see you. I was so very disappointed when you disappeared last year without any explanation. May I ask why you chose to do so?"

Her face floods with red but she appears to arrest it—mind over matter—and thrusts her chin up, as if defying her own nature. "I think you know why, Ian. Let's not bother with playing games."

His head snaps back in surprise at her tone; clearly Ms. Strong has come into her own. "I know you were angry with me but I don't think it warranted the drastic actions you took. Obviously, you do?"

"I did at the time. Perhaps in retrospect it seems a tad excessive."

"Hmmm. When did you learn of your fellowship?"

Again she flushes. "The letter of acceptance arrived in the morning mail the very next day." She smiles, satisfied. "I had less than two weeks to pack up and get there before classes were slated to begin."

What incredibly bad timing for him. That damn letter arriving that day brought him a year's worth of misery.

She clears her throat. "Ian, I don't mean to be rude but I would really like to cut to the chase. Do you mind?"

Again the door opens and the waiter steps over to take their dinner order.

Ian leans back in his chair, feeling his equilibrium return to him, and casually sips his wine. His hand must be played oh so carefully—no need to rush it, despite her impatience, or rather because of it. He just watches her react to his presence and enjoys her unease. Or is it disdain? Perhaps his power no longer affects her quite so dramatically? The distinct possibility leaves an acidic taste in his mouth.

"So," she starts.

She's decided not to wait for his lead, then. Let's see where she goes with it.

"I understand you consider my book a violation of the contract you had me sign when we first met. May I explain the circumstances to you?"

He gestures with his hand for her to continue, and by his manner keeping the pressure up and on her. He just isn't sure it matters anymore.

She launches into her explanation. As she recounts the story, Ian watches her face closely, scrutinizing her for lies or half-truths. None. It seems as if she's being honest. He has to suppress his laughter at the impossible situation in which she finds herself, through no fault of her own, not really. Poor Ella: not good for her but excellent for him.

Initially, it was to his consternation to learn she had ignored the CA and in the most public of ways, by writing a damn book! The news had taken him aback for it didn't seem like something Ella would do, to tread on someone else's privacy so thoroughly. But when Delacroix read the book—and enjoyed it immensely, so he said—and saw there were no identifying details, Ian had felt better. Still, there remained a lingering sense of betrayal about the whole affair, over the fact that she profited monetarily by disclosing intimate details, however anonymously. Now that she explained how it unfolded, he can find it comical.

She flips her long hair back off her shoulder, distracting him from his thoughts and continues to speak. "The question now becomes what exactly will you accept as restitution for your injury? I'm perfectly willing to consider anything you put on the table, Ian."

A brow goes up. "Anything, Ariel?"

No blush—ten points for her. "Within reason. I just want to clear this matter up."

"You could have turned down the offer from the publishing company, you know."

She shrugs, bringing attention to her bare shoulders. Now on her second glass of wine, she's removed her sweater and her tanned shoulders gleam in the low light. A shiver runs up his spine: he wants her in his bed tonight. Is it within the realm of possibility? Her voice interrupts his reverie. "By that point it had been all over the Internet. It became a matter of continuing to give it away or make some money on it. Seemed like a no-brainer."

"Indeed. Allow me to say I have no interest in sharing in the monetary profits from the sale of the book or the film rights. None at all."

Her face registers her suspicion. "Go on."

"Nor do I wish to see the book pulled from the shelves; I'm rather flattered that it's so popular, as a matter of fact."

"So, then, I don't understand. What's the purpose of the lawsuit, Ian?"

"Very simple, Ariel: I want you to accept my original offer to you to become my submissive. The only difference is in the length of time. I'm extending the trial period from six weeks to six months. Should you satisfy the terms of our agreement, I will relieve you of all liability now and in the future for this specific book."

"Six months? You've got to be kidding."

"I'm afraid not, Ariel. Six months. And I want your definitive answer before we leave the restaurant this evening." He peers at her, his face now devoid of any amusement. "In fact, I'd like to begin the arrangement tonight."

Words apparently fail her. Instead, she turns a full-on glare at him, her eyes never wavering in their focus or intensity. Their verbal exchange has now evolved into a stare down. Neither wants to be the first one to look away. He knows his eyes are daring her to challenge him, reflecting confidence, arrogance, even expectation. Hers are blazing with disbelief and outrage. Either it would become a showdown or she'd capitulate—though he wouldn't bet on the latter based on her body language at the moment.

Pushing her chair back from the table, she practically spits at him. "Excuse me, please."

He rises with her, as ever polite, noting she leaves her sweater draped on the chair back. *Good*, he thinks, *she's not planning on ditching me, but still...*

"May I ask where you're going?"

"Not that it's any of your damn business but I assured my attorney that I wouldn't agree to anything without his prior approval. Since you demand an answer tonight, I need to speak to him first," and with that announcement, she flounces out of the room, her spiky heels clicking furiously on the marble floor. Worried he may have overplayed his hand, he watches her hips swing back and forth, and pulls out his own phone.

"How did it go, Ian?" Delacroix answers on the first ring.

"I'm not sure, Jackson, but not as good as I'd hoped or anticipated either. She was a lot more malleable when she was fresh out of college and without resources, and, more to the point, had no attorney to help fight her battles. What do we know about this Stephen Buchanan person? He's advised her not to commit to anything until he gives his okay."

"Buchanan? He's known to be a bit of a shark in protecting his clients' rights to their intellectual property. In other words, he's usually sitting on the other side of the courtroom—his clients are mostly victims of copyright infringement. Other than that? Nice guy. Late thirties, handsome, comes from an old family, tennis aficionado."

"Married?"

"I'm not sure—he was at one time. Is it material?"

"Hmmm… I'm sorry?"

"Why do you ask?"

"Oh, just wondering if he has more than her legal interests at stake. He wants her to get his approval first—I realize, of course, that she engaged him for legal counsel but after hearing my proposal, it's become more of a personal matter at this point, hasn't it?"

"Yes and no. First, he doesn't know about your intentions or didn't until now. At the very least, he'll expect to draw up papers for you to sign, relieving Ms. Strong of all liability if she satisfies your requirements, so you might as well disabuse yourself of the notion that you'll have company for breakfast tomorrow morning."

He laughs. "Well, I can always invite you."

Chuckling, Jackson disconnects the call, leaving Ian alone with his thoughts, to contemplate what he should do in either case. Ariel struts back into the room before he expects her return. He leaps to his feet as she approaches the table but she makes no move to sit down. This doesn't look good, Ian thinks, but he waits patiently for her next move.

"I accept your offer, Ian, with limits, naturally. I'd like you to draw up a list of all the… *obligations*… you'll require of me—everything; I want no surprises. Also, I need to know where I'll live while we're engaged in this relationship. My attorney will draw up a waiver for you to sign, relieving me of any legal liability for the specific book, as you put it."

"Very good. Shall I assume these conditions must be met before we begin? Or is it possible that we may start tonight before the paperwork is signed?"

"We can start tonight."

Chapter 8

I decide the best way to handle Blackmon is to lull him into a false sense of security. I could not believe the unmitigated audacity of the man to demand what he did of me. Yes, I'm still obscenely attracted to him, and yes, I'm probably still half in love with him... but I have absolutely no intention of becoming his submissive and allowing him to abuse me, physically or otherwise. Is he genuinely mad—as in out-of-his-mind crazy?

The last twenty-four hours have been exhausting. After Ian and I arranged to meet at the restaurant, I went to bed early, knowing I had to be on my A-game the next day, but sleep proved elusive. I finally conked out just before dawn, so I was grouchy all the next day, snapping at people a number of times—behavior that I instantly regretted and for which I apologized. I got myself ready and went shopping.

I opted for pants since I always feel more powerful when my legs are covered, for some reason... but I wanted to feel sexy, too. I knew Ian would look fantastic—he always does and so effortlessly—and I didn't want him to best me in anything. I needed every ounce of mojo available to me in order to pull this off. And pull it off I would.

At 1:45, the plane took off from a private airfield not too far from Burbank Airport. I got into Portland at about five and went straight to my hotel to check in. Seeing the familiar city again gave me a pang of nostalgia and I realized I had missed it. While I was here, I would go visit Mariah and a few other friends, for sure. Tonight I had to meet Ian at eight, so I had enough time to shower and dress at my leisure. Though I never drink anything stronger than wine, I nonetheless help myself to a bottle of Absolut from the mini-bar. It infuses me with calm and maybe a little bit of courage. I need all the help I can get.

As I see it, I have to anticipate what Ian's going to say. There are three possibilities: first, that he wants money. But I tend to doubt it. Ian Blackmon has more money than God. Going after my wealth would be small fry to him.

Second, that he wants to have the book pulled from bookstore shelves. That's a greater possibility but it seems silly. After all, so many people have already read it and there are millions of copies in circulation so pulling it wouldn't really achieve anything at this point.

The third and most probable possibility is that he wants something more personal: perhaps he wants to reestablish our relationship? But that also seems insane. Why would he? He could get any woman he wants. Plus, I left him in a hurry without even a phone call. He never tried contacting me after his first few attempts. At one point, I felt sure he'd put his considerable resources to use, easily finding me and showing up at my flat in the UK. But he never did.

I could only surmise that he didn't care... and it didn't matter anyway since *he whipped me*. I just couldn't get over that experience. Who could?

Here's what I figured I'd do: show up at the restaurant, find out what he wanted from me, and as soon as I learned his demands, I'd call Stephen and he would tell me what to do. But I must admit I didn't handle it well at all when he told me what he wanted. His fucking submissive? Really? I thought at least he'd upgrade me to the status of girlfriend. At this point I probably wouldn't take that either.

I took my time getting ready to meet him. I slid into the tight black pants and very high heels, softening the look with silk and silver. Checking the mirror after dressing, I nodded: it made just the right statement, sexy but powerful, feminine but not a pushover. I carefully applied some make-up—enough to look good but not too much. Ian didn't like garish... and then I remembered that I didn't care what Ian liked, damn it. The make-up was war paint and I was dressing for battle.

After he makes his outrageous proposal, I step away to call Stephen as promised. It is quite a conversation.

"Let's have it, Ella. What does he want?"

"I warn you it's shocking, Stephen. I think Blackmon has lost his mind."

"Don't' fret: I've been around the block a time or two. Try me."

"Okay. Well, you know what my book is about, right? It seems that Mr. Blackmon would like me to assume the role of his submissive for a period of six months in order to rid myself of any liability for his injury resulting from my big, bad book."

"You've got to be kidding?"

I manage to squeeze out a brittle laugh despite the fact that my body is as taut as a bow and arrow tensed to fly. "My words exactly, Stephen. But, no, he doesn't appear to be joking. Further, he wants a definite answer before we leave the restaurant and, here's the best part: he wants to begin this relationship tonight."

"Not going to happen. Let me think a minute, Ella. We don't want to give him a definite answer—that won't work for us."

"Originally I planned to placate him to the best of my ability. Should I just agree to everything and then we'll plan from there?"

"Agree to begin tonight? How will you handle that one?"

"Well, I figure I can go with him to his place and begin by asking him to lay everything out in front of me. After, I'll go back to my hotel. I'm not going to sleep with him or even spend the night, obviously."

"I'm just concerned that if you agree to his terms and then renege, it might just piss him off enough to really go after you, Ella. Blackmon has a reputation among his adversaries for going right for the jugular and not stopping until there's a river of arterial blood at his feet. I'm not convinced it's a smart thing to do."

"So then what do you think I should do at this point? Let's face it: whichever way I go, I'm going to piss him off... unless I do what he wants and I'm not going to do that. Never."

"I suppose our choices are limited right now so go ahead and agree for now. Meet with him in private and have him tell you in no uncertain terms what he requires. Then let's talk again. Okay?"

"Yes, okay, and thanks, Stephen. I appreciate your support."

"You're welcome. Good luck, Ella."

When I agreed to begin tonight I could tell by the astonished look in Ian's eyes that he didn't expect that answer at all. That was satisfying on some small level. He pays the check, both of us silent, and then ushers me into a black limo for the ride back to his place. My heart is slamming against my rib cage, but I try like hell to look calm and collected. I do not want any cracks in my armor to show, none at all, even though close proximity to him is wreaking havoc on my equilibrium. God, but the man is smokin' hot. Why oh why must he be so beautiful? It's not fair especially when he could be such a pompous ass. I glance over at him, sullen in my space at one end of the back seat, as far away as I can get without being too obvious. Interestingly he makes no attempt to close the gap.

He is quiet, too, and he looks solemn, glum even. Why? As far as he knows, he's won. He should be triumphant, taking a victory lap. But he most definitely isn't and it gives me pause to wonder if he is aware that my capitulation isn't genuine. Bizarrely, I feel regret for my deception and almost come clean. Almost. But I have to remember he is looking out for himself so I have to do the same.

When I walked into that restaurant and got my first

eyeful of him, my knees wobbled—I hate when that happens, when knees just give out so readily. It's downright scary, especially when one is wearing stilettos. Anyway, tonight he's wearing a navy blue suit, white shirt, and dark maroon silk tie. The suit fits him so well, the pants highlighting his slim waist, narrow hips, and long legs. He's always so put together, as well. Have I ever seen him in an off moment? Not really, even after we had passionate sex and rolled all around the bed pawing at each other, he still looked fine afterward. I was the one whose hair stuck out in every direction and whose cheeks were chafed red by Ian's five o'clock shadow (not to mention having sore nips from his loving attention and aching legs from being held open too long by a certain someone with very strong hands). These ribald thoughts are making me sort of desperate to jump into bed with him. Bad Ella. I begin to think of the devastation from the latest hurricane in the Midwest.

Traffic is light so we arrive at our destination, an impressive apartment building, in under ten minutes.

I glance sharply at him. "Have you moved?"

"No," he answers in a soft voice. "I use this apartment to house business associates from out of town. I thought it would be best to work out the details of our arrangement on neutral territory."

Nodding in agreement, I step out of the sedan. The doorman holds the elevator for us and, luckily, there are two men already in the car so that saves us both from any stilted conversation. Finally, we reach his place and he settles me in the living room and goes to the bar to get some cognac. When he returns to me, my stomach sinks and I know it's show time.

I twist my hair behind me and then over my shoulder, pulling my sweater around my body a bit tighter. "So. Here we are."

"Yes." He hands me a cognac.

For a minute, he doesn't look like the big, bad CEO who wants to manipulate me. Instead, I see a flash of boyish charm and insecurity in his countenance. It gives me pause but I try to collect myself quickly, reminding myself that he is an adversary and a formidable one at that.

"Okay, Ian. I agreed to begin tonight because I want your cards on the table. I want to know every single thing you'll require of me during this time we'll be together."

"So are you saying that you didn't really agree to it back in the restaurant? First, you want to see everything it entails?"

How to proceed? Should I just spill the truth?

"I agreed, yes, and I don't plan to renege. However, the devil is always in the details... and that's why I need to know them. Maybe before that, I'd like to know why you're doing this, why you would try to coerce me into this situation when you could have any woman you want with a snap of your fingers? It seems very strange to me."

Running his hand through his hair, he looks me directly in the eye. "I'm doing it because I want you back, Ariel. Coerce? Well, last time I gave you free rein—and you ran from me. You never even gave me a chance to apologize... didn't even give me the courtesy of a phone call." He stops there, as if he's said too much. Did I hurt him? Does he realize how much he hurt me?

The strident tone in his voice changes to a softer one, almost a whisper. "Ella, I believe if you give this situation a real chance, it may turn out to be a life-changing event. But you won't know if you don't try."

"Life changing?" I chuckle but it's laced with bitterness and he recognizes that.

"You see? Your attitude may preclude us from having any success in this endeavor. As for the details, they're simple. This type of relationship requires a power exchange: you allow me to have all the power and in return I take care of you. By putting a time limit on it, it may be easier for you to relinquish power in the short term, knowing it's for a finite span. Six weeks was never enough but six months will give you a good idea of what this particular lifestyle entails. It is my hope that after six months, we may both decide to continue together, one way," he sips his brandy, keeping his eyes trained on mine, "or another."

"Why would you want to?"

He sighs, clearly exasperated. "I like you, Ariel. Do you find that so impossible to believe? You're intelligent, you're beautiful, you make me laugh, you're sexy, and I was your first man. I like that, too." He stops, waiting for something; I'm not sure what.

"Must I live very close to you?"

"I'd prefer you live *with* me, actually."

I allow myself to gasp. "Live with you? Are you insane?"

"I might be, but not because I want to live with you. Why is that insane?"

I swallow loudly. "So I may infer from your reply that I would need to live near you since I'd never agree to move in, Ian. That's asking too much. What about the whole punishment-reward thing?"

"What about it?"

"Will you insist upon the punishment part?"

"If you're referring to the whip, no. But there are other forms of discipline that don't hurt as much physically. We can start slowly and take it from there."

"That's what you said the last time," I grumble. "Didn't work out that way."

"True. And I am very sorry for what occurred. I think it was because you were so natural at everything, a true submissive, that I got carried away in the moment. It won't happen again; I promise you, Ella." His hand reaches for mine resting on the sofa and I pull it away before he can touch me. He looks injured and again a pang reverberates in my chest. Am I being a cold bitch here? Or just sensible? Why is it that I'm not sure at all?

He sighs again. "I wanted to begin tonight, Ella, because I wanted to touch you, to hold you... so much. It's been a long year." He pauses, his eyes shifting to the floor. "But I can see that hope was overly optimistic... and it's not going to happen."

After he lets that observation hang in the air for a long moment, he looks back up and smiles sadly at me, and then flicks his wrist to check his watch. "It's getting late and you've had a long day. I'll take you back to your hotel now and you can think about everything we've discussed tonight and give me your answer tomorrow night. Okay?"

"You called me Ella," is the only thing that comes out of my mouth.

"Yes," he whispers softly, his eyes filled with... what? Is it uncertainty? Regret? I just can't tell. I think about spending the night with him, in bed together, holding him, and having him hold me... and my chest tightens at the thought. I want to! So badly. But I shouldn't want to. He's a bastard who's suing me. How much more kicking do I need before I get it through my head, for God's sake? Why on earth do I still want him?

"That sounds like a rational plan," I respond, my voice sounding perfectly normal—there's no hint of the turmoil raging within. I'm surprising myself tonight. "And, yes, I am exhausted. Thank you, Ian."

He drives me to my hotel himself, in his little two-seater sports car. When I turn to say goodnight, I extend my hand to him. He accepts it but uses it to pull me closer and kisses me gently on the lips. No force, no tongue—just a soft kiss that confuses me even further.

"Good night, Ella. I look forward to seeing you again. Thank you for coming to Portland to meet with me."

I nod my acceptance. "Good night, Ian. I'll speak with you tomorrow evening."

He assists me out of the car. Right before I step through the revolving door entrance of the hotel, I chance a look back. He's standing by the passenger door, leaning on his car with his arms crossed and his long legs tilted outward. His whole demeanor is melancholy and it makes me sad, too. I wave and muster a small smile before heading into the lobby with a heavy heart and a guilty mind

Chapter 9

She was just playing him.

She never had any intention of agreeing to any of his demands. As soon as she returned from making her phone call to her attorney, he pretty much knew he'd lost the game. His sweet, innocent little Ariel had become a force to be reckoned with and getting her back wasn't going to be easy—perhaps not even possible. He might have to tell her how much she had come to mean to him in their brief time together, how he actually loves her. Tell her even before he is sure of her feelings for him.

He shakes his head. *Never.* He'll never give someone—a woman—that much power over him. If she knew how she could use it to destroy him...

After he'd had time to consider the evening, he realized that his plan never stood a chance, not a ghost of one. Out of the two of them, an open court battle would hurt him far worse than her—he had the most to lose, and surely any two-bit attorney would recognize that truth immediately. He would tarnish his sterling reputation, his business credibility, the respect of the corporate community... What would Ella lose? Right now, her public name was built on a sexy book. If anything, it could only help cement her reputation as an author of risqué prose.

If Ian could recognize it even from such a subjective position, certainly she and her high-priced lawyer could, too. That meant they would call his bluff and when he thought about it, he really had no other hand to play: he might be the dominant personality, but she held all the strong cards.

He has to smile. When he first set eyes on her, she appeared so shy, so easily flustered. When she handed him his purchase at Archipelago that day they met and called him sir, it set all his instincts as an aggressive male and a sexual dominant on fire. But one small, uttered word did not a submissive make.

Still, he's certain she has submissive inclinations— it's in the way she responds to a sharp command—but perhaps she is willing to give up control only in a sexual context and only sometimes. He knows that is often the case with strong women who wield a lot of power in their careers, their lives in general. He'd probably asked her for too much control and she was only willing to give up some. And the pain? No, she won't accept it, at least not the kind delivered from a whip.

Pity. The crack of a whip is so sexy, and seeing it dance and flicker across the silky skin of a squirming girl excites him beyond belief.

But surely he can live without it.

He could live with or without just about anything if he could get her back. He just doesn't know how exactly to go about it. So far, he'd only managed to alienate her further... and in the process cost her money and royally piss her off. Gone is the shy, innocent girl of last year, and in her place stands a kick-ass, confident young woman with a fat bank account and a pricey attorney. Perhaps the best thing to do right now is retreat. By doing so, he'll run the risk of never seeing her again. But right now he holds a purely sucky hand and it is time to fold. The thought depresses the hell out of him.

He wakes up before dawn the next day and immediately the preceding night infiltrates his brain, depressing him again. He'll call Jackson today and tell him to withdraw the lawsuit. He won't sign a waiver relinquishing his right to sue but he will let it go... let Ella go. If she doesn't come back to him, well, that is that. He'll manage to forget her and find someone else eventually. After a year of celibacy, it is high time.

"What? Why are you cutting and running, Ian? Are you actually letting this little girl win so easily?"

He laughs lightly, no heart in the forced humor. "Jackson, I know when to call the game. She was playing me for a fool last night, allowing me to think she'd acquiesce to my demands when she had no such intention. Let's face it: I can't let this get to court and she knows it. Just drop the suit and advise her attorney. I have no plan to speak directly with her any further."

"Okay, Mr. Blackmon. You're the boss. I'll give Mr. Buchanan the good news right now. I guess I'll see you this weekend?"

"I'll be there."

Before going in to the office, he visits the gym on the lobby floor to get in some exercise, wanting to burn off some negative energy. As usual the receptionist—Stephanie, is it?—tries her damnedest to engage him in conversation. He smiles politely and keeps going.

Thinking about Ella's reaction when her lawyer tells her he dropped the suit makes him grin. She'll certainly be happy and relieved... but will she also feel disappointed that she won't see him again? At this point he really doesn't know worth a damn. For a man adroit at reading people as easily as others read the newspaper, Ian can't begin to assess what is going on in that little minx's head—and that is probably part and parcel of her allure for him.

Since his defeat last night, he'd made a few decisions. Probably the most important one is that he would now begin to move on, starting immediately. He was planning on going to the club Saturday night and playing with one of the subs there—he is not cut out to be a monk, for God's sake. Getting laid will surely improve his disposition. He was looking forward to being in that atmosphere again, with like-minded people—he and Jackson would go there after the *Tae Kwon Do* tournament at the dojo.

Rubbing his face, Ian leans back in his chair and stares into space. His back aches from sitting all day, despite the fact that he'd dropped a small fortune on the ergonomic chair in his office. *I have to get out of here,* he thinks. He'd been spending ten-hour stints at work nearly every day since his firm acquired a failing solar panel manufacturer that he and his team were trying to prop up—make it solvent and then hopefully profitable. It was a lot more work than they'd bargained for when they purchased the damn company.

He'd go to the club tonight—this time definitely. It had been three weeks since he'd dropped the lawsuit against Ariel and he hadn't heard from her, not a peep. He'd planned on going to the club weeks ago but then business picked up to a frenetic pace and he was just too tired to do anything other than some exercise and plopping on the sofa, using the remnants of his energy to hold up a glass of wine and a remote control. Yes, he'd been too tired to go to the club—it had nothing to do with hoping Ella would contact him. Nothing at all.

No, he was looking forward to going out tonight and spending some time with a warm and willing woman. Checking his watch, he realizes it's already seven. Time enough to go home, shower and change, and make it to the private club before all the available women are spoken for. He clears off his desk and picks himself up out of the chair, a physical and mental effort at this point.

"Ian, about time you showed your ugly mug around here."

He had just walked into the main room of the club and Jackson was threading his way to him through the throng of people. "Finally. Are you drinking this evening or planning to play?"

Looking around at who was already in the room, he nods in approval. "Play, I think. Anyone new and interesting tonight?"

"As a matter of fact, yes. I did see a pretty redhead I haven't seen here before. I went to the restroom, though, and couldn't find her when I returned. Maybe she went downstairs." His bright eyes continually scan the room.

The club lighting is dim, the music pulsing so loudly and so heavy on the bass, it resonates inside the body. All the elements of the club—the dark, the rhythm of the bass, the scent of sweat and pheromones—combine to evoke the cradle of humanity, the primacy of the jungle and all things primal. It gets the heart pumping ferociously, and adrenaline surging through veins. There's a dance floor and a huge circular bar on the first floor. All the action takes place in the dungeon that begins in the rear rooms and spills down to a floor below. Because the club is private, everyone pretty much knows everyone else, at least by nodding acquaintance, and new people are allowed to join based only on recommendation by longstanding members or by satisfying a lengthy application process. The annual membership fees are hefty enough to keep out all but the most determined and well-heeled patrons, as well. Privacy and discretion come at a premium.

Club members are allowed to bring guests, however, so around the bar there are usually fresh faces. Guests don't generally wander too far afield their first night there and aren't allowed in some restricted areas of the club.

"Ian!" A pretty dark-haired woman runs up to him, leaping into his arms.

"Juanita?" He looks at her admiringly, assessing the woman from head to foot. "What's different?"

The young woman laughs. "Oh, about twenty pounds and a new set of boobs." She swivels from right to left, sticking her chest up. "You like?"

Laughing, he nods in assent. "Very much. Though I liked them well enough before, too."

She pats his cheek. "You're so sweet. It's so good to see you back here. Are you topping anyone tonight?"

"I just arrived a minute ago." He winks. "I think I might have a drink first."

"Okay, well find me if you're interested. I'll be on the

dance floor showing off my new cleavage."

"Will do. Jackson, a drink first?"

"Sure, why not? I want to see if I can scope out that redhead again."

The two men walk over to the bar. "Ah, thar she blows."

Ian arches his brow. "I don't think any woman would appreciate your using that reference about her."

Jackson's grin is rueful. "No wonder I never get laid." He tosses his head back with a spurt of laughter. "I never know whether being seen with you is an asset or liability. Either I might bask in your reflected glory having your stupidly handsome face by my side or I might wither in comparison. But since I'm a loyal friend, I'll err on the side of camaraderie."

"Much appreciate it."

"Ian?"

He turns to see a tall, slender blonde strolling toward him. "Kim." He leans over to give her a kiss on the cheek. "God, it's good to see you. How's everything?"

"Much better, thank you. It is so great to see you, too, Ian. I never had the chance to properly thank you."

He smiles. "Can I buy you a drink? We were just heading to the bar. Jackson, do you know Kim?" He almost forgot and tacked on her last name—club etiquette dictated that surnames not be used.

Jackson is too busy gaping at the blond woman for intelligent conversation. Ian understands: utterly beautiful, Kim attracts attention wherever she goes. Even more appealing than her incredible physical beauty is her genuinely kind personality. Kim is an absolute sweetheart.

Ian slings his arm protectively around Kim as they continue to the bar. While Kim and Jackson converse, Ian glances up and directly into a pair of very determined, very surprised, perhaps even angry blue eyes.

Ella? Here?

Chapter 10

I'd been rehearsing what I was going to say to Ian when I called him back the next day to give him my answer, when Stephen's call came in. My nerves were so on edge that I jumped when Aretha started singing. I grabbed for the phone to quiet it.

"Yes?"

"Ella, Stephen. Incredible, great, fantastic news. Blackmon dropped the lawsuit."

"What? Just like that?"

"Just like that. I just got off the phone with his attorney. He said as far as his client is concerned the matter is closed."

"Wow. I'm... confused... happy, but confused. It doesn't seem like him to just change direction like that with no explanation."

"I think Blackmon realized he was going to go down in flames so he cut his losses. He's a smart man, Ella, and he couldn't win this one. I was really surprised he tried at all but after getting to know you a bit, I may understand his motives."

I laugh nervously; Stephen has never said anything untoward to me so I wasn't expecting that compliment. "Well, thanks for letting me know. Do I need to do anything now?"

"Anything? You mean like send him a thank-you note?"

"Uh, yeah, I guess so. Is there a proper etiquette for situations like these?"

His responding laugh is sharp and loud. "No, Ella, not really. My advice is to do nothing, just go on with your life as if this upsetting little event never happened—unless you want to celebrate your win over the big, bad Ian Blackmon, for it is a win. In fact, why don't I take you out for a celebratory dinner?"

"Oh, thanks, but no, Stephen. I think I'm going to head back to L.A. sooner than later. But thank you... for everything. Really."

"No thanks necessary, Ella. I'm taking a vacay on your dime, after all. Take care and please let me know if you need me for anything."

"Yes, thanks, Stephen. Oh, and enjoy your vacation." I disconnect quickly, horrified that he was hitting on me. Or was he? I don't trust my own judgment these days. Do I even want to go back to L.A.? I have some thinking to do now that the lawsuit's been dropped. Even though I know I should feel elated, somehow I don't. In fact, I feel let down in some way. How odd.

That night I have dinner with Mariah. I haven't told anyone what's been going on for to do so, would be to further infringe on the CA. It would be great to have a friend with whom to commiserate but it is what it is, as Stephen would say.

"So," she says between bites of a plate of *enchilada mole*, "how long will you be staying in Portland?"

I shrug, eyes scanning the crowded restaurant. I find myself doing that every time I leave my hotel room. Who or what I'm looking for, I don't know. "Not sure, honestly. If the whole crazy book thing never happened, right now I'd be applying to doctoral programs and looking for an interesting internship. Having all money worries removed is liberating to be sure, but it also makes goals less clear, if you know what I mean."

"Mmm, wish I did, Ella, but, no. I'm still a working stiff. I do have your old bedroom still vacant and I could use the extra rent if you're interested in hanging around for a while?"

"Hmm, maybe. Let me mull it over tonight and I'll let you know tomorrow. Good enough?"

"Absolutely. Mmm, you have to taste this, here," and holds a forkful out to me.

We spend the rest of dinner stuffing our faces while Mariah gives me all the details on her recent trip to San Francisco.

A week later I move into her spare bedroom, to Mariah's relief. I've decided to stay in Portland for a month while I decide what to do with my life. After, I'm going to visit my parents, and then maybe make a quick trip to New York to meet with my agent and visit some museums. I've decided to put my real estate search on hold until I make decisions on my immediate future—it would be silly to do otherwise.

I never called Ian and he hasn't made any effort to contact me. I know I should be happy; I know I should feel nothing but relief... but I don't. I mean, I'm definitely relieved about the lawsuit going away and there was never any real chance that I'd actually become his submissive. But if I'm brutally honest with myself, I'm also massively disappointed. I'm sort of crushed that I won't see him again. I've been pining for the man for the entire past year and I have to remind myself of the reason why I wrote the book in the first place: *I missed him*.

How can I possibly have fallen in love with a man after knowing him less than a month? But then I think, who wouldn't fall in love with him? Even with his deviant predilections, he's an amazing man. He's wickedly intelligent, incredibly competent in so many ways, he's funny, he's gorgeous, he's generous with his money if not himself, and he treated me very well—apart from the little matter of the whipping.

But I agreed to it. It wasn't as if he forced me into it. I was curious about the whole thing and I never expected he would strike me that hard. Why did he? That's what I don't get.

I've been reading up on BDSM and I understand it a little better than I did back then... but understanding intellectually is not the same as living it. I've always been able to see how erotic it can be… but I'm not certain I'm wired for it. And I take exception to the fact that Ian called me a natural submissive. I'm not. I'm strong and capable and independent—I don't plan on submitting anything to anyone. So there, Ian Blackmon. Have a nice life.

The intercom rings one Friday afternoon. Mariah's not home from work yet and she didn't mention she was expecting anyone. I pick up the intercom. "Yes?"

"Yes, Ms. Strong. I have a Naomi Lewis here to see Mariah?"

Naomi Lewis? Yes, Mariah mentioned she might be hanging with us this weekend; she just didn't say to expect her. "Oh. Okay, send her up."

"You must be Ella," the redheaded woman shouts, as I open the door and she flings herself into my arms. "I've heard so much about you!"

"Good things, I hope?"

"Oh, yes, Very good things. You are Ella, aren't you?"

Laughing, I admit it's me. "Naomi, it's nice to meet you. Mariah speaks highly of you, too."

"Now you're just lying," she chuckles. "Mariah thinks I'm completely insane. And I am, FYI. But it's a fun insane, not a dangerous, creepy insane."

I like her instantly. Still giggling, I go into the kitchen to get us some wine. "White or red?"

"Ooh, definitely red. What do you have?"

"Is Cabernet okay?"

"Perfect. Thank you."

I pour out two glasses and we bring them into the living room. Digging out my iPod from my oversized bag, I park it in the dock and put on some Chili Peppers.

"So," Naomi says, leaning back into the sofa. "Has Mariah mentioned what we're planning for tonight?"

I swallow a sip of wine. "Planning? No, she hasn't said anything."

"Really? Hmm, I wonder why. Okay, well I'll wait until she gets here to explain."

"That sounds mysterious. What's in the bag?" I gesture to a large silver shopping bag she's parked at her feet.

"Weeeell," she says, stretching out the syllable, "that's part of what we're doing tonight."

"Okay, well, now the suspense is killing me. Spill your guts, Naomi."

At that precise moment, the key turns in the door and in struts Mariah. When she sees Naomi, she drops her coat and bag and makes a beeline for the woman. "You made it! I was sure you'd bail on me yet again. I never get to see you anymore."

"My job has taken over my life... but I'm all yours tonight and Ella here was just about to extort our plans for the evening out of me. How come you didn't tell her?"

Mariah shrugs. "Nothing nefarious afoot; I just wanted it to be a fun surprise."

My eyes volley back and forth, feeling as if I'm watching tennis. "What, damn it?"

"We're going to my club tonight."

"Your club? That's the surprise?"

"It's a very special club, Ella. Isn't it, Mariah?"

"Oh, yes. Mucho special."

"Really?" I ask. "What's so special about it?"

The look on Naomi's face has me worried. "Well, considering the racy book you wrote, you may not find it all that unusual, but it's a private BDSM club and I'm taking you and Mariah as my very important guests."

"You are?" I look helplessly at Mariah. "We are?"

Mariah nods slyly. "I thought it would be fun—and educational—to see a real club after reading your imaginative novel. C'mon, Ella, it will be epic."

Naomi jumps in. "And trust me, there are hunky men always lurking about there—always. Beautiful men, both Dom and sub, whatever trips your trigger. What do you think, ladies? Are you all in?"

I take a big swig of wine, gulping it like water. "So what's in the bag?"

Shrugging again, Naomi casually says, "Oh, some

fetwear, and some plain but sexy clothes—things for you and Mariah to pick through and try on. I have mine on already." She stands and removes the tunic-type sweater she's wearing and underneath she has on a very short, very tight black latex dress that zips up in front from bottom to plunging neckline.

"Oh. Wow. Okay, let me think about this idea for a second." I try to clear my head but the wine is already causing my brain to buzz. "Are we allowed to just sit at the bar and observe? I mean, we don't have to do anything, right?"

"Noooo, but you very well might want to, once you get an eyeful of some of those men. Sometimes members even bring guests who aren't into this particular thing so you can meet conventional people there every so often. You know, normal men."

Mariah claps her hands. "Oh, no, I want to meet the abnormal ones! Normal is boring."

I look at both of their eager faces and shrug my shoulders. "Oh, what the hell? What's the worst that can happen?"

"Famous last words. Didn't Napoleon say that ere he saw Elba? Or was it Anne Boleyn? General Custer?"

I laugh. "Okay, Mariah, I take back the fate-tempting words. Sorry."

Mariah leaps to her feet and grabs my hand. "Come on, let's go try on some bad-girl clothes."

Two hours and two glasses of wine each later, we're dressed for the night out. Mariah is wearing a black leather corset that makes her body look killer—she can't breathe but it's worth it. A short black leather skirt—so short it's almost not there—completes the outfit. Her shiny reddish-blond hair is piled high on her head and she's doubled down on the eyeliner.

I opt for a black leather bra that happens to fit me as if it were made for me personally. Over that I'm wearing a sheer white see-through long-sleeved top. It has a vee-neck that plunges down low enough to allow the top of the bra to peek out. Naomi wraps a pewter choker around my throat—slave chic, I suppose. Since I wasn't about to wear the ridiculous skirts she brought for us (they looked like broccoli rubber bands), I slide into—and slide is the operative word—a pair of super tight Lycra jeans-style pants, and my black stiletto shoes. I leave my hair down and put on some extra make-up.

"Excellent!" Naomi exclaims when she sees us. "We all look so hot we're gonna set the place on fire. It's just about seven-thirty now. Should we grab a bite on the way there? The club usually doesn't start hopping until about nine."

"Are we really going to go into a restaurant dressed like this? I don't think so—unless you let me wear a fake nose and mustache to disguise myself."

Laughing, both Naomi and Mariah roll their eyes and Mariah says, "Ella, I swear I don't know how you wrote that dirty novel of yours. You're such a prude. A babe but a prude."

I stick my tongue out at her. "Am not," I huff. "Just sensible and slightly dignified."

Naomi solves the problem for us. "How about we go to the diner on the same block as the club? They're used to seeing it all."

"Okay," I say in defeat. I have a strong feeling I'm going to be overruled in everything we do tonight. I have to admit, though, I'm having fun for the first time in... well, since I can remember.

We get to the club at nine on the dot. Naomi signs us in and we have to show ID and sign disclaimers relieving the club from any liability for insult or injury—not the most reassuring thing in the world. As soon as we enter the room, my blood pressure rockets up: it's scary. Everyone is in various stages of undress and/or outlandish clothing. There are very big, scary men dressed in black leather, strolling around, coiled whips and handcuffs dangling from their belts. One even smiles at me—an evil smile—and I get icy shivers sprinting up and down my spine. He sees my reaction and his grin gets wider. I reach for Mariah's hand and clutch it for dear life. All of a sudden this is not so fun anymore.

"Naomi," I shout over the din of the loud music, "dumb question: do you know most of the people here?"

"I know many of them by face, not name. I've been a member for about two years already so, yeah. But there are always new faces cropping up."

I notice an older blond man checking out Naomi and she looks back at him with interest. Maybe she'll go a separate way tonight? And that thought leads me to a chilling one: what if Mariah and Naomi both hook up and I'm left by myself? No, they wouldn't do that to me. Would they?

"Come on," Naomi shouts into my ear, "let's go to the restroom and freshen up." I nod and the three of us head over to the ladies' room line. It take us nearly twenty minutes to make it to the front, use the facilities and wend our way back to the bar. Phew. I think I've already seen enough and that was just from the ladies' room queue alone. I need a strong drink and soon.

Somehow, we manage to snag three bar stools, moving them into a contiguous row, and order drinks. Naomi is looking around and speaking to Mariah. I hear her say, "Oh my God, it's Ian! He hasn't been here in ages." My head jolts up when I hear the name and I see the man she's referring to right away.

It's *my* Ian.

Well, it's Ian Blackmon. Shit!

He hasn't spotted us yet so I watch as first a brunette throws herself at him and then a gorgeous blonde. Ian seems happy to see them—in fact, I've never seen him so relaxed and smiling as he is now. I feel a hot rush of jealousy surge through me when the woman touches his chest. Why is he carefree with her and all stern and dominant with me? Does he consider me beneath him or something? I have to wonder. Naomi turns and catches me staring."

"You like?"

"Ian?"

"Yes, he's gorgeous, I know. But be warned: you and

every female in the world like him. And he's *très* picky."

"I know him," I say, my heart pounding so hard and fast, it seems to eclipse the volume of the blaring music.

"You do? By the look on your face, it's not a good memory. You look terrified, Ella. Are you okay?"

I nod weakly.

"Huh. Have to say, I'm surprised to see him here—he hasn't been at the club in, oh, it has to be a year or more. I assumed he got married or moved away or something."

I close my eyes and try to think. Should I leave now or wait until he spots me? I want to see him so badly but I know I shouldn't. For whatever reason, all logic flees me when the equation contains Ian Blackmon as a variable. Right now I can't think at all. I down the rest of my drink in one big swallow and nearly choke at the burn. I don't want to look at him again but I can't help myself. And just as I look up at him, I see another woman rush in and grab at him, kiss him, and white-hot anger infuses my system. What is wrong with me? He's not mine and I have no right to be jealous. But I am—so fucking jealous.

I watch as he swings an arm around the beautiful blonde's shoulders and feel another injection of adrenaline pump into me. They start walking toward the bar, *toward me*. The woman is speaking to another man—the blond man who earlier caught Naomi's attention—who seems to be with them and Ian happens to glance up and that's when he sees me.

His pretty eyes lock right into mine.

The look on his face is one of utter shock. I continue to watch as various emotions flash across his beautiful countenance but they fly by so fast it's impossible to grab them long enough to discern exactly what they are. He says something to his friends, disengages from the blonde, and then heads straight in my direction. My legs begin to tremble as the bartender replaces my drink with a fresh one and I smile up at him gratefully.

"Ian." My voice comes out more breath than voice.

I'm so nervous that my whole body is shaking at this point and, please God, I don't want him to notice.

"Ariel. You look surprised to see me here."

"I might say the same to you. And, yes. I guess I'm not surprised that you're here but I wasn't expecting it... and I *am* surprised at your... uh, demeanor."

One brow rises and there's a hint of a smile on his lips. "My demeanor? Care to elaborate?"

I shift my weight on the stool, trying for comfort in a wretchedly uncomfortable moment. For a moment I lose his attention. ADHD? "It's just that you seem so, um, friendly? I watched two women maul you just now and you actually smiled and chatted with them."

"And you find that unusual?"

"Well... yes, for you. Normally you're kind of aloof. And I thought you didn't like people getting too close or familiar with you."

He leans in and speaks directly into my ear so neither of us has to shout or strain to hear over the music. "I apologize if I gave you that impression, Ariel. I myself tend to avoid unfair generalizations when possible."

My face gets hot and I know I must be scarlet with embarrassment. He was always so good at verbal sparring—always, as in all twenty-five days we spent together. But still I try to dig myself out. "When I went to your office? You seemed quite cool with the women you employ... and yet you see them daily..." I trail off weakly, realizing I'm just making things worse for myself.

"True, but then I don't put my staff in bondage and do rude things to their bodies, either. That kind of proximity tends to breed familiarity."

My cheeks are now on fire; any moment now I'm expecting to spontaneously combust. He's discomfiting me on purpose and enjoying my misery. I mutter under my breath, *Thank God for small favors* but I'm not sure he hears me so I speak up, "And these women you do?"

"Some of them," he says mildly, glancing around. "In the past." He focuses on me again and stares me in the eye. "Your turn now. To explain, I mean," he adds with a wicked grin. "What the hell are you doing here?"

He's pissed that I'm intruding on his stomping ground? "I came at the urging of a friend who's a member here. It was just meant as a lark. If my presence makes you uncomfortable, I'll leave. Actually, I wasn't planning on staying beyond a few minutes anyway."

"Please don't leave on my account, Ariel." His eyes begin to gleam and his lips stretch into a smile. An evil smile. "In fact, would you like me to show you around?"

Mariah and Naomi finally take notice of the spectacularly gorgeous man in front of me. "Ella?" Mariah nearly shouts over the music.

"Naomi, I believe you know Ian?"

She nods. "I used to see you around... though not lately. Glad to see you've come back."

Ian nods his head in greeting.

"Mariah, this is Ian Bla—" Oops, almost forgot the no surname rule.

Mariah smiles, trying to make herself heard over the music. "Yes, I remember Ian. He came to our condo looking for you after you absconded from the country last year."

He offers a restrained smile to Mariah. "Nice to see you again, Mariah. And it's also very nice to see you again, Naomi. I'm going to steal Ariel away from you ladies for a little while... if that's okay?"

Both of them turn to me and I nod my assent nervously. Mariah looks admiringly at Ian. "Sure. Just make sure to bring her back just the way you found her, please."

He flashes them the most devastating smile in his arsenal, the one that should come with a warning label that says *Caution: dangerous to your health and mental well-being*.

"I'll be sure to do that. Excuse us, please. Ariel?" He holds out his hand.

I slide off the barstool. "Can I take my drink?"

He assesses me up and down. "I think maybe you've

had enough." He goes to put the glass back down but I swing it out of his reach.

"No, Ian, I haven't had enough. As a matter of fact, I don't think there's enough alcohol behind that bar to be enough for me tonight." And I walk ahead of him, drink in hand.

He was right though: I'm wobbly on my high heels so drinking more would be foolish. I whip around, by some miracle not stumbling, and hand him my glass. He merely smiles with approval and places it on a small table near a sofa crowded with people, some seated, others kneeling on the floor. *Subs.* I shake my head.

"Ariel, I should warn you: if you found my small dungeon disturbing, the things you'll see here will give you nightmares. Are you sure you're up for this tour?"

"Sure, why not? I should also take this opportunity to say thank you for dropping the lawsuit. I was surprised... but grateful."

"So grateful you didn't bother to call me, I noticed."

I gape up at him. "I wasn't sure if you would have welcomed it or not. My attorney told me to refrain from doing anything."

"Your attorney probably doesn't welcome the competition. Jackson told me he seemed more than professionally interested in your welfare."

I roll my eyes—he always did think every man wants to sleep with me. "Jackson?"

"My attorney. Anyway, I appreciate your gratitude. You're welcome."

"Hmm. Will you tell me why?"

"Why?"

"Why you dropped it?"

"After you explained how it all happened, my sense of betrayal and outrage dissipated. I didn't want to hurt you." He turns and puts his hands on my arms. I want to throw myself at him, embrace him, kiss him, and in my mind's eye I do it. In reality, I stand there stiffly and wait for his cue.

"I care about you, Ariel. I wanted you back in my life but blackmailing you into it didn't seem the right way to go about it." He laughs.

Wanted? His use of the past tense stabs me in the chest. "I care about you, too, Ian. I'm sorry if my book hurt you, truly I am."

He leans in and kisses me gently. "Come on, let me show you just how mild a Dominant I really am. Maybe you'll look more favorably upon me."

We walk down a long hall. On either side are rooms where people are doing... *things*. Various things. Terrifying things.

"The whip frightened you so much that it might be prudent to show you just what punishments are available, to show you how lightly you got off—and by got off, I mean got away with." He grins wickedly at his dirty little joke.

I blush on cue, as he knew I would. Just then I hear a woman scream—I wouldn't call it bloodcurdling—but it was bad enough to scare me. I must have turned white as a sheet because Ian moves his body closer to mine as if my terror beckoned him.

"Okay?"

I nod.

He leads me deeper into the darkness. I don't care to examine the reasons why but I feel completely safe with Ian. When I was with Mariah and Naomi, I still felt like prey sitting there at the bar, but I feel protected with him by my side. We hear a woman sobbing and we follow the sound.

My eyes are taking in the scene but there is a sharp disconnect between the images being absorbed by my retina and my brain's processing of the information. What in hell is going on? I glance up at Ian.

He must feel my eyes on him or he just anticipated my confusion. Without taking his eyes off the scene, he explains it to me. "That submissive's crime must have been severe—accordingly, so is her punishment. She's riding what's called a wooden pony."

He turns and whispers in my ear. "As long as she remains on her tiptoes, she can hold herself off the pony. Once her calves become strained and she is forced to put her weight on her full foot, she will come down on the pony... and it will hurt her most tender parts." He says that with a smirk but his eyes look troubled. I look again in sheer horror.

The girl is stark naked. Her arms are chained overhead and she is holding onto something—I suppose for balance. Her legs are straddling a piece of wood about two by four inches with the narrow part turned up. Apparently she was on it long enough to have to come down on the wood already and she is weeping pitifully and continually adjusting her position, seeking to escape the pain, no doubt. Her movements mimic riding an actual horse and I suppose that's how the torture implement got its name. I want to rescue her but the man standing right next to her, observing or perhaps providing her punishment, is big and very mean looking. I feel like a criminal just standing there and doing nothing but what could I do? God, these people are cruel bastards.

"Do you know what she did to deserve something so harsh? She didn't violate a CA, by any chance?"

A beguiling smile is my response. Why does he have to be so damn beautiful?

"No. I don't know what she did—I just arrived a minute or two before I saw you. This is the first time I've been to the club in well over a year." He looks at me pointedly as if that's meaningful to me. Does he mean that he hasn't been here since he met me? If that's supposed to make me feel better, well, it actually does.

"But, to answer your question, they usually don't use the pony unless it's something egregiously bad. The last time I saw it used, the sub had done something to cause another sub to get hurt because she was jealous the girl hooked the Dom she herself wanted. She paid for it and still didn't get the man."

"How do they know how long to put her on that

thing? Or do they just make it so lengthy a session she's bound to be badly hurt?" And my words are exactly right: she's bound for the express reason of hurting her.

If he notices the pun, he chooses to ignore it. Obviously I'm not making light of the situation. "They look at her body, her weight, her age, and how toned her muscles are, and they estimate how long she'll likely be able to stay on her toes. Then they double that time for the punishment. That way, no matter how strong or how stubborn, she will get the pain."

"Ah." I cringe, my muscles contracting in sympathy. "Such devious minds."

"That punishment is as old as the hills. The most inventive tortures were conceived in the Middle Ages. Some are still used."

"Are Doms ever punished or is it just the poor women?"

"First of all, some men are submissives and some women are Dommes, though admittedly it usually skews the other way. And, yes. Though Doms are not usually punished, I have been witness to a few. There was one just recently that a friend told me about."

He looks at me, one brow raised, as if challenging me to ask about it. Normally, I wouldn't, since I like to be difficult with difficult people but I desperately want to know. "Okay, I'll bite. What did he do?"

"Ignored a safe word. That's probably the worst possible offense a dominant could commit. Because he was a longstanding club member who had lost his temper and acted uncharacteristically irrational, the owners gave him a choice rather than just kick him out: he could either forfeit his club membership or accept a whipping by the club's most vicious sadist. The *caveat* was that he would not be permitted a safe word, since he tried to deprive a submissive of the right. He chose the punishment and it was quite severe, so I'm told."

A violent shudder reverberates through my body and Ian sees it, smiling gently. "Come. Let's go see some more. That is, if you're up for it?"

I nod. In for a penny, in for a pound, I suppose. This club was really like a chamber of horrors. Why would anyone choose to do these things?

"Ian, why would that man choose the whipping over losing his membership? Aren't there other clubs around? Is the membership that valuable?"

"To some it is. There aren't any other private clubs like this one in the area. The public ones are not as safe, or clean, or interesting. He knew he was in the wrong; it was worth it to him to take the whipping and continue. It's a community here and people feel free to be themselves within these walls."

We walk past a woman being spanked on this obnoxious looking bench. Her skirt has been flipped up her back and every passer-by could see all she has to offer. Apparently no one believes in underwear here. Another shiver runs up my spine.

He pauses to give me a long look. "Have you seen enough or would you like to continue?"

"Is there a lot more to see?"

He laughs. "Yes, lots more, but frankly, I'd just as soon not show you. Come on. I'll take you back to your friends."

Relieved, I nod. "Okay, thanks, Ian." As we're walking back upstairs, my hand in his big, warm, masculine one, I realize that I'm suddenly depressed: I'm going to leave this place and he's going to stay. And do things. With women. The idea makes me sick to my stomach.

Just before we reach the bar, he pulls me to a stop. "Poor thing, you're so pale. This outing probably wasn't a good idea for you." He looks at the bar. "But your friends look like they're having a good time."

I follow his eyes. It was true: both Mariah and Naomi are talking with men and looking as if they are having a grand time of it. "Mmm, I guess I'll be going home alone tonight," I laugh but he doesn't join in. Instead, his eyes sparkle with some secret devilry but before I can read it, it's gone.

"Are you living here now?"

"No. Just staying for a few weeks before I go visit my parents and then on to New York."

"New York?"

"Just for a quick trip. I'm not sure where I'll end up—somewhere with a good doctoral program, I suppose."

"Any chance it will be here?"

I shrug. "It's not impossible but it's unlikely."

He's staring into my eyes and I'm so turned on by him I want to launch my body at his... instead, I retreat. "Well, thanks for the tour, Ian. It was nice to see you and I'm glad I got the chance to tell you I really appreciate your dropping the lawsuit. It was kind of you."

"Would you like to have lunch with me tomorrow? The weather is supposed to be nice and I thought to perhaps take a drive."

"Um, okay. Yes, I'd like that. You have my number, right?"

"Yes. Why don't you go see what your friends are planning to do? If they want to stay and you want to go, I'll take you home."

"Oh, that's okay. I know you just got here, Ian. I wouldn't want to spoil your evening."

He laughs. "Spoil it? Funny. Go check, Ariel. I'll wait."

His eyes look stormy and I wonder what's going on in that Machiavellian mind of his. But I want to stay with him, I do. I may be crazy but whatever. So I march up to Mariah who is presently chatting with a ruggedly good-looking man—he looks like a cowboy. But that's impossible, right? I mean, this is a BDSM club, after all.

"Mariah? Can I have a minute?" I have to yell to get her attention.

"Sure. Will you excuse me for a moment?" I hear her shout to her new friend.

"I'm leaving, Mariah. You look like you want to stay. Ian offered to take me home. Do you want me to accept?"

She looks at me oddly, then glances over to Naomi whose lips are currently locked together with those of Ian's blond friend. "Yeah, looks like Naomi's occupied for the evening. And I'd like to stay," she says excitedly and turns her head away from her cowboy. "Isn't he gorg?"

I smile and nod. "Okay. I'm ready to go home so I'll take Ian up on his offer. I'll see you later or tomorrow."

I thread my way back to Ian. "They're staying; I'm going. If you really don't mind, I'll take you up on your generous offer."

"Let's go." He offers me his arm.

"Don't you need to tell your friend you're leaving?"

He shakes his head. "He'll figure it out. Come on."

My heart is beating wildly again. In the club we couldn't get too intimate but now we're outside—it's just he and I, without the lawsuit clouding the energy between us. As we walk to his car, parked in the lot behind the club, I allow myself a long look at him. There was too much going on earlier to check him out thoroughly. He's wearing black jeans that fit him like a snug glove, and a black tee-shirt that stretches tautly across his broad chest. Black boots, black belt, a high-tech black rubber watch. The man in black—I really like the effect though it does make him look a bit like Satan, if Satan was a breathtakingly handsome man.

"Where am I taking you, Ariel?"

I suck in a deep breath. Should I do it? If he turns me down, I'll be crushed. Oh, what the hell—you only live once. I thrust my chin up. "Your place?"

His head rears back in surprise. "Are you saying you want to spend the night with me, Ariel?"

I nod, not trusting my voice to hold up. I can't believe I just said that—just propositioned him. It's a first for me.

He's looking into my eyes without saying a thing, just gazing, as if he's reading my mind or soul. *Say something for God's sake.* Yes? No? Maybe so? Absolutely not? Something, damn it.

His fingertips brush across my cheek lightly and he takes my hand and kisses it. "Okay. Let's go."

Chapter 11

Life is truly a theatre for the absurd, Ian thinks, as he floors the accelerator once he merges onto the highway. There he was, scheming and conniving every which way to get Ella back into his life and he failed miserably. *Miserably.* And then all it took was a chance encounter where she happened to see him with other interested women and she asks to come home with him. He shakes his head.

Jealousy. No one is immune to it, man or woman. All one has to do is read a little Shakespeare to see how even the high and mighty fall upon its sharp and sometimes double-edged sword, eyes wide open. Why it didn't occur to him to use it to his advantage was the real mystery. He'd known Ella had a robust streak of the green-eyed monster right from the start. Their first night out together, he'd run into a female acquaintance. When the woman put her hands on him, he'd glanced at Ella and saw her eyes simmering at the proprietary insult. He'd seen no reason to tell her that he didn't even like the woman—Ella's reaction had amused him at the time because they'd just met and had no claims on each other. Not that they ever did... but he would like to now. Very much.

In the club, she'd looked angry at first, too. He had his arm around Kim—perhaps that was why. Seeing Ella there, against a backdrop of a multitude of beautiful women, all dressed—or undressed— to look their hottest, it was patently obvious to him that Ella left them all in the dust. The girl is seriously beautiful—and the thing he might love most about her is that she genuinely doesn't appear to be aware of her beauty. Or if she is, she doesn't take it too seriously.

He almost can't believe that events happened as they did, but a quick glance over at the passenger seat and there she is, in all her auburn glory. She catches his eye and he smiles, reaching for her hand to give it a reassuring squeeze—he can tell she's nervous. How many other men has she been with since she left him last year? He's burning to know but he's too polite to ask and she probably won't offer the information. After all, it isn't really his business, is it?

Would she be surprised to know he hadn't been with a single woman since her? He wonders.

"Aren't we going to your place?"

He looks over at her, smiles enigmatically, and nods.

"Didn't we just pass your exit?"

"I don't live in the glass house anymore, Ella. I moved out last week."

"Oh? Where?"

"You'll see. We're almost there."

"What prompted you to move?"

"I bought the new place a year ago but I've been having it remodeled. The renovations were just finished a little over a week ago so I moved in and put the other house up for sale."

"A year ago? Seems a lot of things happened with you last year."

He keeps his focus trained on the road ahead, choosing not to acknowledge her observation. It must be so obvious that I fell apart when she disappeared, he thinks. But I won't confirm it—that would give her too much sway over me and I simply cannot allow that to occur. Not yet. Perhaps not ever.

As he turns his little black Lexus sports car into the marina parking lot, Ella's head whips over to look at him. "No way! You bought a houseboat?"

Smiling, he nods. "I needed a change and I love the water. I have to say, I'm really loving it—I don't think I'll ever leave." He parks the car in his designated space and quickly jumps out to open Ella's door. She waits, remembering that he has these ingrained manners and expects her to abide by them.

Once outside the car, Ella jumps up with excitement, clapping her hands. "I'm impressed, Ian, so impressed. I would never expect you to live on a houseboat—but I love it!"

Laughing, he cocks his head in that way she loves. "Why? Wouldn't you expect it?"

One corner of her mouth turns up in a crooked grin; she seems elated at the prospect of visiting a houseboat. "Not luxurious or formal enough for you. I don't know, Ian, but you seem different to me now—much more relaxed about life, more inclined to enjoy it. Am I mistaken?"

She takes his extended hand, both of them reveling in this one small touch after so long apart, and they walk toward his boat. He doesn't answer right away; instead his eyes scan the dark water, lights from the row of houseboats shimmering on its surface. "Perhaps not," he says after a pregnant pause, "I suppose I went through a bit of a personal crisis last year, Ella." That's as much as he plans to admit to her. He could tell she's dying to ask questions but he doesn't encourage them. There's only so far he's willing to open himself up to her. No, he has to be careful, never relax his vigilance. He'd learned his lesson quite well. Five years ago. *So fucking well.* But no, he thinks, shaking off the old demons; he refuses to conjure the ghost of Natasha tonight.

"Here we are."

Ella stops dead in her tracks and gapes at the house. "Oh my God, Ian, it's… magnificent. Just, like, drop-dead gorgeous."

It looks like a villa one would see on the banks of the Grand Canal in Venice. The house has two stories and a roof deck on top, with glass panels wrapped around the perimeter of the roof for safety without obstructing the view. The façade is a textured plaster in Tuscan Gold and all the windows, both arched and square, are floor to ceiling height and wrap around the entire house. Ionic columns enclose the first floor to form a portico extending around the entire house while the second story has four columns in front from roof to ground that harbor a balcony within. The same glass panels protect the entire second floor, whether a Juliet balcony or the larger terrace in front. There are huge pots of colorful flowers anchoring the roof on all four corners.

"Can I assume you like it then?"

"It's all right, I guess," she says, affecting a nonchalant tone, her eyes glowing with delight. "I'll bet it's even prettier by daylight."

"Oh, I don't know about that. The light shimmering off the water makes it pretty special, don't you think?'

"Mmm. This was such an excellent choice, Ian. I'm jealous."

Smiling, he unlocks the door and steps aside. "After you. Would you like a formal tour or would you prefer to just wander around and acquaint yourself with the premises?"

"I'll wander."

"Okay, then I'll go get us some wine. Unless you'd prefer something else?"

"No," she shakes her head with a rueful smile, "wine is perfect. Perhaps just half a glass for me, though. I drank a bit too much already today."

"Good enough. Feel free to look around and make yourself at home, Ariel." He tilts his head back. "You look good in this house."

Her voice drops in volume, sounds strangled even, as she replies, "I *feel* good in this house," and then quickly turns away.

Ian's own equilibrium shatters at that point and he realizes with a start that he's nervous again, too. When was the last time he was nervous around a woman before meeting Ella? Fourteen years ago when he was fifteen, probably. But Ella frequently made him nervous, especially now, when he'd spent so many months missing her, thinking her lost to him forever. Tonight was his chance to win her back. Feeling a lot is riding on tonight is what is making his heart pound. It's an alien sensation and he doesn't like it. Not in the least.

Returning with the wine, he finds her sitting at one end of the sofa. Ian considers trapping her there by placing himself in the middle, thus invading her personal space, but instead decides to go slowly, so he seats himself at the other end, after handing her the glass. It feels relaxing to quietly sit and listen to the soft music and sip the wine—not at all how he'd originally envisioned his evening. Still, he couldn't say he was disappointed. Quite the contrary.

After a few minutes, he looks at her and pats the cushion next to his lap. "Come here, Ella."

After a slight hesitation, she rises to her feet and walks over to stand in front of him. He watches, waiting to see what she'll do. Moving closer to him, she straddles his legs, sits on his lap, sets her hands on his shoulders... and then leans in to kiss him. Bold move.

He'd forgotten how soft her lips were... *are*. While she's occupied with his tongue, he reaches his hands under the loose white shirt and up to her breasts, exploring with his fingers and then yanking her bra down to expose her breasts. A small moan is her only response. When she pulls her mouth away from his, he slides his hands to her waist and lifts her body as he stands—an impressive display of strength. "Wrap your long, sexy legs around me, sweetheart."

As she complies, he carries her upstairs. As he walks, he talks. "Allow me to give you the abbreviated tour. This is the staircase to the second story. This is the hallway. Here's the master bedroom," he says as he enters the room and then drops her gently on the bed so that she's lying across the width. "And here's the bed. You have too many clothes on."

He leans over her and pushes her arms up, sliding the shirt up and off; the leather bra, already half off, follows quickly. "By the way, I like the bra on you... but I like it better off." He grins wickedly and then hooks his fingers in her waistband, unbuttoning, unzipping, and yanking off the pants. He leaves on her panties.

His eyes are focused intently on her, appraising her body up and down. "You've lost weight," he notes. "Intentional?"

She shakes her head.

"You're beautiful, Ariel," he says as he leans back in to start kissing her, "I've missed seeing and touching you." Beginning at her throat, he works his way down, kissing and nipping. By the time he reaches her hips, he could see her skin is glistening with sweat, as she squirms underneath him—but he won't let that hurry him. He takes his time: he's waited a very long year for the privilege.

As he kisses, touches, licks, and rediscovers her body, a possessive instinct washes over him and he wants desperately to ask her if she's been with other men... but he can't... he won't.

No. It would be wrong. But he wants to know...needs to know.

But why? Would it make any difference? No, it really wouldn't.

He won't ask.

"Have you been with other men since we parted?"

He fucking asked! Stupid.

"No... have you? Been with other women? I probably don't want to know how many, right?"

"No, Ella. I haven't been with anyone since you," he admits and before he can watch her eyes reflect the dawning comprehension of what those words mean, he quickly dives down, kissing her between her legs, getting her mind off the exchange they should never have just had... but that he's so glad they did.

She hasn't been with anyone else. There was room for hope.

He'll reward her for her fealty with an outstanding orgasm. The piece of lacy fabric between her clit and his tongue serves only to drive her frustration ever higher as it prevents a complete connection. Her body burns hotter, so hot it's nearly on fire. When he thinks she's had enough teasing, he slides the panties down her legs, gripping her thighs so there's no room for her to move, no outlet for the tension, and his relentless tongue sends her into a screaming climax. He looks up to watch; he can't remember ever being as hard as he is right now, seeing her come undone. When her breath returns, she looks at him with glazed eyes. "Why am I naked and you still have all your clothes on?"

He points to the top of the bed. "Move up, baby. My clothes are coming off now."

She sidles up to the top and center of the mattress as he sheds his clothes quickly and efficiently and unfurls a condom. Lying on top of her, he takes her hands and brings them over her head, wrapping her fingers around the iron posts of the headboard. "Keep them there, no matter what I do. Can you do that?"

She nods. He chuckles—she'd probably agree to anything right now.

"Open your legs. Wider." She complies and he leans back to bend her knees, pushing her legs up as far as they'll comfortably go. "Leave them in that position; don't move them an inch."

She nods again and licks her lips. "No cuffs or ropes?"

"I don't need them—you're bound by my will. Just as effective. Do you like it, Ella?"

"Yes. What happens if I move?"

"Torment."

"No whips, right?"

Her question stings him. "No. Of course not."

"So," she says hurriedly, as if anxious to move past the moment, "torment." She smiles sweetly. "Don't move. Got it."

"We'll see," he says, an evil smile animating his face as he moves in toward her.

Two hours in bed with Ella—Ian definitely considers it a night well spent. An entire year of wanting her and missing her, of monkish celibacy... but tonight all of the suffering seems worth it. He looks down at her, dozing in the crook of his arm and thinks that maybe, possibly, he could marry this one, make a life with her. But how would that ever happen if he were afraid to let her know how he felt about her? He just can't do it.

She sleeps for about a half hour and when she wakes, he wraps her in a silk kimono and throws on his jeans and they go to scare up some food. They take the laden plates with them into the living room and he turns on the television.

"Well, you spent a lot of time in the UK. Want to watch *Little Britain*?"

"How did you know I did? I don't recall mentioning it."

"How *did* I know? Hmmm." His grin is downright devilish. "I don't suppose you're aware of my superior stalking skills, Madame."

"So you knew where I was then?"

"That time I actually had to hire a professional. You certainly covered your bases quite well."

"If you went to the trouble of locating me, why didn't you contact me?"

"Not that I'm avoiding it, but do you suppose we can table this conversation until next time? I'm not feeling up for it right now."

"Okay," she shrugs slightly and grins happily at him. "I feel agreeable tonight—for some strange reason."

"Do you? I wonder why, Ms. Strong. Could it be the gentle waves lapping at the houseboat that are lulling you into a good mood?"

"Yes, I'm sure that's it. Definitely. Okay, so *Little Britain* it is."

Inching closer to her on the sofa, Ian flicks on the show with the remote and then angles his body so he could look at Ella.

"So now that you've had time to process it, what do you think about what you saw in the club?"

She shakes her head. "Still horrified. I just don't

understand why people put themselves through such humiliation and pain. The whole public aspect of it probably bothers me the most. Some things should be private—always."

"Hmm, for some people, yes. Not for others."

"Why did that girl let them hurt her like that? That's just plain crazy."

"When a person joins the club, he or she agrees to certain conditions. Discipline is one of them."

"Doms, too?"

"To a lesser extent, but yes. Everyone needs to respect the rules of the club. They're there to keep it safe and enjoyable for all."

"If it's such a serious transgression to ignore a safe word, why'd they let that Dom continue?"

"It was a complicated situation but normally a person doing that would automatically be kicked out. To ignore a safe word... well, it amounts to a criminal assault and the sub could have reported it to the police and brought the house down on the club. But he chose not to."

"He? The sub was a he?"

"Mmmhmm. From what I gather, the Dom in question had a long-time sub—his girlfriend—to whom he was very attached. The male sub somehow connived to get the girl to leave her Dom—I don't know the exact details. Needless to say, the Dom was pissed off, to say the least. He ran into the male sub one evening at the club, told him he deserved a whipping, and the male sub agreed to take one. I suppose it began as more of a negotiated scene than an assault. When it started getting rough, the sub used his safe word and instead of stopping, the Dom gagged him and kept going. It took a while for someone to hear him using the safe-word signal for a gagged sub.

"What the male sub did, getting between a Dom and his sub, was rather inexcusable and since the male sub didn't care to pursue it, the club owners gave Jared— that's the Dom's name—the choice. He opted for the whipping."

"Must have been horrible. Was it done at the club?"

"Oh, yes. They scheduled it for a Thursday, so the club wouldn't be full but when the news went out, everyone and his brother showed up for the spectacle. It was packed to capacity, so I hear. Not only that, my friend told me it was the first time in his experience that all other play stopped so everyone could watch the whipping. Had to be intense."

"Why would they all want to watch it? Does everyone dislike Jared?"

"Not at all. He's popular at the club." He pauses. "To answer your question, it probably drew a crowd because it was a Dom getting whipped, as opposed to a sub. It's unusual enough to make a stir. Plus, whippings never happen without a safe word so that made it highly unusual."

"Were there any rules?"

"Probably just the common sense ones that there should be no permanent scarring and obviously it had to stop short of the mark of requiring a hospital visit or medical intervention of any kind."

Ella shudders. "The pony was disgusting. What diseased mind thought up that horror?"

"Actually that one, with variations, has been around since the Roman Empire—of course the one they used ended up being fatal, with limbs being dislocated and that sort of thing. Our Roman friends were a bloodthirsty bunch—lead in the water will do that. Then a similar device was popular during the Inquisition. There was one used doing the Colonial War. They called it riding the rail. Another one used in the Civil War was employed in conjunction with weights to increase the fun. The one in the club is fairly mild in that the sharp edge is just the narrow part of the wood, rather than an actual point, the way the torture was originally intended." He glances at her. "Still must be rather unpleasant, no doubt."

Ella smiles impishly. "How do you happen to know so much about it, Ian?"

"I was probably as disturbed as you when I first saw it—prompted me to do some research on the device. Luckily, it's not often used at the club."

She puts her plate on the coffee table. "Well," she says, snuggling up to him, "Thank God for small favors. Now, let's talk about something infinitely more pleasant, such as how it's possible for a man to be as beautiful as you are, Mr. Blackmon?"

Chapter 12

I hear his sharp intake of breath when I ask why he is so beautiful. Did he really expect the same shy girl of last year? So much life has happened to me in the last twelve months—that girl is no more, not that she really ever was.

Will he like the new me? In truth, I was never really that shy, easily flustered girl he thought me—it was just that he completely intimidated me. Still does. His is a very commanding presence. In addition, he's rich, handsome, powerful, and smart. Oh, and tall. How could someone not be intimidated? In addition to all of his other overwhelming attributes, his dominant tendencies tend to cower me. It's up to me now to ensure he doesn't know the effect he has on me—he may try to use it against me. But all alone with my private thoughts, I can admit how much his dominance turns me on. And I sort of hate that it does.

I don't want to be submissive. Even the word pisses me off. Centuries of subjugation will do that to a girl: women are kind of sensitive about any show of weakness, or any masculine show of force. Well, most of us anyway, but certainly not all those women in scanty clothes at the club.

Okay, I don't get that at all. Maybe it's because I'm sexually naïve? Or maybe I'm just built differently... but I just don't find pain erotic and I don't understand anyone who does. But damn: that club was sure jam-packed Friday night with people who do.

I must accordingly concede one point to him: sexually, I like his being in control—at least my body likes it, responding instantly to his commands. Matter of fact, it's damn irritating how my body betrays my mind—he'll do something and I'll tell him I don't like it and then he touches me—you know where—and instantly knows otherwise. So unfair.

So here we sit, in his beautiful new living room on his beautiful new houseboat, watching a silly British comedy, of all things. So not Ian Blackmon. He's laughing at the show—a sketch about an overweight support group. He must feel my eyes on him because he swivels his attention from the television and looks over, catching me staring.

For a long minute he just looks into my eyes and I try like hell not to break first. But I do. Of course.

He suddenly stands and holds out his hand. "Come."

"Where are we going?"

"I thought a steam shower would be nice."

"First give me the unabbreviated house tour." I place my hand in his and he pulls me to my feet. Smiling, he leads me first to the kitchen.

His new houseboat is charming and relatively simple, though luxurious. The floors are a dark gleaming wood throughout. The walls are all done in Venetian plaster, with bronze old-world style fixtures. The kitchen is state of the art, naturally, since he does so much cooking—not.

Upstairs, each bedroom—and there are three—has its own en suite bath. The guest rooms are not large but comfortable, however, the master is sumptuous, and leads to the balcony I spied from outside. Inside the room, across from the sleigh bed, are a wood-burning fireplace and a magnificent Persian rug gracing the wood floor. The bath is done in Carrera marble subway tile from floor to ceiling and the furnishings are all dark wood with brushed nickel fixtures. There's a huge double steam shower and a big, rectangular whirlpool tub. Very masculine but the height of luxury as far as baths go.

"Bath or shower?" he asks.

"I'd prefer a shower, if you don't mind."

"A shower it is then." He reaches in and turns on multiple sets of showerheads that protrude all the way down each wall. "After you, Madame."

I slip off the robe and step into the shower. The water is steaming hot, too hot for me, and as I move to retreat a step, I run into a wall. Of man.

"Not so fast."

I can feel his enormous erection pressing into my back and it stops me dead in my tracks. Talk about hot... whew.

Reaching for the shower gel, he soaps up his hands and begins to wash my back... and everything else.

The water is still hot enough to scald but I am getting used to it. Why do men like such hot water? My father is like that, too. The thought of my father right now where I am is disturbing so I banish him from my brain. It's my turn to wash Ian and as I do, I once again marvel at his physique. "How many hours a week do you spend working out?" I finally ask.

"Generally, two to three hours about four times a week."

"That's a lot. When do you find time?"

He shrugs dismissively. "My trainer comes to me at the office during the week and we get together on weekends too."

"Hmmm. What kind of work-out?"

"Kickboxing, running, some weight training. I don't want to bulk up too much—just keep my stamina high and the fat off." He grins. "So far, so good."

"Not bad," I say with a smirk, as my hands travel from his throat down, washing him slowly and thoroughly and seeing evidence of his enjoyment grow bigger before my eyes.

We make love twice more before we fall asleep. Ian has mostly kept the kink out of the bedroom tonight—I suppose the whipping is ever-present in both of our minds. Still, with his overpowering personality, he yet manages to exert control over me in some measure and I find I don't mind it. The last time we were together I felt I was tolerating the whole thing. Now, for whatever reason, I actively like it. The idea of submitting to him turns me on, makes everything seem hotter. This night has been one of the best of my life and I don't want it to end.

But despite how happy I feel right at the moment, I realize that nothing's actually changed between us. If he wants me long-term at all, it's as a submissive, which is no commitment at all—I mean, what do I get out of it but a broken heart at the end of a rutted road?

When I open my eyes the next morning, I glance over and see that I'm alone in the bed. The sun is high enough to stream in through the windows, reminding me that I never let Mariah know where I was. I'm not worried though, for Mariah surely can figure out where I ended up. I do need items in my bag, though, and I left it downstairs. Damn. Quickly, I wrap a sheet around my body and go in search of my bag and thus my toiletries. On the stairs, I hear Ian's voice in a one-sided conversation: he must be on the phone. He sounds angry.

"I don't give a damn, Jonas. It's not going to happen. Get on the phone with Keppler now and make sure he understands our position. We are not going down with this one, no fucking way. What else?

"Who? You've got to be kidding me? How the hell did she get your number? No. Do nothing; say nothing. Just ignore it and let's hope it goes away by itself. I'm going to try to enjoy my weekend now, if that's okay with you? Fine. Till Monday then."

Timidly, I step downstairs, hoping I could snag my handbag and get back up before he spots me.

"Ariel. Good morning."

I stop short, feeling sneaky. It also doesn't escape me that he called me Ariel again. Last night I was Ella. "Good morning. Is everything okay?"

"Yes, fine. Sleep well?"

"I did, thank you. I thought I'd take a shower."

"Ah. Are we still on for the car ride today?"

I nod my assent, feeling very shy all of a sudden. Last

night I did every imaginable thing with this man and yet I have the nerve to stand here this morning with blushing cheeks? Gives new meaning to the term cheeky.

He nods, also smiling. Did I put his smile there? "Good. I'll take you home to get changed. In the meantime, I've left a tee-shirt on the chair in the bedroom for you to wear over that sexy bra. Come down when you're ready for breakfast."

I stand there stupefied. "You made breakfast?"

He raises his left brow. "I take exception to your implication, Ariel. It's extremely sexist of you to automatically assume that I can't cook because I'm a man."

"Not because you're a man," I say, shaking my head. "Just because you're you and you always have staff doing everything for you. This is a new side of Ian Blackmon that I've not seen before."

"I'm glad you can see I'm multifaceted. If you must get technical, perhaps *cook* is not the most appropriate verb to use in terms of what I did for breakfast."

I cock my head. "Is *heat* more appropriate?"

His lips twitch. "I think *bought* would probably suit best."

"Aha. I knew it!" I giggle, strolling over to my bag and snatch it up. "I'll be down in five."

Before I can leave the room, he makes a sudden lunge for me, catching my arm and yanking me close to his body. "When you giggle it does things to me and, besides, you look too delectable not to manhandle this morning, Ella."

Oh, good, we're back to Ella. He nuzzles my neck, holding me tightly. "It's incredibly nice to see you wake up in this house—you've christened it for me, baby."

I lean into him and inhale that delicious Ian Blackmon scent. Mmm. Just as I'm burrowing in and getting comfortable, he smacks me on the butt—hard. "Okay, off with you now before I forget about breakfast and eat you instead."

I gasp, unsure if I'm gasping at the hard smack or his

dirty words. I sling my bag over my shoulder and with a haughty look thrown back at him, make my way upstairs to shower and get dressed. I hear him laughing in my wake and my heart feels happy and full to listen to such wonderful music.

I end up spending the whole weekend with Ian and can only use superlatives to describe it. By Sunday night, I'm feeling depressed, knowing that it's time to say goodbye. We can't make any future plans—for one thing, I no longer live in Portland and have no idea whatsoever where I'll be living. For another, Ian never gives me any direction in terms of where this thing between us may be heading.

But he also seems a bit out of sorts when the weekend rolls to its close. He drives me back to Mariah's, both of us brooding and silent, only the music softly playing. Beck is the only one vocalizing his feelings in the tiny car.

When he pulls in front, he reaches over and presses the ignition off. "So," he angles his body toward me, "do you have any idea as to when you'll know where you'll be landing?"

I shake my head. "No idea. Right now I'm looking for either a doctoral program or an internship of some sort—whichever one grabs my attention first."

"What kind of internship?"

We'd avoided discussing anything of this nature all weekend, possibly for this reason. "Not sure yet. I was thinking maybe of trying to work with an historian researching a book. Or maybe a television show, perhaps something associated with PBS. The other alternative is to go the academic route. Maybe teach as an adjunct professor while I scout out the right doctoral program. I'm just not sure."

"Why were you in L.A.?"

"Honestly? I didn't know where else to go. The unexpected windfall from the book provided me with a lot of options... but in giving me all those choices, it makes decisions considerably more difficult. And I'm indecisive by nature."

"Could have fooled me, Ella. You seem exceedingly directed to me." He reaches over and caresses my chin, his fingers butterfly soft. "I'd like to see you again soon. Is that a possibility?"

"Yes. I'm not going anywhere for the next two weeks, at least."

"Next weekend? Can you stay with me again?"

"Yes," I say, my voice so faint and breathless I'm surprised he hears me. But he does and smiles in response, kisses me softly.

"Good night, Ella. Thank you for a wonderful weekend. Come, I'll walk you to the door."

So now I have a week to think, to mull, to obsess— before I see him again. First things first: it's time to face certain truths and the biggest one is that, for better or for worse, I'm in love with Ian and I have been probably since the day he strode into Archipelago all those months ago.

I also need to contemplate all the drastic changes I've seen in him in the past few weeks. The radically important question for me is whether or not these changes are real and going to last? Has he truly evolved or is he playing at something? With Ian, I never can tell.

When I met him, he was so... distant; perhaps inaccessible is the right word. He held himself apart from others, locking himself away in that ivory tower of his, the glass bubble set high up in the clouds, looking down on everyone else, both literally and metaphorically. He had staff to do everything for him—to keep him at a remove from everyone else in the world and provide a protective buffer zone between him and daily, messy life: grocery shopping, car parking, errands—all these activities wherein one might actually have to interact with other human beings. I snort, thinking it's surprising he bathed and dressed himself. Wonder why he didn't have a personal valet to do it for him, a Mr. Bates-type staff member?

Even the most intimate of encounters—sexual relationships—he'd conduct within the strict confines of BDSM. One doesn't need to be a psychologist to see why he found that lifestyle attractive, perhaps even necessary. Let's face it—he's a young, healthy male who wants sex. But he doesn't want emotional entanglement. What better way to get one without the other than by restraining your partner—both literally and figuratively—from getting too close?

Plus, it's very clear he has a dominant personality—it's quite evident, apparently, in his business dealings. When I first met him, after a small argument about negotiation and compromise, I ducked into a bookstore on a rainy day to buy him a joke gift, a book called *Negotiating for Dummies*. I began chatting with another customer who noticed me buying the book and as fate would have it, she used to work for Ian. She told me that when Ian Blackmon walks into a board meeting or conference, the whole room goes silent, as if he sucks all the oxygen out.

And controlling? Ha! There's probably a thumbnail picture of his face next to the definition of the word in Merriam-Webster. He just cannot function unless he has complete control of himself and everyone around him.

Ian's twenty-eight—twenty-nine now—and he wants to be master of all he surveys. The perhaps impressive yet also frightening part is that he's actually managed to accomplish it—and rapidly. But something happened last year. Something happened to Ian to make him take a long, hard look in the mirror. It was now for me to ponder what that something was. Could it possibly have been me?

He's given up his luxurious and cavernous house in the sky for a considerably smaller, friendlier, and more accessible houseboat. I saw him laugh and talk with friends at his club, so relaxed, so different from the Ian Blackmon I had known previously. In recent weeks he hasn't been constantly surrounded by staff, nor has he seemed paranoid about security, as he used to be. Has he really changed or am I witnessing an anomaly, a blip in his normal routine? One thought repeatedly niggled at me though I continually dismissed it as preposterous: was *I* responsible for the sea change in him? Did losing me force him to do some serious introspection?

I make it through the week in relatively good shape. Of course, I have help. On Monday I receive two dozen long-stemmed roses. On Tuesday, a case of the wine I'd liked while at his house arrives. Fed Ex delivers a package on Wednesday with a CD he'd burned with songs he thought I might enjoy, and Thursday a gorgeous little black dress and black lace lingerie are delivered. The shelf bra is scandalous—it barely covers the girls. Still, when I try it on I have to admit it's sizzlingly hot.

Mariah can't help but notice Ian's attention. This is so not good.

"Ella, looks like someone is smitten. Doesn't it now?"

I don't care for the scrutinizing look she gives me. "I suppose he enjoyed my company last weekend?"

"Uh-huh. Not just last weekend, either. He did come looking for you right after you left for London last year and I could see some serious panic in his eyes when I told him you'd left the country. You didn't say fare thee well to him before you flew across the pond?"

Now I'm feeling desperate. Mariah's no dummy. She can so easily figure out that my little fiction book is actually nonfiction if she makes some very simple connections—especially now that she knows that Ian is a member of that stupid BDSM club. Damn, but I should have seen this coming—preferably before I wrote the stupid book. I have to do damage control and fast.

"Um," I say, my thoughts frantically cobbling together a response, "we only dated once or twice and I realized he was just miles out of my league. The fellowship award came and I kind of just booked. I'm sure I left a message with his assistant. No biggie." I force myself to casually shrug.

She gives me a skeptical look. Uh-oh. "Really? I

wonder why he came running over here looking for you then? Maybe she screwed up and didn't give him your message?"

"Yeah," I say, looking down so she won't see my telltale lying face, "that must have been it." I make a show of glancing at my watch. "Oh, shoot! Look at the time! I have an appointment in less than twenty minutes. I better fly. See you later, Mariah."

I'm not sure I dodged that bullet but there's nothing to be done about it. If she knows, she knows. I recall Stephen's words to me about the story having identifiable details even if I didn't realize it. He was surely right.

Here's what happens on Friday: at seven a.m. I get a call from a man named Lucien Phillips. My friend Lara in L.A. gave him my number when he mentioned to her he was looking for someone to work with him on his documentary film on the women of famed artists of the early to mid twentieth century. His project is still in early stages of compiling research and taping subject interviews. He was so happy to reach me so quickly, he says.

"I'm leaving for Paris tomorrow evening, Ella, and I really need someone here to keep working on the research and possibly shoot an interview or two. Is there any way you can get to New York before tomorrow afternoon to meet with me?"

"Uh, I suppose I could do that." The voice in my head is screaming, *No, No, No. You're going to be with Ian this weekend*. But I hear the sensible girl looking for something worthwhile to do with her life agree to get to New York by tonight.

"Excellent, Ella! I'm really looking forward. Call me as soon as you get to the city, no matter the time and we'll set up a meet. I have a good feeling about this partnership—it's going to work. We'll talk soon."

I flop down on Mariah's sofa, wondering how best to handle this situation. Ian will be displeased. More important to me, he'll be disappointed—as I am. Then a thought occurs to me: perhaps he can come with? We could have a weekend in New York together. I decide to call him.

And that's the precise moment I realize he never gave me his cell phone number. I used to have it but I don't anymore. Glancing at the clock I see it's just after eight. A bit early for him to be at the office so I use the next hour to make my travel arrangements and pack a bag for the trip. My flight leaves at noon and I need to be at the airport by ten so I jump in the shower, write a note for Mariah, and by 9:15 I'm in a taxi on my way to the airport. I pull out my phone and call Ian's office. His admin picks up his line.

"I'm sorry. Mr. Blackmon is not in the office today." A crisp, professional voice informs me.

"I see. Do you know when he'll be in?"

"Mr. Blackmon will be away most of the day, I'm afraid. May I take a message?"

"Uh, it would probably be best if I left my message on his voice mail..."

"I'm sorry, but Mr. Blackmon doesn't use voice mail. I'll be happy to convey your message, however."

"Yes, fine. Please tell him that Ariel Strong called and—"

"Ariel Strong? Please excuse me for interrupting but Mr. Blackmon left instructions that your calls be put right through to him. The problem is he's really not here now; he's in a conference meeting with international associates. What I can do is give him the message as soon as he checks in. Can he reach you at this number?"

"Uh," I stammer, feeling self-conscious at the change in her tone, from cool and professional to obsequious. "I'll be on a plane in a couple of hours so I won't be able to take any calls. Please tell Ia... uh, Mr. Blackmon that he can send a text with a contact number and I will get back to him as soon as my plane lands."

"I'll tell him, Ms. Strong."

"Okay, thanks."

My cell chimes with a message as soon as I am seated on the plane. It's Ian, asking me to call him on his cell as soon as I get his message. We have a few minutes before takeoff so I call him now.

"Ariel. Where are you?" His voice is low and tinged with emotion. Is it anger?

"I just boarded a flight to New York. I received a call early this morning about meeting with someone for a job that sounds pretty perfect for me. He's leaving for Paris tomorrow so he asked me to come to New York right away to meet with him. I'm really sorry to cancel our plans at the last minute, Ian."

"I'm sorry, too. Who is this person with whom you're meeting?"

"A documentary filmmaker. His name is Lucien Phillips and my friend Lara recommended me to him. I can come back to Portland directly after I meet up with him and still spend Sunday with you."

"That's unnecessary, Ella. You'll be exhausted if you do that. Didn't you say you had business in New York anyway?"

"Yes, I was planning on visiting in a few weeks. I guess the sensible thing to do is just stay and get it all done." I pause, wondering if I should even mention my idea. What the hell? "I don't suppose it's possible for you to come to New York too?"

He's silent long enough that I think the call's been dropped but then I hear background voices on the other end. "No, that won't be possible, not this week, Ella. Perhaps we can reschedule for next weekend?"

I try not to laugh at his use of the word reschedule, as if I'm a business appointment. "Definitely," I say.

"Oh, wait. I just remembered I'm going to be out of the country next weekend. Why don't we play it by ear for now? Call me when you get back to Portland."

"Will do. Oh, and Ian? I just want to tell you I received all of the gifts you sent and I very much appreciated them. I was so looking forward to this weekend and I'm really disappointed."

"As am I... and you're welcome, Ella. I hope you have a good trip and I'll speak to you soon."

I disconnect, feeling depressed. If it weren't for this last-minute trip, I'd be getting ready to spend my weekend with Ian and now I don't know when I'll see him again. I'm beginning to regret not telling Lucien I couldn't make it. I shut off my phone and put my iPod headphones on, cranking up the music to take myself out of my head for a while. I already miss him so much and it's only been a week. God, but I'm pathetic and stupid.

Chapter 13

Fuck!!!!! The urge to send something breakable sailing across his office is nearly irresistible. This past week had shaped up to be one of the suckiest in recent memory. The only thing that had gotten him through it was the prospect of spending the weekend with Ella, and now she's going out of town—to meet with a man, no less.

At least she'd invited him to accompany her. On the spur of the moment, he got an idea to surprise her there but he'd told Ella he couldn't make it—just in case circumstances made it impossible, then he wouldn't disappoint her.

He picks up the phone. "I need a security check. Right away. Lucien Phillips. Double ell, I think. Try it both ways. Filmmaker, New York. That's all I have. Get back to me ASAP."

Ian slams the receiver back down into its cradle, finding it somewhat satisfying to vent his frustration on an inanimate object. Nothing but problems this week, starting with that big loser, Solar Systems, Inc. The cash-bleeding company he'd taken on was going down in flames, despite his firm's hemorrhaging more money into it, throwing good money after bad. The government was backtracking on tax breaks he'd been counting on—it was a big part of the impetus for giving it the green light in the first place. Now for the cherry on the cake of his day: their Japanese partners in the electronic security systems manufacturer that they finally brought back into black ink with the military contract they'd been awarded, were getting antsy over new tariff regulations that just passed Congress. He had to fly to Tokyo next weekend to placate them.

As if all of that weren't enough to ruin his week, that crazy bitch Alexis had begun to stalk him. He rubs the back of his neck, massaging the stiffness out of it. He'd hardly dated the woman; she was a mistake from the word go. The barely-there relationship was a consequence of his dedicated effort to give up on Ella: he went to the club one night, about six months after Ella absconded to Britain, and he met Alexis Martinez.

She was very attractive and friendly, bubbly even, intelligent—all positive attributes in his estimation. He'd taken her out—what? Twice? Dinner and nothing else. He found he couldn't shake off his obsession with Ariel. When he demonstrated no interest in continuing the nascent relationship, Alexis seemed to move on, bearing no grudge. Yet now, five or six months later, she was beginning to hound him at work. She'd called ten times over the last four days, trying to reach him, refusing to leave any message other than to say she called. He assumed by her failure to do so, there was no emergency that prompted her contact with him.

Thank God, she didn't have his new address. Of late, he'd begun to get lax about protecting his privacy. Stupid. He'd learned an inordinately painful lesson five years ago and he never wanted to forget it, lest history repeat itself.

He leans back in his chair, realizing he's exhausted already, and it's barely two o'clock. Long day. New York is almost certainly out of the question—not after the meeting he just took. Too many things require his constant attention to avoid all-out disaster. He'd have to work over the weekend—get some paperwork done that he'd neglected over the past week while he was actively engaged in damage control. Trying to squeeze in a ten-minute power nap, he closes his eyes.

Returning to the office after yet another time-leaching meeting, Ian finds the security report on Lucien

Phillips sitting on his desk. He nods in appreciation—fast work. When he opens the folder, an 8x10 glossy spills out. The masculine face in the photo smirks obnoxiously back at him, confident in his fashion-model good looks.

He quickly rifles through the paperwork: Lucien Phillips, age 27, filmmaker, director. Born in San Francisco, raised in Paris, now resides in New York City. Studied at Juilliard, earned both undergraduate and graduate degrees from the esteemed school. Won accolades for his debut film that premiered at Sundance. *Naturally.* Well-respected, up and coming, work in demand. Personal life: recently terminated relationship with long-term girlfriend (Eliza Littleton, 28, actress), and currently single.

Oh, I don't think so, Monsieur Phillips. Ian slaps the paperwork down and depresses the speaker button on the phone.

"Janine, call Scott Weldon and tell him I'll require the use of the Gulfstream tonight. Yes. New York. Have Scott call me for details. I'm leaving the office now; he can reach me on my cell."

Assuming Scott was available to pilot, he'd leave around eight and should make New York by early tomorrow morning. Perhaps he could even accompany Ella to her meeting? No, she would perceive that as too pushy. But, damn. Was it asking too much from the universe for Lucien Phillips to be short and bald? He didn't want Ella to be alone with the man. Not now... not ever.

He finally indulges himself and throws that thing across the room—a crystal paperweight that shatters into a hundred tiny, sparkling shards—and smiles.

By eight p.m. he's in the air, sipping a glass of ruby Cab and trying to slough off the filth of the day and week. He leans back into the leather headrest and allows his thoughts to float away with the soft jazz playing in the cabin. There's nothing like Connick to soothe the savage beast.

Fortunately, Scott was available so Ian didn't need to pilot the jet himself but since Scott needed to get back to Portland immediately, Ian would have to catch a commercial flight back home. No problem, he thinks, checking his watch again. Ella would be getting into New York in about an hour. Would she try to meet with Phillips later tonight or wait for morning? Common sense would dictate morning but Ella didn't always display an overabundance of sense.

Once he'd seen to all the exigencies of travel, he'd texted her, asking where she was staying. He decided to go straight to her hotel and surprise her before she could get going for the day. Hopefully, it wouldn't leave her a wealth of time to meet with Mr. Phillips. Now that he'd seen the man's photo, he really hoped the job wouldn't pan out.

New York: he hasn't been there in almost two years. What could he do to make it special for her? As far as he knew, she'd never set foot there before. Well, there was the Empire State building, of course. And Ellis Island, which garners one a beautiful view of the Statue of Liberty as the ferry crosses the river.

She'd mentioned going to museums; New York had among the finest ones in the world. They could spend a week going to a different museum each day and still not run out of options. A helicopter ride by twilight? A midnight cruise up the Hudson on a yacht? Endless possibilities. After another glass of wine, Ian rises from the chair, stretches his long legs, and makes his way into the bedroom to finally get some sleep. He's going to have to pay for this impromptu trip with some torturously long workdays next week. Might as well tank up on some sleep while he can.

It's six a.m. in Union Square. New York City is dark and dreary with pounding rain, and since it's Saturday, only a few shift workers are scurrying about the wet streets. Now what? Should he go straight to her hotel? If he doesn't, there's a chance he'll miss her before she heads out for that meeting with Lucien Phillips.

If he does, she might be a tad ornery at the early hour and be unable to show her appreciation for all the trouble he went to in order to see her. He decides to pick up some lattes and take his chances with the rude awakening.

"Ian!" She flings herself into his arms—a very good sign—and he kisses her hello. "I can't believe you're here. I thought you said you wouldn't be able to come to New York?"

He gifts her with an ear to ear grin. "Turns out I could."

"Please tell me that's coffee I smell in the shopping bag."

"Indeed it is. If you invite me into your room, I'll share."

"Oh, sorry. You totally caught me by surprise. Come in." She steps aside to allow him entry.

"Have a seat, Ian. Just give me five minutes to take a quick shower and I'll join you."

"I have a better idea. How about we drink our coffee now while it's hot and then I'll join you in the shower?" He arches his brows suggestively.

"Okay," Ella agrees, laughing, and accepts a cup from him, curling one leg under the other as she perches on the chair. He eyes her: she looks sexy in a pair of drawstring pants and a slinky camisole. What would she do if he just began to peel them off her, with no preamble whatsoever?

"Tell me your plan for the day, Ella."

"I'm meeting this man, Lucien Phillips at ten and then I'm free for the rest of the weekend."

"Where are you meeting him?" Ian asks as he reaches for a bagel, acting as if his question is very casual when it's anything but.

"Um, at his loft in Soho."

He sits back, his posture unnaturally erect. "You've never met this man before, know nothing about him, and you're going alone to his apartment?"

Flushing, she tries to defend herself. "Lara... my friend, Lara, knows him quite well, Ian. I'm only meeting him there because he's really pressed for time. He's leaving for Paris this evening and he has a lot of things to do beforehand. I was just trying to make things easier for him..."

"At your expense, no doubt." He exhales audibly, casting a sharp glance in her direction. "In that case, I'm accompanying you, Ella. I'll sit quietly and wait until you're done and then we'll go to the Met and look at some wonderful art. Agreed?"

She rolls her eyes at his overprotectiveness. "Fine. You can come with me though I'm going to feel silly having my chaperone along. Now, since we have at least two hours before I need to get ready, what should we do?"

"I can think of a few things... but every single one involves taking off that sexy little camisole and pants. Are you game?"

Just as she did the first night at the houseboat, she climbs on his lap, facing him, and wraps her arms around his neck. "I'm very happy to see you, Ian and I'd like to show you just how happy I am."

His lips smile but there's heat in his eyes. "Please do. It's been a very long and tiring 24 hours and I've been a very good boy. I would definitely like proof that patience is a virtue and not its own reward."

Chapter 14

As soon as I walk into Lucien's loft, everything becomes clear to me. I immediately understand, a.) why Ian rushed to New York, and, b.) why he insisted on coming along with me on this interview.

Lucien Phillips is fucking gorgeous.

I won't say he's better looking than Ian because that would be humanly impossible. But I will say that Lucien gives Ian a definite run for his money.

He's about an inch shorter than Ian, if that, and he has dark blond hair that he wears long, about chin length. His eyes are dark and smoldering and he has model gorgeous features. If I had to describe him in one word, face and body, it would be chiseled.

Plus, he is an absolute darling! Although he seems slightly surprised when I introduce Ian, he nonetheless rises to the occasion. He invites us both into the living room of his beautiful loft and we begin to chat. One of the things I find admirable is that he is unfailingly polite to Ian, including him in the conversation, even though this is supposed to be an interview to see if he and I might work well together.

While Lucien leaves for a moment to fetch some contractual paperwork, I take the opportunity to look around. The loft has its original wide-plank wood floors, and though refinished, the wood still bears the multitude of scars from its long industrial career, adding so much character and history. The walls are all cream, which provides a blank canvas for the artwork that covers many of the walls, from black and white photographs to driftwood sculpture. All the furnishings are modern and in quiet shades of brown and gray: very beautiful, very masculine... and very expensive. Either Lucien's films do very well or he's a trust-fund baby.

"Here, Ella. Look these over and let me know what you think. If you decide to sign on, I'm going to ask you to get started while I'm in France. Most of the research can be conducted online or in a decent library but there are two interviews I need taped: one in San Diego, and another in New York. The one in New York is the problem, since she's traveling and will only be back in the city for two weeks, as of Tuesday. I won't be back for nearly a month, so I'll miss her.

"As for recompense, there are two options: a flat fee or a percentage of profits. The producers are trying to get an extended release in art theatres in every major U.S. city plus a few international houses but they're also courting academic institutions. If that happens, profits will be robust. Unfortunately, at this point, opting for the profit sharing is somewhat risky. It's your call. What do you think so far?"

I clear my throat, acutely aware of Ian and wishing he weren't here with me. I can feel his jealousy hanging weighty in the air. "Lucien, I'm intrigued by the whole project and it does seem rather perfect for me, considering my academic background. I'll read over the paperwork and consider what we've discussed this morning, but I will say that right now I'm inclined to accept if you're inclined to offer. It's almost too good to pass up."

Lucien's handsome face lights up at my words. "I'm delighted to hear you say that, Ella." He takes his wallet out of his jacket pocket and fishes out a card. "Here's my business card. It lists my cell number as well as my email address. You can contact me at either one. May I ask you for a definitive answer in 48 hours? Normally I wouldn't rush you, but I need that interview with Picasso's assistant's daughter and I'd like to nail it down as soon as possible."

"No, I understand. I'll give you my answer within 24

hours, Lucien. Sound okay?"

"Absolutely. I cannot stress enough my gratitude in your coming here on such short notice. It's very much appreciated."

"No problem. I was casting about for something worthwhile to do when this just fell into my lap. I feel like the fortunate one." I look over at Ian but his face is inscrutable. "Well, Lucien, we're going to leave and let you get back to your packing. I'll be in touch very soon."

"Thank you, Ella. Would you happen to have a card with your contact info on it?"

"Uh, yes, actually." I dig in my bag and find a couple, handing him one.

"Great. It was a pleasure meeting you," he says, shaking my hand and then extends his to Ian. "Mr. Blackmon, very nice to make your acquaintance."

"Likewise. Enjoy your trip to Paris. It's lovely this time of year."

"Yes. Certainly. I get homesick for the city every now and then, especially in autumn, for some reason."

After we leave Lucien's, we head straight to the Met and spend three hours wandering the galleries. Never having been to New York City before, I am simply amazed at the sheer number of famous works located in one place. It's beyond exciting, especially for me, since art history is my academic focus.

Ian takes me out to lunch at Balthazar's, a restaurant that's apparently impossible to get into most of the time but he somehow manages it. We head back to the hotel around six.

After a two-hour nap, he wakes me up by undressing me and kissing me up and down my naked body. There are worse ways to wake up.

"Do you want to play tonight?" he asks me.

"Play how?"

"My way," he answers, his eyes gleaming.

"Do you mean by going to a nasty club?"

"No, that's not what I mean. But I do mean kinky fun.

Are you in?"

I narrow my eyes, mulling over my answer. "Okay. What do you have in mind?"

"You'll see."

He leads me into the shower and we take turns washing each other. I never realized how much fun a shower could actually be before I met Ian. By the time we're through, he has a huge hard-on and I'm hot enough to make friends with a doorknob or something. The strange thing, though, is he makes no attempt to scratch the itch—for either of us. I'm beginning to wonder if his version of kinky fun involves sexual torment and I have a strong feeling it does.

Ian dries us both off and we go into the bedroom to get dressed.

"Here. Wear this one," he says, pulling my short black cocktail dress out of the hotel room closet. The dress is made of slinky fabric and it has three-quarter sleeves and a plunging vee-neckline that's held together by satin lacing, providing peek-a-boo glimpses at what's inside.

"Okay." I take the dress.

"Do you have a garter belt?"

"No. But I do have silk stockings that stay up without a garter. Do you want me to wear those?"

He nods. "And your black stilettos, please."

It's not until we get in the taxi that he makes his next request. Once he gives the driver an address, he leans in to whisper in my ear. "Take off your panties."

I look at him as if he's lost his mind. "What?"

"You heard me. Do it."

"In here?" I screech, thinking about all the people and... stuff... that's been on these car seats. "It's not hygienic."

He shakes his head, a gesture he uses when he is dismissive of my concerns. "Keep the dress underneath you, but do as I say, Ella."

I look at him with suspicious eyes but my hand slowly travels under my hem. Watching the driver in the rearview mirror, I surreptitiously slide down my panties, being extra careful that my butt does not touch the icky car seat. When I work them down off my ankles, Ian holds out his hand and I give them to him. He pockets them without taking his eyes off me and those eyes? Smoldering.

"I'm not sure I like this, Ian." My voice is shaky.

His voice is smooth and deep. "My money says you do. Care to make it interesting?"

"How interesting?"

He shrugs. "We'll keep it manageable. Say a thou?"

I chew my lip nervously and nod my assent. His hand snakes up my dress and he touches me intimately, then thrusts a finger up into me. Then two. After only a moment, he withdraws his hand and holds it up in the glare of the streetlights outside. His fingertips are glistening. "I win," he whispers and licks my ear. Again I glance at the driver and see his eyes in the mirror. Nosy bastard is watching us and I can only hope he didn't manage to see anything worthwhile.

In a few minutes we reach our destination. Ian comes around to open my door and help me out—and, believe me, with no panties, a rather short dress, and high heels, I need help. He pays the driver and leads me to a shop front. I look up. A jewelry store?

"Why a jewelry store, Ian? And why is it still open at nine o'clock, by the way?"

"No questions. Tonight you're my sub: just be quiet and follow my lead. Okay?"

I nod. I can do this—it's exciting and it may just be fun. I'll play nice for now. "Lead the way."

Before we could get in, his phone rings. Checking the caller, he frowns but takes the call. "Talk," he orders the poor slob on the other end of the line.

He listens for a long moment. "Please tell me you're not kidding? This is good news, Jonas, the best news. Have Terence get his ass on a flight to Beijing ASAP. Oh? Well, then, have him follow them to Hong Kong or around the fucking world, for all I care, as long as he gets to them quickly. No, Terence speaks fluent Mandarin and can muddle his way through Cantonese; he needs to be the one to court them. And notify Jackson Delacroix about the offer. Tell him we're definitely interested but we need to show a healthy profit on the sale—we've sunk too much into it already. Have accounting do their best to pretty up the books—to the legal extent possible. Keep me posted."

"Good news, I take it?" I ask after he disconnects.

"If I ever say I don't believe in God, remind me of this day, Ella. I just received a gift from heaven, routed through China. We've been bleeding out on this solar panel company we took on, hoping for tax waivers into 2020. With recent budget cuts, the government phased out the waivers starting next year. We were set to take a bloodbath on it. A Chinese firm offered to buy us out. They can make it profitable because it's an open secret that the Chinese government illegally subsidizes their green energy companies so that no American company can effectively compete. If they take it on, it's a win-win for everyone involved. Especially me."

"It's a good night for you; you also just made a cool thou in the taxi."

His response is the most lascivious grin I've ever seen on anyone's face—it travels right into my girly parts—as he takes my hand and we enter the store.

It looks like an ordinary jewelry store—nothing different at all. The saleswoman is a blonde, mid forties, tan and fit. She immediately assesses Ian, up and down. I know what she's doing: besides ogling his beauty, she's appraising him for wealth. Having worked in an upscale shop, I know how these commission hounds operate—especially in New York, where they can tell volumes about a person just by his or her shoes.

Ian is cool as he asks, "May we shop in the rear store, please?"

Blondie nods impassively and steps over to a door, rapping her knuckles on it twice. I hear it unlock and then the door opens and Ian leads me inside.

Oh. My. God.

Inside the rear store is a sex shop that has every imaginable (and many unimaginable, believe me) toy and accessory anyone could ever want for sex. I've never seen anything like it and I'm pretty sure I don't want to see it again. It's the dildo section that causes me the most distress while also fascinating me: every shape, size, color, and material, is on display. Are there people who will shove anything remotely phallic up there? I gape at Ian and he smiles reassuringly before he begins to completely ignore me. Oh, that's right: I'm the sub—or second-class citizen—tonight.

Taking my wrist, he pulls me toward a counter that has silver and leather chokers. It takes me a minute before I realize what I'm looking at. Not chokers, dear stupid Ella.

Collars.

There's a thirtyish woman in purple hair and black leather, manning the counter. If I had to choose one adjective for her, I'd pick formidable even before female. "Can I help you, sir?"

"Yes," Ian replies smoothly, "I'm looking for a gold or sterling collar. Something with clean lines, simple yet elegant."

The woman looks at me curiously as I watch her. Ian catches her glance and whispers in my ear. "Eyes down, Ella."

Oops. I'm a bad submissive, apparently. After a second, I realize that eyes-down is actually a kindness in this place. I hope he doesn't think I'm going to kneel on this scuzzy floor, though.

"I like this one. Do you agree?"

I look up to answer him, only to realize he's speaking to the saleswoman, not me. Apparently I'm not to be consulted for my own collar—and that sounds just so wrong.

"Yes, that one would look lovely on her." She hands it to Ian and he sweeps my hair to one side to put it around my throat. "Yes. We'll take this one."

Chancing a glance up, I see the woman looks delighted. I take a wild guess that the collar is pricey and she just scored a hefty commission.

"Here's my credit card. Don't close out the balance until we're finished shopping.

"Of course, sir. Will she be wearing the collar or would you like it packed up?"

"Wear, I think." Still holding my wrist, he leads me to the other side of the store. An older man, also in black leather, is managing this side and I immediately feel way more uncomfortable, especially seeing the items Ian is homing in on. Oh, no.

"May I see that one?" he asks the man. "The one with the gemstones?"

The man says nothing but efficiently removes the item requested, handing it to Ian. I sneak a peek, trying to figure out what it is. It's sterling silver and it's thicker on one side but the narrow side ends in a wider piece and is surrounded by those gemstones. I'm not sure but I think it goes up a person's butt so the gemstones stick out—jewelry for the ass is taking the whole concept of adornment a bit far, in my opinion.

While I'm keeping my eyes down, Ian buys some other things. I don't even want to look anymore: I'm so ready to leave. After he pays for the items he's selected, he asks for the use of a private room and the redhead ushers us through yet another door. I feel as if each door sends me into an alternate universe. Now Ian and I are alone in a small red and purple room with a huge gilded mirror and an antique plush-velvet couch.

He sits on the couch. "Ella, come here. This," he holds up the silver thing, "has been sterilized—I just watched the salesman do it. I'm going to put lubrication on it and insert it in you. I want you to wear it until we get back to the hotel. Any questions?"

"Just one. Where are you going to insert it exactly?"

"In your pretty little hindquarters."

"I don't think so, Ian."

"You agreed to play with me tonight: my way, my

144

rules. Leave everything to me. Now turn around, bend over, and grasp your ankles. It will only take a few seconds."

I stand there, chewing my lip. I did agree to play tonight but I didn't know playing involved sticking things up my butt. However, what's the big deal? I'll try it and if I don't like it, then I'll remove it. No big whup. I spin around and bend over, trying not to dwell on what I must look like in this position.

I feel him pull my dress over my back and hear him opening a package. Then something trespasses in a place that should be entirely private. It's his finger. He pushes it in and out a few times and then I feel something cold and heavy start to slide in. "Push against me, Ella, and it will be easier."

I do and it goes in slowly and uncomfortably. After a protracted moment, he pulls my dress back down and adjusts it. "All done."

I stand up and turn around and as soon as I move, the plug shifts and sends all kind of strange sensations through me. Ian sees the look on my face and smiles. He knows what I'm feeling—which is precisely why he wanted it there. He's going to drive me insane with need before he slakes the thirst.

"Where's yours?"

"Mine?"

"Don't you get anything up your ass?" I ask sweetly.

"Not tonight," he grins. "Just you. Do you want to see how pretty it looks?"

Shaking my head, I say, "Not particularly. I can feel how pretty it looks—those gemstones are not the most comfortable thing, you know."

His eyes sparkle with evil intent. "Wait until you sit on them."

"Something to look forward to, I guess. Now what?"

"Now," he says rising to his feet, "we go out for dinner." He kisses my nose.

I knew it. I'm not going to get any satisfaction for hours and by the time we get back to our hotel, I'll probably let him do anything he wants—and he's counting on that, the Machiavellian bastard. I just know it.

It's bad enough that I have no panties on, but when you add a short dress and a butt plug to the mix, it makes for one uncomfortable Ella. Ian takes us to an elegant French restaurant on the Upper East Side that serves dinner until eleven. We just make it in by 10:30.

"A little late for dinner, don't you think?"

"This is the city that never sleeps, Ella. When in Rome..."

"We're not in Rome," I say grumpily—those gemstones are starting to smart.

All through dinner, he pays constant attention to me: hanging on my every word, smiling, winking, and oozing charm in general. He also touches me quite a lot, his fingers brushing across my shoulder or the middle of my thigh. At one point he places his hand on the small of my back, almost on my ass but not quite. I'm sitting on the plug—carefully—and it's becoming excessively uncomfortable, despite my frequent squirming to make it less so. By midnight, I'm more than ready to get back to our hotel downtown and deal with it all.

We get into another taxi but Ian doesn't give him our hotel address. To my consternation, he takes us to a club. I look at him questioningly, my disappointment surely on my face.

"An after-dinner drink, Ella. Then we'll go back to the hotel."

"Why can't we have the drink at the hotel bar?" My voice sounds whiny.

"You'll see. Let's go."

He leads me into the club that's literally wall-to-wall people: there's barely room to move through them to the bar. After about twenty minutes we finally get there and Ian orders two scotches, neat and straight up. "I'm drinking scotch?" I ask.

"Apparently." He lifts one glass to my lips, offering me a sip and then we go in search of a place to land. Of course there are no tables available but we find a piece of a wall we can claim that has a shelf nearby for our drinks. Ian puts his arm around me and pulls me close.

"Now," he says, "you wanted to know why we couldn't go to the hotel bar? I'll show you." I feel his hand go right up my dress and he starts finger fucking me right there in full view of everyone. I whip my head around, horrified, but no one seems to be paying us any attention. The room is dark, crowded, and loud with voices and music. My knees have just about gone out on me. Between Ian's fingers and that damn butt plug, I'm seconds away from an orgasm. He knows it too because just as things start to contract, he stops completely, taking back his hand and kissing me deeply as I feel my climax melt away entirely. I can't help it: I stomp my foot.

"That was mean!"

"I'll make it up to you soon, Ella. Just hold on a bit longer."

"Why?"

"Do you really want to come here, with all these people around you?"

"Right now I don't give much of a damn. But you know that, Ian, since you're the one doing it to me."

His hand goes back up my dress but this time he starts pulling on the plug, inching it out and then back in and twisting it back and forth. With the same hand, he slides his thumb into me in front. It should be obviously apparent to others around us as to what we're doing since he has to bend his knees to put his hand up my dress... but the idea that people may be watching does not horrify me as it should. What is wrong with me? When my eyes are locked with Ian's, the whole world recedes into the background like a blurry photo of a crowd. My knees buckle again and I lean my head on his shoulder. Just as I move into the orgasm, he stops again.

Okay, fine! Two can play at the same game. Without caring if anyone can see, I put my hand over his crotch and start rubbing it in earnest. He smiles and remains perfectly composed. How the fuck does he do that? I'm never going to win with him as my opponent. Ever.

Nevertheless I keep it up (excuse the pun). When I feel him get even harder than he was already, I stop and wait a few moments. Then I start up again. While I'm rubbing him, I kiss his throat, lick his ear, suck his earlobe, and finally bite his neck—hard. As soon as he feels my teeth sink into his flesh, his eyelids flutter closed for a brief moment, and then he grabs my hand, roughly leading me out of the club and right into a waiting taxi. I can't help but smile.

After giving the driver the hotel address, he leans back and looks at me. Seeing my triumphant grin, he merely raises a brow. "Battle conceded, war still up for grabs," he says as his hand goes back up my dress.

Chapter 15

Despite heavy Saturday night traffic, they get back to the hotel in ten minutes. Ian had his hand up her dress for the whole ride—inching her inexorably to the cliff edge and then easing her back—and she is seconds away from coming when the taxi pulls in front of the hotel. As they wait for the elevator, Ian sees Ella's face is flushed and her eyes are bright and shining.

"Have I ever told you that you'd look beautiful in silks?" he asks, as soon as he closes their room door behind him. He slides off the black leather messenger bag slung over his shoulder and begins to remove the items he purchased from *Get your Kinks*. Ella is watching, mesmerized, as he pulls out the long silky scarf-like binds, the blindfold, clamps, and butterfly vibrator—he remembered she liked that the first time he used it on her.

When he finishes taking the items out, she catches his eyes and slowly raises the hem of her dress higher and higher until it goes over her head. She's practically naked now, since he deprived her of any underwear. She's wearing only her thigh-high black silk stockings, the new collar, her kick-ass shoes, and the bejeweled butt plug. She looks ridiculously sexy, Ian thinks, his pants becoming uncomfortably tight. He shifts his hips, trying for a more comfortable position.

"I do wish you were wearing a tie tonight, Ian, so I can lead you to the bed by it. I always wanted to do that to a tall, dark, and handsome stranger. You fit the bill."

He smiles, going for a rakish look. "I'll put one on if it means that much to you, baby."

She eyes him up and down and he thinks she likes his attire by the hungry look in her eyes—or is she focused only on what's underneath? Though he took time in selecting the clothes he'd worn tonight—black tailored pants, a charcoal silk shirt, and a black cashmere cardigan, his prized accessory is the one causing the trouser tent in the front of his pants.

Stalking towards him, her head tilted down in a predatory fashion, she replies. "Not strictly necessary. I can improvise." She reaches him and grabs his collar with both hands, yanking him with her as she steps backward toward the fluffy white bed. Apparently she doesn't intend to let him continue with the program, if she could help it. Ian, however, has other plans.

"As I said, you will look so very good in silks, Ella. So indulge me," he gently removes her hands and steps back over to his goodies, grabbing the silky scarves.

He sits on the edge of the bed and pats the mattress next to him. "Come here." She immediately moves to him and he kisses her, long and hard, holding her head to his so she cannot move. "Lie down in the center of the bed." His voice has quickly slid from seductive lover to demanding Dominant with no segue. The unpredictability is intentional: it will keep her off balance.

Playing nice, she does as he asked. Ian takes a moment to admire the scene: enfolded in the downy comforter, the contrast of her long, dark hair, black stockings and shoes, and kohl-rimmed eyes against the crisp white is visually alluring. Again, he has to adjust his pants. He takes the first scarf and ties it to her right wrist, checking to make sure it's not too tight. Drawing her right knee up, he ties her ankle to the long end of the wrist cuff. "It's really too bad that hotel beds have nothing to lash these to, but I'm a determined man."

Ian repeats the process on her left side so her arms and legs are bound together but not lashed to the bed. She tests the binds by closing her legs and looks satisfied at her relative freedom of movement. He picks up a third scarf and his lips stretch into a wicked grin. He ties one end to her right cuff and then runs the scarf under the mattress to the other side, where he ties it to the other. Now she can't move, nor close her legs. She's at his complete mercy.

"Okay?" he asks.

She nods, her eyes wide and slightly panicked. Perfect: a little apprehension will only enhance the experience for them both. Ian reaches into his pocket and then crawls on the bed with one knee, leaning between her legs. "Now, I will allow you to come anytime or as much as you want, Ella, but you may not move an inch or make any noise whatsoever," he warns as he places three cobalt blue marbles on her belly, in a straight line. One immediately sinks into her navel. "I will not appreciate it if you make me lose my marbles. Are we clear?"

"I'm afraid that ship has long since sailed," she says with a breathy laugh. "What happens if the marbles roll off?"

Shaking his head and tsk tsking, he says, "You don't want to know. Trust me—it will be ugly."

"How ugly?"

"Hmmm, let's see. Spanking? Perhaps. Tickling? Almost definitely. Orgasm denial? Without a doubt. Giant anal plug? Possibly. I might even give you another go at it if you lose a marble or two but if I do permit that generosity, you will get nipple clamps first. Then if one or two marbles slip, it will earn you a tug on the clamp chain. Let's just see how it goes, shall we?"

With that comment his head dips down between her legs and his tongue begins a relentless, unerring torment. Two of the marbles slide off almost immediately.

His head comes up; he attempts an expression of profound disappointment while trying hard to mask his amusement. "Oh, Ella. You didn't even last a few seconds. Is that really the best you can do?"

"Just so we're clear, Ian, I want you to know that I plan to murder you in the most painful way possible as soon as you untie my hands and legs. Don't say I didn't warn you."

He wags his finger back and forth. "Eh, eh, eh, you do not have permission to speak." He gets up and retrieves another item from the pile on the table. "I'm going to choose to be generous and give you another chance."

He takes her right breast into his mouth and sucks so hard she gasps sharply. When he pulls away, he replaces his mouth with the clamp. It stings but it's not too bad—that is, until he tightens it beyond endurance.

"Ow! That really hurts!"

"Take a few deep breaths and it will subside." His voice is confident and reassuring. He does the same with her other breast. Running down from each clamp is a delicate silver chain and the two connect together into one chain—a leash of sorts—that dangles down past her belly.

"Ready to try again?"

She whimpers. "I'm going to lose them again; I know it. Damn it, Ian: do you think you could do it? It's damn near impossible."

"Control, Ella. You need to work on maintaining better control."

When his head dips down again, she stops him. "Wait. What do I win if I manage to keep the marbles still?"

"You get a big—giant, really—and hard... kiss." He pauses for a long beat. "...as I fuck you into next week." And he begins again.

Motivation. This time she manages to keep still for a little while but not silent. Far from it: does she even realize she's moaning loudly the whole time? Ian can't help but smile against her flesh. He stops to unzip his pants and put on a condom and then leans in to continue.

"Oh, no, you don't. I want to see you naked. It's only fair," comes her husky voice and she picks up her head, expecting him to comply and to watch him undress.

Fair enough. He straightens and removes his shoes by pushing one off with his other and kicking them away. Unbuttoning his shirt, he keeps his eyes on hers the whole time, enjoying how they seem to darken as the pupils dilate with her excitement. It's proof she finds him as attractive as he finds her, and it strokes his ego. When he's entirely naked but for the condom, he slides back down between her legs to give her that long awaited orgasm. She earned it and fair is fair.

The marbles stay on her abdomen until the top of her climax when they come rolling off as her hips jerk up into the air as high as the restraints will allow her to move. As promised, he jerks the chain attached to the clamps and is rewarded with a high-pitched shriek. The slight bit of erotic pain will only enhance her orgasm, whether she knows it or not. He continues tonguing her until the last spasm and then in one fluid motion pulls up and pushes deeply into her. The plug makes it an extremely tight fit, plus she can't move much at all and that sense of helplessness, combined with the extra friction, sends her over the cliff and she comes again within seconds. The clench of it is so strong that she almost takes him with her, but he manages to pull back in time so he could keep going. He waited all night for this ride and he's going to make it last.

Sounding excited—almost desperate—Ella cries out, "Ian, I want to touch you; unbind me please."

"How much, baby? How much do you want to touch me? Tell me," he says in a voice deeper and huskier than usual.

She whimpers. "Please, I want to hold you... so very much."

"That much, huh? Enough to turn down the job with Lucien Phillips?"

She looks at him, startled, and they both freeze. It's an awkward time for this discussion but he needs to make her understand how he feels. What better way to have her complete attention?

"What? Are you kidding?"

He shakes his head very slowly, his eyes boring into hers. "No, baby, no jokes tonight. What will it take for you to turn down the job?"

"I…"

He swivels his hips then swings them back slowly before driving into her forcefully. Her eyes begin to glaze over as lust replaces confusion. Leaning his head close to hers, Ian whispers into her ear. "You're mine, sexy Ella, all mine. Turn down the job."

It's the last thing she hears before her world contracts and explodes in an incredible orgasm.

Chapter 16

It doesn't take a genius to figure out why Ian doesn't want me to work with Lucien Phillips. If anyone could give Ian some competition, it would be that blond Adonis. But I'm not looking at Lucien as romantic potential: I want to work with him on his documentary—badly. Besides, in the few minutes we spent together, he demonstrated no interest in me other than purely professional—for all I know Lucien might even be gay. One thing I definitely do know: I am taking the job, come hell or high water.

The adjectives I've come up with to describe what Ian did last night are unconscionable, bizarre, outrageous, infuriating, and punishable—a crime worthy, in fact, of imaginative punitive measures. If I hadn't been so irrevocably in the moment, I would have kicked him. Oh wait: I couldn't do that with my legs bound, could I? He'd covered all his bases.

I have to admit the undeniable: sex with Ian is incomparable. It's true that, technically, I have nothing to compare it with since he's the only man I've ever been with intimately, but I've had enough conversations with my friends and read enough *Cosmo* articles to know that sex with Ian is not the norm. Not even close. I know I should want to experiment with other lovers but I'm so certain they'll come up short that it almost seems an exercise in futility. It's important to Ian—he's made it abundantly clear—that he's my first and only man, so I need to consider that going forward. Ironic that in the beginning my virginity bothered him but it's come to be something he highly values. Still... he's made no commitment to me nor have I to him. Do I even want a commitment so early in the game? I'm only twenty-three.

I open my eyes the next morning and realize I'm immobilized. The reason why becomes clear quickly: Ian has his arms and legs wrapped tightly around me—even in his sleep he restrains me! If I as much as take a deep breath, I'll wake him. I crane my neck to see his face just above my head and he wears such a serene expression that I don't have the heart to smack him upside the head, as I almost certainly should. I remain in my human cage for a few more minutes, using the time to think and trying not to dwell on the fact that my nose is itchy.

I will call Lucien and accept the job. It means I'll have to stay in New York to interview the Picasso woman. Lucien had mentioned that he has a film crew on standby for the purpose. After, I can go back to Portland and try to conduct as much research there as possible, using my laptop and the library. At some point, I may have to do more travel but that's fine. I sigh, realizing that if I stay with Ian in whatever this thing we have going is, it means many more fights on the horizon and the thought is depressing.

"Why the frown?"

He startles me: I thought he was still asleep. "Just thinking."

"About?"

Inhale, Ella, and just go for it, I tell myself. "The logistics of my new job."

I can feel his whole body stiffen around me. "So you are taking it, then?"

"Yes." The least said the better, I think. I dare a peek at his face.

He looks pissed: his jaw is clenched and his eyes narrowed—quite a marked difference from the sleeping angel of a few minutes ago. "I see. I need to go to Tokyo next weekend and I thought to ask you to accompany me. Is that at all possible if you accept the position?"

"I'm not sure, Ian. I'll have to stay in New York to do that interview that Lucien has been waiting for. That might take me past the weekend..."

"Too bad. It would have been nice to have you along. This will be only the second time I've visited Japan—it would be wonderful to have you there to sightsee with me."

"Oh, I would love that, actually." I know I shouldn't feel guilty one tiny bit... but I do. I really do. Stupid, I know.

He says nothing, just swings his long legs over the side of the bed to get up. I watch his lean, graceful body as he stretches. Lean but powerful. Ah. *The glory of young men is in their strength*. He turns to see me ogling him and gifts me with a small smile. "Shall we go out to breakfast or call for room service?"

"Go out, I think. I want to see more of the city."

"Okay. I'm getting in the shower."

I surprise him in the shower, tiptoeing in silently, and grab him from behind... but he's waiting for me, the sneak. In one fluidly efficient motion, he spins me around, pins my arms over my head, pushes me against the wall, and rams into me as the water turns scorching, scalding us both.

"Too hot!" I yelp and he turns up the cold water with his knee.

"Are you mine, Ella?" His face leans heavily on my cheek, his lips on my ear; I can't escape any part of him.

Panting, I try to avoid answering.

"Ella, answer the question." He continues thrusting his hips forcefully, making any coherent thought impossible. With one hand he's holding my wrists, the other is brutally gripping my right hip, holding me in place.

"Right now I am." I move forward, rest my face on the cool tile: I want to concentrate on feeling rather than thinking.

He falls silent then, instinct swamping intellect, and I fall with him, switching off my mind to revel in the physical wonder of what boy plus girl can equal.

"Ella, fantastic news! I'm excited," Lucien says as I reach him in Paris a few hours later. "In the paperwork I gave you yesterday, you'll find the contact information for both my crew and the interview subject. Her name is Maya St. Sauveur and she promised me that she'll be back in the city by Tuesday afternoon. If you can shoot the interview, I think you can probably head back out west afterward. Also, can you sign the contract and send a copy to my New York address, as well as to my attorney's office that's listed on the back of the contract?

"Absolutely. I noticed you provided a list of questions you'd like me to ask her. Do you want me to go beyond those or adhere strictly to the script?"

"At your discretion, Ella. As long as you cover my questions, feel free to ask your own—within the bounds of the subject matter, but I know I don't have to tell you that. I included a DVD of some of the interviews I've already taped of others so you can get a feel for how to approach it."

"Oh, that helps. Alright, I'll spend tomorrow reviewing all the material and getting ready for Tuesday."

"Great. I'll be back in the States before the end of the month. Will you be able to return to New York at that time so we can work with the editor on the new footage and perhaps splice it with the others?"

"Not a problem, Lucien. I'm really looking forward to this project. Do you have a projected completion date?"

"We're aiming for end of March so it can go into post-production and be ready for release May one."

"That seems like plenty of time. Okay, I don't want to keep you on the phone, Lucien, so I'm going to compile a list of questions and email them to you—that way you can answer at your leisure. Sound good?"

"Perfect, Ella. I'll look forward to it. Enjoy your stay in New York—there's no better city in the world... except maybe for Paris."

"Thanks, I will. Bye, Lucien." I disconnect and try to avoid looking across the table at Ian. I don't need to look because I can feel his eyes on me, hostility radiating out like an atomic cloud threatening to engulf me.

Focusing his attention on his breakfast, Ian says nothing but I can feel the tension charging the air between us. "When do you have to leave for Tokyo?" I ask, after about five minutes of no conversation.

"I have meetings lined up for Tuesday and Wednesday, so I should probably leave sometime on Saturday, which will give me a day to acclimate."

"Assuming I can't come with you, will you stay to sightsee or return home after your meetings?"

He shakes his head. "I've made no plans yet. Since things are frenetic right now at Excalibur, I probably should come right home."

I nod. Excalibur is the name of his umbrella enterprise, which is a holding company for all the smaller ones in which he owns majority stock. Apparently, his first company, named eponymously, went belly up about five years ago, which is when he established Excalibur. "I should know by Tuesday or so how long I have to stay in New York. Tomorrow I'll get up to speed on my new job and I'll pop over to see Mo Jackson, my agent.

Once Ian gets over his snit, we end up having the most fantastic time together. He is so relaxed and charming when taken out of his element, and we have a leisurely day visiting Hayden's Planetarium and the Empire State building. It's after four when we get back to the hotel and decide to have a drink at the hotel bar. Because the weather is chilly and damp, Ian orders us each an Irish coffee and then finds a quiet corner table. I spend a moment feeling grateful for the little joys in life, such as a hot drink and a beautiful man's strong, warm hand holding mine.

His left brow arches. "What's the smile for?"

"I was just thinking how much I like being with you."

Now he smiles, his eyes alive with affection. "Well, the feeling happens to be mutual."

We sip our drinks and I look around. It's nearly the dinner hour so the bar is relatively quiet. Yes, I can see Ian's point about not coming here last night—not for what he had planned anyway. His deep voice interrupts my wayward thoughts.

"Ella, in all likelihood, I'll have to go back to Portland tomorrow."

I nod, disappointed but expecting it.

"I'd like to have an honest discussion with you about where we stand right now... in terms of you and I, our relationship, if that's what it is."

"Okay." My heartbeat begins to take flight. I wasn't sure we even had a relationship. Ian never wanted anything but a sexual arrangement with me—in the past, anyway. I always thought he didn't consider me good enough for a genuine romance. I should just ask him. My voice falters but eventually I spit it out. "I was under the impression that you weren't interested in a relationship... at least not with me."

His expression freezes with astonishment. "Why would you think that, Ella?"

I shrug. "Because you only ever offered me a sexual arrangement. I figured that's all you wanted with me."

"I... no, that's not true. If it ever was, it's no longer true, anyway." He seems to be taking his time, considering his words carefully. "I'm not very comfortable... I'm used to setting the parameters of my... intimate... relationships and knowing exactly what to expect. With you... well, it's very different. I'd appreciate knowing how you see me, where I fit, I suppose, in your life."

"I'm not sure either, Ian. Last time what wrecked everything was the... well, you know what. I remain uninterested in exploring that part of the lifestyle you're attracted to. If my reluctance is a deal breaker then I suppose we don't have much of a relationship."

"And if it's not? A deal breaker?"

"Then I'm in," I say, feeling a spot of heat on each cheek. It's hard to talk honestly with someone you're involved with—especially if that someone is as intimidating a presence as Ian Blackmon.

He nods. "Are we exclusive then?"

I glance up to scrutinize his face: he looks serious and even a bit anxious. "I... uh... would prefer a relationship that is exclusive. How about you?"

"Absolutely. So can we agree on this aspect?"

"Yes, I can agree to that—happily. What about," I drop my voice to a soft whisper, "the BDSM? Where does that fit into the picture?"

"It can fit in wherever you want it to fit in. We'll only do what you're comfortable doing, Ella. How does that sound?"

He looks so sweetly sincere as he waits for my answer that I can't keep from jumping up to embrace him. He wraps his strong arms around my waist and I hold his face in both my hands and kiss his beautiful lips. "That sounds perfect, Ian, absolutely perfect."

He smiles and kisses my hand. We finish our drinks, listening to the piano player and then escape to our room, spending the rest of the night in bed, touching and tasting each other leisurely. As far as evenings go, it ranks up there with the crème de la crème.

Ian leaves New York the next morning and I allow myself a half hour to cry because I begin to miss him the second he walks out the hotel room door. Terribly. The room seems desperately lonely without his commanding presence.

I'm meeting Mo at one o'clock and my taxi is stuck in midtown traffic. "I'll just get out here and walk," I say to the driver, handing him a twenty-dollar bill. The fare is fifteen dollars and change, and I'm not sure the tip is big enough, considering I left him stuck in a traffic jam but I hope it is. "Thanks."

Mo's office is on 57th street and I get out on 51st so I just need to walk six blocks—in the rain. Luckily I have my umbrella. I'm rushing to cross a street before the light changes when my cell phone starts singing.

Checking the caller, I see it's Lucien.

"Lucien, hello. What's up?"

"Ella, some not so good news, I'm afraid. I just got a call from Maya St. Sauveur. She's in Venice and apparently cannot leave until some legal matter can be cleared up. I'm stuck in Paris for the next 48 hours at least. Maya claims that if her legal matter takes much longer than two days, she might not have time to go to New York. She's due in Bali for a wedding early next week. This interview is proving to be a massive pain. Is there any way you can get to Venice to do the interview? You can take Gerard, my cameraman, and just knock out the interview that way."

"I suppose I can do that. I'm meeting my agent now and then I have no other business in New York. If I could get a flight out tonight, I might be able to pull it off."

"Ah, so good to hear. I'll phone Gerard and let him know."

"Sure. I'll call the airport as soon as I get back to my hotel."

"Just to be on the safe side, Ella, I'll call and buy the tickets for you now... in case the flight gets booked before you get the chance. I'll call you back or text you with the details."

"That sounds fine. I'll speak to you later, Lucien."

Well. I suppose I'm going to Venice for the first time in my life. If only Ian could accompany me, it would be grand. Not only will going to such a romantic city alone be a bit pathetic but then I'll also have to deal with Ian's inevitable wrath. I glance at my watch: he's still in the air so I can't call him. I'll text him after my meeting.

"Ella! It's so good to see you. Come, let's have lunch. My treat."

"Thank you. I'd like that."

"It's the least I can do considering how much money you've made me," she says with a chuckle. "How about a glass of wine and a Caesar salad?"

"Perfect. Let's go."

Mo takes me to a small café that boasts of selling only fresh food, locally grown. I observe her as she places her order. I've never met her in person before today, handling all our business by fax and phone. The woman is a powerhouse but, physically, she's tiny. She has dark red hair, big eyes, and a penchant for highly tailored suits, I see. She's wearing very high heels but I suppose that's because she's so petite. Though small in stature, she has a booming voice and a huge personality, as well. I like Mo a lot, I decide all over again.

"Ella, I heard from the film production company last Friday. They're starting to cast, you know. Beth Furman, the assistant CD, asked me if you would want any weigh-in on the leads since it's not explicitly stated in your contract—but they don't want to get your nose out of joint, apparently. I suppose they're hoping for a sequel," she snorts.

"I wondered about that. I don't know anything about casting or film production, in general, but I'd like to get a final approval on their choices, as well as possibly offer them my idea of the characters' physicality."

"You describe them in the book," she points out, breaking a bread stick in half. "That's what they're using as a jumping off point. Trust me," she says, waving the bread stick at me, "they do not want to piss off your legion of fans. The fans are the ones who will pony up the dollars to see this movie; they want them to be pleased as punch with the actors cast in the roles. I think it's a good idea to give them your take but not to hold their feet to the fire. How does that sound?"

"Fine, Mo." I tilt my head in consternation. "Do I look like the type to hold anyone's feet to the fire?"

"No, Ella, you certainly don't. You also don't look like the type to write a naughty book so appearances apparently can be deceiving."

I have to laugh. If she only knew... or does she know? The thought makes my face grow hot. Shit, I'll bet she knows; Mo looks awfully crafty, I suddenly think, eyeing her suspiciously now.

"How long are you in the city?" She interrupts my miniature panic attack.

"I'm leaving for Venice tonight, hopefully." I look at my watch. "I need to hurry."

"Business or pleasure?"

"Business. I'm working on a documentary and I just found out the woman I need to tape an interview with is not going to be coming to New York after all. She's in Venice right now."

"Oh? What's the documentary about?"

"It's about the women—wives and mistresses—of three famous 20th-century painters. The one I'm meeting is the niece... or is it daughter? I think daughter... of one of Picasso's mistresses."

"Oh my God. Don't tell me you're working with Lucien Phillips?"

"Yes, I am. Do you know him?"

"Not that well—although I'd like to," she laughs. "I met him at a gallery opening a couple of weeks ago. Talk about eye candy, my God. I see good things in store for you, my girl."

I blush again. "I doubt my boyfriend would like that very much. He wanted me to turn down the job."

"I can't say I blame him. Lucien is hot."

"So is Ian... my boyfriend."

"Well, aren't you the lucky girl. That's nice for you. Tell me about Ian."

I shrug my shoulders nonchalantly but inside I'm thrilled beyond belief that I get to call Ian mine. *Mine!* I still can't believe it. "He's a businessman in Portland. Wealthy, gorgeous, you know, run of the mill."

"Let me see: wealthy, gorgeous, Portland, Ian. You're not going to tell me he's Ian Blackmon, are you? That would be too much of a coincidence."

Again, she stupefies me. "How can you possibly know Ian? You live in New York and he's a businessman from Portland."

"He used to spend a lot of time in New York City. A lot." She laughs so loudly that she startles me. "As for how I know him? That, my dear, is something I think I'm going to keep to myself. Suffice it to say, your Ian had sown a reputation among the ladies. But I'm sure that's all in the past now that he's met you." She winks.

"It had better be," I say, but I can feel my heart sag inside my chest. I hope Ian isn't planning on bringing me more heartbreak because I'm just not up for it these days.

After saying goodbye to Mo, I go back downtown to my hotel. As soon as I get there, I check the tickets that Lucien purchased for me, and then text Ian to let him know what's going on. Texting is much better than phoning him since I won't have to hear the displeasure in his voice if he gets pissed off about it. I snort. Not *if* but *when*. Exactly fifty-six seconds elapse between the time I hit *send* and the time Aretha starts wailing for respect on my cell pone. Oh, shit.

Chapter 17

He is furious. He knew that son of a bitch Phillips was an operator: he could tell he was up to no good right from the start. If there was anything Ian knew, it was human nature. He had the bruises to show for it. Ella picks up the call on the third ring.

"Hey, Ian. How was your flight?"

"Venice, Ella?" He yells so loudly the cab driver jumps in his seat. He makes a gargantuan effort to rein in his anger.

"Phillips told you the woman would be in New York and now he has you traipsing to Italy? What kind of bullshit is he up to? I don't like it, Ella. You hardly know the man."

Her loud sigh comes clearly through the phone line. "Ian, please tell me how you really feel—don't tiptoe around the issue."

Ignoring her attempt at humor, he continues as if she hasn't spoken. "Ella, my instincts tell me this guy is up to no good. Tell him you cannot accommodate his request and come home directly. Now."

"What? No! Ian, you cannot order me around. I'm going to Venice to conduct the interview and then I'll fly directly to Portland. I just might make it in time to go to Tokyo with you."

"Are you traveling there by yourself?"

"No. Gerard—the cameraman—is coming with me."

"Another man you don't know. You're basing all of this trust on the word of a single friend with whom you had, at best, a superficial acquaintance. Answer me one question: are you being sensible in your hellbent determination for this job? Tell me, Ella."

"I don't have time to argue about it, Ian. I'll text you when I get there since it will be the middle of the night in Portland."

"Fine." He disconnects, not even saying goodbye. Right now, it's the smart thing to do. Glancing at his watch, he sees it's too late to go to the office so he decides to head straight home to get some paperwork done there. His housekeeper should have been in this morning, cleaning, organizing, and stocking the refrigerator so he didn't need to go out again. He leans back into the seat to try to center himself, wishing like hell that Ella was with him now. What would it take to get her to open her eyes about men? She was so naive it bordered on gross stupidity, for God's sake. She's a beautiful young woman—she's going to be prey for every piece of shit lowlife horny bastard out there. She has to accept reality.

Twenty minutes later, the cab pulls in front of his houseboat. He unclips a fifty-dollar bill and hands it to the driver. "Keep the change. Thanks." The driver hops out of the car to carry his bag to the front of the entrance. Ian nods his thanks.

As soon as he opens the door, he sees her. Can this day get any fucking worse? How the hell did she get into his house? The first thought that crosses his mind is to wonder if the woman is dangerously unstable. If so, he must proceed carefully.

"Hello, Ian. Long time no see."

Treating her like a wild animal, unpredictable in her behavior—in her case, crazy rather than feral—he slowly puts down his bag, careful not to make any sudden moves lest he provoke an attack. He nods to acknowledge her without saying a word.

"What's the matter? Cat got your tongue?"

He stands in the hall, still about twenty feet from where she's sitting. "Alexis, what are you doing in my house?"

"I came to see you, of course. You've been avoiding

me, Ian, and that's just not nice."

"I'm not avoiding you, Alexis. It's just that you and I have no relationship. You've been calling me and I'm not returning the calls because we have nothing to talk about. Do you understand?"

She stands up to move closer to him. "Now, that's just not fair. We're friends, aren't we? I like you, Ian."

"And you show it by breaking into my house? You do realize that in addition to being insane, it's also against the law. Correct?"

She takes a moment to admire her lacquered fingernails. "Oh, pish posh, mere technicalities. What're a few laws between friends? I tried calling you… numerous times, but you never called me back. What else could I do?" She pouts exaggeratedly, her full lips coated in scarlet lipstick.

"How did you get in?"

Shrugging her reply, she flips her long dark hair back behind her shoulders. "I just told the housekeeper I was your sister. She's new, isn't she?"

"What do you want, Alexis?"

She glides over to him: she's wearing a very short black dress with white polka dots and very high black heels… and not much else. He could see her breasts about to spill out of the low-cut *décolleté*, "I want *you* of course. What do you think?"

"Alexis, first of all, I'm not interested in you in that way. Second, I happen to be involved with someone right now. And third, I make it a habit never to date women who break into my home."

She's now inches away from him. "I think you are interested in me, Ian, but for some reason you're resisting.

"Okay, look: I'm tired, hungry, in need of a shower, and have an almost insurmountable pile of work to do. Please leave now, or I'll have no choice but to contact the police to intervene."

"Where's all your usual security, Ian?"

"Right now, they're on their way," he bluffs. "They're

coming from my office building where I was supposed to go. Instead I came directly home from the airport. Please leave before they get here and are forced to physically remove you from the premises."

Putting her arms on his, she leans into him, pressing her body against him. "Okay, I'm going... for now... but only because I have an engagement. I don't expect to be ignored." She leans in to kiss him but he rears his head back and away. She smiles and then releases him.

Without another word, she walks over to grab her purse off the sofa and, slightly unsteady on her heels, walks toward the door, "And by the way, Ian, I really don't care if you're involved with anyone or not. I've decided that you and I belong together. I'll see you tomorrow?"

"No, Alexis, you will not. Please don't force me to take legal action against you. Go away and stay away."

"You're not being very nice to me. But I'll forgive you your bad mood this time." She blows him a kiss on her way out the door.

Sighing, Ian finally exhales, realizing that Jared was right about the houseboat being impossible to secure. He might just have to pull the glass house off the market and move back in there... as long as crazy Alexis is running around. He especially doesn't want her to get near Ella.

Ella.

He can't even think about her right now; he's still too upset. Frustrated beyond belief that he couldn't just up and fly to Venice, he has to sit here in Portland knowing she's in that romantic city, possibly with Lucien Phillips. He can only hope that she gets back in time to accompany him to Japan. He checks his phone and sees she called earlier. He'd decided to let her stew for a while since he is so angry, it will do neither of them any good to speak. Let's see what the silent treatment will net him—it's better than yelling.

He quickly scans the room, ensuring that everything is in place. What the hell was she doing here? Did Carrie, his new housekeeper, actually let her in without checking with him first? He tended to doubt it. He also doubted that Alexis broke in only to say hello to him— there must have been something she was after. But what?

Chapter 18

I meet up with Gerard when I get to JFK Airport. I wanted to get a flight out of Newark, which would have been much faster but Lucien booked one out of JFK. It took me over an hour to get here from midtown so Gerard beats me there.

He seems like a nice guy—jovial, at least. He's stocky, about 5'9" and has merry eyes. Dirty blond hair sticks up in short spikes from his big head—everything about him is big, now that I think about it: big jaw, big body, big teeth, big laugh. I like him immediately.

Our flight actually takes off on time, is peacefully uneventful, and we arrive at Marco Polo Airport within minutes of our ETA.

"Ella, have you heard from Ms. St. Sauveur yet?" Gerard asks me in the taxi to our hotel.

"Yes, we're meeting her later this evening for dinner at her hotel—eight o'clock. That gives us time to check in to our hotel and have a long nap."

"I need to pick up some things so after we get settled, I'll head out. I guess you don't really need me at the dinner meeting, unless we're taping tonight. Are we?"

"I'm not sure what Ms. St. Sauveur's schedule is like so I figured we should be prepared for anything... so, yes, you should come to dinner. If she says we can tape in the morning or later, then you're free to leave. Does that sound acceptable?"

"Yes, Ella, perfectly."

The hotel Lucien selected is a small European-style affair, luxurious by most standards. The lobby has creamy marble floors and dark wood wainscoting on the walls. The upper part of the walls is painted a creamy beige tone to coordinate with the floor but it's done in Venetian plaster so it has depth and character. Everything looks brand new—the hotel must have been recently renovated. All the rooms have private baths and are tastefully furnished. Gerard and I part company as soon as we get our room cards, agreeing to meet at 7:15 in the hotel lobby. As soon as I close the door to my room, I plop down my bag and then drop into bed, exhausted. I don't look at my text messages for I don't want Ian to upset me. I also shut off the ringer on my phone. I'll deal with him later when I'm feeling stronger.

We're to meet Maya St. Sauveur at a rooftop restaurant at a nearby hotel. Gerard and I arrive for our eight o'clock meeting at 7:45 and cannot be seated until the entire party arrives so we stand awkwardly just outside the entrance, near the elevator bank. At exactly eight on the nose, the stainless steel doors slide open and out strides an elegant woman. I know instantly that it's her.

"Ms. St. Sauveur?"

"Yes. Ella Strong?"

I nod. "And this is Gerard Brolin, our cameraman. Gerard accompanied me in case you're interested in taping tonight. Can you give me an idea as to your preference?"

"Oh, no, dear. Not tonight. I just thought we'd meet and have dinner. I rather hoped we could do the interview in the late morning tomorrow."

Her accent is interesting: perfect Queen's English with some French thrown in as well. "Actually tomorrow morning will be perfect. Gerard?" I look at him. "You're free to head out to your own pursuits, then."

"Very good." He extends his hand. "Nice to meet you, Ms. St. Sauveur. I look forward to seeing you again in the morning."

She nods her regal head, perched on a very long neck. "Thank you. Till tomorrow then."

A maître d' comes to seat us a moment later and greets Maya like an old friend, so of course we get an excellent table by a window with a magnificent view of the city and Grand Canal. Venice is romantic and I wish Ian were here with me to enjoy it. With that thought I shake my head: I'm getting too attached to him way too soon. I have to stop it. Plus, right now he'd be lousy company since he's fit to be tied.

"I told Lucien Phillips that I'd be done with my engagements by late next week and that I could meet with him in Paris. Apparently that wasn't good enough for him?"

Maya St. Sauveur is not the type of woman to cross. She is nearly six feet tall, thin but not painfully so, and has such an erect carriage that she must have been a dancer at one time. She wears her light brown hair in a loose chignon and is dressed all in black, slacks, sweater, and flat loafers—elegant but formidable. I'd much rather be her friend than foe.

"I do apologize if this taping is inconvenient for you, Ms. St. Sauveur. Am I pronouncing your name correctly?"

"Yes, your pronunciation is fine. And no, it's not inconvenient, per se. It's just that that man irritates me. I'm doing him a favor, not the reverse, and yet he's quite demanding nonetheless." She assesses me slowly before continuing and I feel myself wilt beneath her sharp gaze. "Be careful with Phillips, Ms. Strong. He wants what he wants when he wants it. He'll run ramshod all over you."

"Are we talking about the same man? Lucien has been unfailingly polite in my dealings with him thus far."

"Oh, really? Perhaps it's just me he annoys with his impatience and exactitude. I am not a woman with whom to trifle, and Monsieur Phillips doesn't appear to comprehend this factoid."

I begin to get a slightly uneasy feeling about Lucien: first, Ian, now Maya. I dismissed Ian's instincts as jealousy automatically because he seems to overreact to any men having any dealing with me. Maya, however, does not seem the type to rush to judgment so I put more stock in her opinion—which is weird because I don't know her at all. My instincts tell me Lucien is a nice guy—and I like him just fine, so far. I hope my instincts prevail.

Dinner is excellent and I end up having an interesting chat with Maya—as she instructed me to call her. She's had a fascinating multicultural life and she could be the subject of a film herself. We decide to meet in her suite at eleven the next morning and I walk back to my own hotel two hours later, enjoying the stroll in such a beautiful city. Along the way, I pass a bent old woman, dressed all in black, feeding a group of stray dogs. There are six or seven skinny mongrel waifs and they're surrounding her as she hands out food. I can't help but smile because the scene seems straight out of a Fellini film, many of which I watched in my undergrad cinema class.

The canal waters are shimmering with reflected lights and I watch as the *vaporetto* slides into a dock to unload its passengers. Tomorrow I'll go to the Bridge of Sighs and Piazza San Marco to feed pigeons. I'm actually thrilled to be here in Venice.

It's almost eleven when I get to my room—that means three in the afternoon in Portland. Time to call Ian. I muster the courage to look at my messages: none. Uh-oh. I call voice mail: there's one from my mother and another from Lucien, asking me to call him to give him an update.

None from the man in Portland. A cold, slithery worm of anxiety works its way up my spine. What's going on with him?

Lucien gets a quick text message to let him know that Gerard and I have arrived and that we're meeting with Maya in the morning at her hotel. I grab a bottle of Drambuie from the minibar to fortify myself for my call to Ian. By the time I reach the bottom, I feel warm and courageous. I punch in his number on the speed dial.

The call goes to voicemail.

I start to feel ill: he hasn't called nor left any message and now he's not taking my calls. What exactly is he trying to tell me? My first instinct is to cry—I don't know why but I feel as if I should, as if I've lost him before I ever really had him. Did I do wrong? Wasn't he being unreasonable? This job does mean something to me, after all. Shouldn't he support me in my career ambitions? I would certainly do the same for him.

But maybe I pushed him too far too soon. Though it seems incredulous for a man of Ian's looks and stature in society, he is incredibly jealous, possessive, insecure... and crazy. I need to take all of that into account when making decisions. And Lucien has been imposing on me all at once, I suppose, if I try to see it from Ian's perspective. My head starts to hurt from all this thinking I'm doing.

It occurs to me that I'm truly exhausted and that I should go to sleep. I'll feel better in the morning. After washing up and brushing my teeth, I hit the double bed with the fluffy feather top and I'm out as soon as I close my eyes.

Waking up early, I go for a jog in one of the most glorious cities in the world, and pick up a huge latte on my way back to the hotel. By 10:30, I'm showered, dressed, and have my script for the interview ready and in hand. Still not a peep from Ian. I shrug off my worries to focus on the job at hand. If I'm lucky, tomorrow I'll be back in Portland and I'll deal with the fallout then, whatever it is. For now, I'll do my job and enjoy Venice.

Just as I'm setting up for the shoot, Gerard walks in and he's accompanied by... Lucien? My face must register the shock I'm feeling because both men smile.

He's even more gorgeous than I remember. His black cashmere vee-neck sweater clings tightly to his chest and shows off his superior physique. He looks taller today though he's wearing loafers. I can't seem to keep my eyes off him, while at the same time, my heart's gone into overdrive at the fact that he's here.

"Ella, I know it must be a surprise to see me today. Allow me to explain," Lucien says smoothly, as he walks over to me and greets me with a kiss on both cheeks. "I was meeting with an attorney over a contract dispute and my appointment was for tomorrow afternoon, which is why I couldn't make it to Venice on time to meet with Maya. However, last night as I was having dinner in a bistro on the left bank, the attorney in question came into the same restaurant and we were able to amicably settle the matter like gentlemen over *appertifs*." He smiles. "By the time our discussion was concluded, you were already in the air. I decided to come here so we could do the interview together."

"Oh. Well, that works out nicely, then," I say, darting my eyes to Maya who is wearing a self-satisfied smile. I feel the flush come over my face as I consider her warning in light of this new development.

Maya is calm and collected as Lucien and I sit opposite her to ask the questions. Our voices will be edited out so it will seem like a seamless conversation. Lucien is friendly and charming with Maya but she holds her reserve with him: it's obvious she doesn't like him and I'm not entirely sure why. His insistence on the interview being done quickly seems like a minor thing to hold a grudge over. I can't help wondering if these two were romantically involved at some point.

Three hours later, we're wrapping up and Gerard is packing up all the gear. Maya goes into the bedroom of her suite to make calls, saying her goodbyes before she does. She tells me to look her up the next time I'm in New York.

"Ella, may I take you to lunch?" Lucien asks, as we're about to leave.

"Sure. That would be nice." I check my phone: no calls, no messages, my heart sinks. "Let's go."

"I know of a great little *trattoria* not far from here. They have the best *cioppino* I've ever tasted. Are you game?"

Having no idea what *cioppino* is, I am nonetheless on

board. I give a little shrug and smile. "I'm game. Lead the way."

Once we're seated, Lucien takes some papers out of his messenger bag. "Ella, these are for you: you'll find more information on the people we need to interview and the research required. Also, this is the credit card I obtained for you; please charge all business expenses to this account, and here's a check for cab fare and tips. I didn't want you to wait until we ironed out the compensation details. I very much appreciate how flexible and accommodating you've been."

"Not at all, though in retrospect, I didn't need to come at all since you were able to make it."

"No, I think it's a good thing that we got to work together on this one. Now you'll feel more confident for your next interview. Can you tell me what your schedule is for the next two weeks or so?"

The waiter interrupts then to take our order. In what seems like perfect Italian to my untrained ears, Lucien orders our lunch—the *cioppino*—and a bottle of wine, winking at me when the waiter says something in response. Since I don't speak or understand Italian, I have no idea what the waiter said. Lucien later told me he commended his choice of wine but I'm not sure I believe him.

"So," I pick up the thread of our conversation, "the next two weeks? Tomorrow I'm going back to Portland and I believe I'm going to Tokyo with Ian on Saturday. I don't think we'll be there for more than a few days, however. When I get back to Portland, I'll get started on the research." I pause. "Actually, I'll get started as soon as I return tomorrow."

Nodding, Lucien says. "Why are you going to Tokyo? Is it just for pleasure?"

"Ian's going for business and wants me to come to take some time to sightsee."

"Ah. Are you two serious?"

I play dumb because I don't really want to discuss it with him. "Serious?"

"I mean in terms of commitment. I assume you are romantically linked with Mr. Blackmon?"

I can't help it; I blush. I barely know the man and he's asking personal questions. Why does he care?"

"Uh, yes. I suppose you can call it a committed relationship," I reply, thinking in my head that often I think Ian should be committed—to an institution—so, yes.

He smiles. "He's a lucky guy. Is he comfortable about our working closely together?"

"He's fine." I change the subject. "So, are you going back to Paris now?"

"Tomorrow."

The waiter returns with our wine, pouring Lucien the first sip and then fills both glasses after he approves the wine with a nod. I take a sip and it's delicious: Lucien must know his wines. Ian does, too. Every time I think of Ian, my heart hurts. I don't understand why he's avoiding speaking to me and it's leaving me unsettled.

"Oh, my literary agent mentioned that she knows you, Lucien."

"Really? What's her name?"

"Mo Jackson? She said she met you at a gallery opening?"

"Ah. I can't say I recall the name. Describe her to me."

I do, and he nods his head. "Yes, I recall meeting her now. She seemed very interested in my project. So, she's your agent? I wasn't aware that you're a writer, Ella. A woman of many talents, I suppose."

"Hardly. I wrote a book on a lark, as a Christmas gift for my friends. They started sending it around and it went viral online. Before I knew it, I had a contract and a film deal. It was rather absurd."

"A film deal? Really? What's the title of the book?"

"Oh, do I have to tell you? I'd rather not." Saying that to him is like dangling a carrot in front of his face. Now, of course, he's dying to know what book it is. "Can we discuss the St. Sauveur interview?"

Smiling with an enigmatic look in his eyes, he allows

the conversation to move on. Whatever else he is, Lucien is a gentleman. "Surely. Do you have any questions?"

We discuss the interview in minute detail throughout lunch—which was absolutely delicious. After we polish off the bottle of wine, Lucien asks me to take a walk with him, agreeing to show me the Bridge of Sighs and Piazza San Marco. He even buys me a bag of food to feed the pigeons, an experience so exhilarating and terrifying at the same time. Anyone who has ever seen Hitchcock's *The Birds* can't help but think of it when all those pigeons come swooping down toward the poor person holding the feedbag. I throw the rest of the bag of food down in a big hurry, and run toward Lucien, who is laughing so hard he's clutching his stomach.

"Oh, Ella, it hurts to laugh so vigorously on a full stomach. Did you not expect that outcome?"

I shake my head, a rueful grin on my face. "No, I suppose I don't always think ahead. Where to next?"

"Let's take a look at the Palace of the Doges," he suggests and takes my hand unexpectedly. I don't pull it back but I'm immediately uncomfortable. It seems an awfully intimate thing to do and inappropriate for our relationship as colleagues who've just met recently, no less. Once again, I think of Ian's reaction to Lucien and wonder if it indeed has merit.

After seeing the Doges' palace, we stop for espresso at a bar. I have to admit that Lucien is a lot of fun to hang with. All around us, women are eyeing him as if he were made of chocolate. When I'm with Ian and other women flirt and swoon over him, it makes me jealous and insecure because I consider him mine, right or wrong. With Lucien, though, it's fun because they all think he's mine, yet I don't mind the flirting since he's not. I can and do appreciate his finer qualities and I wonder what might have happened between us if I hadn't already been with Ian when this job arose.

At dusk, Lucien walks me back to my hotel. As soon as we step into the lobby, I turn around. "Thanks, Lucien. I had such a good time. I appreciate your showing me around the city."

"You're so very welcome, Ella. I like working with you and I'm looking forward to getting back to New York and further collaborating." He grasps my hand and brings it to his lips, kissing it softly. "I hope you have a safe trip back to Portland. I suppose I'll see you in a few weeks."

I jerk my head. "Yes," I say quickly. Having him this close is tipping my equilibrium. I mean, yes, I'm faithful and monogamous, but I am female and only human, for God's sake, and Lucien is a rare specimen of gorgeous male. He smells good, too—like an expensive man.

Kissing me on both cheeks, he says goodbye and takes his leave. I rush to my room to pack and text Ian, letting him know I'm coming home and what flight I'll be on. I sit down to worry about what awaits me when I get there and began contemplating how strange it is that life took me to Ian in the first place.

My flight is delayed by nearly an hour so I arrive at Portland International at 11:03 a.m. that same day. It was odd because I'd left Venice at 10:30 in the morning and I arrived in Portland at eleven so it was as if I never lost any time. I am startled to see that Ian is waiting for me just past the security gate as I make my way out. Seeing him stops me in my tracks for a moment: he looks mouthwateringly good. Before I even know what I am doing, I run into his arms.

"Ian!"

He catches me, but is clearly not expecting my... enthusiasm. "Ella. Did you have a good trip?"

"Yes, but why didn't you call me or text me or take my calls?"

He ignores my question. "Do you have luggage to collect?"

"No. I only brought my carry-on. I'm an efficient packer."

He takes my hand and leads me toward the exit and parking lot.

"So… are you going to answer my question?"

"I was angry, Ella. I didn't think it productive to continue to argue with you and I knew any conversation would devolve into an argument. I've made my feelings crystal clear when it comes to your job."

"Yes." I bite my lip, wondering whether I should tell him about Lucien showing up in Venice. I decide to put it off for now and change the subject. "Ian, how do you know Mo Jackson?"

His expression is blank. "Mo Jackson? I don't."

"She claims to know you… or know of you."

"Describe her to me." Funny that he uses the exact same words as Lucien did before him.

"Tiny, about five feet without heels but she wears giant ones, dark red hair, cute, sort of elfin face, late thirties, maybe early forties, dresses very expensively."

"And she claims she knows me?"

"Yes."

"Mo," he says, thinking. "Mo is short for Maureen, isn't it?"

"Is it? I don't know."

"A few years ago I was spending months at a time in New York—almost relocated there, as a matter of fact. I still own my downtown loft in the financial district, though currently there's a tenant subletting. The woman I was… seeing… had a friend who threw these BDSM-themed parties in a loft in the meatpacking district. That's probably how she knows me. I seem to recall someone of that description being one of the regulars."

"There is no way Mo is a submissive. She's crazy strong."

"I didn't say she was a submissive. But there was a tiny, redheaded Domme…"

The laugh that erupts from my throat sounds more like a death rattle. "You have got to be kidding me? Is everyone in the world some kind of deviant?"

He gives me a sidelong glance and smirks. "Everyone in New York, certainly. Personally I felt very comfortable there… Now, tell me about Venice."

Chapter 19

"Venice?" she repeats, as if stalling for time. Ian doesn't like the hesitant look on her face. "What about it?"

He couldn't wait for Ella to return to Portland, and unequivocally refused to analyze his feelings for her—mainly because it rather terrified him. Ever since Natasha, he'd managed to keep emotionally detached from every woman with whom he'd become sexually involved, no matter how attractive or affectionate she turned out to be. After what he'd endured five years ago, he vowed never to let down his guard and he hadn't. For some reason, though, Ella Strong wasn't letting him get on with the program.

What was it about her? Not only did he immensely enjoy her company, the joking and the verbal sparring, but he also felt very protective of her. Right now those protective instincts were kicking into high gear over the prospect of Alexis getting anywhere near Ella. He'd already pulled the glass house off the market and his staff would move his things from the houseboat to the estate while they were in Japan. He'd tell Ella about the threat once they were out of the country—he didn't want to worry her. He was pissed because he'd been really enjoying his life on the water with fewer layers between him and the rest of the world. Now he'd have to retreat behind his self-constructed walls again... but he aimed to take Ella with him this time around.

And that was the one thing that scared him most— the fact that he never wanted to say goodbye to her, needed to keep her close at all times. That propensity was the most disconcerting of all to a dedicated bachelor like himself.

Ella had texted him her flight information so he left the office at ten to ensure he'd be waiting at the airport when she arrived. He'd almost sent Brad, his new driver, but he wanted to see Ella badly and he didn't want to wait until the end of the workday—and, by all indicators, today was going to be a tediously long one. He'd have to immediately return to the office once he deposited her home. He didn't dare take her to the houseboat.

Now he tries to chuckle but the look on her face chokes it off. "For one thing, your impressions. You've never been there before, correct?"

She nods, a slight smile on her lips.

"Also, your business there—how'd it go? How was the flight? What did you see?" He raises a brow. "Lots of things about Venice to discuss."

"Okay," she begins haltingly, "To start, Maya St. Sauveur was a most impressive woman and I enjoyed meeting her. She was a bit miffed at Lucien's impatience to get the interview on tape... but other than that, she was charming."

"Obviously I'm not the only one he rubs the wrong way."

"No, apparently not. Um, what else? Oh, I fed pigeons in Piazza San Marco and they scared me witless... I think I gave everyone in the plaza a good laugh. We went to see the Palace of the Doges . . ."

"We?" The volume of his voice escalates—there should be no *we* in Venice. The look that descends over her face chills his blood because he recognizes it as one of guilt and his stomach twists.

And here comes the deep flush that colors her face instantly. "Uh, yeah, I was getting to that. Lucien showed up unexpectedly at the taping."

"Oh?" He could hear the ice in his own voice as he struggled for control. Right now if that blond bastard was in front of him, he'd definitely take a swing at his stupid pretty face. Pretty faces irritated Ian—even his own.

"Yes. I was annoyed at first since if he was able to do the interview, I wouldn't have had to drop everything to go to Venice. But he explained that he only realized he'd be able to make it once I was in the air so..." She lets the sentence lay where it drops.

"Things have a habit of working out conveniently in Phillips' world, don't they? So... he took you sightseeing then?"

"After the taping we went to lunch and he accompanied me when I went to see the Doges and the plaza. That's it, Ian; nothing inappropriate happened and he knows that you and I are involved."

"How observant of him. Tell me, what tipped him off? Could it have been my presence at your interview with my arm around you? He's obviously quick on the uptake."

"Stop it. You're going to have to get past this antagonism. I'm going to be working with Lucien until June and then it's done. Please tell me you're not going to keep it up that long."

"There's something slimy about the man, Ella. I've learned to trust my gut instinct about people. It's never let me down yet."

"I promise, Ian, if Lucien does anything untoward, you'll be the first to know. Okay?"

"So then I can assume from that comment that he behaved himself during your time together? He didn't touch you?"

"Yes, he behaved admirably."

"He didn't touch you?"

"Ian! Stop it. As I said, if he did anything, I'd tell you. So, when are we leaving for Tokyo?"

She's avoiding answering my question, Ian thinks, and wonders what exactly it means. Had Phillips touched her and she set him straight? Or maybe he touched her and she interpreted it as benign? There was something there—Ella was a God-awful liar. He decides to let it go for now.

"We're leaving day after tomorrow. I'll take you to Mariah's so you can rest and get packed for Japan. I'm going to have a late night tonight at the office so I'll head directly home and I'll pick you up sometime tomorrow afternoon. Be packed and ready."

"Oh. I was hoping we could have dinner together tonight."

He touched her cheek affectionately—it was so incredibly nice to have her back with him. "I'm sorry, baby. I'm swamped at work—there's too much going down next week to prepare for and I'm going to be away, obviously."

"How long are we staying in Japan?"

"I need to be home by next weekend at the latest so I thought Thursday or Friday. I know it's a short stay for such a long trip but it's the most I can manage right now."

"That's fine. I have work to do here anyway."

He pulls up the SUV in front of Mariah's apartment complex. "Look at that: a parking spot right in front. How auspicious," he notes, smiling. "Come on, I'll walk you to the door."

"Okay. Thanks for meeting me, Ian. I know you're busy so it's all the more appreciated." She reaches across the console to kiss him sweetly.

"I wanted to see you," he says simply and honestly, and that earns him a beaming smile from her. When they reach the door, he sets down her bag and draws her into his arms. "I can hardly wait until tomorrow. A whole week I get to spend with you, Ella. We'll have a very nice time, I promise."

"I know we will, Ian. If you change your mind about tonight, just give a holler."

"Will you hear me?"

"I'll keep my window open," she replies, her voice deepening in a very sexy way. When her voice deepens, other things happen in and on her body, Ian knows, and suddenly he can't wait until tomorrow. He pulls her to him for a kiss that just gets deeper and deeper. Finally he manages to end it—very reluctantly.

"Are you sure you have to get right back to the office?" she breathes. "We could make it quick?" She puts the key in the door and twists it open.

At that invitation, his eyes darken and with one hand he grasps hers and the other reaches for the bag, swinging them both inside the apartment. Ian drops the bag in the hall and bends down, his shoulder dipping into her stomach, picks her up and tosses her over his shoulder like a sack of potatoes. She yelps but starts laughing so hard that she can't catch her breath enough to complain.

Chapter 20

I can't sleep. My circadian rhythm is all screwed up from the back-to-back travel I've been doing. It's five a.m. and I've been staring at Mariah's guest bedroom ceiling for an hour, noting all the imperfections in the paint that the soft lamplight allows to show. Giving up the fight for more sleep, I decide to shower and dress. I'll go buy breakfast and surprise Ian with it. We're leaving for Tokyo tomorrow afternoon and he told me he was taking today off to get ready for his trip so I know he'll be home. Anyway, I'll get there well before seven.

As soon as I finish my shower, I throw on my favorite jeans and a cotton sweater, and grab my phone, which I left charging the night before on the kitchen counter. There are several messages and I scroll down to see two of them are from Lucien. I read the most recent.

Ella, something's come up and I have 2 travel 2 L.A. tomorrow. I will b there 4 a week at least -- if I'm still there when u get back from Tokyo, can u meet me? We could tape interview w/Stieglitz/O'Keefe subject and go 2 exhibit at Getty Ctr 2 c his NY Gal collection there. Keep me posted RE ur sched. LP.

Ugh, I think. Ian is not going to like that one little bit. Am I going to have a steady diet of stress from him until I complete this project and finish working with Lucien? And what about the next project that I get involved in? Do I have to work with only women and ugly old men to make Ian happy? He'd probably be jealous of ugly old men, too, now that I think of it.

Well, yesterday I got everything packed, paid bills, called friends and family, and even had time to hike over to the library to do some research on the subjects we'll be focusing on in the film. Mariah and I had dinner together at a neighborhood bistro and I soaked in the tub for an hour, then crawled into bed exhausted. I actually feel pretty good today and I'm dying to see Ian. Though we only had forty-five minutes or so together yesterday, every second was golden. He's so yummy that the more I have, the more I want: I can't seem to get enough of the man.

So, happily I head out into the still-dark morning in search of breakfast and my beautiful boyfriend.

A half hour later, just as the sun is poking through the cloud cover, I arrive at Ian's houseboat. Curiously I find the front door open and an alarm bell rings through my brain. It's certainly not like Ian to leave the door open—quite the contrary; he leans to the more paranoid side. Debating whether or not I should go in or call someone instead takes up five minutes. Who would I call? I don't know Jarvis' number—his head of security at Excalibur. Finally, I very cautiously edge the door further open to peek inside. Nothing looks amiss so I step in, all the while looking all around me. So far, so good, but my heart is thudding in my chest. I make a quick detour to the kitchen to grab a weapon and put the breakfast bag down, feeling foolish but better safe than sorry, right?

Good thing I'm wearing my comfortable jeans and my low-heeled biker boots. That way, I can run fast if I need to—but also kick worth a damn. I regret they don't have steel toes. As I make my way up the stairs, kitchen knife in hand, I can't help but feel like the idiot girl in a horror film, the one at whom the audience is screaming not to go inside, open the door, go down to the basement, answer the phone, or whatever she's doing that's egregiously stupid. We all know she's in mortal danger by the music scoring the scene. If only real life had a soundtrack to let us know when danger is near, it would be very helpful.

I get to the top of the staircase and nothing looks to be out of order. I don't hear anything, either. I tiptoe to Ian's bedroom door and ever so slowly turn the handle. Luckily, everything in the house is new so nothing creaks, squeaks, or clicks. Pushing the door inch by inch, all the while holding my breath, I finally have it open enough to peer inside. And what I see almost sends me into cardiac arrest.

Ian is sleeping peacefully in his big bed, wrapped in his 600-thread-count Egyptian cotton sheets. His lustrous dark hair spills upon the white pillow and his face is serene as he slumbers, his tanned, muscular arm wrapped around a dark-skinned, dark-haired woman—who is naked. At least I'm assuming she's naked by the upper part of her body that's not covered by the sheet. Ian's arm is slung around her waist and her huge breasts are resting on his forearm. It also appears that Ian has his leg across her. He wraps around me like that, too.

Or at least, he used to.

I back out and leave the door slightly ajar, my guts twisting tightly as if a hand is wringing them out like a sponge, inside my body. Bile rushes up my closing throat and I think I'm going to puke, plus I'm shaking like a leaf in an approaching hurricane. I hurry down the stairs and right out of the house, pulling the door shut behind me. Too late I realize I left the breakfast I'd bought in the kitchen. Oh well. I guess the cat's out of the bag now: he'll know that I know when he sees the food there. Just as well since I never plan to see him again... ever.

First, a white-hot anger takes charge of me: I feel it inhabit my body and it makes me want to kill him, the fucking bastard! How dare he do this awful thing to me? Now I know why he didn't want to spend the night with me last night. Stupid, stupid, stupid girl that I am, it never occurred to me that Ian might be a player, a cheater. Why not, I wonder in retrospect? True, he never seemed to look at another woman with any interest at all when he was with me. But the man is rich, gorgeous, and relatively well known: he can have just about any woman he desires so why did I think he'd possibly be exclusive to me? Because he said so?

I scoff at my sheer gullibility. I don't know why but I believed him. Somehow I'd convinced myself that he had feelings for me, and only me. I know I have strong feelings for him—I'm pretty sure I'm in love with him. And that, more than anything, is my personal tragedy.

Then dire misery—a combination of sadness and acute pain over the betrayal—sucks me into its dark, inescapable vortex: the tears cascade down like rain, with almost no warning. I stagger over to my rental car, barely able to see a few feet ahead, I'm crying so hard. How am I going to drive? I have to calm down but I can't. I'm sobbing and I can't stop so I sit in my car, switch on the ignition and turn on the A/C so it's blasting cold air in my face—I figure if I'm so freezing cold, I won't be able to concentrate on the burning pain flaying open my guts right about now—and I manage to slow down the weeping long enough to shift into drive and pull out of the marina parking lot.

Somewhere along the highway, I find enough resolve to help me make it back to Mariah's apartment. The pain I'm experiencing is so intense, I just want to shrivel up and die. Fleetingly I wonder if anyone ever dies of grief? Surely the answer is yes. I allow myself an hour to curl up in the dim room and wallow in the abject misery that grips me.

Since my bags are packed already and I'm not going to Tokyo after all, I decide to go straight to the airport and wait for the next flight to L.A. I'll drop the rental car off at the airport and I'll go back to my leased cottage in Los Feliz where the deep pink *bougainvillea* will be in full bloom.

So that's exactly what I do. Along the way, I open my window and say my final goodbyes to Portland and all its denizens.

Chapter 21

The solar rays streaming through the window shine directly onto his face, warming it and gently edging him toward a conscious state. He keeps his eyes closed, enjoying the heat of the sun that so rarely makes an appearance in Portland in such potency. Next to him, he can feel the added warmth of body heat.

Mmm, Ella.

He snuggles up to her. It takes a few moments to remember that Ella wasn't with him last night and, as if someone jammed his thigh with a hypodermic of adrenaline, he jerks his head up to look at the woman in his arms.

The *naked woman* in his arms... who's not Ella. "What the fuck?" he screams and Alexis jumps up, startled.

"Chill out, lover boy," comes her throaty voice. "One would think you'd never seen a naked woman in your bed before."

"What the fuck are you doing in my house, Alexis? Was I not crystal clear the last time you broke in? Do you have a yen to go to jail? Because that's exactly where you're headed."

"No," she purrs, reaching out to brush the lock of stray hair out of his eyes. "I have a yen for you."

He slaps her hand away viciously. "Don't touch me," he says in a scathingly cold voice as he jumps out of the bed and pulls on a pair of jeans, grabbing his phone and punching in the number for Jarvis' cell.

"What the fuck is wrong with you?" he screams into the phone when it connects to Jarvis' voice, thick with sleep. "Were my orders not explicit enough? I told you to watch Alexis Martinez 24/7 until I left town. Which part did you not understand, Jarvis?"

The voice on the other end is suddenly on high alert. "Mr. Blackmon. We've tried to comply but she never came home for us to pick up the tail. It's impossible to follow someone you can't find."

"Well, that's because right now she's in my fucking bed, Jarvis. Get someone here now to get her the hell out."

"Do you want to bring in law enforcement at this point?"

"Use your professional judgment. If you do bring the cops in on it, make sure you tell them I've already left the country. I don't want my trip delayed by this bullshit. Just get here now!"

He shrugs into a tee-shirt and snatches his leather jacket out of the closet before heading downstairs. Running his hand through his hair, he realizes how lucky it was that Ella wasn't with him last night. Would Alexis have hurt her? There was no way he was bringing Ella to this houseboat again. They'd both be safer in the glass house

He puts on his running shoes, sans socks, since he doesn't want to go back upstairs and see the crazy bitch again. She can't leave from the upper story unless she wants to break a limb or two. There's no climbing down unless she knows where the ladder is concealed. Shit! She might just know it, the crafty wacko. He runs back upstairs to check on her.

Alexis is not in the master bedroom when he gets there. Thinking she went out the window, he's about to check the roof garden when he hears water running in the master bath. Talk about calm: she's freshening up for her arrest? The door opens a few moments later and she's fully dressed. She smiles.

"A dress, Alexis? Do you have something a bit more casual for jail?"

Laughing, she says, "Oh, Ian, you know I'm not going

to jail. I know you don't want negative press right now when big things are happening at your company. Being involved in a sordid stalking won't calm your investing partners' anxiety."

His eyes narrow menacingly as he takes a long, hard look at her. What exactly is going on here? Choosing his words carefully and struggling for calm, he says, "At least you acknowledge that you're a sordid stalker. Exactly who are these investing partners to whom you refer, Alexis? Please, enlighten me."

She shrugs. "Oh, you know very well who they are. I do my homework, baby. So... when do you get back from Tokyo, you and what's-her-name?"

His blood boiling, Ian grabs her upper arm and hauls her out of the bedroom and down the stairs. When they reach the living room, he forces her into a chair to wait for Jarvis to arrive. Fortunately, his residence is five minutes away so he should be able to get here soon, providing he can get a back-up team together. In the meantime, Ian attempts to extract more information from the woman.

"What's this all about, Alexis? Who are you working for?"

"Working for? Why would you assume that, Ian?"

"Obviously, you're trying to glean information about my company... and what's with the sudden obsession with me? You didn't seem so broken up when I stopped seeing you. Methinks I sense a nefarious plot afoot."

Tossing her glossy head back, she laughs. "Paranoid bastard, aren't you, Ian? I hate to disappoint you but I'm just your standard garden-variety stalker. I don't take kindly to men dumping me, baby. That's really all there is to it. And what does what's-her-name got that I don't?"

There's a loud knock on the door and he gets up from his perch on the arm of an upholstered chair to open it. That was fast: Jarvis and three of his men rush into the house.

"Mr. Blackmon, we'll take it from here."

Alexis looks surprised that the men are actually

there. She rises to her feet and begins to back away from them, but the two stockiest go after her and easily restrain her. Ian watches as they drag her out of the house.

"Don't touch me," he hears her scream. "Rape!"

One of the men claps a hand over her mouth and she bites him and yells again as he mutters a curse. They push her into a white van they left running in front of the house. Jarvis watches from the door. "We'll let the police know you'll be available next week but honestly I don't know if they'll hold her without you personally pressing charges, Mr. Blackmon. Is there any possible way you can just put in an appearance at the precinct today?"

Ian runs his hand through his hair in agitation. "Yes, I suppose I will if it means they'll hold her. Something like this, they'll almost definitely set bail and expect me to take out a restraining order—am I correct?"

Jarvis nods. "That's usually the way it goes, yes. Let me see what strings I could pull. I know one of the desk sergeants at that precinct.

"Very good. Keep me posted."

Ian glances at his watch, wondering if Ella would be up by now. It's after nine so she's almost certainly awake. Taking the steps two at a time, he hurries into the bathroom to take a quick shower, only to find all of Alexis' toiletries on the vanity—she truly made herself at home. Sweeping his arm across the lot of them, he pushes them into the garbage in disgust and then pops into the shower. He needs to get to Ella and explain about Alexis—he is not going to take any chances.

Before getting into his convertible, Ian tries calling her on her cell but it goes directly to voice mail—he bangs his hand on the steering wheel in frustration. Then he tries Mariah's home phone. Mariah answers, her voice groggy.

"Mariah, it's Ian Blackmon. Is Ella there?"

"Uh, I don't know—I was sleeping. Can you call back in ten?"

"I'm on my way now. I'll wait till I get there."

"Okay. I'll make coffee if Ella hasn't already made some. See you soon."

Why isn't Ella picking up her phone? He's trying to push down the anxiety that's creeping up his spine but he can't stop its encroachment.

Pulling up in front of the apartment, Ian takes a deep breath, trying to quell the premonition that something's truly amiss. He strides with purpose toward the front door, anxious to see Ella.

The apartment door opens as soon as he knocks.

"Ian. Come in." Mariah looks subdued, even troubled.

"What's wrong? Where's Ella?" Now the knot in his stomach tightens painfully.

"She left."

"What do you mean, left? We're leaving for Tokyo tomorrow."

"She was gone when I woke up... she left a note."

"May I see the note, please?"

Mariah looks hesitant. "Come in and sit down, Ian. Let's talk for a bit. I'll get you a cup of coffee."

He has no choice but to play by her rules so he complies but as every minute ticks by, he feels the meltdown approach ever nearer. Right now, his body feels as tense as a bow the moment it's drawn.

"What happened?" Mariah asks, handing him the coffee mug. "What sent her running?"

The hot coffee anchors him to the sofa: if he weren't holding it, the adrenaline in his body would force him to his feet. "I'm not sure, Mariah. I need information."

Ella's friend is thinking, mulling something over, and it makes him wonder what the hell the note said. Did Alexis contact Ella? Hurt her in any way? What the hell was going on?

Clearing her throat, Mariah begins again. "Did something... *unusual* occur between last night and this morning, Ian?"

"Yes."

"What?"

He sighs. "A woman is stalking me. Sometime last

night she broke into my home... and got into bed with me. I didn't discover her presence until I opened my eyes this morning to a rude awakening. Very rude," he adds sardonically.

"Ah, that explains things." She pulls a piece of paper out of her robe pocket and hands it to him. "Have a look."

Taking the paper, he quickly scans it. Now a lump of lead sits in his chest as he begins to put two and two together.

Mariah, I'm sorry I didn't get to say goodbye but I had to leave, like, right away. I won't be coming back to Portland. I'm going back to L.A. to stay and it happens that Lucien is there and asked me to meet him so it works out conveniently. I'm including the rent check for next month since I didn't give you any advance notice. If Ian calls, please don't give him any information. He and I are through (I'll explain next time we talk).

All love,
Ella

Ian sits staring at the paper long after he finishes reading, imagining the possible scenario. "Did Ella leave the apartment anytime last night?" he finally asks.

"I don't know but it looks that way. Either that or the stalker contacted her and somehow convinced her of something she didn't like. You have to leave for Tokyo soon, don't you?"

Not bothering to answer, he asks, "Where is she? Do you happen to have her address in L.A.?"

Mariah gets up, her bare feet padding across the hardwood floor to the breakfast bar, where she pulls an address book off the corner. Flipping through it, she finds the page. "Yes." She tosses a pen to him and he catches it, turning over the piece of paper to write on the back. Mariah reads off the address.

Checking the time, he wonders if she's already in the air or if he could still intercept her at the airport. Traveling on a commercial flight takes time to book, make it through security, board the plane, etc. He might just get lucky. The other option is to take no chances and just get there, possibly ahead of her.

Always decisive in crisis situations, Ian reaches into his pocket for his phone. "Jonas. Is the Gulfstream available this morning? Good. Call Scott and tell him I'm on my way and I need to get to L.A. If he's not available to pilot, I'll do it myself but ask him if he could at least file a flight plan for me. I need to get in the air ASAP. I'm on my way to the airfield right now. Thanks."

Less than two hours later, Ian buckles his seat belt and leans back into the buttery leather chair as the plane taxies down the runway. Fortunately, Scott was available to pilot the plane, allowing Ian to make calls and try to resolve some problems during the flight. Right now what's eating away at him the most is the possibility that Lucien will get to Ella first. Would she succumb to his charms if she thought Ian was cheating on her?

Either Alexis somehow got to Ella or Ella walked into the bedroom and saw the psycho in bed with him. Knowing Ella, rather than confronting him then and there, she would run. That's her MO. He's trying, with monumental effort, not to be angry with Ella for rushing to judgment—after all, what other conclusion could she have drawn? He hadn't yet told her about the woman stalking him. Besides, how many women would want to have a scene with her lover while he was in bed with a naked woman? Rather intimidating, he'd think.

His phone chimes. "What's going on, Jarvis?"

"Mr. Blackmon. Alexis Martinez was arrested and booked but was released on her own recognizance. As your head of security, they permitted me to press charges against her for stalking, as well as breaking and entering, but the bail assigned was paltry and she made it within a half hour. I went back to your houseboat and secured it."

"Good. Do we know how she got in?"

"Not yet. The lock on the door wasn't jimmied—in

fact, a lock like that is virtually jimmy-proof. It looks like she had a key, believe it or not. We also found a bag of take-out coffee and croissants in the kitchen. Did you put it there?"

He closes his eyes in frustration. "No, I didn't... but I don't think it was Alexis who did, either. I think it was my girlfriend who apparently came over unexpectedly. Now at least I know why she left town."

"I'm sorry, sir. We have someone on Martinez now. She won't pull a stunt like this one again."

"I'll hold you to that promise, Jarvis. I want this matter dealt with expeditiously—and harshly. I suspect the woman is working for someone... might even be corporate espionage at play here."

"Yes, sir. We'll handle it. I'll let you know if anything else comes up."

"Good." He disconnects the call.

He gets to Los Feliz by three o'clock. If he and Ella are going to make their flight to Tokyo from Portland tomorrow, he'll have to be quick about it. Pinning his hope that she goes to her rental house first, before she does anything else, he hasn't allowed himself to consider alternatives. She had better not be with Phillips because she might do something very stupid out of hurt and anger, something that will compromise their relationship permanently. And he, in turn, might do something very stupid out of hurt and anger.

Following the GPS, he finds the house and notes that there's a car in the driveway. Did Ella mention that she owned a car? He can't remember, but hopes it's a rental auto she picked up at the airport, and expertly pulls his rented car into a space partway down the block.

Pausing at the front door to listen, he can hear the faint strains of music. His racing heart slows down a tiny bit. He barely notices the charm of the cottage, the arbor dripping with pink-flowering vines, the Mexican tile paths and steps, the tall drought-resistant grasses swaying in the gentle breeze. All he can think of is finding

Ella and setting her straight.

Ian raps the knocker hard against the door since there's no bell. He can hear footsteps coming closer and he's careful to stay out of view lest she spots him and refuses to answer the door. He's counting on her naiveté to just swing open the door without checking to see whom it is first. She doesn't let him down.

As soon as her eyes take him in, unadulterated shock drops her jaw open. "Ian! I have absolutely nothing to say to you," she spits at him and attempts to slam the door in his face.

Anticipating her reaction, he slides his foot between the door and jamb so it's impossible to close, then pushes his way in.

"Get out now or I'm calling the police."

"No," he answers, closing the door behind him.

"What do you want?"

"Are we alone, Ella?"

"What difference can it possibly make? Yes, we're alone. Say your piece and leave."

"Okay, I will," he says, advancing toward her. Her eyes widen, in surprise or fear, he can't tell. Might as well have a bit of fun for all the trouble she put him through.

She stands there—back straight, eyes wide, saying nothing now. He looks right into her eyes, smiles, and says one word.

"Strip."

Chapter 22

I'm gaping slack-jawed at the tall, enigmatic man standing in front of me, trying not to dwell on the fact that he looks good enough to bite. "Well, that answers one lingering question I've had since I've known you, Ian." I aim for a flippant tone but my heart is hammering in my chest and all the spit in my mouth has evaporated. I don't want him to see me this emotionally vulnerable—he's arrogant enough as it is.

He cocks his head, his eyes inscrutable. "Am I supposed to ask what question?"

I shrug, feigning nonchalance. "Ask or not, it makes no difference to me." I begin to turn away and he grabs my elbow.

"Fine, I'll bite: what lingering question, Ella?"

"Whether or not you're insane—now of course it's confirmed."

He raises an eyebrow and smirks. "Well, good, now that that's all cleared up, do as I said or I'll do it for you."

"If you actually think I'm going to have anything to do with you after what you did, Ian, you really are completely delusional. Now remove yourself from the premises. I have matters that require my attention. Not everyone in the world kowtows to the almighty Ian Blackmon, you know."

He laughs. Laughs! And says, "Either you'll take off your clothes or I'll take them off for you—and I won't be careful about it." He makes a show of looking at his watch. "In less than five minutes after I've explained the matter to you, you're going to apologize to me and, consequently, I'm going to punish you for making me drop everything to run here to get you, Ella. I'd simply like you to be ready for it."

"Fuck you, Ian," I snap and attempt to leave the room. I'm supposed to meet Lucien in a few hours in West Hollywood and I need to shower and take a power nap. I'm done crying over Ian Blackmon, really I am. I spent the whole morning doing it and I have the red, swollen eyes to prove it.

"Ella," he says, spinning me around. "You really do owe me a heartfelt apology," he says as his hands go to my shirt and rip it open, buttons flinging everywhere. I gasp so loudly and strongly that I almost choke on my own saliva.

"You ruined my shirt!" I've often been told I have a talent for stating the obvious. Blackmon totally ignores my shock, his face a wooden mask of impassivity—but his eyes? His eyes convey a quite different story.

His eyes are scorching. It's beyond fascinating how every nuance of his mood is readily reflected in the depths of those strange eyes.

"I believe I told you to do it or I would." He's staring, mesmerized, at my breasts, encased right now in a skimpy lace shelf bra that barely covers the girls. "Every single time I see you without clothes, I marvel at the texture of your skin, Ella. No manmade material could ever approximate the exquisite feel of it," he says hoarsely as he runs just the tips of his fingers across my collarbone and down to my hip. Everything from my navel down lurches into sharp contraction and instantly feels liquid. It's in the midst of this elastic moment that I know I will submit to him, regardless of whether he deserves it or not, and I sway on my feet.

"Now, allow me to return to the reasons to prompt your apology: first, for having absolutely no faith in me," he says, his voice dropping into a deep, husky register while his hands rapidly slide the arms of my cotton shirt off my shoulders. He effortlessly unclasps my bra and slips it down.

"Additionally," he adds as he moves to the belt of my

jeans, "you obviously put no stock in my word, my vow to be monogamous."

Feebly, I try to resist him, but I'm restricted by my arms pinned behind me by my own damn shirt—it's currently half on and half off my body. His deft fingers skate over to my breasts, eliciting more immediate response from my disobedient body.

"Now that I have your unwavering attention, allow me to explain—the explanation you should have demanded from me this morning when you visited my bedroom unexpectedly."

He drops down to his knees gracefully, taking my jeans down with him in a fluid motion, every move efficient and almost balletic. I'll admit that I'm not struggling as much as I know intellectually that I should but I'm flustered by his undeniable sexual gravity. Seriously, I'd like to meet the woman who could resist the libidinous magnetism of Ian Blackmon—I'll buy her a new pair of *Blahniks*. Still, I make a halfhearted attempt to give him a hard time.

He looks up at me, his eyes alight with a fiery glow. "Do you still have that lovely antique four-poster you used to have?"

I ignore him, suppressing an urge to stick out my tongue. The stupid, arrogant, perplexing... gorgeous bastard with the dazzling smile.

He rises to his feet, his shoulder dipping into my stomach to lift me over his shoulder—again!

"Ian, for fuck's sake, I'm not a sack of potatoes!"

I know he's smirking as only he can, a look that says *I see you... and I raise you*, as he chastises me, "Tsk, tsk, such language, Ella. I think I'll add a few extra swats to your punishment."

With his free hand he grabs a leather duffel bag from the chair where he deposited it and begins searching for my bedroom. In this vintage house, all the doors look the same, so the first one he opens is a closet, the second one a bathroom. The whole time I'm shouting profanities and pummeling his muscled back and lovely, tight little ass with my fists as hard as I can, but he just ignores me as thoroughly if I'm an annoying gnat. Finally, he finds the master and that four-poster bed... and drops me unceremoniously upon it. Quickly he finishes removing my shirt and bra and, wrapping his hand around my throat in a blatant display of dominance, gently pushes me flat onto my back.

"Don't move," he orders, "not an inch." My eyes dart up at him and note that any amusement whatsoever has drained out of his face and his mood has visibly shifted in a markedly different direction. Aha, alpha Ian returns for a visit.

Well, tough. "I'm not done cursing at you, Ian. I still haven't heard your so-called explanation." His eyes are devoid of any color right now and look so odd that for a moment I'm transfixed. I shake myself out of it—my wits cannot escape me, especially at this particular moment.

He inhales deeply as if collecting his patience with my infernal interruptions to his attempt to torment me. "It seems I have a stalker and that's the woman you saw in my bed. Sometime last night, she broke into my house—and I still don't know precisely how—and got into bed with me. I didn't discover her presence until I opened my eyes this morning."

I bestow upon him my most skeptical frown ever and say nothing, as if his explanation does not even merit a verbal response.

"I should have told you about her sooner, Ella, but I didn't want to worry you and frankly, I thought my security staff had everything under control. I came home from the office very late last night—it was close to midnight. I had a fierce headache so I took a couple of Tylenol PM and went directly to bed. Honestly, I slept like the dead all night long and woke up to a rather titanic shock."

He reaches into his bag and pulls out some things—looks like some kind of nylon twine and a small metal ball. I'm wearing nothing but my ivory lace panties that seem to mock me now, as if I wore them to entice him—I probably did, now that I think of it since early this morning I still liked him. He lays the objects on the bed and sits down on the edge of the mattress, crooking his finger at me. I shake my head no.

"Oh, yes. I think you owe me that apology now."

"Ha, forget it. Assuming your story is true, and the jury's still out on that one, you should have told me about this woman sooner and I'm still having a hard time believing you knew nothing about it. You had your arm around her, for God's sake, Ian—you had your whole *body* around her!"

If I didn't know Mr. Cool and Aloof better, I'd say his expression actually became contrite.

"In my sleep, I thought she was you. She's been arrested, Ella."

He's silent for a moment, letting his words hang between us. Then a sharp light comes into those mesmerizing eyes and that infamous smirk makes its appearance as he says, "Now come here and tell me how sorry you are for inconveniencing me to this very considerable extent."

"No." I cross my arms for punctuation. "I'm not sorry."

Without another word, he reaches his long arm over to yank me by the wrist, pulls me over his lap and swings his leg over mine so I can't move. I'm hanging off lopsidedly so my feet are off the floor. He's done this purposely so I have no leverage to pull myself up. I feel him touching my posterior and then, slam!

"Ow! That hurts, you bastard!"

He hits me harder this time. "Ahh!"

"Until you stop cursing at me and start counting respectfully, your count remains at zero."

"What? That's incredibly unfair. I didn't even agree to this punishment and I'm not the one who should be spanked, damn it. Ow!" Another one. They're getting harder and harder.

"Count, Ella, and start from one."

Wiggling doesn't help and I can't stand up. My butt is

on fire already and I don't how many he's planned. Do I truly owe him an apology? Wasn't the conclusion I'd drawn the only reasonable one to reach? He hits me again. I refuse to count—I don't care how many times he wallops me. So he keeps on swatting me with so much force that my hindquarters are growing numb.

"Okay, then. I was going to give you twenty but now I'll just keep going until my hand gets tired."

"Good. I hope your hand hurts like hell, you asshole." I pay for that remark with the next slap but it's worth it in satisfaction.

When he is finally done, he flips me over on the bed and I can barely tolerate even the silky sheets on my tender skin. I watch as he takes the nylon twine and stands to tie it from the right post at the head of the bed to the left post at the rear. He orients my body so that I am in the center of the queen-size bed.

"How did you have time to bring your bag of toys? Wasn't this an unexpected trip?"

He barely looks at me to answer, so engrossed he is in what he's doing. "I'd left the bag in the jet when I flew to New York—which is why I had to buy new toys in New York. It worked out nicely this time, though." Cocking his head, he finally glances at me, waiting for some response. "Well? Am I going to get that apology?"

I shake my head emphatically—I still feel as if I were wronged.

"In that case, you're not permitted to speak any more."

I finally give in to my baser instincts and stick out my tongue at him. If he has any reaction, he chooses not to show it.

He clips leather cuffs on my wrists and thighs and secures them to chains he wraps around each of the head posts. I'm not fighting him but I'm also not helpful. Instead, I'm watching his every move, suspiciously eyeing that diagonal line above my head. I see him remove something else from the bag and then he leans over me and his mouth descends on my left breast, and he sucks... hard... almost painfully. I close my eyes to process the sensations when I feel something bite into me. My eyes fly open: he's attached a jeweled clamp to it with a long delicate chain hanging from it. He does the same thing to the other breast.

I gasp. "These really hurt; they're too tight."

"Just breathe, Ella. The pain will fade to something more bearable in a few moments." He watches intently until I somewhat relax and then he drops a kiss on my lips and continues to do whatever he has planned.

"Now," he whispers, "I'm going to help you keep quiet. Remember last time you had some difficulty?" He holds up the metal ball: it's the size of a large walnut, made of metal, and doesn't look very intimidating. He attaches a nylon rope section to it and then clips the rope to the chain that links to the two nipple clamps, tossing the ball over the other side of the nylon string above my body.

"Here's how it works," he says, feeding the rope slowly over the twine until the ball lands on my stomach and jerks the clamp chain up, tugging painfully on my nipples as I swallow a shriek of pain. Then he pulls the ball back up and takes the slack rope and puts it between my teeth and tells me to bite down... and smiles the most malevolent grin I've seen in a long time, if ever, and his eyes are filled with carnal promise.

"If you keep the rope in your teeth, you'll be just fine, Ella. But if you attempt to talk or even scream in ecstasy, then you'll lose the rope, the weight will pull down on the other side of the twine and it will yank up the clamp chain. Might hurt a bit. So you see, incentive to keep quiet and all without a gag." He leans his head close to mine and whispers in my ear, "You're welcome."

If looks could kill they'd be digging his grave by now. I flash him the filthiest possible one ever and he couldn't seem to care less. Truly.

He holds my face in his hands and gazes into my eyes, his expression entirely unreadable. If I were forced to guess, I'd say he looks... *hurt*. Ian is so mercurial, his mood changes are so fast and frequent, they're dizzying. He takes the rope out of my mouth to kiss me—deeply—and I realize with a start that he is expressing himself. He's upset at the rift between us and he's trying to make it better in the only way he knows how. In light of this revelation, I feel the sexual pull to him grow ever stronger and gain momentum.

He puts the rope back into my teeth, "Bite down," he commands and I comply. "So, Ariel, I've taken away your autonomy and movement. I've taken away your ability to speak." He picks up a satiny black blindfold off the bed. "Now I'm taking away your sight, so you'll feel everything more intensely. You're entirely exposed, open and available to me, and at my complete mercy. Right now, to be perfectly honest, I'm not feeling inclined to have any. Of course, if I receive a penitent apology, I might change my mind and develop a bit."

How I'm supposed to deliver the penitent apology is anyone's guess since I can't open my mouth—I can' t say anything or the clamp chain will pull up and it will feel like fingers tugging viciously on my breasts. Sharp fingers.

My mind stays focused on the hurt look in his eyes. Finally, after a year of mental anguish caused by meeting him, then falling for him, I feel that I have a clear insight into Ian now. Though he's scrupulously honest, he has great difficulty sharing his emotions—or admitting he has any: if he is guilty of any lies, they are lies of omission. Instead he uses sex to communicate the feelings he has that he can't share. He'll never be honest with his feelings because he denies them even to himself, I suspect. Displaying feelings shows a chink in his armor.

I hear him moving around my bedroom but I can't fathom why until I hear strains of music, a trumpet and piano, and I realize he was looking for a dock for his iPod. The composition is achingly familiar to me but I can't identify it and I obviously cannot ask him... anything. I refuse to give him the satisfaction of losing the rope between my teeth. Not for the first time I wonder if the man is a sadist.

As I wait, anticipation building—which I'm sure is the point—my mind shuttles back to the day Ian first showed me his dungeon and explained about himself. As I strolled through the room, examining his lovely little torture chamber, he'd regarded me intently, alternating between agitation and fascination. He'd been nervous on the way there, even apologetic, yet he went through with it anyway. He could have instead tried to establish a normal relationship with me, but, no: he didn't want it. Everything always has to be on Ian Blackmon's terms.

I consider my own reaction to him during our first discussion, after that initial encounter at the shop. Everything about him seemed either anachronistic, as if he belonged to another era in time when men had to keep their emotions in check, or somehow forced, as if he were an actor playing a role. It's almost as if he started with a blank slate, zero personality, and researched the kind of man he wanted to become. Perhaps he read 19th-century literature for manners and studied the robber barons of the same century for disposition and reputation. Or even more likely, the Marquis de Sade.

What I do understand thoroughly now is that he has a knack for speaking directly to my body, completely circumventing my mind, and it infuriates me at times. Whatever my brain may instruct me to do in an act of self-preservation and sense of self, my body is heedless, wantonly falling prey to his every whim and dictate. Perhaps other, stronger women could suppress libido for intention and I applaud them for it. Personally, I find I cannot manage it comfortably—not with Ian, anyway. He is the one man who has been able to shut off my mind and turn on my body—I just have to go with it. I send my female brethren, my sisters in arms, a silent plea for forgiveness, and await his next move.

"I do hope you're not attached to these sexy little panties, Ella," he says as I hear cutting sounds and feel my panties slip away from my body. "Like unwrapping a gift, you know; it increases the anticipation and isn't that what it's all about?"

Time ticks by slowly and I'm feeling increasingly desperate. Nothing is happening—I don't even hear him moving about and it occurs to me that he must be watching me lie here, watching the edges of panic begin to claim me. As if in direct response to my thoughts, he runs one finger down my arm for reassurance so I know he's there but the only sound is the soft music playing. Not being able to see ratchets up the stakes exponentially; I have no idea what's coming so when I feel something very hot splatter on my belly, I begin to scream and catch the rope between my teeth in the nick of time.

"It's only hot wax, Ella and it won't get any hotter than that."

He drips it up my belly, around first one breast, then the other. Each sensation seems to travel directly to that heated spot between my legs and by the time he finishes circling each breast, I'm beginning to feel an urgency for satisfaction. Something tells me, though, that it will be a long time in coming—as I will be too. He circles each breast again and then a hot drip lands right on top of one captured nipple and this time I don't catch my shriek in time and the rope slips and the tug burns; I scream again from the pain.

He sighs dramatically. "Ella, you must be more careful to keep the rope in your teeth. Now, bite down again," he says, as I feel the burn ease and I want to cry in frustration. He starts up again with the other breast. This time I'm prepared for the nipple splatter and I manage to stop myself from making any noise. The hot liquid works its way back down my belly, down one thigh and calf and up the other. Now I understand what his ultimate target will be and I begin to perspire, a sheen of sweat covering my entire body. Will I be able to keep the rope from slipping?

The drips get closer and closer and then move away again. By now I'm hurting for the physical satisfaction he's been denying me. When he finally runs out of thigh, I hold my breath, and he seems to pause... and then splat! Right on top of my clit and the orgasm just rips right through me. I don't even realize I've screamed and lost the rope until I feel the aching burn of the clamps as they get jerked up.

I hear a deep laugh and then he removes the clamps entirely. The pain is worse when they come off than when they go on and I whimper. He soothes the pain with his tongue on each one and then lifts the blindfold. My eyes take a moment to adjust to the light.

"Hi there," he says softly, and I feel close to him again. I badly want to touch him but my arms and legs are still restrained. He kisses me, and this time I'm an active participant, entwining my tongue with his eagerly. Ian has beautiful sculpted lips and they're velvety soft. His tongue is warm and wet, and touching it with mine makes things deep inside of me dance.

He sits up and begins to take off his clothes, treating me to an eyeful of his Greek-god physique... and his monstrous erection. My anticipation begins to grow potent again.

But instead of getting on top of me, he dives down between my legs and whispers softly, erotically, "Watch, Ella, keep your eyes on me" and then that tongue, the one I was just marveling about a moment ago, begins to relentlessly circle my clit until I feel like an overfilled balloon about to burst and forever disappear from the face of the earth.

I can't watch—I don't know exactly why but I can't. He's beautiful and sexy but I can't do it so I close my eyes. After another astounding orgasm, he looms over me. "Untie my hands, please, Ian. I need to touch you."

He unclips one, then the other, but leaves my legs chained, open with knees bent. I wrap my arms around his head, running one hand through his silky hair as he pushes his huge erection into me. We moan in unison and I watch his face as first he coaxes another orgasm out of me, commanding me to come for him, then as he struggles to defer the inevitable, wins a few times and then finally surrenders to it, coming with my name on his lips and a violent jerk inside me.

Minutes later, we're still lying in the same position, perfectly spent, when the doorbell chimes. Ian picks up his head. "Are you expecting anyone?"

I shake my head, "No. I'm supposed to meet Lucien later but not here."

Jumping up, he pulls on his jeans and shirt.

"Uh, Ian? Are you forgetting something?"

He grins in delight as he reaches over to unclip my legs, removing the cuffs and massaging my hips and shoulders. "I'll go see who it is while you get dressed. Then we'll talk about our schedule."

I want a shower in the worst way but I know I first have to deal with Ian and the timetable for the trip to Tokyo. I guess it's back on for me and I have the rare pleasure of pissing off both Lucien and Ian in the same day. I should not have told Lucien I'd be in L.A. so fast but stupid is as stupid does. I hear Ian say something to someone and a deep voice responding as I throw my clothes back on and run my fingers through my wildly messy hair. When I look up, Ian is in the room and his narrowed eyes are cold and angry.

"Your employer is here, Ella. Get rid of him, please." His voice is like ice.

Shit, he's massively pissed. I quickly slip into my shoes and go to speak to Lucien.

Chapter 23

Seething, Ian follows Ella back into the living room where Phillips is waiting to speak to her. He purposely left his shirt partially open and his feet bare, so it would be exceedingly clear to Phillips what they were doing when he so rudely interrupted with his visit. What Ian knew he'd really like to do is flatten the pretty, fair-haired boy for once and for all, and his hand is already closing into a fist. He forces it open: Ella might not get over such an event easily, and he'd just managed to make things right again after the Alexis debacle.

Alexis. What exactly was that woman up to? It reminded him all too well of what happened with Natasha five years ago. He'd stupidly trusted her—and she'd virtually destroyed him and everything he had worked so hard for, and he'd vowed to himself that it would never happen again. Can lightning strike twice?

"Lucien," he hears Ella exclaim. "Did I get my wires crossed? I thought we were meeting later in West Hollywood?"

"Ella, hello." Lucien reaches across to greet her with a warm handshake. "No, you didn't get anything crossed. I had planned to meet later in Westwood, actually, at the UCLA film archives. Allow me to say I'm sorry to catch you at an inconvenient time— I managed a good few hours of sleep on the flight here so I thought we could get a quick start on the archival footage. I see you're otherwise engaged, however?"

Phillips does not look like he just got off an international flight: his clothes are impeccably crisp and unwrinkled, and every hair is in place—he's since grown a neatly groomed beard since he's seen him last. Ian couldn't hate the man any more if he tried with all his might. Plus, his innate radar for liars was going off like crazy: the man is slimy—Ian is one hundred percent certain of it. What he finds perplexing is how Ella, a very intelligent young woman, is blind to it. She's always unaware of men trying to get into her hot little pants. Perhaps it's because she's not one to trade on her good looks? Ella has integrity so she probably expects others to have it too. What Ian was trying to prevent was her learning her lesson the hard way that it's not the case. He turns his attention back to the conversation…

"…and I apologize, Lucien. As a matter of fact, I jumped the gun a bit when I told you I could meet you in L.A. so soon. My trip to Japan is back on and I have to return to Portland today. I won't get back to L.A. until next weekend at the earliest." She glances at Ian and he eyes her steadily, nodding slightly to confirm that yes, she needs to get back to Portland tonight.

"Ah, that won't do. I'll probably be gone by then. I have to make a quick stop in New York before I return to Paris but I do need to be back in France by middle of the following week."

"Hmm, that's unfortunate." Ella says softly; she's feeling anxious about the situation she's created—albeit unintentionally.

Lucien's face gives nothing away but he's got to be annoyed by the unexpected turn of events. Ian smirks, pleased to be getting in Phillips' way time and again. And rest assured, dear Lucien, I will continue to do so, he thinks and smiles broadly at the happy thought.

Checking his calendar on his phone, Lucien says, "I'll just have to accomplish everything here myself then. It would have been helpful to have you along but I see it's not possible," he throws a cool glance at Ian.

So he doesn't like me either? Ian thinks. I just may go home and weep over it. He returns the look with a glare that he usually reserves for his business rivals, shriveling even the most redoubtable corporate gangsters.

"I might be able to take care of whatever it is you have to do in New York... that is, if it's work-related?"

Now Phillips smirks. "Yes, actually, it is. That may be quite helpful, Ella. Thank you, I'll consider it and get back to you."

Relief washes over her face and Ian can see her shoulders relax. "Okay, I'll wait to hear from you then, Lucien. Please email me all the information—it might behoove me to fly directly to New York from Tokyo."

"Very good, Ella," he reaches over to take her hand again. "I hope you have a nice time in Japan." He nods curtly to Ian. "Blackmon."

Ian nods his head almost imperceptibly in acknowledgement. As soon as Phillips leaves, he pulls out his phone.

"Scott? Are you still in L.A.? Excellent. I'll need the Gulfstream to return to Portland." He looks at his watch as he speaks. "Two hours? Perfect."

He punches in another number. "Jackson? Ian Blackmon. Yes, I received your messages. Anything to report?" He's listening to Delacroix but his eyes are on Ella, watching her every move. He didn't like how agitated she'd been about disappointing Phillips. " I'm in L.A. right now but I'll be returning to Portland later tonight. We leave for Tokyo tomorrow afternoon. Any chance you can meet with me in the morning? Yes."

"Do you ever say thank you or goodbye to anyone?" Ella asks when he slides the phone back into his pocket. She's also been watching him since Lucien exited the house.

"I show my appreciation in more concrete fashion, i.e. dollars and cents. Verbal niceties are a waste of time. I'm a man of few words, Ariel."

She rolls her eyes. "It's called manners, Mr. Blackmon, not a waste of time."

"Ariel," he says in an admonishing tone of voice, his eyes and the set of his jaw telling her to stop dissing him; he holds out his hand to her. "Come. Let's take a shower. We need to leave for the airport in an hour."

After a long, hot shower, they prepare to leave for Portland. "It's just seven now. We'll probably hit the tail end of the L.A.-rush-hour, so we should head out now. We'll dine on the flight to Portland, if that's okay with you, Ella?"

"Yes, that's fine. Will we be staying overnight at the houseboat?"

"No. I've moved back into the glass house—it's more secure. I don't intend to have any more middle of the night visitors."

He looks at her from the corner of his eye when her head whips back to look at him. "No, we wouldn't want that, would we?" She smiles shyly.

At ten the next morning, Ian meets with Jackson Delacroix. When he arrives at the café, the blond attorney is waiting for him.

"Ian," he gets up to shake his hand.

Ian nods, shaking his hand and pulling out a chair. "You mentioned a similar situation?"

Delacroix chuckles at the lack of pleasantries in Blackmon's repertoire—he always gets right to the point. "Please, have a seat and order some coffee. I'll make it quick, Ian; I know you're pressed for time."

He sits and Delacroix signals the waiter. "More coffee, please?"

"Yes, sir."

Ian watches him patiently. "You mentioned over the phone that you've seen a similar situation?"

Delacroix nods, sipping his coffee. "After we spoke and you updated me on what happened with that woman, I felt a sense of *déjà vu* and I couldn't recall exactly why. I began to think of your situation five years ago, Ian: all your troubles began when you raided the energy company. Correct?"

He nods. "Yes, and that was the last hostile takeover I've ever executed, too. It was the day I developed a more honorable code of business ethics. So?"

"I happen to have a friend—probably the best

corporate litigator in New York—by the name of Bradley Butler. His son Daniel is, for want of a better term, a venture capitalist. He basically does what you do: rescues ailing companies and shores them up again by infusing lots of cash and focusing on strengths. In return, he gets a controlling interest in the company. Although Daniel's wildly successful, his father tells me his son is a reluctant participant in the corporate world. He fell into it when friends needed bailing out and he had the cash.

"Anyway, Butler was in the UK for personal reasons right after he rescued a friend's energy firm—name of GeoTech—and set it on the road to black ink when the shit hit the fan. He had to rush back to the States to do major damage control. Here's what happened.

"The company was holding an inordinately valuable patent on a new extraction technique and holding capacity for a geothermal system capable of high vertical density energy output—as in New York City- or Chicago-capability. It's green, fairly inexpensive, and in such abundance, it's ridiculous. The stock was going through the roof based on this patent that could potentially redefine the entire energy industry and give the oil companies serious competition. Daniel was sitting on the patent, not selling it or developing the system beyond a prototype, but instead using it as a bargaining chip for lucrative government contracts that Daniel was courting.

"He engineered the whole comeback based on this one patent that was already in development when he signed on. The company was cash poor precisely because it poured all its resources into R&D and had several patents pending. Daniel hired a brilliant PR team to make noise about it. He has a knack for making people sit up and take interest and so the company was rebounding without even utilizing the patent.

"This is where the criminal raiders come in," he pauses for effect, seeing he has Blackmon's complete attention. The waiter serves the coffee while the two men stare at each other. Ian is beginning to feel ready to explode because he senses what's coming and it's setting his blood to boil. It's happening again, he thinks with incredulity.

"While Daniel is out of the country, these ghosts start acquiring as much stock as they could get their hands on. Daniel had controlling interest but he didn't have enough to ensure it—I think he owned something like 40 percent. They managed to acquire nearly that in a few short weeks. Daniel got back and bought out the stock of his friends and all the employees to give him over fifty percent so they couldn't wrest away control regardless. He figured he'd eventually give it back to them when they could get their hands on the stock held by the raiders.

"So, now, they can't get to the patent legally, they resort to illegal measures. They use a blond who looks like she could snag the Sports Illustrated Swimsuit cover and have her go after Daniel's partner in GeoTech, a guy by the name of Stephen Hemingway. They begin dating, get hot and heavy, and she's trying to get info on the design so they could at least try to steal much of it, regardless of the patent. Plus, she's looking for any intel they could use against GeoTech. Daniel had managed to put out the fire but the blond subsequently did enough damage with the information theft that the company almost went under again.

"Fortuitously, GeoTech was already in the final stages of negotiation with the state of New York, for new building projects. Plus, they had quietly approached an established green-energy company about purchasing the patent and working in concert with them to develop the system. In effect, the criminals were a bit late with the espionage or it might have worked.

"I discussed the whole matter at great length with his father and we concluded that it had to be the oil companies behind it. The attempt was well financed and executed professionally. The only reason it didn't succeed was because Daniel was able to keep the lid on the patent until he was ready to move on it. Nothing was ever proven, of course, but Mr. Hemingway is a lot more careful with his romantic prospects." He laughs.

"I am beginning to think the espionage that brought down Blackmon Enterprises may have been engineered by the same raiders, Ian. Fits the MO. You had acquired a green-energy firm, one of the earliest success stories in the burgeoning industry. They used Natasha Grierson to get to you. Unfortunately, that time they were successful. Still, you didn't have to dismantle the entire corporation over it. I never understood your motivation for going to such an extreme."

Ian can feel a tight knot congeal in his stomach. The betrayal was by far the worst of the whole ugly affair. He loved Natasha, had trusted her, and she sold him out to the highest bidder. That unforgiveable betrayal had led him straight to the dark doors of BDSM, where he found a way to get his physical needs met without engendering any emotional risk.

He attempts a cavalier façade for the attorney and shrugs his broad shoulders. "I was ready to move on—I didn't like the man I'd become. Hostile takeovers are not honorable endeavors merely because they're euphemistically called M&As. It's outright theft, no matter what anyone names it, and it causes a lot of people to lose their livelihoods. Frankly, I couldn't sleep at night after a while. I much prefer the considerably more civilized approach we take at Excalibur."

Delacroix smiles. "I think you mentioned that Ariel has to go to New York on business periodically?"

"Yes, that's correct."

"Might I suggest you accompany her next time and have a meeting with Daniel Butler? He just might be able to shed more light on this matter before the situation escalates."

"Very good. I'll do that. Can you text me his contact information and advise him of our conversation so he knows to expect a call from me? Ella will be traveling directly to New York from Tokyo, and if things permit, I'll travel with her at that time."

"Good. Yes, I'll call Daniel in the morning. How long

will you be in Japan?"

"Only till the weekend. While I'm gone, I'll make sure Jarvis increases security both at my estate and at Excalibur. Alexis Martinez was arrested but as I told you, she was summarily released on her own recognizance. I don't think they'll use her again but we'll want to be on high alert in any case."

Finishing their coffee, Ian signals the waiter for the check and hands him his credit card. "I do appreciate your taking the time out of your weekend to meet with me, Jackson. I'm going to leave you to your breakfast now since I have to take care of a few things before our flight leaves."

"Okay, thanks for breakfast, Ian, and I'll be in touch soon. Adios."

The first-class cabin is only half full so the flight is peaceful, evocative of the days when air travel was not such a fraught ordeal. Still, ten and a half hours is a long flight and he is glad when it's over. He'd been able to knock out some paperwork while Ella slept and even squeezed in a hour's nap himself. Noticing Ella rousing as the plane begins its descent, he grasps her hand.

"Hi. How are you feeling?"

His reward is a megawatt smile and his heart lurches upon seeing it. "I feel ridiculously good, considering how much time I've been spending on planes these days."

"Yes, you've been the world traveler of late, haven't you? Well, Ms. Strong, you are now about to set foot in Japan. What would you like to see while we're here?"

"Definitely Fuji. And I want to take the bullet train.

"Modest enough aspirations. We can do both in one afternoon. Anything else?"

"Lots," she nods. "I'll need to do some surfing on the Internet to decide what to fit into this short trip." She squeezes his hand with hers. "When will I be on my own?"

Glancing sharply at her he asks, "On your own?"

"I mean," she says flushing, "when do you have to

work?"

"I have a meeting set up for early Tuesday morning with a group of my investors. At that time, I'll determine how much time and effort I need to invest in them. May I get back to you on that?" He smiles sardonically.

"Yes, you may." She stretches and yawns. "I can't wait to get off this plane. Where are we staying anyway?"

His lips twitch. "Some dump called the Imperial Hotel Tokyo."

"Ah, I've heard about that fleabag hotel. Couldn't we do better?"

"You know, while I have to work, you should treat yourself to some spa time at the hotel. You deserve it," he says, kissing her hand. He's beginning to understand how much he cares for this girl and it's massively unsettling. All those months apart when she was in Cambridge, he'd begun to believe he was in love with her. When he'd failed to get her back, he somehow convinced himself it was all just a delusion on his part. But now? Now he was once again faced with the uncomfortable truth: it took his breath away if he allowed himself to dwell on it.

"Let me know when you hear back from that smarmy guy you work with about going to New York." He looks at her, brazenly challenging her to complain about his characterization of Lucien.

She doesn't take the bait. "Why?"

"I need to meet with someone in New York. I may just travel with you directly from Tokyo, depending on the timing and what's going on at the office."

She snuggles up to him and he puts his arm around her. Mmm, she smells so good, like sunshine with a hint of sandalwood. He's looking forward to having her in his arms tonight; he never enjoyed sleeping with a woman so much as he did with Ella. In fact, he rarely did sleep with anyone before meeting Ella. She'd inspired him to break so many of his own habits and rules, all without even knowing it. He shakes his head in consternation. Just as that thought dissolves, he feels the landing gear gently bounce on the runway. Ah, Tokyo.

Chapter 24

I never knew I could be so attracted to a man in a suit, I muse. I'm lying in the fluffy bed in our hotel room watching Ian get dressed for his meeting. It's funny: casual is practically my middle name. I've pretty much lived my entire life in jeans and tees, wearing a dress only if the occasion absolutely demanded it. I used to like to look at men in casual clothes, clothes that showed off their efforts in the gym. That was all pre-DWB (Dorian Wesley Blackmon), though. Since meeting Ian, I now get hot whenever I even see a suit from a distance—he has rewired me that way.

But, trust me, suits never look as good on anyone else the way they do on Blackmon. Eyeing the charcoal gray Versace suit he's donned for his business conference today, I can't help but want to drag him back into bed. The pants drape down from his slim hips, highlighting that trim waistline and tight butt, and flare down his long legs. The light blue shirt hugs his buff torso like a lover and the jacket plays tease, offering glimpses of its luscious contents as it sways with his motion. Mmm. He catches me looking and gifts me with a wolfish smile—I know what he's thinking now.

I put my arms behind my head to further enjoy the view. "Have any idea how long you'll be?"

He looks down his nose at me. "Why? Will you miss me?"

"Always. Should I make my own plans for the day or wait on you?"

He considers my question. "Why don't you shower and have breakfast? I should have an idea where this will go by the first hour or so. As soon as I have more information, I'll text you and you can take it from there. Sound okay?"

I nod and stretch languorously—multiple orgasms right before bed do wonders for a person's morning outlook. Ian finishes dressing, adding a silvery blue tie, gives me a quick kiss, and reminds me to check my messages before taking off for the day.

It turns out he's gone for most of the day so I end up walking the streets of Tokyo—um, wait, that didn't come out right. I *toured* the local neighborhoods of Tokyo, took the train, and bravely ate food from street vendors. I stopped to chat with the man selling tofu pudding—he spoke fairly good English and said his name was Kiko. Fascinating me with trivia, he explained that street vendors were ubiquitous in Tokyo once upon a time but by the 1970s were all but gone, replaced by convenience stores. In recent years, there's been a resurgence of the vendors, selling healthy alternatives filled with fresh vegetables and tofu. The woman next to him was selling piping hot sweet potatoes and the comforting scent filled the air.

The city is densely populated, both by people and architecture. Wending my way through both, I window shop and gape at the unusual style of building, both in style and material. Stopping into a small boutique, I buy a new dress to wear to dinner. It's very short, in fact, barely there, and I wonder what Ian will have to say about it. By four o'clock, I haven't yet heard from him so I return to the hotel to soak in the huge whirlpool tub and have a glass of wine.

I hear the door open at ten minutes to six, as I'm attempting to do research on one of the film subject's native origins. Leaping up, I race to the door and as soon as he closes it behind him, I have at my gorgeous CEO, jumping into his arms and hoping he'll catch me: he does.

"Now that's what I call an enthusiastic greeting. Miss me?"

"Nah, not really," I breathe, my hands reaching up to caress his face as I kiss him.

"I'd like to be greeted like this every day, Ella. Can you see to that?"

Laughing, I slide down his body, making sure I press closely against every inch of him on the way down. "Highly doubtful, sad to say. Hey, I bought a new dress. Want to see it?"

"Absolutely," he replies, putting down his messenger bag, and taking a seat near the sofa. He sits there like the king he is—the king in my realm anyway.

I retreat to the bedroom, rip open the bag and lay the dress on the bed. Oh. It's even shorter than I remember, I think with dismay. There's almost no way that Ian will go for this one. I pull off my tee-shirt and yoga pants and lift the dress over my head. The light blue slinky material feels cool and slippery as it settles over my body. Now I remember why I bought it—it's amazingly comfortable yet it highlights my best assets. I sidle into the other room to show Ian, feeling suddenly shy and almost silly. When I walk in, his head jerks up to look and I see shock etched into his face. Uh-oh.

"What do you think?" I ask coyly, even though I kinda know the answer just based on his expression.

"It's quite short."

"Is it? I hadn't noticed. Anything good to say?"

"The blue matches your eyes and... you look very sexy. Much too sexy. I'm not good at sharing, never have been, and I do believe you're aware of that inclination."

I shrug my shoulders. "I like it. I was hoping to wear it tonight?" I frame the thought as a question.

He sighs. "Wear what you want, Ariel. I'm sure you'll look beyond fantastic. Be warned, however, that I will go to whatever lengths necessary to keep other hands off. Understood?"

Mutely, I nod, trying to imagine what lengths he'll deem necessary to go to; I suspect Ian doesn't have too many boundaries when it comes to jealousy. Perhaps I should wear another dress?

"Oh, by the way," he adds, "I have something for you that will look good with the dress." He gets up and goes into the bedroom. When he returns he has a piece of jewelry casually draped over his fingers. When he hands it to me, sans box, I assume it is a piece of costume jewelry but when I touch it and get a good look, I gasp. It's a platinum gold bracelet and it's studded with diamonds—not chips, mind you, but actual diamonds. The piece must be worth a fortune and I'd be terrified to wear it.

"Are you insane, Ian? This gift is a bit over the top, don't you think?"

He smiles and shrugs. "I actually bought it for you over a year ago, Ella."

Over a year ago? Before I left him and fled to Britain. My stomach lurches as if someone just delivered a swift kick to my abdomen.

"I never got the chance to give it to you, to say I was sorry. Will you accept it now in the spirit in which it was intended?"

Gulping, I nod, blinking away the tears. "Of course, Ian. It's unbelievably beautiful."

He takes the bracelet from me gently and drapes it over my wrist, clasping it. "Very pretty," he says and kisses my hand. "I made reservations at a restaurant I think you'll like but we don't have to leave for another couple of hours."

"Oh? Hmm," I tap my finger to my lips as if in thought. "What should we do in the meantime?" Finally I get my chance to grab him by the tie and lead him to the bedroom by it. His eyes light up and he doesn't put up much of a fight.

When we get to the bed, I shove him down onto his back and start to undress him. "You'll be wanting to change out of this fussy suit, anyway. Right?"

He just smiles but his hand goes up my dress. "Mmm, there are benefits to very short dresses, aren't there?

Ignoring him, I don't stop until I've removed every last article of his clothing and he's lying there with only what he came into the world with—of course, it's a lot larger now and that suits me just fine. I quickly tear off my own clothing while he observes with a heated expression. Let's see how far he'll let me take this enterprise, I think, as I grab a condom off the bedside table and climb on top of him.

Shockingly, he doesn't stop me; he just lets me have my way with him. I have his wrists in my hands and I'm still on top, regulating our movement, along with his escalating passion and my own. I'm surprised he hasn't wrested control from me by now but he's lying there passively, watching me. Just as I'm about to gain the apex, seconds away really, he swiftly frees his hands, lifting my hips so high I can barely reach him to mount again and my momentum toward orgasm crashes and burns.

"What?" I pant, only managing the single word.

"You may be on top but you don't have control, Ella. It's mine and I decide whether you come or don't. I haven't given my permission yet, now have I?"

Oh, I want to slap him so badly right now. To think he let me do all the work and just as I was about to attain my reward, he snatches it right out from under me—literally. He's still holding my hips, his eyes filled with amused satisfaction and I'm tempted to take myself up and away and deny him for the rest of our trip.

In fact... Just as I'm about to act on that impulse, he slams me down onto him and I forget what I was about to do. He raises me up slowly and slams me down again. I can't think of anything else, not a single other thought besides waiting for the next slam to happen. By the time he gets me back to where I was when he stopped it, my body is slathered with sweat and my legs are shaking almost violently.

His eyes like melted silver, he's holding me back, keeping me poised on the edge of the precipice, and finally he says, "Now," and yanks me down onto him very hard and fast, once, twice, and the room flashes white with the explosion happening inside my body.

The next day we take the bullet train and go to Mount Fuji. I never before realized how beautiful a country is Japan—the architecture is spectacular but the natural beauty is nearly sublime. Wednesday we spend traveling to Kyoto and Thursday we stay closer to see the Meiji Shrine and take an enchanting evening cruise on Tokyo Bay.

On Friday, we fly to New York though Ian is on his cell every minute we aren't in the air, barking instructions to Jonas, Jarvis, and Jackson—the J men, as I now call them. I've never met any of them though I saw Jackson Delacroix briefly in the club that first night—but I feel as if I know them simply from listening to Ian's side of the conversation over and over again. The one person I really am burning to meet is his executive assistant Claudia, who works most closely with Ian when he's in the office. I'm desperate to see what she looks like and why she hasn't tried to make a play for Ian herself. Wouldn't most women?

The matter I need to handle for Lucien is pending. Apparently there's some legal problem with a release for one of the subjects so I need to wait until he Fed Exes me some paperwork, and then meet with the attorney. Lucien seems to have gotten over the last bump in L.A. without any problem. I know Ian doesn't like him but Lucien seems perfectly reasonable and even considerate to me.

Ian has a meeting while I schedule time at the library and the Museum of Modern Art. When I'm finished I still haven't heard from him so I text him: *Can I meet u wherever u r? I'm finished 4 the day and am in the mood 2 meet a tall, dark handsome stranger. Know any? Ella.*

His response comes back a few minutes later: You can't get much stranger than me. I'm at the Russian Tea Room on 57th St. I'll be the one wearing the big grin when you walk in. See you soon. I.

His message makes me smile and suddenly I can't

get to him soon enough. He must have gone to the iconic restaurant because he knew I wanted to see it and we had planned on hooking up at whatever place his meeting would be held. I push through the doors of the Museum hurriedly—I'm definitely growing much too fond of him and moving into the red zone for heartache if something goes wrong.

I'm ever so glad to arrive at the restaurant for it's started raining—teeming really—and I have no umbrella. Normally difficult to get a cab in New York, it's impossible in the rain—you probably have a better chance of winning the lottery, I think. As a result, I resemble a drowned rat as I rush through the entrance, attempting to shake myself out, sort of like a dog in a bathtub. The maître d' comes over quickly.

"I'm meeting someone? Ian Blackmon? He's already seated."

"Of course. Please follow me, Madame."

As we walk, I look around at the fantastical atmosphere. Colorful comes to mind. In the main room where we are now, the leather banquettes are a bright red, the walls a hunter green with framed paintings on every inch. The floor is covered by a vibrant red, patterned carpet, and the ceiling is a warm wood that reflects all the amber light bouncing around the room. The maître d tells me that each dining room has a different décor and one is all gold with blue glass walls and another has some very unusual light fixtures.

When I spot the table, I see Ian is sitting with another man but I'm focused on my dastardly handsome man so I'm not paying attention to his companion—that is, until I approach the table and both men rise politely.

"Ariel," Ian leans over and gives me a peck on the cheek. "This is Daniel Butler. Daniel, my girlfriend, Ariel Strong."

The man swivels his eyes to me and nods politely. "Hello, Ariel. It's a pleasure to meet you," and extends his hand.

I'm frozen in place and struck dumb. The man just

shimmers with some kind of potent energy and his eyes, like light green glass, seem to penetrate right through me. I'm also taken aback at his utter masculine beauty. If any man can ever give Ian real competition, it's this one standing in front of me. I quickly gather my wits about me to avoid scrutiny from Mr. Blackmon. Sheesh, lately I've been surrounded by such beautiful men—I must be doing something to please the gods.

As handsome as Lucien is in all his blond perfection, he doesn't move me the way Ian does. There's some kind of magnetic field around Ian that just sucks me in— probably sucks in most people. Consequently since I've met him, I've never really looked at another man—not in *that way*.

But this man, Daniel Butler? Whatever *it* is, he has it in spades. He's golden, but not fair, with blond streaks throughout his brown hair and a bronze skin tone that nearly matches. Piercing light green eyes that have incredible depth peer out from thick lashes, and his physique, well, I'm not going to even go down that road because Ian is watching me ogle him and that can rapidly deteriorate the situation, making my night ugly. I lightly grasp Daniel's outstretched hand and murmur, "Likewise," and drag my eyes away, focusing them back on my own hottie.

"I'm sorry," I say, swallowing reflexively. "I thought your business was concluded. I didn't mean to interrupt..."

"Not at all, Ariel. We were just finishing up." Ian looks at Daniel.

"Yes, of course. Please have a seat and join us," Daniel says, gesturing to the empty side of the booth. The booths are U-shaped with the longest part connecting the two sides. The men sit across from each other so I slide into the wide bench between them while Ian is still standing.

"Ariel, Ian tells me that you're frequently in New York on business?" Daniel asks.

"Yes, for the next few months anyway. I'm working

with a filmmaker on a new documentary film he's producing."

"Yes, so I'm told. Fascinating work, I'm sure."

I eye him closely again. Not as formal as Ian, he wears charcoal gray fitted trousers and what looks like a cashmere sweater, black and vee-neck. He's certainly polite, pleasant even, but he holds himself at arm's length. I suppose he could be called reserved. "Yes, it's interesting," I reply to his comment.

Daniel nods. "My fiancée and I have just purchased a brownstone on the Upper West Side. Please consider joining us for dinner if you find yourself at odds in the city. Olivia loves to show off the house—she and her father have been renovating it a bit together."

"Ella," Ian says, "Daniel's prospective father-in-law is the sculptor Derek Girardi. Do you know his work?"

"The name sounds familiar."

"He's quite renowned," Daniel adds and checks his watch. "I should get going. It was a pleasure to meet both of you," he says, standing.

Ian stands also, and they shake hands as Daniel says, "I'll get back to you with more information when I have it, Ian. I wish you good luck in fending off the barbarians."

Ian laughs, but it sounds bitter or perhaps angry. "I gave in and let the bastards feed at the trough last time. They won't find me so accommodating again."

Nodding his head in satisfaction, Daniel says, "Good. You should never allow parasites like that to win the day—it just encourages the behavior. I'll be in touch," he says in closing and nods at me, before leaving. I look at Ian, wondering what the hell they were talking so cryptically about. Should I ask? I also wonder how many gorgeous men are there out in the world and how sad it is that each girl can only have one.

While I'm watching them exchange goodbyes, I am trying desperately to keep my thoughts clean but they keep drifting into the gutter. Imagine having both of them? At the same time? At one point Butler glances sharply at me and I blush, feeling as if he could read my mind. That would be horrible, wouldn't it? Sometimes when I have a bad thought, I begin to think that someone in a crowded room knows what I'm thinking. It's terrible enough to force me to keep things clean, even inside my head.

Once we're alone I wait for Ian to explain but of course he doesn't. I always have to pry information out of him—it's like pulling teeth. "So, what parasites was Daniel referring to, Ian? Is everything alright?"

"Yes. Did you get everything done today?"

Tricky man always flips the conversation back to me. "Yes, pretty much but I may have to either stay here longer than planned or return at the end of next week when Lucien is due back so we can begin editing footage. Also, there's an art historian he wants to interview about Stieglitz... oh, and Mo invited us to a party tomorrow night. I told her probably not, just in case it was *that* kind of party. I was afraid to ask."

Ian smiles. "It might be educational for you."

"Mmm, sometimes ignorance is bliss."

Chapter 25

It is a beautiful autumn morning in New York City, the kind of day New Yorkers always say they woke to on 9/11, when nature's beauty makes it glorious to be alive, the sky a startling blue, the cool air crisply fresh, without a hint of the usual amalgamation of offensive smells that come with a densely populated city. Well, except for all the motor vehicle exhaust clinging to the air currents. Halting his jog to catch his breath, Ian leans, hands on thighs, and watches the cars swing onto the FDR entrance ramp in rapid succession. Doing something healthy like running while sucking up all the fumes of New York City traffic seems rather self-defeating yet here he stands, drawing in deep lungfuls of the tainted air. Despite the drawbacks, he desperately needed exercise and often found he did his best thinking while physically exerting himself. Well, not during *all* physical exertions—just the monotonous ones like running. And Ian had some serious thinking to do, too. Things were beginning to move at warp speed and this was precisely how mistakes got made, grave mistakes. Taking the time to carefully consider his moves was imperative in this chess game of very high stakes.

He smirks: history repeats itself. Five years ago, he was riding high on the crest of the tall wave he himself created out of air. Every single company he took over was a resounding success; there was never any backlash or interference. He'd identify a firm ripe for the plucking, usually one that had decent asset to liability ratios but had tried to grow too quickly and was strapped for cash, and he'd make his move. Never once did he fail. In less than four years, he'd acquired a diverse portfolio of firms: media dot.coms, electronic component manufacturers, energy-efficient product design, and even a telecom. No problems until he made the foray into energy. Almost as soon as the ink was dry on the deal, they descended like thieves in the night.

He didn't care all that much about it really: it was one company among many. He could have let it go or fought back: he'd come out smelling like roses either way. It was Natasha's betrayal that forced him off the rails, caused him to reevaluate his life and his business, hold them up to the harsh light of day—and ultimately found both sorely lacking. He was no better than the barbarians who tried so hard to unravel his deal.

He was, in point of fact, one of them.

Mergers and acquisitions is a euphemism for corporate piracy and when he looked in the mirror, he didn't like the thief who stared belligerently back at him: stealing other people's sweat equity under the banner of acquisition, causing employees to lose their livelihoods and calling it elimination of redundancies, capitalizing, in general, on the misfortune of others—all of it. Covering up his crimes with crisp suits and euphemisms was akin to any common criminal laundering dirty money. He was glad to be done with it all. He dismantled Blackmon Enterprises completely in less than a month's time, signed over the companies to their employees, and eventually divested himself of even the minimal shares of stock he'd held. Then he began virgin fresh.

Mmm, virgin fresh. Of course Ella pops into his mind now. He can't wait to touch her again. Last night they'd both been exhausted but tonight? Tonight, he had plans. He shakes off his lascivious thoughts for the moment— running with a hard-on is not a good idea.

He selected the name Excalibur for he needed some magic in his life and work; he hoped it would pave the way to get some. *If you build it, they will come,* right? And it did: it all came so quickly, all over again. He had a Midas touch.

One thing he couldn't fix so easily was his fractured soul: Natasha had wreaked pure havoc with it.

Since high school he'd known her. Ian could even remember the first time she graced his eyes—English class, right? She was sitting in the back, next to the only available seat when he came sauntering in fifteen minutes late. Once he saw her face, well, that was that—instant hard-on, instant adulation, permanent love. He couldn't concentrate on anything academic afterward.

And what a beauty she was—and still is, in all likelihood. Born of Russian émigré parents, she bears classic Slavic features: high cheekbones, crystal-clear blue eyes, and such beautiful lips. Her hair so blond and naturally so. After she cut him down, he began to gravitate toward brunettes, as if blondes were evil. Yeah, Natasha did that.

For months after that initial meeting they were inseparable but then college divided them: he went east to Harvard; she went south to Stanford—both of them geniuses and the schools they each applied to recognized it. They planned to get together after graduation: work together, play together, live together.

And they did: their teenage plans actually came to fruition. Natasha returned to Portland, came to work for him, and they moved in together. He was content with her and believed—wholeheartedly—that she was, too, with him. They worked in sync and when he discovered Natasha could be cutthroat in the boardroom, he'd considered it an asset, not a liability. He thought ruthlessness was a positive trait in the corporate jungle.

He thought it until she royally fucked him over.

Paranoia followed on the heels of heartbreak. Ian chuckles as he recalls Ella's facial expression when he produced the paperwork and pen with a flourish for her to sign on their first date. He was certain she thought he made her sign away any rights to disclosure to keep his sexual proclivities confidential since he showed her his dungeon almost immediately afterward, and to some extent it was true. Especially, perhaps, when he was young and just starting out in business, he worried about his reputation, back when he wasn't sure of himself or his place in the world.

After a few years of consecutive successes, he learned who he was and what he deserved from the universe, what he'd earned with his genius and iron balls. It became less important to worry over someone learning about his unusual sexual appetite. Moreover, that appetite pretty much grew out of Natasha's betrayal.

No, the restrictive legal agreement was necessary as one of many tools to prevent more of the same bullshit he'd contended with from the hostile takeover of Total Energy Solutions, orchestrated by one very beautiful and treacherous woman named Natasha Yenin.

But Ella didn't have to know any of that, now did she?

The moment that Excalibur became interested in rescuing a green-energy outfit that was having growing pains, things began to go awry. A break-in, important papers misplaced or missing, high levels of their system hacked into... the same shit that happened the last time. Only this time, he was going to fight back with every gun he had at his disposal. If this were Natasha, et al., again, they'd shortly find out they can bleed too. Oh yes, and bleed copiously.

Jackson Delacroix had given him the name and number of someone who'd endured a similar situation, a man named Daniel Butler. Ian called him the moment their plane landed at JFK. It was the second reason he came to New York.

The first reason, of course, was preventing Lucien from getting Ella alone. He didn't trust that SOB, at all. Butler agreed to meet him the next day for lunch. They decided to go to the Russian Tea Room since Ella was anxious to see the iconic restaurant and she was to touch base with him there after his meeting with Butler was concluded.

Already seated at a table, Ian eyes the man

approaching his table. Over six feet tall, mid to late twenties, expensively dressed, good comportment, a little too pretty but he couldn't really throw stones in that respect—overall, Butler looks like a man to be reckoned with. He stands up to introduce himself as the man reaches the table.

"Daniel Butler? Hello, I'm Ian Blackmon. It's very nice to meet you."

After a quick appraisal, Butler takes his extended hand and offers a slight smile in return. "Likewise. You mentioned a mutual acquaintance—Jackson Delacroix?"

"Yes. Delacroix recommended I speak with you over my current situation fighting off a hostile takeover of one of my companies. He said you encountered a similar situation."

"Delacroix is an associate of my father's. Dependable, I think."

"That's been my experience certainly."

"Mmmhmm. Let's sit, shall we?"

Ian seats himself and waits for Butler to get settled and order a drink. "So," he says, looking pointedly at Ian, "tell me what's going on."

A half hour later, Ian finishes recounting to Daniel the sordid details of what was currently going on and his experience five years ago. The man impressively listened without interruption, carefully considering everything Ian told him.

"I can state unequivocally, Ian, that Big Oil is behind every last one of these takedowns. The major players in the industry know their fat revenue stream is entirely dependent on a dying industry and they're panicking from all sides. Stupid, how they go after every endeavor with great potential, no matter the size. Ridiculous, really, but it's been an effective strategy for them thus far: attack them when they're small and weak—they never get big."

"Why don't they themselves simply get into alternative energies? It makes the most sense, doesn't it?"

Butler shakes his head. "They will never cannibalize current revenues for future profits—goes against their outmoded business model. Quite frankly, they don't think they have to. It's not very farsighted, I agree, but there it is. They'd much rather sabotage every viable effort to bring renewable energy sources to a large volume of people, keeping everyone small and of no threat to their gargantuan market share. For God's sake, they've been squashing the electric car since the 1970s. The technology has been here that long and so has the desire to make it happen. It's absurd."

"So exactly what did you do to fend them off?"

Daniel shrugs. "Well, my situation was a bit different in that we were poised to make a deal when they struck. We pushed it through quickly and rendered their efforts fruitless. I had to rush back to the States from Britain and buy up every share I could get my hands on to keep my majority percentage. I suggest you do that to the extent possible, even if it means buying—on paper—all your employees' shares, friends' shares, whatever, and holding them until the threat passes. Erect an immediate and united front. If there are any deals in the works with any outside contractor, expedite them. The more auxiliary business you could attach to your firm, the more difficult it will be for them to destroy."

He stops speaking for a moment, tapping his finger on his lips. "May I ask why you walked away the last time?"

"Personal reasons: a friend's betrayal and a long, hard look in the mirror. I redirected my efforts into supporting privately held enterprises and earning the stake in the companies rather than taking them over and wringing out all the capital. Everyone gets to keep his or her job and I still see a healthy profit margin. Win-win and I go to bed with a clear conscience."

Grinning broadly, Butler says, "Good for you. Have to say, I hate those M&A types. They are fucking leeches, aren't they?" He leans back, watching Ian's reaction to his comment. "So... I understand you make regular trips to

New York?"

"Lately I have been. My girlfriend took a job with an art film producer and director. She's been traveling back and forth between NYC and the left coast."

"Ah. Who's the filmmaker?"

"A man named Lucien Phillips. Know him?"

Daniel tilts his head back, considering the name. "No, I can't say I do. My soon to be father-in-law probably does, though. He knows just about everyone who is anyone in the art world."

"Oh? Who is your future father-in-law?"

"The sculptor, Derek Girardi?"

Ian nods, looking intrigued. "Yes. I know his work very well—very talented artist. He's an interesting man, too, from what I've seen and read about him. Married to an African model, isn't he? Very thin, very beautiful woman?"

"Yes. Mia is Ethiopian."

"She's not your fiancée's mother, is she?"

"No. Olivia's mother is Derek's first wife."

"Yes, the model looks too young to have grown children."

Daniel chuckles. "Actually, Olivia's mother is but a couple of years older than Mia. Her father, too. Her parents married and had their two daughters very young. Neither of them has breached forty yet. Both terribly good looking, too."

"So you're practically a contemporary of your future wife's parents?"

"Sort of. There's not much more than a ten-year gap. Derek often feels more like a rival for her affection than her parent. They're too close in age, among other things, and due to their past history, he's far too territorial about her. Strange, even uncomfortable dynamic at work."

"Sounds like it. How old is your fiancée?"

"Young. Very. Not yet twenty. But she's an old soul, and I'm a possessive sort: there are too many people—both men and women—trying to get at her." He laughs. "It's easier to pluck her off the market than beat them all back."

Ian raises his hand up and grins. "Kindred spirit, here. Can you ask Girardi about Phillips? I did have a security check done on him but it came up clean. Still, there's something about the man that doesn't sit well with me."

"Yes, I will. We're actually seeing them tonight for dinner. I'll give you a call tomorrow if I learn anything of value."

When Ella returns to the hotel from her meeting, Ian is lying in wait for her. As soon as she walks through the door, he's on her. Putting one hand on the back of the door, he slams it closed the moment she's inside the room.

Ella looks up at him, startled. "What—"

"Take off your clothing. All of it. Now," he orders.

Her eyes open a bit wider as she leans over, slowly easing her satchel onto the floor, without taking her eyes off his; she's prey, avoiding motion so a predator won't strike. "May I go into the bedroom first?"

"No." His voice was cold, brooking no argument whatsoever. "Do it here; do it now. No discussion, no hesitation."

He could see the wheels turning in her head. With Ella, it's hard to shut off that overactive brain of hers but he manages as long as he gives her something to worry about, focus on. Right now, he shows her his iron will to claim her full attention.

"What's this all about, Ian?" Almost inaudible.

"I want more time with you. Starting right now."

She forces out a feeble laugh. "We've been together, just about 24/7 for over a week now. How much more do you want?"

"More time but more... *everything*. I need to dominate you. I need to see your eyes dilate and your muscles give out as you surrender to me. I need to hear you scream from the fury of your orgasm." His voice drops to a soft whisper. "What do *you* need, Ella?"

After the briefest hesitation, she answers, "The same will do."

"Begging the question, *Will you?* Will you accept your nature, finally, and submit to me, Ella? Or will you continue to struggle against it for all you are worth?" His hands are on her now, helping her to disrobe. Hers are fumbling, inefficient; his are not. He strips her in less than a minute. "Come."

Once in the bedroom, he points to the foot of the bed. "Sit on the end of the bed, in the middle."

She complies as he reaches into his bag to get a pair of ankle cuffs. "You didn't answer my question, Ella," he says softly, as he buckles the cuffs onto each ankle. "Will you embrace your sexuality or will you continue to deny it?"

Her voice husky with arousal, she gives him a long, hard stare. "Why are you so sure it *is* my nature, Ian? How can you be so certain of me when I myself am not?"

"Experience," he replies confidently as he attaches wrist cuffs. "I've been dominating women for enough years to be able to spot a submissive. I can usually identify submissive males as well, without too much trouble. They all respond in similar fashion to a sharp command by a Dominant, even without sexual tension. Any other questions?"

She shakes her head, chewing over what he just told her probably. "Good. You may not speak at this point unless you need to say your safe word. Do you understand?"

No answer.

"Ella, I asked you a question. Do you understand?"

She grumbles out an affirmative. He hides his smile.

After attaching her wrist cuffs to the ones on her ankles, he flips her over, gently pushing her head down onto the bed. When he spreads her legs wider, she is precariously balanced on her knees, having little or no control over her body in this position. "We talked about anal sex. I've used a fairly large plug on you, in you, I should say. We'll use another tonight so that next time, you will be ready to take me in. Yes?"

"Am I allowed to answer?"

"If you're asked a question, Ella. Of course. I expect an answer."

"It scares me."

"A little fear is welcome. But it needs to be tempered with arousal, of course." He hand moves between her legs and he laughs quietly. "And yes, you're aroused by the idea, Ella. Does the thought of being taken that way excite you?"

A pause. "No, I told you: it frightens me."

"Your mouth can lie, Ella, but your body betrays you every time. You're very wet." He thrusts a finger inside. "Are you sure you're not excited by the idea of being taken from behind? Picture it, Ella. Your ass high in the air, your wrists cuffed at the small of your back and me firmly behind you, not allowing you to retreat, thrusting, filling, wakening all those dark sensations." He laughs when she clenches tightly around his finger. "Told you so," he whispers, kissing the base of her spine as his hands continue to make her body rev up.

When she moans, he replaces his finger with himself, after sheathing his erection in a condom. She has to passively take whatever he gives her because in her current position, she has no leverage, no purchase with which to move. He pushes out her legs even wider, balancing her so tenuously she must just accept his pace, his whims. Ian proceeds to tease her, keeping his rhythm erratic so she can't move too close to a climax—it's always inches out of reach… and her frustration mounts as palpably as the layer of sweat forming on her body. How long will she tolerate the burn before she loses her temper? Not very long, he'd wager.

As he feels her muscles coil, moving into orgasm, he pulls out and stops, waiting for her body to calm. Her tension is building, like guitar strings tightened too much and threatening to pop. He begins again, and repeats the same cycle. And again. On the third time around, her willpower gives up the game and she whines her frustration.

Ian gets up and removes the plug and lube from his bag, returning to her when it's ready to insert. "Take a deep breath, baby," he says, "now exhale," and giving her no time to think about it, presses it in against her natural resistance. "If you push against the invasion, it makes it easier and less uncomfortable, Ella. Try to remember that for next time." Once it's in place, he waits a few moments before moving. "How does that feel, baby? Is it okay?"

"It's okay," she manages to get out, her respiration drawing down.

Sweat is pouring out of him, dripping off his chin, running in rivulets down his chest; it's strenuous work staving off ejaculation. Especially with the toy: it's a much tighter fit when a plug occupies so much space. Ian knows he can't hold out too much longer so it's time to finally give Ella her well-earned orgasm.

"Let me know if there's a problem, Ella. I'm going to go hard and fast now. Baby? Are you with me?"

"Mmmhmm. Do it."

Grabbing the one part of her body he'd carefully avoided until now while she did everything she could think of to direct him, hand or mouth, to it, he pinches hard as he thrusts his hips forward almost violently. Her scream is worth everything he did to elicit it. "That's my girl," he says softly and he finally lets himself come on the heels of her satisfying wail.

Chapter 26

I open my eyes and the room is pitch dark. For a moment I have no idea where I am but as my eyes adjust to the darkness, I begin to make out the room and remember I'm in a New York City hotel with Ian. My hand reaches out for him but comes up empty. Sitting up, I look over but the other side of the bed is empty. It makes me feel empty too... so I go look for him.

He's in the sitting room of the suite, reading some paperwork directly under a soft lamp. Soft music plays from the iPod dock on the table. He looks as melancholy as I feel right now.

"Ian?"

Glancing up, he stares at me for a long moment and then gives me a megawatt smile, lighting up the room for me. "Did I wake you, Ella?"

I shake my head. "I don't think so; I don't know what woke me."

He holds out his big, wonderful arms. "Come here, baby. I need to touch you."

I walk quickly to him and fold myself into those warm, hard, protective arms, feeling for the thousandth time that there's no better place to be.

"Is everything okay, Ian?" I mumble into his chest while staring into space.

"Everything's fine, Ella. Just a lot of work to do always... and I'm tired." He pulls his head back to examine me from a distance. "Did you have fun tonight?"

"Fun?"

"When we played? Do you like it when I take control of you, Ella?"

I shake my head. I don't know why exactly, but I feel like crying. He's not going to let it go, though. If he did, he wouldn't be Ian Blackmon.

"Ella?" His voice is silky but determined. "Yes? No? Talk to me."

"Honestly? I'm not sure how I feel about it, Ian... but I do notice that when you're stressed about work, you come at me in full-on Dom mode." I crane my neck to look up at him.

He just gazes back, his face impassive, eyes inscrutable.

"Why were you so cold?"

A weighty sigh escapes from him. "Cold?" he asks. I don't answer and a protracted pause ensues, the quiet of the night closing in around us. Though we're physically close to each other, a yawning distance begins to emerge, grow. It's weird but I can actually feel him emotionally pulling away from me. I wait, barely breathing lest I push him even farther into the darkness.

A few minutes later, his cool voice perforates the wall between us. "I didn't like the way you looked at Butler yesterday, Ella. I was reacting to that, I suppose."

My head whips up, taken aback. What? Shit! I thought he'd forgotten but I should have known better. "I..."

"I've told you before and I'll keep reminding you, Ella. I don't share and I'm jealous when it comes to you. You're mine and I would appreciate it if you remembered that when meeting handsome men."

"But ugly men are okay to gape at then?"

He doesn't laugh. Oh, for God's sake, this man is too fucking much.

"Regardless. You had an intense orgasm. Isn't that good?"

I feel a scalding heat rush up my neck to my face. "Yeah, well. It's not the dominance I was reacting to, necessarily."

"No? What then?"

"You. You turn me on, Ian: your body, your gait, your

eyes, your voice. Do you need any further elaboration?"

"Maybe just one more noun." He gives me a wicked smile. "That's nice to know, Ella. But tell me," he leans closer and his voice gets rougher, darker, "doesn't it make the experience better when you're restrained, open, and completely at my mercy? You trust me, don't you?"

I nod. Where's he going with this?

"That's all you need, *we need*, is trust. You trust me to do what I think best and so I will. That way we can both enjoy ourselves. Stop obsessing about semantics, anyway. It's just the word and its implications that bother you, isn't it? Submissive?"

This subject is tiresome already but he won't give it up, will he? He wants what he wants but I'm a bit obstinate myself. I envisage a future of push and pull between us. Could be worse, I suppose.

"Perhaps. Yes, probably. If you were a member of a group that's been subjugated by almost every society from ancient history to the present, you'd be a tad touchy when someone tried to do it again, even in the name of sexual gratification. Don't you think?"

"Good point, as always, Ella." His eyes shine with an unholy light. "But that's not going to stop me from tying you down and having my wicked way with you, baby. Never. You're my sexy girl, my lo..." He broke off.

What was he going to say? My love, perchance? Damn it.

"You're mine, Ella, all mine. Make me jealous and I'll make you pay... one way or another." He tightens his embrace. "I'm getting very fond of holding you. Do you know that?"

"Me, too."

"Mmm." He kisses the top of my head and that's probably the only apology I'll get for his boorish behavior earlier. I hate to admit and will never tell him, but I kinda like it when he's a bit nasty. Scary yes, but he makes me wet. There, I said it.

"So... you don't think you like playing the

submissive, then?"

"Ian, I'm not comfortable talking about these things but... I don't think I'm submissive."

"No? Would you want to tie me up and take charge in our next encounter?"

I squirm. He's backed me up against the wall: if I say yes, then I might have to do it and it doesn't appeal to me in the least. If I say no, he'll say that means I'm a sexual submissive and I don't like that label either. I try to avoid answering but of course he won't allow that either.

"Well?"

"Let's just go back to bed, Daniel... I mean, Ian." I try to keep a straight face when I see the look I put on his, but I can't and burst out laughing. To his credit, he manages to maintain a stern expression but I see his lips twitch despite himself. I grab his big, beautiful hand and lead him back to bed: I feel an attack of my oral fixation coming on.

Ian leaves the hotel early the next morning, promising to be back to take me to lunch but has to call to cancel. Dinner then. I've a feeling he's going to have to return to Portland before I can go and the thought depresses me; I'm getting too used to having him around.

To cheer myself up, I decide to go hunting for new clothes—in what better place than the concrete retail jungle that is New York City? I head downtown to Soho to seek out some edgy boots and maybe a sweater or two. By the end of the afternoon, my arms are laden with high-end boutique bags. Um, I bought a few more things than I anticipated.

It's always strange to go shopping now that I have real money in my bank account—I get a little shock every time I realize I don't have to shop by price tag anymore. Often I even feel guilty, as if I didn't really earn that money. The way it came to me, so much of it, so quickly, so unexpectedly, I feel like a fraud or a thief.

Then I think of all the women who have written to me in the last year, swearing I've saved their marriages and sex lives, telling me about the babies conceived because of my book... and bone-deep satisfaction washes through me. I can pull out that credit card with a bit more confidence, knowing I inadvertently helped a lot of people with my sexy little book and it makes me feel empowered. I didn't find a cure for cancer or end world hunger... but every little step toward reaching self-actualization helps, right?

Picturing Ian's face when he sees my new lingerie hastens my step in hurrying back to him. It's the sexiest I've ever purchased for myself: a bustier and a matching—and skimpy—thong. Harlot red is the actual name of the color. The bustier pushes up my girls so I look even chestier than I am, and the thong... well, it's a thong.

The dress I purchase to wear for dinner tonight is alluring but elegant: navy blue and tight, with a square-cut but revealing neckline, size 4. Can I say that again? Size 4! All this travel has helped me lose weight, not to mention being around exercise-mad Ian Blackmon. I also treated myself to a new pair of shoes to go with the dress. Ian likes stilettos—I guess every man with a pulse does. I never do find the right boots, though. The quest for the perfect boots must continue another day.

While I'm shopping I duck into an Armani shop and choose a beautiful cashmere sweater for Ian. I'd admired the one Daniel was wearing a few days ago and thought Ian would look great in it. I opt for a soft charcoal to set off his light eyes. Yes. He'll look downright scrumptious in it: I can't wait to get back to the hotel.

But he's not there when I return. I lie down on the bed to wait for him but when I wake up almost two hours later, the room is dark and I'm still all alone in the suite. My pulse picks up as alarm settles over me like a mist: it's not like Ian to be late without calling. Where is he?

I check my phone: three messages. Whew. When I play them my heart sinks: he had to go back to Portland today. No! I feel the ache in my gut instantly as I start missing him already.

I can't call him because he'll be in the air so I text him my unhappiness and decide to try to get some work done. Pulling out my laptop, I hunker over it, wondering if I should just order room service when my cell vibrates. I grab for it hopefully. Ian? No.

Lucien.

"Hey, Lucien. How are you?"

"Very well, Ella. It's good to hear your voice. Is all well?"

"I'm still waiting to hear from the attorney. Nothing's moved on it since last we spoke. Are you in Paris?"

"No."

He pauses and I wonder why. For a moment, I think the call has dropped. "Hello?"

"I'm still here. I'm in New York, Ella. I just got in a little while ago."

"Oh? So does that mean you'll take over handling the legal issue?"

"Yes, I will. But before you head back to Portland, I thought we could meet with the editor and start making some preliminary edits with the footage we've already shot. We do have more than half the film in the can, so to speak. What are your plans for the next two days?"

"Um, well, Ian had to go back to Portland today... unexpectedly. So..."

"Oh? Well, then, why don't you have dinner with me tonight?"

Is it my imagination or does his voice suddenly sound more upbeat? No, I chastise myself. Looks like I'm starting to buy into my own press clippings and thinking no man can resist me, or some such nonsense. Lucien's just being nice and I'm actually happy to speak to him. I'm so depressed that Ian left without time for even a goodbye that distracting myself with Lucien and work sounds like a good idea. "Yes. I'd like that. Where and when?"

"I'll pick you up at your hotel and we'll decide from there. Weekdays are usually doable without reservations. Text me your hotel info, Ella, and I'll be there at seven. Is that acceptable?"

"Yes, absolutely. See you then, Lucien."

I disconnect the call, my mind racing a hundred miles a minute. I know Ian wouldn't be pleased to know I'm having dinner with Lucien but he is my boss or colleague or whatever we are. And Ian's not here. Justified or not, I feel abandoned and dinner with Lucien seems a far better choice than the pity party I'd planned for myself, complete with *Ben & Jerry's* New York Super Fudge Chunk ice cream... and straight-up tequila. I've done it before certainly and I can't recommend it. Not only do you feel disgustingly slothful the next day, but you also have a killer hangover, and hair of the dog never works with tequila. I go back to my laptop but I can't concentrate because I miss my Ian so much, it actually hurts. Oh, boy, am I in trouble.

At precisely seven, Lucien appears in the lobby of my midtown hotel. Hmmm. I have to admit I'd forgotten just how attractive the man is. His blond hair has gotten longer since first I met him and again he has it neatly tucked behind his ears but he's grown a goatee in the last week or so since I've seen him, lending him a slightly sinister look... sinister but likeably so. He's wearing dark blue jeans, a dark silk shirt, and a black leather car coat—very much the young urban hipsterish *whatever*. Or perhaps some would uncharitably call it the Euro-trash look?

"Ella!" He steps over to greet me, kissing me on both cheeks. "You look great. How was Tokyo?"

"Really..." I reach for the right word, "fascinating; I just wish we'd had more time to explore. Any updates for me?"

"None since we last communicated. Everything's going according to our timetable. A few blips, here and there, but those are to be expected. I have some news, however, but let's scout out a restaurant first."

He takes my arm and links it through his. I know if Ian saw him do that, he'd have a coronary, but I'm unsure how I personally feel about it. Do I tend to overreact about these kinds of things?

If I asked Mariah, she'd roll her eyes and tell me to get over it, that he's just being friendly. If I asked my childhood friend Carrie, she'd say it was definitely inappropriate, *overreaching* is how she'd put it. I'm somewhere in the middle: it wouldn't overly bother me if it weren't for the fact that I know it would massively piss off Ian. But he's not here now... so I smile and say nothing.

Walking outside, I shiver and pull up the collar of my jacket. The air has a biting chill, a definite promise of the winter fast approaching. We walk a few blocks uptown, ending up at a small Japanese restaurant famous for its soba noodle dishes. The ambiance is perfect: small, intimate even, yet not romantic. The lighting is high and the tables are situated close together, inhibiting any PDAs among diners. As soon as we're seated, my phone starts singing. I don't even have to check to know who it is and as usual, his timing is perfect.

"Excuse me for a moment, Lucien," I say, getting up to take the call privately. I answer right before I reach the front door and step outside into the frosty air, shivering.

I'm elated to speak to him so I feel like acting silly. "Hey there, handsome. How's it hanging?"

"Did I get the wrong number?"

I laugh.

"It's hanging low because you're so far away. Baby, I'm so sorry I had to take off without telling you. It happened so fast: we had an emergency arise quickly here and I had to get back ASAP—fires to put out, people to slap around. You weren't answering your phone so I texted you from the airport. I left some of my clothes in the room so please check the closet before you check out."

"Okay."

"Ella? Are you okay?"

I'm choked up just hearing his voice and I don't want

to even examine my feelings for him right now—they're so overwhelming, it's scaring me. I clear my throat, stalling for a few moments to collect myself. "Yes. I... um... I miss you so much."

"And I you. Why weren't you answering your phone?"

"I was probably in the subway when you called. No reception underground."

"Why you take the subway is beyond me, Ella. It's a disgusting ordeal."

Giggling at the face he's surely making when he says that, I shrug. "I like the immediacy of it. It's like life: pulsating, smelly, crowded, loud... you name the adjective and it suits. I bought you a present."

"Did you now? Well, I can't wait to get it. When are you coming home?"

Home.

Is Portland my home? Or is it that Ian himself is? That's the million-dollar question these days. "As soon as I can. Lucien called me today... as a matter of fact, I'm having dinner with him right now. He wants me to work on some editing with him before I leave." I say the words really fast hoping it lessens their impact.

"Does he now?" His tone is acidic. "Ella, please get home as soon as you can. I miss you, too, baby."

"I will, Ian. I'll try to fly back day after tomorrow. Okay?"

Sigh. "It will have to be, I suppose. Keep your guard up around Phillips. My instincts say he wants more than just your professional acumen, Ella. Trust me on this matter and be cautious."

"I promise I will, Ian. I'll ring you when I get back to my room. Okay?"

Mollified, I think, his voice changes timber. "Don't forget. I'll be waiting."

"I won't forget. Talk to you later." I disconnect before I can say too much, before I can tell him I love him.

Chapter 27

The intercom on the massive glass and steel desk chimes elegantly.

"Yes, Claudia?"

"Everyone is assembled in conference room B, awaiting your arrival, Mr. Blackmon."

"I'm on my way."

Plucking his navy suit jacket from the chair where he'd flung it earlier, he shrugs into it and tightens his copper raw-silk tie, a gift from Ella and recently used to tether her wrists to the bedframe so he could play without her interruption. Shaking off the bolt of lust that arrived with the thought, he trains his focus on what's immediately ahead: close eyes, inhale deeply, visualize triumph in all things—*ready*. Striding purposefully into the outer office to ring for the elevator, Ian realizes he's far too impatient, and instead takes the stairs one flight up to the tenth floor, long legs scaling three steps at a time.

The moment he enters the large air-conditioned room—he intentionally keeps it at a chilly 64 degrees to ensure that cool heads prevail—an immediate hush drops over the suits clustered around the long mahogany table. Ian is used to silencing a room with his entrance—he actually feeds off it, savoring the tension percolating just beneath their polished veneers as they adjust their clothing, pick up pencils, avert eyes, or clear their throats. Nodding to each person in acknowledgement, he convenes the meeting.

"We all know why we're here so I won't waste time on pleasantries or preliminaries. Jarvis, an update on

Alexis Martinez, please?"

Jarvis leans over the table, checking his notes. "Yes. Last night I received intel from the twenty-four-hour tail we placed on Ms. Martinez. Currently, it appears that Ms. Martinez didn't satisfy and is no longer an engaged player. Night before last she left town rather precipitously with two large pieces of luggage. We checked and she turned off her power and phone and a quick check of her condo revealed measures in place that suggest an extended absence."

Smirking, Ian comments, "I won't ask how the condo tour was accomplished." His eyes make a complete circuit of the table, scanning the faces that watch him with rapt attention. "The other good news is that we now have photos of the two people who broke into our building last week. They're grainy but Belarus has managed to clean them up enough for facial recognition and comparison. I've had copies of the photos Fed-Exed to an acquaintance in New York whose firm experienced a similar attack. It's a long shot but it's prudent to leave no stone unturned. The CEO in question will compare them with those he has on file for his raiders.

Struggling for calm but finding it elusive, Ian hones in on Belarus. His voice is low but sharp enough to draw blood. "Can you give us an update on what's happened since last we spoke?"

The words Blackmon flung at Belarus yesterday were not quite as diplomatic. While he was in New York with Ella, Excalibur's system was hacked into yet again, the accomplishment of which smarted like a vicious slap in the face, a kind of *we can always get in no matter what precautions you implement* type of thing. Ian came roaring back to Portland, determined to send heads rolling like bowling balls.

Fortuitously for Belarus, his head of tech security, he was miles away in New York City at the time of the breach, for Ian's blood was bubbling over, superheated by flames of black fury. He loathed incompetency and any evidence of it served to drive him into a feeding frenzy, searching out the scent of blood. "Can you tell me" he'd shouted to the tech expert, "why the hell I'm paying you a king's ransom if you can't keep the system protected? Remember, I pulled you out of the gutter for God's sake, Belarus, one step back from a long jail sentence and a boyfriend named Bubba. What the hell am I wasting my time and money on if you cannot succeed in keeping the integrity of our system inviolate?"

Right now the Russian whose nickname is Belarus boosts himself up in his upholstered chair, straightening his back, and shifts his eerie blue eyes around the room, ending reluctantly upon Ian Blackmon. "Once again, our system was compromised at the highest level—their hacker is world-class and has breached every firewall we erect to obstruct him. I contacted Peerless, the best tech security firm available, bar none—the government uses it for classified document retrieval and storage—and PPS will develop another tier of protection for us. Meanwhile, I've implemented other interim protections; I won't get too technical here but I'd say we are as protected as it is possible to be with current technology."

Ian nods and with his peripheral vision sees Delacroix make a slight hand gesture. He swivels his frozen gaze to the attorney. "Jackson? You have something to add?"

And so it went.

Most of the afternoon was spent in the closed-door conference. He'd included Jonas, Jarvis, and Belarus from Excalibur, and they joined a complement of corporate attorneys—M&A specialists—who Delacroix pulled together to keep control of TES. The good news was that most of the best legal minds with whom they'd consulted agreed their chances of maintaining both the control and integrity of the energy firm were more than excellent. The most harm that was done came out of the system hacking, getting their hands on confidential and delicate correspondence. Now the hackers could go after the government contracts Excalibur was courting—the closed bid amounts were contained in the compromised files so they could easily undercut Excalibur's bid submissions. Still, it wasn't the end of the world and if he could prove exactly how they undercut Excalibur's bids, their bids, winning or not, would be nullified.

Each member of the meeting offered information or advice and by five o'clock, Ian Blackmon began to feel significantly more confident about the state of affairs at Excalibur. Only one thing continued to gnaw at his mind: he hadn't been able to reach Ella today.

Last night she'd called him when she got back to the hotel from dinner.

"Hi Ian. Just providing you with your goodnight call."

"So you're in for the night, Ella?"

"Very much so. I miss you."

"And I you. I'm... sleepless without you."

"Sleepless in Portland? Doesn't work as well as Seattle."

"No, I suppose not. Good night, baby. Call me when you're done for the day tomorrow. I'll be waiting."

"Yes, I will, Ian."

She sounded fine and he stopped worrying for ten seconds. Within the next breath, his heart lurched in his chest again.

"I'm going to do some editing tomorrow with Lucien and then I'll return to Portland the following day. I booked a very early morning flight, Ian."

"Where is the editing to be done?"

"Um, at Lucien's loft. There will be two other people there with us."

"I'm very uncomfortable with that idea, Ella. No."

"Ian, I'm not going to argue about it. This is my job."

"I really don't give a damn, Ella. You are not going to the man's loft unaccompanied. You barely know him, for God's sake. Why do you take such ridiculous chances with your safety, Ariel?"

"What's ridiculous is your reaction. I'm not taking chances: I'm a grown woman, a *summa cum laude* graduate with a master's degree, working with a filmmaker whose work is fairly renowned, albeit in esoteric circles. I realize I don't know him all that long or well but he's not a stranger either, Ian. And I resent your implications, as if I'm a wayward child incapable of looking after myself. Now I'm going to hang up. I will phone you tomorrow afternoon once we conclude and I leave Lucien's company. Goodbye."

She hung up after that and a knot formed in his stomach. He considered flying back to New York but he had to again meet with Belarus tomorrow, after Peerless was through working on their firewalls. They had to protect the files.

But Ella seemed to need protecting too... and she was far more important than any damn files. He raked his hands through his hair, indecision a rare and uncomfortable experience for him.

By the next morning the knot in his stomach was twisted and bucking in his viscera like a living beast with a mortal wound. Ella hadn't returned any of his calls. Checking his phone, he saw a single text message and quickly opened it.

Ella.

"Ian, all is fine. Just very busy. Talk soon. Later, A."

Nausea rushes in, overwhelming his gut. *Later.* Remembering a lighthearted discussion he and Ella had about language, how it evolves through misuse and slang. They talked about their pet peeves—*later* as a form of farewell was one Ella's. She hated it. Why would she use it now? Was she trying to tell him something?

Glancing at the antique Arts & Crafts grandfather clock in his library, he sees it's just after nine p.m., New York time. He puts in a call to Daniel Butler.

"Hello, Ian. How goes it?"

"Daniel, not too bad. We're holding our own. Tell me, did you speak to Girardi about Lucien Phillips?"

"I did, and yes, he knows Phillips but very minimally. He didn't have much to say about him, really, said he seemed nice enough. But Ian..."

"Yes?"

"I'm not sure how to say this without sounding a bit off... but I have... let's call it enhanced intuition, if you will. I don't want to alarm you but I think the man might be dangerous in some way."

Ian's entire body flash freezes at hearing that word: *dangerous*. Scrabbling for a breath of air to inflate his lungs, he makes a titanic attempt to keep calm; nonetheless, he feels the panic slide in, his skin going cold, his blood running hot, and the nausea escalating, rising to his esophagus: a full fight or flight response, but at Ella's peril, not his own.

"Ian? Are you there?"

"Yes," he manages to spit out but his voice is strangely hoarse, "I suppose my instincts are enhanced too because I've felt that way all along. What's more, Ella was working with him yesterday and now I can't reach her. I've received only one text message from her and it was... odd."

"Odd in what way?"

"The phrasing was... unusual for her. To say I'm concerned would be vastly understating my current disposition."

"Do you want me to pay Phillips a visit?"

"I think I'm going to scare up the Gulfstream and return to New York immediately. However, since I can't get there for some hours, I'd be grateful if you could manage a quick visit on some pretense." He pauses. "I realize it's quite an imposition on you, as I'm little more than a stranger to you, and the hour is late, but I would enormously appreciate it, Daniel. Deem it a second marker in your column."

"Consider it done. I'll bring one of my security people as well and I'll phone you as soon as I have any information, Ian."

"Thank you."

Placing the phone down, he nearly clutches his stomach in pain from an imaginary kick to the gut, as ugly fear transforms into a physical response. Something's wrong: he can sense it. That motherfucker

Lucien Phillips has finally made his move and Ella is in danger... and right now there's not a thing he could do about it. Not a fucking thing. Kicking his foot out violently, he sends the umbrella stand flying across the room.

An hour later he's driving to the small airfield by the office, where Scott left the plane to be serviced and refueled. Ian had called him earlier and told him to stand by. Fortunately, Scott was available to pilot or Ian would have damn well done it himself. Time was of the fucking essence.

His phone rang as Scott was taxiing to the runway and Ian was about to shut if off. Daniel Butler. He answered it quickly. "What happened?"

"Nothing good. There was no one at his loft but I sense she's with him... somewhere else. Did you check with her hotel?"

Ian leans his head back and closes his eyes: he's so close to a nuclear meltdown and he's mustering all his strength to remain in control of his savage temper. "She checked out early this morning. The hotel manager informed me that she handled the check-out by phone call. Hence, she never returned to the hotel yet all her things were packed and gone."

He heard a muttered curse on the other end of the line—it was one more sharp pointy thing poking in his viscera.

"Ian, I'm very sorry to alarm you but there's something... *amiss* in this situation and the sooner you get here, the better."

"I'm sitting on the plane as we speak, taxiing to the runway."

"Very good. Would you like me to continue to look for her?"

"What do you suggest?"

"The address you gave me is not Phillips' official address: the deed is in a company name, Expat Films. Phillips has an Upper West Side address on file. I'll start there."

Action. Action is good, necessary, moving toward resolution. "Excellent. Please text me that address, Daniel; I'll go directly there when I land."

"Yes. In the interim, I'll scope it out. I should be able to tell whether or not she's there." His voice drops lower. "I know the situation is terrifying."

"More than you know. I'm in your debt, Butler, and it's an uncomfortable place to be but right now, I'm willing to take it on. Thank you... and please keep me posted. I'll text you the telephone number on the plane so I don't have to use my cell. Call me if anything new develops."

"Affirmative."

Chapter 28

I feel hands. Cool, silken skin touching me, *feeling* me—my face, my breasts, my bare shoulders.

Ian.

The hands are gentle but insistent and in the next moment, there's seductive warmth: tiny pockets of heated, humid air skimming my throat. Floating in some state of disconnect, neither dream nor awareness, my sluggish brain scrambles to make sense of the tactile sensations and somehow I manage to decipher what it means: a lover's breath. He's close to me, so close. His proximity comforts me and I surrender to him, drifting back into the undulating rhythms of Morpheus's arms.

Music. Plaintive notes waft in, as if through an open door from another room. It's a familiar composition but I can't place it: my ears discern the distinctive harmonies of harp, cello, violin—angel music.

Now there are voices, low and deep. Male. The phrase *sotto voce* springs to my mind and I try to smile. *Inside voices, children,* Mrs. Lowell would say to our kindergarten class when we got rowdy.

Surfacing gradually to consciousness, I drag my eyes open but see nothing. Too dark. My mind is yet hindered by cobwebs of sleep, and my body aches all over.

Where am I? The last thing I remember clearly is finishing up the editing conference with Lucien and the two editors we're working with—Michael and Nico.

I lick my dry lips but even my tongue is too devoid of moisture to make any difference: there's a terrible taste in my mouth. It reminds me of the time that Carrie and I, along with Emily Pedersen, the girl who lived around the corner from us and still wore diapers at age five, were sucking on pennies just for the fun of it... until Carrie's mother caught us and washed our mouths out with yellow Listerine. No matter how long I live, I'll never quite forget the taste of copper on the tongue, a sensory experience that sticks like glue. So does yellow Listerine.

Right now I need water so I attempt to sit up, to seek out hydration, but my body will not serve its master. That is the precise moment when my heartbeat begins to take flight. Something is very wrong with me.

A disembodied voice reaches my ears. I don't recognize it at first.

"Good. You're awake. I've been waiting such a long time to speak with you."

Not Ian. Who then? The voice is familiar but my brain is slow, synapses misfiring, and the room is pitch black, disorienting in the extreme. I can't see anything and I'm starting to panic.

"Where am I?" A shout in the dark.

Laughter. The harsh sound of it grates on my nerves: it's not melodic; it's... *sinister*. And then recognition rushes in; I know. The voice belongs to Lucien.

"What's going on? Why do I feel so ill? Where am I?"

"Relax, you're fine. You passed out, Ella. I put you on my bed. Can I get you anything?"

"Water. Please. And can you switch on a light?"

"Hmmm. I'm going to leave you in the dark for now but here's some water." I feel his hand lift my head and bring a glass to my lips. He tilts it and cool water flows into my mouth. Ah, thank God. Better already.

"Lucien?"

"Yes, Ella?"

"Can you tell me what happened? What's going on?" I again try to sit up but can't move and I'm not exactly sure why. It's too dark and my thinking is foggy.

"Yes, but I thought I'd give you time to fully awaken. I can tell you're not up to snuff just yet."

"How can you tell?"

"That will be my little secret for now, Ella. Just drink your water and try to relax."

"Yes, but... I need to call Ian. He'll be worried..."

"I texted your oh-so-important boyfriend from your phone. It's fine."

"Trust me, it won't be fine unless I actually speak with him. He tends to overreact." And right now I'm so grateful for Ian's overreacting tendencies. I'll take it any day over Lucien's creepiness. "Lucien, where am I? I'm feeling very anxious. Please turn on a light."

A long sigh made louder by the insulating dark. "Very well."

I can feel his body heat move away and then a lowlight flashes on—a small lamp set on a table a few feet from the bed. I quickly take stock of my surroundings: it's a room, a bedroom of sorts, but one I've never been in before. The walls are black and there are strange implements mounted on the walls. I feel something acid rush up my throat but I can's sit up. "I'm going to be sick, Lucien—I need a bathroom!"

In seconds, he produces a plastic bucket—as if he expected me to vomit—and lifts and turns my head to the side so I can regurgitate into the bucket. My body heaves as everything in my stomach comes gushing up, burning my throat on the way out, and nothing can stop my stomach from its pumping imperative. It continues until I'm dry retching, my throat raw and fiery.

"I'm sorry you're so ill, Ella. Would you like a cup of tea?"

"Yes. Please, Lucien. May I also call Ian to let him know I'm okay? He is a worrier."

"I'll bring you some tea. How do you like it?"

"It doesn't matter."

While he's gone, I chance another glimpse around the room. My mind cannot accept the images my retinas are relaying to it. It's not possible. Please, God, this is a nightmare. Now I finally see why I can't manage to sit up: I'm tied down to the bed, naked but for my underwear. My wrists and ankles are restrained and there is a long leather strap that runs from one side of the bed to the other, pinning me down like an insect on a glue strip. I have some movement, but not enough to sit upright, and my whole body feels weak.

I am so screwed, is my first thought. My second one is, Motherfucker, Ian fucking Blackmon was right all along about this little prick Lucien Phillips. If I live through this, I'll never live it down.

If I live.

He returns with the tea, tilting my head up to allow me to sip it. I take a huge burning gulp, swallowing greedily, siphoning more into my mouth, and lay my head back down. I don't want his smarmy hand to touch me any longer than strictly necessary. "May I sit up?"

"How do you feel?"

I snort. "I've been considerably better, obviously. What's this all about, Lucien? Why are you doing this to me?"

"Don't be coy, Ella, acting as if you don't know."

"Coy? Lucien, I have no idea whatsoever. All I do know is th—"

"Enough! Fine. I'll indulge you in your silly little game and explain. First, I should say that I left all your belongings, including your cell phone, in a storage locker in midtown, safe and sound. When we're done here, I will provide you with the location and the key. I sent Blackmon a message, ostensibly from you, from your phone, telling him you were busy and would be in touch. Obviously, that won't hold him off for very long but it should put him off long enough for you and I to conclude our business together."

I begin to ask him something but he holds up his hand, his eyes dead-fish cold, effectively silencing me.

"I'll ask the questions, my dear. First, which lovely lady put you up to it? Was it Eliza or Maya St. Sauveur? I'm anxious to know."

"Put me up to what? And who is Eliza?"

"Oh, I see this is going to be like pulling teeth." He looks at me with evil intent. "Perhaps I should actually pull your teeth. Will that convince you to talk?"

I slam my head back onto the pillow. He doesn't look insane yet he must be. Obviously he thinks I've done something to him but I have no idea what or why. I don't know how to handle him because I don't yet know what his problem is. I just wait, hoping my silence will prompt him to spill more information.

My plan works. As the seconds stretch into minutes, he begins to talk again.

"You will be telling me who was behind your little exposé, Ella, your attempt to ruin me. You will also provide me with restitution, i.e. the monetary profits you netted from your ill-gotten gains. After both of my requirements have been satisfied, I will liberate you."

Lucien is watching me closely, searching for a reaction. I have none because I haven't the slightest idea what he's prattling about. I only know that, one, I have to pee like a racehorse, and, two, I hate this son of a bitch with all my heart. When I think of all the times I defended him to Ian... it makes me want to rip out his pretty blond hair, follicle deep.

"So, if it wasn't Eliza I must then surmise it was Maya. Correct?"

"Maya? Who did *what*?"

He slaps me. Hard. There's something about a slap to the face: it not only smarts but it somehow shames as well. I gape at him, tears in my eyes from my stinging cheek. I wish I could smack him back. First chance I get, I will. That's a definite promise.

"You know, I didn't want to do that, Ella. Despite myself, I actually like you. If I didn't know what you're capable of, we could have been such good friends. I would have happily welcomed you into my personal life." He begins to stroke my face and I turn my head the other way to escape his touch, eliciting a chuckle from him.

"Oh, sweetheart, I've touched much more than your face. Do you realize you're nearly naked?"

Clouded memories of hands touching me fill my head. I grimace as I try to pull my hands free but they're tied down tautly. I whine in frustration.

The sound I make prods him to move. His hand skims my flesh, causing goose bumps to emerge. They are from utter disgust, not excitement. I hate him so, so much.

"You're very beautiful, Ella. Blackmon is a lucky man." His hand moves to my breasts now.

"Don't touch me! Just tell me what you want from me so I can escape this hell you've consigned me to—for whatever twisted reason."

My words must inflame him for his eyes hold heat now. He yanks down the cups of my bra, exposing my breasts and starts fondling them, pinching me until my eyes water, his eyes boring into mine. The strap across my belly precludes me from shrinking away from his touch. Again I yell. "Stop, Lucien! Tell me what you want, for fuck's sake, and I'll try to make it happen. Please!"

Ignoring me, he continues to run his hand over my body. Now he's touching me intimately, through the scrap of silk that is my panties. For the first time in my life, I wish I were wearing huge granny bloomers. The pig.

"I hold all the power, Ella, see? I can touch you; I can finger-fuck you... or a great deal more. Right now, if I choose. There's not a thing you can do to stop me, either. So be a good girl and play by my rules or you'll be punished. Severely. I will forewarn you: I'm not a kind master."

I stop talking, hoping his anger will wane. Obviously yelling at him is not the brightest thing I can do—it's tantamount to playing with fire. I close my eyes and try to pretend he's not touching me. It's impossible but I keep trying because if not, the rage I'm feeling might strangle me to death if I allow it free rein.

"What's the pin number on your debit card and how much is in your checking account?"

"The pin number is 8989GTH... there's about nine thousand in there now."

"Okay. Where's the rest of the money?"

"The rest of it?"

"Your profits from the book: where did you put the money?"

I clear my throat. So that's what he's after? My money? "Um, I invested much of it in mutual funds and a commercial real estate venture. I do have another bank account but my broker controls it, too."

"Well, by the end of day tomorrow it all has to be in my account in the Cayman Islands so we'll get right to work on it first thing in the a.m. It's not that I need the money, you understand. Far, far from it. It's just the principle of the whole thing.

Now, I'm going to offer you a choice, pretty Ella. Either you tell me who gave you the lowdown on me, or I will show you firsthand what pleasures and pain await you in my special little room here. Which will it be?"

"Please just tell me what you mean by the lowdown, Lucien, and I'll tell you. I swear."

Rolling his eyes, he sighs again. "What I mean is who told you about me, my particular appetite, my little hobby, my room of torture as you so charmingly named it in your book. *This* room."

A gasp escapes me. "You think my book is about you?"

"No. I don't think; I know. I read your book, Ella. You describe my room down to the doorknobs. You describe the... tools... of the trade. My demeanor, my words—everything."

Shaking my head, I swallow whatever saliva I can muster. I'm in a difficult position here: I obviously don't want to tell him about Ian but I may have to. Will Ian care if it means saving me from possible rape and even death? I doubt he would hold it against me in such a circumstance. I may be overestimating his feelings for me but I think... that is, there's the possibility, however remote, that he... *loves* me. I know in this moment wherein my very life may hang in the balance that *I* love *him*. If I ever am so graced again as to see the beautiful contours of his face, I'm going to tell him, come what may. Life is too short to play games. I want him to know what he means to me. If my love is unrequited... well, so be it. No one ever said that life is fair.

"Lucien, may I have another sip of water or tea, please?"

He reaches for the tea and holds it to my lips and again I gulp it. I'm so dehydrated. "I'm sorry; I'm so thirsty. May I have more?"

"It's the drug that's made you dehydrated. The effect should lessen soon."

"You drugged me." It's not a question but rather a punctuating statement. Of course he drugged me. "With what?"

"Rohypnol. It was necessary to ensure things would go my way." He brushes my hair off my face as he again lifts my head to drink. "You're really a very pretty girl, Ella. In other circumstances... well, it's a shame. I like you very much."

"Lucien?"

"Yes?"

"I didn't write my book about you. I don't know Eliza and I only met Maya when you sent me to Venice. My stupid little novel is purely fiction; I researched it on the Internet and the rest is fabrication. I was really broke and wanted to give my girlfriends a fun Christmas present. That's really what it was about."

"And the apt description of my room was just a coincidence? A figment of your girlish imagination then?"

"Well, not exactly." I see his interest perk up when I say that. He's waiting for me to elaborate.

"I have a friend... he's a Dom and he showed me his dungeon. That was the room I described in my book."

"And does this friend have a name?"

Nodding my head in abject misery, I say a silent prayer to Ian to forgive me. "Yes. Ian Blackmon."

His eyes widen and a look of alarm passes over his face. Clearly he wasn't expecting that answer and I find it gratifying on some level. Still, he's holding all the cards and I remain strapped down and powerless. And scared.

Very, very scared.

I watch as the gamut of emotions flicker across his face, ending with wrath. Not good.

"I'll tell you what, Ella. I'm going to allow you some time to think about everything and we'll have another chat later on. Very early tomorrow morning, we'll begin to set things into motion to give me what I want from you and then, if all goes well, you'll be on your way home to Portland by early evening. For now, use your time constructively to think about the ramifications of lying to me. Look around this room and take note of my pretty little whips and other implements." He leans in to whisper in my ear. "I even have a wooden pony and a wicked little harness to wear while riding it, love. You'd look smashing on it," he laughs, "...and we could take some cute photos. I'm going to have to take some pics of you anyway, to ensure your continued cooperation."

Oh no. No, no, no. I need to escape; I need to get away from Lucien before he damages me to the point of no return. "Lucien, can you untie my bonds a little? Enough for me to sit up and drink my tea?"

"I'm afraid not, dear. But I'll help you drink more before I go."

"But I need to, um, use the bathroom, too."

"Oh, I'm afraid that's impossible right now. Unless you want to use a bedpan?"

I shake my head in disgust. I should stop drinking now so I don't make my situation more critical because dehydrated or not, my bladder is screaming for release... but I'm so thirsty so I take a few more sips of tea when he offers the cup to me. And I curse him to the bowels of hell, the lowest circle, the damned of the damned. If hate were a sharp weapon, he'd be gored down the middle, from nave to chap in Shakespeare's words, right about now. I watch him leave the room.

Then I give myself over, body and soul, to the misery that threatens to consume me as fire consumes dry kindling; I indulge it, even welcome it with open arms, until it is entirely spent.

Tackling each day with all its assaults, both big and small, often prevents any quiet contemplation. Right now I have nothing to do but think and my thoughts are ugly. What if I don't survive this experience? What if I never see my friends or family again? But the worst consequence by miles is the one currently dancing inside my feverish brain and refusing to honor my eviction notice: what if I never see Ian again?

Many minutes pass and Lucien doesn't return so I force myself to relax, to escape into the recesses of my mind—because I have to get out of here, one way or another.

Memory is capricious, entirely subject to perception and accumulated experience. Sometimes I remember that first night with Ian as raw, pulsing, and carnal, a coming together born of base physical need to create the beast with two backs, he eager to make me bleed, and I eager to make him come.

Other times, my memory is of a night of sensory feast: he approaches me delicately, revering my beauty, treasuring my innocence. Instead of naked lust there's refined ardor, more sensuous than crude. He doesn't allow me to see him slip the condoms from his dresser drawer—too clinical. He wants to taste me, as one would sip of a fine wine, not consume me, as a wild animal would gnaw at raw meat.

We were in his bedroom, after he convinced me to allow him to make love to me. I didn't take much convincing for I was more than ready to surrender my virginity and I wanted him to be the man to take it. I stood in the middle of that vast room and watched every move he made. In one version, he stalked me like a predator: head down, shoulders swaying, long legs moving fluidly, one in front of the other. In the other version, he sidles over to me gently, a romantic light in his eyes. When he reaches me, he begins to slowly but purposefully remove my clothing.

I had on a cropped button-down shirt, a short denim

skirt, and sandals. I thought he'd begin with the shirt but instead he reached his hands to my thighs, lightly gripping them and then slid them up, right up my skirt and cupped me from behind.

"I've dreamt of seeing you here, in my bedroom, where I can slowly remove your clothes, like relishing the unwrapping of a priceless gift."

I realized then and there that Ian was a born romantic, whether or not he'd ever cop to it. My knees began to give out at the feel of his strong hands kneading my flesh, making my blood stir. Finally, his hands released their grip and traveled seductively up over my hips, my arms, my shoulders, clavicle, stopping just shy of my breasts, and he began to tackle the shirt buttons one by one.

When it flapped open, he leaned in to kiss my throat and chest; ever so slowly his hand snaked around to the back of my bra and unhooked it on the first try. Of course. The shirt dropped off my shoulders, followed immediately by the lacy bra.

"Beautiful. Very, Ariel." His mouth showed his appreciation of my breasts and that's when my knees gave out altogether. Fortunately for me, his arm quickly wrapped around my waist and caught me on the downslide. Soft, warm lips traveled from my breasts up my throat and kissed my lips with his sensuous ones.

"You know, it's said that offering one's throat to another, an alpha specifically, is the sign of ultimate submission, Ariel. It's the most vulnerable position in which to be. I can wrap my hand around almost the entire perimeter of your lily-white throat." His big hand follows his words and his thumb presses down ever so gently on my windpipe but releases it instantly.

Slightly shaking his head as he gazed upon me, he murmured, "A woman who can send an artist running for his brush. Just your slender, elegant neck alone is inspiration enough." As he admired each part of me verbally, he paid homage to it physically. I knew there was a distinct possibility that I might reach a climax long before we joined together. I was already very, very wet for him. Embarrassingly so.

When I stood before him naked and he'd run his hands over every inch of my body, he peered into my eyes. The lighting in the room was dim but I could see him clearly and his eyes were the color of liquid silver. It was also very apparent by a quick peek at his jeans, that he wanted me a bit.

"Ariel. I've never craved a woman the way I crave you right now. But are you sure you want to surrender your virginity to me tonight? Isn't it possible you'd like to wait until you're with someone you love deeply?"

There was a thought that quickly flitted uninvited through my mind: *I could love* you *deeply*. I shook my head. "No. Tonight. You. This is what I want, Ian. I've waited long enough, too long. Please."

Nodding but saying nothing, he took my hand, kissed it, and then guided me to the bed. He was so sweet and soft with me. When I was lying down and he was beside me, he again began to speak. "You do know it will probably hurt?"

I nodded and licked my lips, unwilling or possibly unable to say anything.

He was still wearing his jeans and tee-shirt so he rose from the bed and quickly undressed, removing his shirt, shoes, socks, and belt. He left his jeans on, while he used his mouth and hands to ready my body for his.

When the time finally arrived, he finished undressing.

That was when I got my first look at a naked Ian and it was as glorious as the first sunset I've ever beheld. My God, it was almost indecent how perfect were his proportions. I think my mouth watered—as well as other parts of me. Yes, I wanted him easily as much as he wanted me. Almost certainly more.

In a few moments he was back with me, warming my body with his own. We kissed for long minutes; he kept at me until I was gasping for breath. "Mmm, your mouth is so delicious, Ariel. I could spend the night just kissing you without doing anything else."

"I want else," I whispered and was rewarded by a megawatt grin.

"So do I." His hand glided down my hip and then up between my thighs until he caressed me intimately. I was embarrassed because I could feel how dripping wet I was but my condition only fanned his ardor. I could hear his sharp intake of breath the moment he touched me. Spurred on, he leaned over me on his knees and spread my legs, his fingers hooking around my knees and pulling them all the way up.

"If I do it gently and slowly, it will prolong your discomfort, Ariel. I'm just going to be quick about it. Okay, love?"

I nodded, both terrified and overwhelmed with excitement. He unfurled a condom over himself as I stared transfixed and leaned in toward me, resting his weight on his forearms. "Kiss me, beautiful girl." His voice had roughened in the last few moments, sounding husky now, even raspy.

I reached up to his lips and did as he instructed, allowing his tongue inside my mouth in a dance that mimicked the other one we were about to do. I felt him, his body heat off the chart, between my legs and then he pressed his hips up, thrusting inside me, and the pain was unlike anything I'd felt before: intense, burning, tearing pressure. He kept kissing me and I tried to kiss him back but I had to focus on my pain, on getting past it. Would it never end? I moaned because I had to but he swallowed my moan, shared my suffering, but kept pressing into me with determination, and finally, finally the hymen broke and he pushed past where the barrier once blocked. Uncharted territory... without any pain.

"It's done, Ariel. Are you okay?" His smile was reassuring but his eyes were triumphant—a conquest for the alpha male that couldn't be denied.

"Yes," I breathed out, just then realizing I hadn't taken a breath in a while. "I'm fine."

He stayed still, allowing my body to acclimate to his

invasion and we just gazed into each other's eyes and that's when I knew I could so easily love him forever. Could he love me? I really had no idea but I was planning to find out. Soon.

"I'm going to move now, Ariel. Ready?"

"Mmmhmm."

"Look at me," he whispered as his hips pulled back at a snail's pace and then thrust in fast. He eyed me carefully the whole time. Whatever reaction he sought, he got, for he did it again. When there was no problem, no protest on my end, he smiled and said, "We're ready to dance, love," and began the ancient rhythm in earnest.

Then there were no more words, just motion. Beautiful, wonderful motion and he was careful to swivel his hips to touch every part of me, as if in search of something. Reaching down between us, he used his fingers to stoke me hotter, and I climbed ever higher, into the clouds, ascending K2, climbing until I ran out of earth and the room flashed to bright white and I came forcefully.

He kept going but I saw on his face the struggle to keep from being dragged into the vortex of my orgasm... but he prevailed. I wanted to see him come badly so I selfishly tried to break his control. I reached my hands around his narrow hips and yanked him to me as I flexed my hips up to him and tightened everything on him. I kept up the torture, trying to keep up with his flawless rhythm but unable to. Still my efforts paid off in minutes as he arched his back and the sexiest of moans traveled up his throat; his eyes closed and his movements slowed and jerked. Then he collapsed and I reveled in his weight on top of me. I wrapped myself around him and wanted to tell him I loved him then and there, but how ridiculous. I couldn't love him. Not yet.

But... I did.

Now I invite the tears to come. Sometimes a girl needs to indulge in, celebrate, hell, even revel in, her right to self-pity. My present circumstances give me full rights. On the heel of that thought, comes the million-dollar question and the one that provokes a full-on crying jag: will I ever see my beautiful Ian again?

Chapter 29

Feeling ready to detonate, Ian takes another swig of his Glenlivet on ice but it doesn't help… not at all. Knowing that Ella might be in danger and being hours away from her is well beyond frightening, and galaxies beyond frustrating. There isn't a word in the English language to call the turbulence roiling inside his head, the turmoil inhabiting his gut. His body, viciously tense, is akin to a bungee cord on the upswing, the reciprocal force being stronger than the original, the reaction far outweighing the original action.

When would Butler reach the apartment and what would he find when he did? He hated putting another person—a total stranger—in harm's way, but he simply had no other choice. Someone had to get to Ella right away and it wasn't going to be him so… His animal instincts, the kind of cues that have nothing to do with rational thought and everything to do with primal sense, told him that Butler was up to the task: there was something about the man that bristled with unabridged power. For now, Ian would just have to rely on his instincts for his choices were nonexistent. Taking another pull on the scotch, he leans back in the plane seat and searches for a way to calm the savage beast within.

Daniel Butler stares at the apartment door, Sean Blackwell and Tom Pierce right behind him. Sean eyeballs the lock and shakes his head.

"We're not going to disable that lock anytime soon, Mr. Butler. The mechanism means business but complicating it tenfold? That strike plate is serious armor. Even a drill won't quickly compromise it. We need to find another way in."

Daniel nods, as if in agreement with Blackwell, but he knows he could get past the lock easily. He won't, however, do it in front of witnesses. He turns his head to the side to address his security team. "Sean, I want you and Tom to case the apartment from the exterior. Figure out how many windows belong to the apartment and if there's a way to get to them. Also, take note of which ones are lit, etc. Meantime, I'll wait here to ensure no one exits. Make it quick."

"Yes, sir. Let's go, Pierce."

Placing an ear to the metal door, Daniel listens carefully. He is fairly certain there's no one in the first room. He knows Ella is in there with Lucien Phillips but he also senses two other men, possibly three. They may be inside or it's possible they were recently there and have since left: he's just not sure. Before his men can return, though, he needs to see to the lock. Marshaling his concentration, he focuses on breaching it and within twenty seconds, the door clicks open.

Tom Pierce looks up skeptically at the long row of windows. "This is not going to be a piece of cake, Sean. It *would* have to be on the third floor, right in the middle of the damn building... and no adjacent neighbor within leaping distance, damn it."

Sean Blackwell tears his eyes away from the bank of tall windows long enough to smirk at the new guy: Tom Pierce had just started working for Daniel Butler the week before last. "Between you and me, Pierce, we won't have to."

Pierce furrows his eyebrows quizzically. "Why not?"

"How much you wanna bet that by the time we get back inside, Butler will have the door open?"

"Not possible. That Medeco is some serious hardware even without the strike plate. It's not gonna happen."

"Care to put some green on it?"

Not a gambling man, Pierce nonetheless is tempted by the easy money. "How much we talkin' about?"

Sean tilts his head in consideration. "Let's keep it little: how about twenty bucks?"

"You're on." They fist bump and Sean says, "Come on, let's go back so I can collect my twenty. I'll use it to buy us a few beers when we're finished here."

Snorting his disdain, Pierce leads the way back inside. The two brawny men, dressed head to toe in black, take the stairs up to the third floor.

Easing the hallway door open quietly, they make their silent way over to their employer. Daniel turns his head as they approach.

"We got lucky. Someone exited the apartment and I was able to get to the door before it locked again," Daniel whispers as the two near him.

Pierce wears the most astonished expression on his pockmarked face and wants to curse out loud badly. He'd been had in a sucker bet, no doubt. Blackwell was right, damn it. Should he wait to pay him so Butler can't see? His partner solves the problem for him by extending his hand, palm up. Scowling, Pierce pulls a twenty out of his wallet and forks it over.

Watching the transaction with thinly veiled amusement, Daniel starts issuing orders. "I'm going for the girl since she's met me before. Sean, I want you to head directly toward the subject whose photo I showed you—Phillips—and incapacitate him as quickly as possible. Tom, you need to take care of anyone else there and if there are no additional bodies, then assist Sean with Phillips. I'm not sure what kind of response he'll give us." He arches his brows as he trains piercing green eyes on both men. "Are we clear?"

Both nod and Daniel inhales deeply. "Let's do this."

The first room is almost completely dark; feeble ambient light radiates from a hallway. Like thieves in the night, the three move single file deeper into the apartment. Daniel is in the lead and ducks his head fast into the first room, pulling it back in case anyone is poised to attack. Clear. He waves his hand to let the others know and they move to the second door.

At that precise point in time miles away, Ian is wondering if he should call Butler. Dragging his hands through his hair, which, by now is so manhandled that it gives him the look of a madman, he considers his options. If he calls Butler and the man is at a crucial moment in the operation, it can screw things up. But if he doesn't call and he doesn't hear from Butler soon, he might just spontaneously combust into flames. Indecisive only when it comes to Ella, he sits uncomfortably in his skin as understanding seeps into his brain, the knowledge that this will be the quality of his life if he succeeds in keeping her—perennially on the edge of his seat, unsure, confused, enticed, and always wanting more. As he acknowledges it, he has his moment of epiphany: he loves Ella. He is in love with her. And if by some divine grace he has the chance again, he must tell her—no more denial and no more prevaricating. Ian knows one other thing for sure: if Phillips was in front of him now, the bastard would die young, but he definitely wouldn't leave a beautiful corpse.

With his acceptance of the status quo, Ian finally finds a tiny measure of peace through resignation, leaning back in his chair to wait for Butler to call.

They find Ella in the third room. She's lying on a bed, the light dim, and she appears to be fast asleep. Daniel waves his two men on to continue the search, as he makes his way into the bedroom. Leaning carefully over the young woman, Daniel touches her hair ever so gingerly. "Ella?"

Her eyes slit open a tiny bit and for a long moment, she just stares at him uncomprehending. Daniel waits patiently until he notices a spark of recognition in her eyes. "Daniel, right?" Her voice is rusty from sleep.

"Yes, Ella. Ian sent me to get you. Are you okay?"

She sits up, rubbing her eyes, and then glances down frantically at herself and then her surroundings. "Where am I?"

"At Phillips' apartment. Come on, we're leaving."

She looks around at the room as if seeing it for the first time. "I was in a black room."

Daniel eyes her closely, wondering if she's been drugged. He also looks confused by where and how he found her. "Listen to me, Ella. Right now all I care about is getting you out of here to safety and calling Ian so he doesn't go into full cardiac arrest. I'm taking you to my house where my fiancée can look after you until Ian's flight gets in. Do you understand what I'm saying to you?"

She jerks her head. "Where is Lucien?"

"Don't worry about him. Let's just get you out of here."

Daniel doesn't want to touch Ella since he's unsure of exactly what she's endured at the hands of Phillips but she's responding too slowly so he needs to help. He reaches his hand to her legs and gently slides them to the floor. She's fully dressed but for her shoes so he looks around on the floor, finally spotting them near a tall dresser. In less than a minute, he's squiring her out the door. Whispering into the mouthpiece attached to his collar, he alerts his men that he's leaving with Ella. Once outside the building, he stops long enough to speak with Sean through the mike.

"Sean? Status?"

"Found him in the next room asleep. We've immobilized him and waiting for your orders, sir."

"Keep him comfortable but restrained until we figure out exactly what went down. Did you search the rest of the premises?"

"Roger on that. Empty."

"Good. Can you both stay or should I order reinforcements?"

"We can stay, sir. The only problem is that he may have more coming and there's only two of us."

"I should know within the hour how I want to proceed. I'm taking Ella to my house and then heading right back to you. Over."

As soon as Daniel flags down a cab and he and Ella are seated inside, he pulls out his phone to call Ian.

"What's going on?" Ian's strained voice answers on the first ring.

"I have Ella, safe and sound. We're in a taxi now, going to my house. I'll leave Ella there with Olivia and then head back to my men at the subject's apartment. They have him restrained, awaiting my orders."

"Do you know what happened yet?"

"No. I found Ella asleep in a bedroom, alone, fully dressed. My men found Phillips in another bedroom, also asleep. That's all I know at this time. What's your ETA?"

"I'm still more than two hours away from landing at Newark. I'd like to kill the bastard but I don't want to keep your men there and in possible harm's way. What do you recommend?"

"I'll question him and see what he has to say. I may have to let him go before you get here, Ian. Let's see how it all shakes out. I'll keep you posted but meantime you can relax knowing Ella is safe."

"Yes. That sounds good, Daniel. I don't even know what to say to you other than that I'm profoundly grateful—to you, your men, and your fiancée."

"I'm sure you'll pay it forward, Ian. I'd put Ella on the phone but she's fallen back asleep—there's a possibility she's been drugged."

Daniel hears a muttered curse on the other end.

"Have her call me if she wakes up before I get there. I'll let you know as soon as I land."

"Very good. Until then."

As the landing gear kisses the ground gently, Ian can barely summon admiration for the pilot's skill: his entire body is vibrating with the need to see and touch Ella. He's decided that Ella's well-being far eclipses his own need for satisfaction so he plans to go directly to Daniel's and see his girl. The moment the plane comes to a stop, he unbuckles and darts into the cockpit.

"Scott, can we keep the Gulfstream here for 24 hours?"

The pilot looks fatigued so he readily agrees. "Just give me about two hours notice when you're ready to return to Portland, Mr. Blackmon."

"Scott, check yourself into the Plaza or whatever nice hotel you like, order room service, and get some sleep. Charge everything to my account, of course. I really appreciate your off-the-cuff readiness. I'll ensure that appreciation is translated into dollars and cents."

Before the pilot can reply, Ian is opening the door and exiting the plane, hoping he can find a cab at this hour of the night. Turns out he doesn't have to for as he exits the airfield, a man in dark clothes is standing there awaiting him.

"Mr. Blackmon? Ian Blackmon?"

"Yes," he replies, eyeing the man warily.

"Mr. Butler sent me to drive you, sir. May I take your luggage?"

Ian had just a small bag slung over his shoulder. "No need, but I do appreciate the ride. Please lead the way."

It's nearly five a.m. when Ian finally gets to Daniel Butler's house. Daniel is waiting for him in the entrance hall so there's no need to knock or ring the bell. Ian had phoned him right before the car pulled up in front of the brownstone.

"Come in," Daniel steps aside, ushering Ian into the house.

"I need to see her first and then we'll talk. Is that acceptable with you, Daniel? I know you're probably exhausted but I have to see Ella."

"That's fine. Follow me and I'll take you to her."

Ian follows Daniel up a long staircase covered with a plush scarlet runner and down a hall. They stop before a closed door and Daniel turns to him. "I'll be waiting downstairs in the kitchen. Come find me when you're ready to talk."

Nodding, Ian says, "Just give me five minutes and I'll join you."

Opening the door quietly, Ian steps in and waits until his eyes adjust to the darkness. There's a dim nightlight not too far from the bed and in its faint glow, he sees her beautiful face and she's sleeping peacefully. He quietly walks over to the bed, leaning his weight down slowly. "Ella?"

No response.

"Ella?" She moans and slowly her eyes open. Ian scowls: Ella is normally a light sleeper so drugs are more than a good possibility.

When recognition sets in, she bolts upright and throws her arms around his neck. "Ian," she sobs and with the utterance of his name, she's off, the tears so violently forthcoming that she soon begins to gasp for oxygen.

Stroking her hair, he tells her to calm down, that she's all right but the weeping is as unstoppable as a storm-swollen river, so he just holds her until she's spent. "Better?" he asks when she begins to quiet.

"Yes, so much better. Ian... I'm not even sure what happened to me."

His brows arch in surprise. "What do you mean, Ella?"

"It was horrible but... when I woke up, when Daniel woke me up... I was dressed and in a different room. I'm not sure what was dream and what was reality. I'm so confused."

"In all likelihood, you were drugged, Ella."

She nods, tightening her embrace.

"Can you tell me what you remember?"

"I went to Lucien's loft for the editing conference. Lucien was there... and there were two other men, Michael and Nico. We discussed the film for about an hour, looked at some footage and..."

"Did you eat or drink anything, Ella?"

"Um, yes. I had orange juice... and I think... yes, I had a cookie, too."

"Okay," he prods gently, "what next?"

She shakes her head, eyebrows furrowing in confusion. "I don't know. I thought I was in a black room and I was strapped down to a bed in my underwear and..." she looks up, sheepishly. "I don't know if this actually happened or not."

Ian knows his expression must be one of utter disbelief but he can't help it. Was Ella remembering what actually happened, or was it a dream or hallucination triggered by a drug? He couldn't be sure right now either.

He clears his throat. "Ella. Did you check out of your hotel?"

"Yes."

"You did?"

"Yes," she whispered softly, "I missed you so much, so I decided to fly home right after the editing conference. I booked an early evening flight to Portland."

"What did you do with your luggage?"

She furrows her brow. "I thought I left it in the lobby of the hotel... with their permission... but Lucien told me it was in a storage locker..."

"I see. Okay. Tell me what you remember, regardless of whether or not you're sure if it really happened. Just tell me quickly so we can move on from there."

So it all comes out in a torrent; she tells him everything, trying to avoid seeing the muscles in his face pull taut with every sordid detail. "But when Daniel woke me up, I was fully dressed and in a different room. I asked Daniel about the black room but he looked confused."

"Okay. I'm going to go have a talk with Monsieur Phillips and get to the bottom of this fiasco. In the mean—"

"Please don't, Ian. If it did happen then he's crazy... and if it didn't, then maybe I am. Either way, I don't want you to get hurt."

"You're not crazy, Ella. He did something to you, even if it was simply slipping you some drugs. You didn't just fall into Alice's rabbit hole."

"Don't leave me," she clutches at him. "Ian, there's something I have to tell you. I promised myself if I ever saw you again, I'd say it."

"I have something to tell you, too. Ella. But I need to go talk to Daniel first. He's been up all night because of us and I don't want to keep him waiting any longer. Can our conversation hold for just five more minutes, baby?"

"Yes, of course. Five more minutes," she repeats like a mantra and then kisses him sweetly. Ian nearly begins to weep—with relief, with passion for her, with love. He loves Ella so fucking much.

Entering the large state-of-the-art kitchen, Ian finds Daniel sitting at the table, two steaming espressos waiting. "Espresso?"

Daniel laughs. "I figured neither of us is going to sleep anytime soon so what the hell. I have to go into the office in a couple of hours."

"I'm sorry about this huge imposition. If you would bring me up to speed on Phillips, I'll take Ella and get out of your hair. I'm not in the habit of asking so much of people I've just met."

"Ah, but you do of people you know a while? I'll bear that in mind before I get to know you any better, Ian."

Ian manages to muster a chuckle. "So what happened when you got back to his apartment?"

Daniel sips his espresso and then shakes his head. "Not much. The man denied any wrongdoing. Said Ella started feeling ill so he put her in his guestroom to rest. What we found didn't contradict anything he said."

"Ella's story was wildly at odds with that innocent account," Ian says, raking his hands through his hair. "But she admits she's not sure if what she remembers is real or dream. It could be that she was drugged and hallucinated as a result. But why would he drug her and then do nothing?"

"Didn't you say he checked her out of her hotel?"

Ian shakes his head. "Turns out she herself did it. But, honestly, I've always felt this guy was a sleaze; there was something about him... Didn't you say you felt he was dangerous?"

Daniel nods tiredly. "Yes. I definitely sensed something amiss there... but honestly it could be danger in the predatory-male sense, and not anything too much worse, Ian. I haven't been around him enough to get a clear bead on the guy."

"So what became of Monsieur Phillips?"

"After we interrogated him—and trust me, we ensured that it was not a pleasant experience for him—we released him and left him alone in his apartment. I could have kept him there but I rightly assumed you'd want to attend to Ella and I had to either pull my guys out of there or send in reinforcements to back them up. We could easily catch up with him again if you require it."

"No, I'll take it from here. Right now I'll take Ella and check into a hotel to sleep for a while. When my pilot is ready to leave, we'll head back to Portland and the mess I left there."

"Forget the hotel. Stay here. Olivia was going to skip her classes to stay with Ella in the morning but since you're here, she'll go to school. I'm leaving soon, too. You'll have the house to yourselves for most of the day. It's ridiculous for you to get Ella up only to go to a hotel. Seriously."

"I am exhausted. Okay, thank you, Daniel. I regret you have to go to work without getting any sleep."

"No problem. I have an early-morning meeting I can't miss and then I'll sack out for a few hours in my office. There's a very comfortable couch in there."

Ian rises to his feet. "I'll leave you to start your day, in that case. I'm crashing from the adrenaline surge of the past few hours so I'll accept your gracious offer and get some sleep. If anything more comes out of this situation, I'll be sure to let you know. Thank you and in the event that I don't have the pleasure of meeting your fiancée, please tell her of our gratitude, both mine and Ella's."

Daniel nods. "I certainly will. Pleasant dreams."

By the time he returns to Ella, she's in a deep sleep once again and Ian doesn't have the heart to wake her. They could have their talk in the morning... or afternoon or whatever time they finally wake up. Quickly brushing his teeth in the en-suite bath, he strips off his clothes and gets into the bed behind Ella, spooning her from behind and saying a silent prayer of thanks that all ended well. When he's finished, he lies in the quiet room, listening to Ella breathing, his hand on her chest as it ebbs and flows with her respiration, and whispers into her ear. "I love you, Ella."

Chapter 30

It's nearly one o'clock in the afternoon when I open my eyes. Physically I feel bizarrely well but my mind is swimming with anxious thoughts. The night with Lucien and all his sinister words seems far away now and based on how Daniel found me, might not have happened the way I remember it. And now I am left wondering if it happened at all.

Next to me lay a sleeping Ian, his face so boyish and serene in slumber it's almost irresistible. I don't think I'll ever get enough of watching him sleep unless he begins to snore or drool—though sex gods like him don't generally have icky tendencies like those, do they?

Last night I wanted to tell him I love him but he had to speak to Daniel and I fell asleep while he was gone. I intend to remedy that negligence as soon as he opens his pretty eyes. I refuse to waste any more time playing games. If I learned anything from my experience with Lucien, it was that.

Lucien fucking Phillips: the new demon around my neck. It would be far easier if my memories were real and I could just cast him off as a sicko fuck whom I will never see again. But what if they were hallucinations? For my whole life, I've always reacted badly to drugs—even cold medicine makes me hallucinate. Not like yesterday, but still. If someone did slip me a drug, it's not impossible that everything that followed was in my mind only.

But the fact remains that he would have still been evil enough to drug me. Why? As far as I could tell, he didn't rape me. In my memories slash hallucinations, he did take liberties, even violated me through unwanted touching. Still, is that reason enough to drug someone? I need to know what really happened. Leaning back on the bed, I close my eyes to think about what I should do next when I feel the bed shift.

"Good afternoon, beautiful."

"Ian."

Concern shades his eyes. "How are you feeling?"

I smile. "I feel quite good, considering. How do you feel?"

"I've been better. But I am overwhelmed with relief that you're okay. Ella..."

"Yes?"

"Scott will be flying us back to Portland later today. But before I go, I need to deal with Phillips. I don't want any argument from you; I promise I'll be careful. I want you to stay here in Daniel's house and wait for me. Will you do that?"

"Please let it go for now, Ian. It's not like we can have him arrested if there's no proof. I suppose I can go to the hospital and have my blood tested for drugs but even so, it's still just a matter of his word against mine. And there's no evidence of any crime. Why prolong the misery?" Before he can even answer, I plunge on. I don't want to be sidetracked from saying what I want to say to him. Nor do I want to have time to chicken out.

"Before we get involved in another argument, there's something I have to say to you, Ian."

Worry flits across his face but he manages to compose his face quickly into a blank expression as only he can do so quickly and so well. "You have my complete attention."

I slide down so my face is level with his, as he is still lying down. Cradling his face in both hands, I peer into his eyes. "I need to tell you something I should have told you a while ago, as soon as I realized it was true." My heart is smashing against my ribcage, terrified he might reject me when I say the words aloud. Only when I remember how I felt when I thought I might not ever see him again do I also remember my courage.

"Ian, I love you." As soon as I say the words I look away; I can't bring myself to look into his eyes after seeing the initial shock that flashed through them. But I bravely forge ahead, my eyes trained on my hand that's currently twisting and torturing the bedsheet. "What I mean to say... is that I've fallen in love with you. I want to be clear."

Silence. I'm still looking down so I have no idea what's happening with him but I just can't look up. Suddenly he takes my hand and brings it to his lips. Does that mean he's not freaking out, or he is and kissing my hand is better than having to say something? The room is so silent but for the rustling of the sheet I'm crumpling with my fist.

"Ella? Look at me."

Finally I drag my eyes up to his: he doesn't look upset but I can't be sure. I wait as he gathers his thoughts to speak, my heart continuing the mad beating.

"I love you, too, Ella. I'm very much in love with you. And I want to take care of you so you never come into harm's way again. I couldn't bear anything happening to you. You mean the world to me; you're the light and the music." He kisses my hand again and then leans in to kiss my lips. When he deepens the kiss, I whisper against his beautiful, sensuous lips, "I didn't brush my teeth yet" and he tosses his head back and laughs. What a beautiful sound is Ian Blackmon's spontaneous laughter and my heart is light again after the darkness of the night.

I hear a knock at the front door and then Daniel enters the hall. Ian and I are in the kitchen doorway, just off the foyer. For a moment, I'm taken aback for I'd forgotten just how handsome Daniel is. I promptly collect myself for I need to express my gratitude to him but I feel so strange: the man went so far out of his way for me and I don't know him at all.

"Daniel," I begin to say, "I can't thank you enough for your help last night. I feel ridiculous that it came to that...

and frankly I'm still confused as to how it did. Regardless, what you did was extraordinary."

The beautiful man smiles at me, his eyes warm for the first time since I met him. "I'm just glad I was able to help. I trust you're feeling well?"

I nod. "Very well. Would it be alright if I take a shower?"

"Of course, please make yourself at home. Everything you need is in the closet in the bathroom."

"Okay. Thank you."

As I exit the room, I hear Daniel ask Ian if he might speak to him for a moment. I'm conflicted: I want to stay and eavesdrop, but I need to shower and dress and I don't want to be caught listening. Maybe I can just stay for a few words...

Daniel begins the conversation. "I have a bit more news, Ian."

"Oh?"

"I sent more men over to Phillips' apartment today to see what's up."

There's a silent pause. Then Ian responds. "Really? Daniel, may I ask why you're going out of your way for us, to such an extent? Forgive me, but you didn't initially strike me as the selfless type. I hope that doesn't sound ungrateful for that's not my intent—I'm just curious."

Another pause ensues. They must be sizing each other up. Two enormously powerful alpha males together in the same room makes for fascinating theatre and I wholeheartedly wish I could sidle back in there, unnoticed, to watch the show.

A throat clears. "No, I suppose selfless is not among the words I'd use to describe myself. Still, I try to live up to the ideal my Olivia sets for me. She's such a pure soul and I know I don't deserve her. Before I met her, I lived a sort of bacchanalian existence and I wasn't a very kind person to others—too absorbed with self-gratification to take stock of those around me. I have much atoning to do to be worthy of my beautiful girl. Consider this a stop on the road."

There's no immediate response from Ian and I really can't loiter any longer, not safely, so I make my way upstairs, back to the room where we slept to take a shower. I'll have to put on the same clothes I wore yesterday because my luggage is still at the hotel.

Chapter 31

Ian stares at Daniel. "So exactly what did they discover?"

Rubbing his eyes with the heels of his hands, Daniel leans back in his chair, his sleepless night catching up with him. "He's not acting like an innocent man. For one thing, he's used the day to pack up much of the apartment. Further, he had a pack of painters in there. Sean Blackwell, one of the two guys with me last night, claims he did see a black room but it looked to be an ordinary bedroom, nothing strange on the walls or anything. Still, it appears that Phillips is planning an extended leave so it might behoove you to pay him a visit before he goes. I can have a security team accompany you. Right now they're on standby waiting to hear from me."

Ian didn't need any convincing. "Have them meet me in front of the building. I want my hands on that piece of shit."

Daniel nods and punches in a number on his phone. "Morell? Is Luna still there with you? Good. Ian Blackmon will be on his way shortly. He'll meet you outside the building in about twenty." He looks up at Ian but says nothing. "Very good. Yes, check in with me before you leave the premises."

He nods to Ian. "It's a go."

Ian stands in front of the apartment door listening. He hears someone moving about within and nods to Butler's people: an African-American man named Peter Morell and a woman, small but built like a tank, Luna

Stephens. Daniel assured him they were both among the best he had. "Ready?" he asks the two.

The tall man nods. "Step aside, Mr. Blackmon."

Blackmon complies and Morell kicks the door in, Medeco lock and all. The man is a martial arts phenom; it takes only three kicks before the door flies open.

Ian gapes at the man and smirks. "Why, thanks. Glad you're on my side." With that comment, he strides right through the door, coming up on one very startled Lucien Phillips.

Phillips is dressed all in black: silk shirt, tailored pants, and boots. His blond hair slicked back, he looks every inch the European artiste. Apart from his initial surprise, he appears calm and expectant of the visit. Ian takes a deep breath, wanting nothing more than to put his fist through the man's face. Keeping his voice light he says, "Going somewhere?" as his eyes take in the suitcases near the door.

"Yes, as a matter of fact. I'm returning to Paris. I suppose you're the follow-up act to last night?"

"Yes, that's right." Ian gestures to the two people standing just to his right and a step behind him. "Meet punch and kick." He leans closer to Lucien's smug face. "And I'm smear," he whispers, enunciating the word clearly. "We're all here to pay you a visit, Monsieur Phillips."

Crossing his arms, Lucien sighs dramatically. "Fine. My attorney will be arriving shortly, just for your information. I would very much like to inquire as to Ella's health but I'm quite sure you won't oblige me. So in the interests of everyone's time, get to the point. What do you want?"

"Apart from a pound of your flesh, you mean? I want answers, fuckhead. Right now. I want to know exactly what happened, minute by minute, after Ella walked through your door. She went to your other place, as I understand it. How did she end up here?"

"We had our meeting at the loft. I was planning on coming back here afterward—alone—but she started complaining that her head hurt and she felt dizzy and ill. I didn't want to just leave her so I put her in a cab and took her here. When we got here, I told her to lie down and rest. She did and fell asleep. She was still sleeping when your friends broke in late last night, as was I."

"Mmmhmm. Who sent me the text message from her phone?"

"I did. Rather than have to explain the long and somewhat convoluted story, I just thought it would be easier for all concerned."

"Where's Ella's phone?"

He shrugs casually. "I suppose it's still at the loft. I really don't know. I took her shoulder bag with us but if the phone wasn't in there, I don't know."

"When I tracked the phone, it showed a midtown location, not uptown. Why?"

"I haven't the slightest idea. Sorry."

"Do you have a black bedroom in this apartment?"

"Why?"

"I'll ask the questions. You'll answer them. Do you?"

"Yes, one of the bedrooms was painted black. I had two of the rooms painted white today so it's not black anymore."

"And why would you have them painted today?"

"Because I'm subletting the place and the tenant asked me to do so before I vacated. She didn't care for the vibrant colors."

"Was Ella in the black room at all?"

"No."

"Was she undressed at any time during her stay here?"

"No."

"Why did you drug her?"

"I did not."

"Was anyone else near her drink?"

"Not that I'm aware of."

"What were you planning on doing with her?"

"Nothing. I was waiting for her to wake up to see how she felt. I checked on her periodically before I went to sleep. She was breathing normally and her temperature felt fine. I saw no reason to call a doctor."

Ian steps closer to Phillips, uncomfortably close until the two are nearly nose to nose. "Allow me to make one thing perfectly clear: I don't believe a word you say, Phillips. You're a slimy liar. If you ever come near Ella again, I will kill you and throw your body to the alligators, even if it means I have to fly it to the Everglades. You are going to cut a check to Ella for all monies you owe her and you will send it to me. And then Ella and I are going to live the rest of our long, happy lives without ever having to waste another nanosecond on the likes of you. Do you understand?"

He scowls. "Yes, I understand. I like Ella, very much, and I tried to help her yesterday. I suppose it's true when they say no good deed goes unpunished. But I agree to all your terms. Now get out."

"Gladly. But first..." he shifts his weight onto one foot and swings at the blond man, his fist making a satisfying thud as it makes contact with Lucien's jaw. Ian follows it up with a left hook to the gut. When Phillips doubles over, Ian bends his leg and grabbing the blond man's head, rams it into his knee, breaking his nose. Then he straightens up, adjusts his clothing, and turns to leave.

"Now I'll get out. Have a nice day."

"You fucking asshole! I'm going to have you arrested for assault, you motherfucker." Phillips is yelling the words as blood spurts everywhere, running down his face, coloring his teeth, and spattering the formerly pristine hardwood floor.

Ian doesn't even turn to admire his handiwork. He only slightly tilts his head so the other man could hear his frigid voice. "A word of advice, Phillips: if you try any retribution against me whatsoever, Ella will file charges of attempted rape against you. We've already had her blood tested for drugs and I don't need to tell you what the results were. There's also that woman whom Ella interviewed in Venice. I suspect she'd have something to add to support our allegations, not to mention your ex-girlfriend. Eliza, I believe her name is? Eliza surely has many colorful stories to share with us. After all, a leopard never changes its spots. I'm a very wealthy man with exceedingly talented lawyers. The only one you'll hurt by trying to get at me is yourself. And I'll come gunning for you again if I have as much as a phone call from anyone in law enforcement. I do hope I've made myself crystal clear."

Ten seconds later, Ian and his security personnel are out the door.

Chapter 32

I'm standing under the scalding hot spray in the large steam shower when it occurs to me that I might be washing off any evidence of Lucien's wrongdoing... *if* there was any wrongdoing. Should I go to the hospital to check for rape? Would they even be able to tell if Lucien covered his tracks and didn't leave anything behind to find?

I rack my brain, trying to remember details. Snatches of conversation with Lucien are within reach... about my book; I can almost feel his hands sliding over my body *gently*.

Gently? The thought alone compels me to scrub raw my skin and every part of my body, rape kit be damned. I just want to put the ordeal behind me.

Without warning, flashes of memory come hurtling at me, staccato—like bursts of machine-gun fire. Lucien's handsome face. A deep voice, *not Lucien's*. Other different voices. Men's voices.

Restraints. I remember being tied down and I raise my wrists up in front of my face. On the left one is a faint red mark but that's it. Nothing on the right: the skin is without blemish. It's impossible to tell what made the mark on the left wrist but it's one thin straight line. Ignoring the built-in seat in the steam shower, I lean against the wall to check my ankles. Nothing. Damn it.

Words rush back at me and I try to force them away: I don't want to think about all the horrid things Lucien said to me, the comment about pulling my teeth, the threat about the wooden pony. Could my subconscious really have manufactured it all? Admittedly, I'd been traumatized by the wooden pony at the BDSM club that long-ago night. Ian was, too. Could that scarring memory have manifested itself in this way? Ian's been continuously telling me Lucien is evil; if I weren't in my right mind, could my brain have created the whole horrific scenario? I just don't know and it is driving me crazy.

Once I'm done with my shower, my skin is hot pink from the dual attack of the hot water and the vigorous washing I gave myself. Quickly blotting the water in my hair with a fluffy white towel, I begin to dress.

Ick. Scrunching my nose in distaste, I begin to don dirty clothes. As soon as I'm ready, I want to go to the hotel and get my things. I suppose I can change on the plane. Once I finish dressing, I apply some light make-up to banish my ghostly pallor and then go downstairs in search of Ian.

He is nowhere to be found, I soon learn. As I'm about to give up and return to the bedroom, the beautiful Daniel emerges from behind a closed door.

"Ella. Feel better?"

"Yes, very much so, thank you. I just wish I had clean clothes to put on."

Nodding, he says. "I sent a driver to pick up your luggage—I just hope the hotel will release it to him. He's in full livery so perhaps they'll trust that."

I feel strange when Daniel looks at me, as if he can see right through me, down to my naked soul. It's probably his eyes: they're very light green and have an incredible depth to them. His satiny voice interrupts my wayward thoughts.

"There's fresh coffee in the kitchen. Would you care for some?"

"Yes. Thank you. Is your fiancée home? I'd like to thank her for her kindness and hospitality."

"No. She has a full day at school today. She probably won't return till evening."

I glance at the mariner's clock on the console table: almost three. "Do you know where Ian is?'

An inscrutable look flickers across his face but disappears just as quickly. "Yes. He'll be returning very soon, Ella. He had a task to attend to. Please make yourself as comfortable as possible; help yourself to coffee and whatever else you desire. I hope you don't think me rude but I'm planning on escaping upstairs for a nap. I don't think I can remain coherent much longer."

"Oh, please. Don't let me keep you up. You must be exhausted, Daniel. I can't begin to tell you how much I appreciate your kindness."

Daniel holds up his hand to stop me. "Please think nothing of it. I'm just glad you're feeling better." He smiles, "If you'll excuse me."

Sipping a cup— a bowl really—of coffee with steamed milk, I wait for Ian to return while my kaleidoscope of mixed-up thoughts keeps me occupied. Evicting all the thoughts associated with Lucien and my time with him, I concentrate on Ian.

So... *I did it*. This morning I told Ian I love him and the earth held onto its axis, Ian didn't cast me out into the cold, and the best part of it all is that he said he loved me, too. I have to wonder, though, if his feelings were just raw from the night we'd had or he really does love me. I've known I love him since the night at the club when I felt such a vicious blast of jealousy seeing other women touch him, even innocently. Afterward, I went home with him and we made love—and it *was* love. Looking into his eyes, nuanced with emotion as we became one, I knew with every fiber of my being that I was irretrievably in love with him. Perhaps I loved him from day one. I used to scoff at the idea of love at first sight, but now... now I'm not so quick to dismiss it.

As for Lucien, I need to put some time and space between last night and my ultimate resolution of the whole affair. Considering the possibility that none of it actually happened is difficult: why would my subconscious fabricate such horrible things?

At 3:35 I hear the elegant chimes of a doorbell and

go to see who's outside. Looking through the sidelights, I see Ian. Standing immediately behind him is a woman, early thirties, with streaky blond hair pulled into a neat ponytail, wearing pale green scrubs. Over her scrubs she wears a jacket, a lined windbreaker. I can't imagine why she's with Ian so I pull open the door to find out.

"Ella, how are you feeling?" Ian asks as soon as he walks through the door.

"Better," I reply, conscious of the strange woman who stands beside him.

"Ella, this is Stephanie Wilcott. She's a nurse whom Daniel kindly requested to come here for your sake. She'll take a blood sample to check for drug residue and she can also check for other things at your request."

His eyes don't leave mine when he says it and I know what he's conveying: a rape kit. If I choose to do it.

I turn to the woman. "Thank you so much. I appreciate your coming here and I'd be only too happy to submit to a drug test. Where shall we go to conduct it?"

Ms. Wilcott removes her jacket and says, "Wherever. It doesn't matter."

"In that case, why don't we step into the kitchen? I was just having some coffee and perhaps I could offer you some?"

"Oh, no, thank you. Lead the way and I'll get this done quickly."

It takes less than five minutes for her to collect the blood and she asks me to provide her with a urine sample so I run to the powder room to comply posthaste. I want to get on the plane and back to Portland as soon as possible. After she leaves, promising to have the results as soon as possible, I sit down with Ian at the refectory table in the kitchen. He looks terrible and I tell him so.

"Yes. I've been better," he sighs, running a hand through his messy hair tiredly. "On my way here I checked in with Scott. He's on his way to the airfield to ready the jet. We can leave anytime you're ready."

I nod, gulping my coffee.

"Why didn't you choose to do the rape kit?"

I don't look up from my bowl of coffee. "I'm confident it didn't happen and I want to put this whole experience behind me, at least for the present."

He grabs my hand and squeezes it and when I look down at our entwined hands, I gasp so strongly I nearly aspirate saliva. "What happened to your hand, Ian?" I practically scream. His knuckles are torn and bloody and large purplish bruises are beginning to form.

He smirks. "You should see Lucien's face."

Another gasp. "You went there and fought with him?"

"The preposition *with* doesn't apply here, Ella. I beat him and he accepted the beating. End of discussion. Come on, let's get ready to go. We've imposed on Daniel enough and I need to get back to Portland to attend to business matters."

This conversation wasn't nearly done but I could continue it during our long flight home. The idea that Ian went there, probably alone, and became embroiled in a physical altercation with Lucien didn't sit well with me. At all. First, he might have been hurt. And, second, I'm still unsure what crimes Lucien committed against me, if any. Until I have some proof, I'm hesitant to thoroughly indict him though it's beyond impossible not to detest him right now. And on the heels of that thought, I suddenly remember giving him or someone my PIN for my bank account.

Shit. I have to check my accounts... and I should share the information with Ian. It's not too much money but it's a significant amount and who knows? It might provide access to other information or monies. While Ian is on the phone with Scott, I place a quick call to my bank.

Relief. No activity whatsoever on my account. I quickly change the numbers. Maybe I shouldn't bother Ian with this recollection then? I allow myself time to mull it over.

The plane sits on the tarmac waiting for us and Scott greets us at the door.

"Good afternoon, Mr. Blackmon, Ms. Strong. Welcome aboard."

Ian nods in acknowledgement. "Thank you, Scott. I trust you were able to rest up?"

"Yes, sir. Thank you. I also managed to wrangle up an attendant to make your flight a little nicer. We'll be taking off within the half hour, I think."

"Excellent."

As soon as we enter the cabin I see the attendant: she's young, can't be much more than twenty, and she's quite pretty. Amerasian, I think.

"Good afternoon. I'm Cassie and I'll be serving you for the duration of the flight. May I get you a beverage?"

Ian eyes the girl with some suspicion. "Pellegrino, please. Ella?"

"The same, thank you."

"Very good," she replies demurely and vanishes into the galley. I dart my eyes over to Ian and decide to just tell him.

"So I remembered having a conversation about my bank PIN during the whole ordeal. I checked my bank accounts before we left Daniel's and all was quiet. I changed the numbers of course."

He turns angry eyes at me. I know he wants to kill Lucien more with every passing minute and I'm just glad he didn't do it when he had the chance. "What else have you remembered since we last spoke about it?"

"Nothing much. Just snatches of conversation but weirdly the voice isn't always Lucien's. I'm wondering if there were others there, talking to me while I was under the influence of whatever drug I'd ingested. I checked my wrists and ankles and there aren't any marks left by restraints, either."

He holds out his hand. "May I see them, please?"

I place my hand in his and he wastes no time in flipping my wrist to check. "Other hand?"

I switch hands and he scrutinizes that one too.

"Ankles now, please."

Sighing, I thrust one leg at him and then the other. Satisfied, he leans back into the roomy leather seat. "He could have used padded cuffs which wouldn't leave any marks. Do you recall anything about the restraints?"

I shake my head. "No, just that I couldn't seem to move."

"Mmm. It's not impossible that the drug rendered you incapable of moving and not any restraints. I'm ready to believe the worst of Phillips but we'll see what the evidence suggests. Regardless of the extent of his culpability, he's no angel, Ella. Trust me: he did not act like an innocent man and Daniel Butler can attest to that fact—and Daniel has no reason for bias, unlike me." He arches his left brow and waits for my challenge. But I have no reason to issue one, so I recline my chair to try to rest for a few minutes.

"Oh, by the way: Daniel's man picked up your luggage and brought it directly to the airport so it's on board with us. If you'd like to change or need anything, it's stowed under the bench seat near the galley entrance."

Hearing that I immediately jump up to change while we await takeoff.

Once we're airborne, I unbuckle my seatbelt to stretch my legs a bit. Bringing Ian a cold beer, I come back to sit down and he bestows on me a smile that can slay even the most impervious among mortals. Shakespeare said there were daggers in men's smiles. Though the bard, referring to backstabbers, meant something very different, every time I see Ian's megawatt grin, that line springs to mind.

Now, those eyes train on me with the hypnotic quality of a crowded opium den. I begin to fidget with myself: first my hair, twirling a long lock around my fingers, then I redirect my energies to twisting the too-large ring on my finger. Mariah gave it to me last Christmas and it's never fit me quite right. I think he wants me but he's probably concerned it's too soon, in light of my recent experience.

It's not. Being with him physically is like a benediction, for in a very tangible way, Ian is a blessing for me, one I need to celebrate right at the moment. I rise to my feet and extend my hand, an invitation in my eyes. When he takes it, his eyes steamy, I yank him up to stand and then lead him into the plane's small bedroom to have my way with him. Once there, I don't give him time to do anything. Before he can even turn around, I push him to the bed and fling myself on top of him. Laughing, he tangles his hands in my hair and begins to chase away all my demons with his sensuous lips and tongue. I wrap my legs around him as he flips us, my pointy heels pressing into his posterior but he doesn't seem to care in the least. In fact, the erotic pain might just be spurring him on.

"It's time to get you naked, Ella." He's sliding my pants down while still jerking his hips, rubbing his huge erection on me. I find the hem of his shirt and slip my hands up his muscled abs and chest, loving the way he feels under my fingers. I push the shirt up and over his head. As soon as it's off, I go for his pants.

He's faster and while I'm still trying to pull off his trousers, I'm pretty much bare. He kicks off his pants, tugs down his briefs and pulls me on him. Before I can think, he's inside me, filling every space, and all I could think is that I want more. More, more, more: we don't stop clawing at each other until nearly an hour elapses and then we just lie there, out of breath and entirely sated.

I'm dreaming I'm back at Lucien's, trapped, restrained, unable to leave. *Ian*. I have to get back to Ian. Then the tears rain down on me, big, salty tears that I can't wipe away because my arms are restrained. It would be my personal tragedy if I were forced to leave this mortal coil without having told him how much I love him, how much I care. Ian, I'm sorry, so sorry. Sorry for not telling you, sorry for not listening to you, sorry I can't see you again... just sorry for *everything*.

If I have the chance, I will tell Ian how I feel about him, that I love him, adore him, maybe even worship him, and am willing to accept the bad with the good—hell, I'll even celebrate the bad because it allows me the blessing of the good.

Abruptly I awaken, sweating profusely from the terror of my dream. Next to me, Ian sleeps serenely, content and beautiful. I remember now: I already told him. I told him I love him and he swore he loves me too. Amazingly, my admission to him of my love has brought me tranquility—at least when I'm conscious. It's important. So very important.

Chapter 33

Though the thermostat on the wall reads a very controlled 68 degrees, the atmosphere is arctic in the sumptuously appointed office of one Ian Blackmon as his hot anger freezes into a calculating fury. Revenge, as they say, is best served cold. Ian carefully and methodically considers his options for retribution against his dual enemies of Lucien Phillips and Natasha Yenin.

What happened earlier in the day solidified his resolve to go after the people who were doing their utter damnedest to wrest control of TES from him. Ian had four hours of sleep before coming straight to the office. He and Ella had gotten in fairly late last night, eaten a quick dinner and after taking laps around the park near his glass house, they'd finally gone to sleep. But Ella's nightmares had intervened, one right after the other, and consequently neither of them had gotten much sleep. By five he'd given up the game and come into work, leaving Ella asleep in his bed, the house heavily guarded with additional security staff and his housekeeper advised to wake Ella if she hears her having a nightmare. No one was getting to Ella—even in her sleep if he could help it.

Why did the bastards want TES so badly? Yes, the P&Ls were good certainly, but not remarkable. There was nothing floating around R&D that would put the company on the map, no deal in the making other than the government bid, which was far from certain. What was he missing?

It has to be personal. Slamming his hand on the desk in frustration, Ian practices a deep breathing technique to bring himself under control. The shit really hit the fan while he was gone over the last twenty-four hours. As he suspected, the files that were compromised when the system was hacked into had provided nuclear ammo for the sneak attackers. Excalibur had identified and been quietly looking into buying a small but highly profitable wind turbine and solar panel manufacturer that had artfully succeeded to bring its costs down enough to be competitive with Chinese producers. The plan was to fold the company into TES, thus making it a more viable energy contender on the world stage. Ah, the best laid plans of mice and me: the CEO of the firm had phoned Ian first thing this morning to tell him they'd received a more attractive bid from another firm. Ian had asked the name of the competing firm but Charles Cosgrove, the CEO of Alt-En Systems, had refused to divulge the information.

Cosgrove had been so solicitous before this incident: he'd been practically bending over and spreading his cheeks. He was hankering to get in bed with Excalibur and he made no secret about it. In the space of twenty-four hours or so, he begins to act like an ex-lover, avoiding phone calls and refusing to discuss the deal they'd been working on for the past month. There was really only one explanation that explained his complete change of heart.

Nastasha.

She was behind this whole thing—Ian just fucking knew it, felt it in his bones. Why the woman had such animus toward him, he couldn't begin to figure out but clearly she was out for his blood. He'd bled for her once. Never again.

"I'm going to crush the bastards, crush her if need be," he promises an empty office. Stupid but it makes him feel better. The intercom on his desk chimes at that exact moment. "Yes?" He manages to bring his voice from furious to curt in seconds. "What is it?"

"Daniel Butler for you, Mr. Blackmon?"

"Yes, I'll take it, thank you. Daniel?"

"Ian. I wanted to check in with you. Delacroix tells

me things have been active while you were in NY. I finally had the chance to compare the photo files and it's a no go. That doesn't mean anything obviously but it's probably a long shot anyway."

Ian rubs his eyes: he's exhausted, mentally and physically and just wants to be home with Ella. "Well, it was worth a try. Anything else?"

"Just one thing relating to the other matter. I know you mentioned you ran a security check on Phillips when Ella first began working with him. I suggest you give it another lookover—a more careful one. Either that or send your man back to the drawing board because I've uncovered some interesting intel on the man."

"Such as?"

"Such as he's royalty. His mother is a second cousin to the Danish queen and his father is a French oil magnate. He's extraordinarily wealthy, Ian: his net worth in almost in the billions."

"Really," Ian's single-word response was spoken as a statement not an interrogative. So Phillips is affluent—he's still a lowlife piece of shit. "So what do you extrapolate from that information?"

"Well, it seems odd that he would be after anything except Ella herself. He certainly doesn't need her money. That doesn't mean he's innocent, far from it. You might try speaking to his ex-girlfriend. They were together for several years."

There's a pause on Daniel's end and Ian is about to jump into the fiber optic void when Daniel speaks again. "I know you're trying to put out fires over there so I tried to make myself useful. I'll bow out now but please let me know if there's anything else I can do. I like you and Ella."

"Thank you, Daniel. The feeling is mutual, I assure you. And you've already done far too much for which we are most grateful. I'll keep you posted on my progress with TES."

"Very good. I'm taking my pretty girl away for a long weekend so I won't be around for a few days. I do check my text messages regularly, however, much to Olivia's continued chagrin, so I'm not entirely incommunicado. I wish you the best of luck."

The line disconnects. Placing the receiver carefully back into the cradle, Ian is deep in thought, pulling at his lower lip as he contemplates the new information.

When he finally surfaces for air, he rings Claudia, his assistant.

"Yes, Mr. Blackmon?"

"Claudia, can you please find something very beautiful and very expensive from Tiffany's or a similar store and have it giftwrapped and sent to Olivia Girardi and Daniel Butler in New York? While you're at it, do some research and see if there are any small Girardi sculptures floating around the market. Call my art dealer, Curtis Wentworth. See if he can get more information. I know Girardi's work has moved into large scale these days but he used to work in different media on smaller pieces. I'm interested in acquiring one or two of the diminutive works. Any questions?"

"No, Mr. Blackmon. I'll get right on both."

"Thank you."

Back to brooding. Shoving Natasha and her motives aside for the moment, his head fills with Lucien Phillips and the hatred percolates up, ascending from his gut like burning acid. He had such a visceral reaction to the bastard from day one. So what if he has money? He could still be a douche and he is one. End of story. He has to keep him away from Ella, whatever his motives are.

But why? Ian is a logical thinker and when things don't make sense, when things are illogical, they itch at his peace of mind. Why would a man with very high connections in the world and inordinate amounts of money reduce himself to the level that Ian suspected Phillips inhabited? Looking at it logically and not emotionally, it just does not make any sense. That aspect of the whole matter is what preoccupies Ian for the next hour until, exasperated by no dawning explanation, he turns his vitriol back to a certain blond Russian beauty.

Chapter 34

Ugh. I wake up feeling mucho crappy. I know it's late in the day because the sun is too high in the sky to be morning. I'm guessing it must be afternoon. I drag my body out of tangled bedcovers (was it me or a whirling dervish who made such a mess?) and stumble off the bed, the bathroom my target.

After a hot shower finished off with a second or two of icy spray just because, I feel like a new woman. There's something about hot water that is so restorative; I find it better than any medicine, better than anything really... except love. And on the heels of that thought, my mind swings to Ian and how much I love him. The one good thing about the whole horrid Lucien debacle is that it forced me to acknowledge my true feelings for Ian to myself and admit them to him. I hadn't realized before how heavy a burden is undeclared love, but I've felt lighter and more liberated ever since.

Another sucky part of the whole thing is that now I have no job. Ian won't let me even release any of my research to Lucien until he pays me in full for my services. Probably not even then. I need to find something else.

A gander at my pathetically pale countenance in the mirror induces me to sigh. How did I ever manage to ensnare a beauty like Ian looking like I do? Granted, I'm not exactly dead-fish white but I am pale, even gaunt these days. I do like my new extra thin body, though. It feels so good in clothes and I can wear just about anything. But Ian keeps trying to feed me. Maybe he wants me to gain weight? I mean, just the *crème brulee* alone that we had after dinner the other night had to be, like, a million calories. So deep I am in my musings, I don't hear my phone singing until it's about to switch into voice mail. Diving for my bag, I'm too late. I check to see who called and it's a New York number. Just as well.

I pull on a black suede skirt, a black, sleeveless knit shirt and high-heeled boots, throwing a black sweater on under my leather jacket. It's imperative for my mental health that I get out today, shop for some new shoes, maybe. Feel normal. I'll start with a trip to Starbucks and go from there.

In the entrance hall, I stop to stow my keys and phone in my bag, and grab a sweater. A door off the hall opens abruptly and I hear familiar footsteps.

"Oh my God, Mason! When did you get back?"

"As a matter of fact, just this morning, Ms. Strong. How are you?"

"Mason," I cock my head, hands on hips, "we've had this conversation one time too many. Please just call me Ella. You and I, Mason... you and I must help Ian to get over his stuffy formality." I pat his arm affectionately. Though I'd like to give him a hug, I refrain from it. "I missed you."

Mason's lips twitch up a tiny bit in what he passes off as a smile, and he slightly shuffles his feet, his discomfiture hardly noticeable but I know him by now. No one has a better poker face than Mason. He's former military so he's stoic to a fault and just simply doesn't show weakness of any stripe. Military people stare death in its cold, black eyes every minute of every day at times; why would they be intimidated by little ol' blue-eyed me?

Weirdly though, Ian told me that Mason acts differently around me. Ian attributes it to my extreme likeability; I attribute it to my extreme obstinacy at taking no for an answer. Either way, it's nice and was even nicer to hear it from Ian's lips. Of course, he was rewarded with two wet, sloppy kisses and an extra special blowjob—er, Ian not Mason, that is. Since then the compliments have been coming hard and fast from him—no pun intended.

"Dubai was a nice place to visit, but it's very good to be home," Mason continues. "I thought when I retired from the military, that would be that, but they keep sucking me back with these independent contracts." He runs his thick fingers through his one-inch buzzed hair. "No more, I've decided. You're a sight for sore eyes, *Ella*."

I give him a big smile, trying for radiant. "I'm just going out for a few hours. I should be home well before Ian returns from work."

"Yeah, about that—Mr. Blackmon asked that I accompany you today, Ella. He's not comfortable with your being on your own so soon after the recent traumatizing experience you endured."

I roll my eyes. "Of course he's not, and I don't want to give you a hard time so soon but I feel ridiculous being trailed by a bodyguard in broad daylight as if I'm royalty or something. Please, don't bother: I'm just going out for some air."

"I gave Mr. Blackmon my word," he says stubbornly.

I'm not going to fight, especially since he's just returned home so I throw my hands in the air in defeat. "Okay, whatever."

First things first: I head to my favorite shoe store, resuming my search for the perfect black boots. I don't find the ones I'm seeking but I find a really sexy pair of red sandals that I know Ian will like so it's not a total wash.

After, I find a perfect little cocktail dress and a more demure one to wear to Ian's next business function that he insists on dragging me to frequently, and I find a beautiful leather jacket for Ian, as well. Thinking about how hot he'll look in it makes me squirm in my expensive lingerie. I also thought I should pick up a gift for Mason since he's had to tag behind me all day, so I buy him a cashmere cardigan and matching scarf.

Fortuitously, since Mason takes the Lexus out of the mall garage, he can't come into Starbucks with me until he parks.

"Why don't you just wait outside? I'll only be a couple of minutes."

"Fine. I'll be right here waiting for you, Ella." He grins and I realize he remembered to call me by my first name. I beam back at him before turning to go inside.

I know I should let him accompany me rather than always giving him a hellish time for doing his job but I really do feel stupid having this super buff guy hovering over me every second, an obvious surrogate for my main and professional hoverer, one Ian Blackmon, sex god and chief worrier. Getting on the long line to order my coffee, I'm barely paying attention to my surroundings and that's how Lucien is able to sneak up on me and shock me spitless.

"Ella. I need to speak with you."

Immediately I begin to wheeze as a noose of panic wraps around my throat, constricting it, and sucking the breath from my lungs. I'm not sure what I find more anxiety producing: the fact that he is here and obviously stalking me, or the condition of his formerly handsome face—it is a total wreck, as if he stopped a bullet train with his nose. He recognizes my terror and tries to reassure me.

"Ella, I'm not here to harm you: I want to speak to you about what happened last time we met. Please, we'll confine our meeting to this coffee shop... if you could lose the goon for an hour."

Closing my eyes and taking a deep breath, I attempt to bring my respiration under some semblance of control and find my center. "He expects me to come right out and I'm sure he'll come in looking for me if I don't."

"Can you tell him you ran into a friend and will be a while longer? I'll be brief, Ella, I promise."

At that moment the barista asks me what I'd like and I place an order for me, and an extra for Mason, trying to disguise the tremor in my voice. Always polite, even with my would-be rapists, I ask Lucien if he wants anything and then instantly realize my stupidity.

"No, thank you," he replies, but quickly hands the woman a twenty to pay for my coffee, before I have a chance to even take out my wallet.

"Come, let's find a table while we wait for your coffee. In the interim, please shake off your muscle for a few minutes. Please, Ella?"

Mason sounds very skeptical when I call him, asking for a few minutes with a friend, but I do my best to reassure him. "I won't be much more than a half hour, Mason. Do you mind waiting? I'll bring you a *Venti*?"

"I'll be right in front waiting, Ella."

"Okay. I won't be too long. Promise. Thanks, Mason." I turn to Lucien. "You have a half hour and the clock starts now," I say looking at my watch. Just then my name is called to pick up the order.

I can barely stand to look at him—his face is a messy swirl of black and blue, and his nose is bandaged across the bridge. The bruises around his eyes are darkest and he can't seem to move his jaw so he's speaking oddly, like an inexperienced ventriloquist.

"Is that all from Ian?" I ask, pointing to his face with my chin."

"Yes. In addition to breaking my nose, he dislocated my jaw so severely it had to be wired shut, and I have a few stitches in my lip. Fortunately I have a great plastic surgeon so I shouldn't bear any permanent physical scars. Mental scars... well." He shrugs.

"I should tell you, Ella: I'm a dedicated pacifist so I refrained from fighting back and didn't call out my own people to dispatch him and his back-up. I understand he was upset but he didn't exactly give me any benefit of the doubt. I can't pretend I give a damn about him or his peace of mind but you... well, you're a different matter entirely."

"Really? How so?" I can hear the dripping sarcasm in my own voice.

He leans in closer to me, his eyes intent. "Ella, what do you think happened the other day? I'd very much like to know."

313

I shake my head—I don't want to go there; it's too fresh to take out for review but I've agreed to speak with him. All I can focus on is the curious fact that his voice has calmed my anxiety rather than stoked it. In fact, he feels as comfortably familiar as he always has and that in and of itself is distressing. Shouldn't I be running in terror from him? Is my radar for monsters broken completely?

"I am not a hundred percent sure what happened, Lucien. Why don't you tell me?"

"Ella, I'd be happy to but it's not what you're expecting to hear. From what I've been able to ascertain, you believe you were attacked at my home? By me? Is that correct?"

He's making me feel stupid, painting me as hysterical. Still, I nod in assent—my mind did not just fabricate all that bizarre shit.

"Can you tell me exactly what you remember?"

"I remember being in a black room; I remember your making threats against me, saying my book was about you and that I owed you the money. I remember you... or someone... touching me inappropriately. I couldn't move freely—I'm not sure why. Someone was saying bad things to me, horrible things, about pulling teeth and wooden ponies..."

"Wooden ponies?" He looks incredulous. "What's the significance of that?"

"You know what that is, right?"

"A carousel figure?"

Is he playing me? I'm not sure but dredging the memories back to the fore of my mind freaks me out and I instinctively push away from the table as the pain begins to poke at me.

Lucien leans in closer to me from across the table in direct proportion to how much I lean back, and lowers his voice. "Ella, shh. It's okay. I'm so sorry for what you endured. I would take your hand to comfort you but I know that would only make things worse. Will you do me the courtesy of listening to what I think occurred?"

His eyes are piercing into mine: if I just focus on the nuanced color of his eyes and not all the bruising around them, I can almost see him the way he should look. "Okay, Lucien. I'll listen but you have to be quick about it. Mason will come in any minute if I don't come out soon."

Nodding, he puts his hands on the table and begins to fiddle with the extra sugar packets. "My father was an extremely affluent man—he dealt in oil commodities. It's impossible to accumulate the vast amount of money he acquired over his lifetime without making a host of enemies... some quite fierce." He cocks his head thoughtfully. "I'm sure much of it was deserved because my father himself was ruthless in his drive to amass wealth.

"Anyway, when I was five years old, we were living with him in Paris, my mother and I, when an attempt was made to kidnap me. I actually remember some of it—to some extent the experience scarred me for life.

"I attended kindergarten every morning and my nanny would pick me up at noon. We would walk to the pastry shop—"

"Lucien, forgive me but what has this got to do with what happened the other day?"

He held up his hand. "I'm trying to explain about what I think happened, Ella. But you need to know some background. If you don't want all the details, fine. But what I need you to know is that the kidnapping was foiled or possibly aborted because two of the men involved... well, I'm not sure if they grew a conscience or perhaps developed affection for me over those few days I was held... but they ended up double-crossing the ringleaders, and went to my father. Without their assistance, the plan very well might have gone off without a hitch and who knows what would have been the end result. It's certainly possible I might have been killed or maimed. These two men, Lithuanians, saved me from that fate... and my parents were forever grateful. My father took the men in, gave them lifelong employment, and treated them generously.

"My father died shortly after my seventeenth birthday— he was an older man when I was born, nearing sixty. As his only son I was important to him, his biological legacy, if you will. Before he expired, he charged those men with protecting me and bequeathed quite a large sum of money to them accordingly. They are still with me today—not just guarding me but protecting me overall."

His elegant fingers start rubbing his temples, drawing my attention back to his battered face. I wonder if the doctors were being truthful with him when they told him he wouldn't have scars. Ian did a serious number on him and came home with nothing more than bruised knuckles. Guess he knows how to fight and maybe even fight dirty. It's an odd juxtaposition thinking of perfectly put together Ian getting down and dirty with a brawl. As my thoughts begin to stray from Lucien's fantastic story, he clears his throat, bringing me back to the table.

"I'm not sure how to say this gently so I'll just say it clearly: these men have been criminals since boyhood. They had compassion for a little boy but it didn't change their inherent natures and so they, at heart..." he shrugs, apology in his eyes, "pretty much remain criminals. Their one redeeming quality is their absolute loyalty and devotion to me. Although I'm little over one decade younger than they are, both men treat me as if I'm their charge... and they have always had considerable affection for me."

Okay, this explanation is so not what I was expecting from him—not that I was expecting anything. I'm sort of riveted to his story because it sounds like fiction. And if it sounds like fiction then... Should I even consider believing him? I do want to hear the rest, especially the part that pertains to my night in hell.

Suddenly I realize I've forgotten about Mason—and his coffee. I look up and right into his eyes: he's sitting at the table directly opposite me, sipping another coffee and watching me like a hawk. Shit. Well, in for a penny...

"Ella? Are you still with me?"

My eyes shift back to Lucien and I flush. "Yes. Continue, please."

"Ian had mentioned a drug test coming up positive. Is that right?"

I press my lips together. I haven't got the blood test results back yet. If Ian told Lucien we had, he must have been bluffing. I counter it with another question. "Why?"

A drawn-out sigh escapes from his lips. "It's possible that my men drugged you, Ella."

"Why would they do that, Lucien? I don't understand."

"Well, this is where my culpability comes in and I'm ashamed of it. I'd been complaining for a while that I could never get you alone. As soon as I met you, there was something about you—*je ne sais quoi*—that I found alluring. I wanted to get to know you beyond that of a colleague. But every single time I maneuvered an opportunity to spend time with you, Blackmon would pop up. I became exasperated. Then the last time, I might have mentioned to them—their names are Lukas and Leo—that I was finally going to have a few minutes with you alone, something that hadn't happened since Italy, and, well, they may have tried to help out."

"By drugging me? That's insane, Lucien!"

Sheepishly, he shrugs. "No one ever said these guys were bright, Ella. They're thugs. Anyway, my theory is that they slipped you a drug and you might have had a bad reaction to whatever it was they administered and began to hallucinate. That's the only logical explanation I could come up with."

"And where were you when all this was supposedly happening?"

He looks puzzled. "Well, initially I was there with you. The problem came later when I had an important meeting I couldn't miss and I wasn't expecting to have you passed out in my loft, helpless. My fath—"

"Lucien, what about the black room?"

"What about it?"

"Is it a dungeon?"

"Is it what?"

"You know, a dungeon with, uh, you know, BDSM kind of things."

"Ella, I'm not the Marquis de Sade, for God's sake. The room is black—or was—because my ex-girlfriend had an odd sense of color. She had planned for a merlot and instead got massacre red, as I used to tease her, so she ended up painting it black to cover her mistake."

"So no wooden pony?"

"I don't even know what that is, Ella."

"What about asking for my bank account information?"

"I didn't do that either. Ella... I don't like to flaunt it or even admit it but I have a ridiculous net worth. My father left me eighty percent of his estate. His older daughter, my half-sister, got very little and my mother got nothing, zero. I take care of both of them. My mother has some of her own wealth, coming from a prominent royal family. Remember Maya? She is, in fact, my older sister and not one of my biggest fans despite my generosity with her. She blames me for my father's ungallant behavior toward her."

"How does Mo Jackson know you?"

"Mo Jackson? No idea. Who is she again?"

"Did you touch me, Lucien?" I lean in to whisper because I don't want anyone to hear. "Intimately?"

Closing his eyes, he nods almost imperceptibly. "Yes, I did. I'm sorry, very sorry, Ella. I was trying to soothe you at first—you were so distressed. But then... my baser instincts took over. But I promise you that all I did was touch. Nothing more."

"Did you take off my clothes?'

He cracks his knuckles, nervously, I think, and somberly shakes his head. "I didn't."

"But someone did?"

"I had a meeting with my attorney that I couldn't miss. The way my trust funds are set up, every time I reach a milestone birthday, I get a new bank account or mutual fund portfolio. Last week I turned thirty and I had to meet with the attorney to sign some paperwork. That's why I left you with Leo. Believe me when I say I didn't want to, Ella. But Peter, my father's attorney, was leaving town the next morning and I wanted to get my hands on more cash for the film distribution. My wealth isn't liquid—not by a long shot—and I've been having problems raising cash for the film; there are just not enough art houses anymore. Every theater is commercial, has to be, in order to operate in black ink. So it may be up to me to make it financially profitable to show the film, even in the smaller venues.

"I was gone for less than two hours. When I left you had all your clothes on... but when I returned you were in your lingerie, under the bed covers. Leo swore he didn't touch you except to undress you and put you in the bed. I believe him, Ella. If he's guilty of anything, it's probably just voyeurism."

I clutch my temples in frustration, wishing I could remember more. "Honestly, Lucien, what I do remember, the fragments have such clarity. It's very hard for me to accept it was all hallucinations. Someone asked me for my PIN—I'm sure of it."

"Did you check your account? Are any monies missing?"

Looking away from him, I scowl in anger because I don't want to answer him. I just cannot believe my mind played such tricks on me—drug or no drug.

"Well?" he prods.

"No. But then, I contacted the bank very quickly and changed everything. Why would I hallucinate such a thing? It seems far too practical a matter to be a drug hallucination."

At that moment, Mason stands up and taps the crystal of his watch with a stern face. I nod at him. "I have to go, Lucien. I do appreciate your traveling all the way here to speak with me but it doesn't change a single thing. Ian doesn't want me near you and since I still don't know exactly what transpired that day and night and likely never will, I cannot have any kind of relationship with you going forward. I will try to convince Ian to let me release my files for the film, however."

He swallows audibly and rises from the table. "Thank you, Ella. I truly regret this outcome, truly. All I wanted was to get to know you better and now I've lost you entirely. I hope that bastard Blackmon appreciates you."

I watch him walk out of Starbucks. From the back, he's still perfect in his well fitting cords and leather coat. I see women checking him out from behind and manage a giggle. If he turns around, won't they have a colorful surprise?

Chapter 35

Dressed all in black, Jonas strides into his office like a dark angel, his face beaming with a broad grin.

"Good news, I take it?"

"The best, Ian. Our friends in China have not only committed to buy out Sol Systems but also agreed to take on our shares of TES—thus, we could dump the bid on Alt-En Systems. They can get into bed with the snakes, the fuckers. We stand to make a very pretty profit plus we're officially out of the energy business. Methinks we should stay out, too, for the foreseeable future.

Ian leans back in his chair, stretching his long legs in front of him. "Perhaps, but I hate to allow them to push me into changing my plans. Anything more on them?"

Jonas frowns and shakes his head. "No, they seem to be backing off a bit. We'll see how they react when TES is swept away and they're stuck with making good on their higher bid on Alt-En. I hope it sucks them dry."

Ian snorts. "That's not going to happen in all likelihood. But one can always hope. I've contracted a new security firm to do all our background checks. Our liaison with the firm is named Thomson. I've asked him to do an extended check on Lucien Phillips as well as Natasha Yenin. Let me know as soon as the reports come in, if I'm not in the office."

Jonas nods. "Understood. Oh, and Ia—"

The intercom buzzes and Ian holds up a finger to silence Jonas. "What is it?" he asks brusquely, disliking interruptions.

"Mr. Blackmon, a Justin Mason is on the line for you."

"Put him right through." He holds his hand over the

receiver. "Jonas, I have to take this call. Can we meet later today for another update?"

Jonas salutes him in military style and quickly exits the office, allowing Ian privacy with his phone call. "Mason? Blackmon here. Anything wrong?"

He hears the hesitation in Mason's voice and immediately gets his blood up. "Mason?"

"Mr. Blackmon. After taking Ella shopping, she asked me to bring her to Starbucks where she requested I wait outside for her. She was taking a long time so I went in to check on her and found her at a table with Phillips, sir."

"With Phillips?" he asked, his tone incredulous.

Mason had to hold the phone away from his ear due to Blackmon's volume. "Yes, sir."

"That son of a bitch! Is he still there with her?"

"Yes, sir."

"Which Starbucks, Mason?"

"The one on 5th Avenue?"

"I'm on my way. Try to keep him there if possible."

"Yes, sir."

On his way out he sees Claudia. "I'm going out for about an hour. Have Jonas update you on what's going on with Sol Systems and we'll meet this afternoon around four p.m. I may have to leave the office a bit early today."

Claudia nods. "Will do, Mr. Blackmon. I'm going to follow up with Thomson to see where he is with the report on Yenin. I thought it might be worthwhile to put a tail on her, see what she's up to."

"Do it. I'll be in touch soon." The elevator appears and whisks him down to the lobby where the doorman flags down a taxi. He arrives at the Starbucks within ten minutes, just as Phillips is walking out the door. Throwing a twenty at the driver, he leaps out of the car and intercepts the man before he could get any farther away.

"In need of another beating, Phillips? Because I'm willing to oblige you—right now if you like."

"Look, Blackmon: Ella doesn't belong to you. She's not one of your possessions nor are you married to her so you have no legal claim either. I have every right to speak with her and I wanted to clear the air between us. I have no intention of harming her and never did. Whatever you think happened did not. That's all I have to say to you."

"Listen, douche bag, I'm telling you to stay away from Ella. She is my girlfriend, soon to be my fiancée, so I have every right to make claims on her. Further, I don't believe a single thing that comes out of your lying mouth. Are you calling Ella a liar?"

Lucien glares at him with seething hatred while Ian examines the man's face in the daylight; he really did a good job on the bastard: dislocated jaw, broken nose, and a veritable palette of bruising. Right now, the man looks exhausted, as well.

"I've already had an extended conversation with Ella and did my best to explain what I think transpired the other day and night. I am now leaving and Ella has said goodbye to me, permanently, so there's nothing for you to get upset about, Blackmon. We're done here and I've achieved what I set out to do, which was to set the record straight with Ella."

"I know you had some ulterior motive for hiring Ella, Phillips. I saw right through your phony façade. I think it all came to pass the other day and for whatever reason you thought you'd get away with it. But I have friends with abilities, fuckhead, and I found you too quickly. Foiled your plans, did I?"

Lucien sighs. "Yes, as a matter of fact, you did foil my plans... but not in the way that you think. The simple truth of the matter is that I was interested in Ella— romantically interested—and you were always getting in the way. I see now that it was never really feasible. Ella and I are parting as friends—I hope anyway. I also hope you appreciate her and treat her accordingly. If I had been fortunate enough to win the day, I would have treated her like a queen—and she'd practically be one, for if she married me, she'd become a part of a royal family, complete with title."

He begins to walk away and then stops, turning back. "One more thing, Blackmon: go fuck yourself. You are truly an asshole."

"You, too, Phillips. I hope you think of me every time you look in the mirror." He smiles malevolently. God, he hates the blond bastard with a passion. Just then, the door to Starbucks opens and out spills a stream of people, all holding cups of various sizes. Bringing up the rear are Ella and Mason. Ella's eyes widen upon seeing Ian standing there. He strides up to her, grasps her hand, and barks out a question to Mason: "Where's the car?"

"I parked it up the block, sir. By the way, I saw you arrive through the window so I allowed him to exit."

Ian nods. "Lead the way."

As Mason walks ahead of them, Ella glances at Ian, trying to divine his mood but his impassive face as always is utterly inscrutable, so she waits. And waits... and still he says nothing. He just grips her hand and walks so briskly that she almost has to run to keep up with him. "Ian."

He glances back at her, one brow raised in query but still no words.

"Are you not speaking to me?"

"Right now, Ella, I think it's prudent if I refrain from conversation. I need to calm down first. Let's just get to the car."

The good news is that Ella doesn't look intimidated, as she almost certainly would have in the very beginning of their relationship. She does, however, look a bit put out and Ian feels a knockdown, drag-out fight is almost inevitable. It's up to him to control the situation, and really Ella did nothing wrong except that she failed to walk away from the man the moment she saw him. But that's not Ella's way... she's too ready and willing to give everyone the benefit of the doubt. Unlike Ian.

His phone chimes and he has to release Ella's hand to pat himself down, looking for the pocket containing his iPhone. "Blackmon."

"Mr. Blackmon, I have news," Claudia announces.

"Go on."

"I just checked your appointment book for the rest of the week to schedule meetings with our Chinese friends, as well as the new security guy, Thomson."

"And?"

"It seems that someone—I'm guessing Janine—scheduled an appointment for you with none other than Natasha Yenin. I'm not sure why she thought it acceptable. She knows appointments must go through me." There's dead silence on both ends, as if the call dropped but the connection is live.

After about thirty seconds, Ian finds his voice again. "When?"

"Tomorrow at four."

The heel of Ian's hand slaps his forehead. "What the hell is she up to? I know she's behind all of this bullshit so why would she want to meet with me? Is it because we outplayed her?"

"I don't know, sir. But I'm certainly not itching to see her again. Should I cancel?"

"Let me think on it, Claudia. I'm going to be back a bit later than I had originally planned. Keep me posted if anything new arises."

"Will do. Let me know when you get back."

He disconnects the call. Ella tugs on his hand, curiosity in her eyes. "What's going on?" She asks the question softly, treading carefully. She obviously does not want to fight with him.

"Nothing much right now."

"It's interesting how you never tell me what's going on in your life yet you always expect me to share. Why the double standard?"

Narrowing his eyes, Ian remembers he's not speaking to her and that she's attempting to out-manipulate him. Not going to happen, Ms. Strong. "I told you we shouldn't speak until I get a handle on my anger, Ella. I'm not there yet. Here's the car."

Mason quickly opens the rear door of the Lexus and Ian places his hand on Ella's back, firmly guiding her inside the car, and he folds his tall frame into the Lexus gracefully, sitting so close to her that he's nearly on her lap. He wants her to feel his control right now. She's been getting too free and easy with him and it's going to stop today. It's going to stop as of this minute, in this car, right now.

When Ella starts to feel closed in, she scoots over a bit and he follows very slyly. She moves again and, after waiting a few moments, he follows her. Using the seatbelt from the middle seat, he clips it on as she does her own belt. Then he moves even closer until his body is pushing hers against the side of the car.

"What are you doing?"

"What do you mean?"

"You keep pushing me over on the seat. You're making me feel claustrophobic."

"I just want to be close to you, Ella." He shifts his body to face her and leans his arm across her face, resting it on the side of the car next to her head. Effectively boxing her in. "Now. Explain to me what just happened with Lucien Phillips."

"There's nothing to explain," she says, but her voice emerges as a strangled whisper. "He showed up at Starbucks to speak with me. I sat with him because he begged me to give him a half hour to explain. I figured, what the hell. He couldn't hurt me: I was in a crowded coffee shop and Mason was right outside. What's the problem, Ian?"

"The problem, Ella, is that you don't see there's a problem. The problem is that you refuse to see the bad in people; you refuse to acknowledge that some people are inherently evil; you refuse to listen to me! That, my dear Ms. Strong, is the fucking problem."

She rolls her eyes, infuriating him even more. "Mason," he spits out angrily, "home, please. Right now."

Mason looks at Ella in the rearview mirror, his eyes reflecting concern, knowing he is to blame for the current situation. Still, he reports to Mr. Blackmon and if he didn't inform him of Phillips' presence, he would be remiss in discharging his employment obligations. She'll probably hate him now, he knows... and distrust him. He sighs, frustrated, because he genuinely likes Ella and doesn't want to see Blackmon shred her for being kind.

They pull up to the circular drive of the glass house; the garage is in the rear. "Drop us in front, please. I'll need you in an hour or two to take me back to the office."

"Very good, sir. I'll park the car and wait for your summons."

Muttering under his breath that at least some people respect his wishes, he climbs out of the car, dragging Ella with him and strides to the front door.

As soon as the door closes behind them, he's on her. He grabs a handful of her long hair and wraps it around his wrist, until it's tight against her nape, then he pulls her head up to look at him. "You belong to me, Ariel. Do you understand?"

He can see her large blue eyes begin to reflect anxiety. He knows she doesn't appreciate it when he gets too possessive, but, when she flagrantly ignores his wishes, he can't help himself. He needs to keep her safe: Ella is too pretty for her own good and that makes her a target for bad people. It's up to him to protect her since she's too kind to be suspicious.

Ella obviously decides to take the preemptive approach. "Ian, don't make this into a big thing, please," her words chastise but her voice is hoarse with arousal and his cock twitches up in response. Ella may not want to admit it, but she likes to be dominated. It turns her on.

Leaning down as if he's going to kiss her, he stops just as his lips are about to touch hers. She's waiting for the kiss but he denies her. He knows she can feel his warm breath on her face as he takes a moment to appreciate her beauty. "Come," he finally says and pulls her into the bedroom with his hand still clutching her hair. When they get there, he bends her over a chair and begins to remove her clothes. "You know, Ella, what caused the rupture in our relationship the last time—the whipping I gave you. I'll never do it again because I never want to lose you... but I confess right now it's all I can think about, pulling off my belt and laying it across your lovely little ass, turning it burning hot and striped with pink. It's no more than you deserve."

He sighs. "But I'll settle for a spanking and I want you to thank me afterward and show me how much you appreciate my concern for your welfare."

"What? You must be crazy if you think I'll thank you for hitting me, Ian."

Before she can get another word out, he yanks down her panties without ceremony. Now she's standing in her black sleeveless sweater, and high-heeled boots, her skirt in a heap on the floor. Seeing her in nothing but those sexy boots does things to Ian and he gets so hard it hurts. He may not last through her spanking, but he'll do his best.

"Tell me why I'm spanking you."

"Because you're an asshole," she says so sweetly.

Smiling, he swings his hand back and slaps her right cheek hard, stinging his hand.

"Ow!"

"Try again. Why?"

"Because you think you're God?"

He swats her left side.

"Hey, that hurt!" she whines.

"That's the point, isn't it? One more time and then I'm just going to let loose on you, Ella. Why am I spanking you?"

"Because I didn't run away from Lucien. I acted like a mature adult with a modicum of compassion and let him attempt to explain what happened to me on that very scary day and night."

Now he gives into his fear for her safety and whales on her backside. She yells out just once after quite a few nasty swats.

"Shall I stop?" he asks politely.

She doesn't answer but her hips sway so he takes that as tacit approval. Her mind and body are at war when it comes to his domination but her body usually wins. He gives her three more swats with a lighter touch and then yanks her up, spins her around, and kisses her with abandon. She won't open her mouth to him so he nips and licks her lips. Still, Ella keeps her mouth tightly closed so he moves to her neck and his hot mouth latches on, sucking hard and then biting down.

"What's wrong with you?" she says sharply as she attempts to pull back. "That really fucking hurt!"

"Yes, I'm aware—again, that was the point. You wouldn't kiss me. Are you mad at me?"

"Damned straight. If you stick your tongue in my mouth, Ian, I promise you I'll bite it off."

"Really? Do you know that you're sending me mixed signals, Ella? Your face and mouth are telegraphing anger but your body is screaming for more. My money says you're dripping wet with want. Care to make a bet?" He could hear the hunger in his own voice as he speaks to her. Can she?

"Fuck you, Ian. You're not checking."

"Oh, I'm checking, baby." Tangling his fingers in her glossy hair, he slides his other hand between her legs and his fingers slip effortlessly past the outer to the inner. "His broad grin is triumphant as he whispers into her ear, "Told you so."

She glares at him but says nothing.

"Now… say thank you to me for caring enough to punish you, Ella."

Her startled eyes could not open any wider; she simply is unable to believe the things coming out of his mouth. "Dream on."

He grinds his hips against her, smiling wickedly because he knows Ella's frustration is mounting and feeling his hard-on is making her hotter. Her fingers begin to unbutton his pants but he pulls back out of her reach, his hands weaving through her hair, massaging her scalp. "I'm waiting for the thank-you, baby."

"Ian, you're not getting one, not today. I did what I thought was right. Sometimes you're going to have to bite the bullet and trust other people's judgment, particularly mine. I know it's difficult for you but if you stay with me, you'll learn. Now forget the thank-you and just do me already."

He turns her around and pushes her down on her knees with her chest resting on the bed, one hand still holding her hair. He doesn't want to let go: he wants her to feel the unbroken connection until she comes, so he fumbles with his fly with his free hand, jerking his pants down only far enough to liberate his rock-hard erection. He reaches around and finds her breast, massaging it and tugging her nipple just to the point of gentle pain, as he uses his knee to spread her legs wider. "Don't move, Ella. Stay perfectly still," he orders as he thrusts inside her. He reaches around to massage her in front in counterpoint to his thrusts, kissing her neck up and down.

"Don't come."

"What?"

"You heard me."

"Ian, I can't."

"If you come, I'll spank you again."

He flips Ella around to watch her face as she struggles to stave off her orgasm but ultimately she can't hold it any more and with a throaty scream, she climaxes.

"Oh, Ella, you disobeyed me." He lifts her leg and swiftly swats her sore backside once and then thrusts into her ferociously and she comes again, a look of utter astonishment on her face. At that point, he lets himself go too, unable to hold back a moment longer, and collapses, spent, on top of her.

"Will you marry me, Ariel?"

"You have got to be kidding me, Ian," she says breathlessly. "Ask me again when we're dressed and you're on bended knee and I'll consider it."

She pushes him off her and rolls over on the bed, pulling the coverlet back and scooting underneath. Her back now to him, she turns her head enough for him to hear her next words. "Until then, I'm taking a nap. You can wake me when you get home from work."

When no response comes, she turns around and sees him standing there, his clothes now set to rights, just staring at her. She can't read the emotion swirling around in the depths. Is it confusion? She just can't tell.

She rises to her knees, crawls over and circles her arms around his neck, kissing him gently. The kiss speaks volumes: he knows in his bones that she loves him as much as he loves her. The contentment it brings him is without parallel.

Chapter 36

When I wake from my nap, it's dark out and the room is shrouded in dusky shadows. At first I panic, disoriented. Familiarity breeds comfort and I soon realize I'm in Ian's bedroom. Instantly I calm, and check the time. Six thirty. Is Ian home yet? I asked him to wake me when he got home.

Stretching my body as far as I can, I feel so good: boneless—all sinew and muscle. Sex with Ian has that opiate effect on me. True, he went all Neanderthal on my ass—literally—and I allowed him to. It's only taken me a year and change but I think I've finally figured him out: I now understand that when he's stressed out and/or having problems at work, his dominance emerges big time.

When I first met him and he showed me his dungeon, I was horrified and intrigued in equal measure. Horrified because... well, that reaction probably doesn't need explanation. Intrigued, because I've always been adventurous and since I kept my sexuality bridled for so long, it was almost inevitable that I'd become a wild child, at least for a little bit, when I finally let loose.

But with Ian and his proclivities, I assumed it was part of his innate sexuality, an alpha-male need to dominate everyone around him, and a raging libido that required exotic measures to quiet. Perhaps that got my back up a bit, at least in the beginning, especially when he took a whip to me.

Now? Now I realize it's not his innate sexuality, per se. He's cultivated this kind of sexual behavior to make sense of his world and his place in it. It's as if he uses sexual dominance to bring order to his world when his control is slipping in other areas of his life. In essence, he uses it as a coping mechanism. That revelation has allowed me to indulge him a little bit more, to feel less guilty that I'm caving in to his violent and macho tendencies.

I've also realized something about myself too and it was a difficult revelation to swallow: I definitely do get highly aroused when he sexually dominates me—*sexually* being the operative word. It seems a strange disposition for someone like me because I think of myself as a strong and even forceful personality at times. Despite my strength of character or perhaps because of it, I enjoy relinquishing control to Ian when we are intimate. It's the ultimate fantasy of the strong male stealing and carrying off the female to ravage—a kind of Bedouin harem fantasy thing—and Ian never forces it on me, always checking to ensure that I want him to continue. It's a game, a dance almost, where he leads and I can choose to either follow or not.

The spanking? Confusing. On the one hand, it's painful and he generally delivers it in anger—never a good combination. On the other hand, it is like a pressure valve for me: the whole ordeal with Lucien brought volatile emotions to the surface and then Ian and I had a very emotional reunion. Being spanked today allowed me to let off steam. As much as I truly fucking hate to admit it, damn it, I do feel better afterward, calmer and relaxed. Go figure. I suppose he feels better too, having vented his frustration on my backside. Win-win?

Then Lucien pops into my head. I try to banish him but he won't quit me. Alright, I'll give him his quarter through contemplation. Here's the thing: his story was so unbelievable but they say truth is stranger than fiction... and in my case, it usually is—witness my runaway bestseller. Lucien's body language seemed honest enough; I watched his every move. Growing up, my best friend's father was a detective and he taught us interrogation techniques and how to tell if someone is lying. I used some of them on Lucien and no red flags came up. Still...

Even if his story is one-hundred-percent true, he still is not without culpability. Even if he didn't know I was drugged—and the jury is still out on that one—he still touched me without my permission. I was in no shape to give consent so legally he sexually assaulted me. Further, even if his kidnapping story was true, why have thugs hanging around? Why not pay them off and get them out? It takes a thug to know one.

I won't forgive him... but I probably won't press charges either. Earlier I received a text saying my blood test results were ready and being mailed to me. I couldn't call because it was too late in New York but first thing in the morning I'll check.

But I already know; I know I was drugged. And it makes me scared. It makes me realize how safety is really just an illusion, a lie we tell ourselves. It's something so tenuous that someone can come along at any time and drug or Taser you and that's it—that's all it takes to overpower another person. You wake up and you've been immobilized and you're at the mercy of a crazy person, just like that. It's that idea and the underlying terror it engenders in me that is pushing me to begin therapy. Soon.

The sound of an outer door closing interrupts my stream of consciousness and a few seconds later, the bedroom door opens. Ian steps in quietly, peering over at me to see if I'm still asleep: he looks anxious and I think I know why. He's afraid of the aftermath of what transpired earlier. I'm not angry with him because I know his reaction stemmed from a good place, a loving place, so I smile and he returns it with a heart-stopping full-teeth beauty, causing my innards to seesaw. The man is one of the wonders of the world—I guess the eighth one.

"How are you, Ella?" his voice is soft, like silk rustling on bare skin.

"Fine. Can we talk? Do you have time?"

"Yes, of course. I was planning on taking you out for dinner. Are you up to it?"

"Um. Maybe. Come here."

He sits on the edge of the bed and I crawl over to him, snuggling under his arm. Mmm, he smells so good: soap and cologne and his own special scent. I inhale deeply.

"I like the way you smell too, you know," he says with a shy smile.

Returning his smile, I reach up and caress his face: I love this man so much that my chest feels tight, so full it's near to bursting. I don't want to break this small communion between us but I need to talk to him about this afternoon, share it with him so he can get past any residual anger. Hesitantly, I broach the topic. "Ian, about my conversation with Lucien..."

"Yes?"

"I just want to tell you what he said. Will you hear it?"

He nods but I can see the new look in his eyes, the very pissed-off look.

"Okay, so here's his explanation..." I say, and launch into the whole saga and how he came to have the thugs in his employ.

"The kidnapping story sounds like utter bullshit to me."

"Does it? To me it seems too farfetched to make up..." I choose my words carefully. "It could be true."

"The royalty connection is a fact, however. I checked."

"You checked? How did you even know about it?"

"Daniel. There's something up with Daniel..." he hesitates, as if searching for the right words, "he seems to know things he shouldn't. If he weren't helping me so much, he'd be suspect. I think... oh, never mind."

"No, tell me."

"No, it will sound too crazy."

"I love crazy! I'm dating *you*."

He smiles and mirth makes his eyes extra shiny. "I

think he may have... extra sensory abilities."

"Like... mindreading?"

"Exactly like it. Yes. He seems to know everything, even before it happens. Anyway, he told me to take another look at the report I had run on Phillips. It wasn't complete so I fired the security firm I was using and hired a new one. The new report was much more detailed and comprehensive. Remember that woman you interviewed in Venice?"

"Maya St. Sauveur. She's his half-sister."

"How did you know?"

"Lucien told me. It explains why she was so antagonistic toward him. According to Lucien, their father left his whole estate to Lucien and not her or her mother or his mother, for that matter. Sounds like a charmer."

"Yes, well, the apple doesn't fall far from the tree, now does it?"

"Hmm. I'm getting the results of the blood test tomorrow—I'm already certain I was drugged. I have a history of severe reactions to drugs—I think I told you how I once suffered hallucinations from cold medicine. If someone slipped me something strong like Rohypnol, I don't doubt that I'd have a bad reaction. Maybe all those things I remembered happening were in fact hallucinations." I look up at him but he makes no comment and his face is devoid of expression. "Do you think?"

Shrugging, he pulls me closer to his chest and kisses my head. "Perhaps, but I'm not inclined to give Phillips any benefit of the doubt. I hold him responsible for everything that happened to you that night, even hallucinations. He should face legal redress, and would, if I had my way."

"It is weird how he told me his whole life story by way of explaining his hoodlum bodyguards."

"He's trying to gain your sympathy, Ella, pure and simple. He admitted to me that he always had an ulterior motive."

My head swings up so fast I nearly get whiplash. "What was his ulterior motive?"

Arching his brows, he says, "Can't you guess?"

"Just tell me, for God's sake."

"He was interested in you, Ella. Romantically. He said every time he tried to get you alone, I'd foil his plans." He grins wickedly. "Told you so."

"Do you believe him?"

"I certainly believe it might be true, since you are rather irresistible. But as for whether or not it was his true motivation... I'm not certain yet. But I will be, once I have all the information to put the puzzle together."

"I'm surprised Lucien even talked to you considering how you artfully rearranged his face."

"Yes, our Mr. Phillips was in a loquacious mood today, wasn't he? Too bad he's such a filthy liar."

"Well, I'm done with him so there's no further need to worry." I stroke his face, hoping he can feel my love through touch—and I think he can. His eyes drift shut and he hums in appreciation. Reaching closer, I kiss his lips softly.

"I believe you mentioned that you want to go out for dinner?"

"Yes," he says, shaking his head to recover his equilibrium, I suppose. "So get your lazy ass up and dressed so I can wine and dine you, Ms. Strong. I'll be awaiting your divine presence in the living room." He gets up and strides out of the room.

I take my time getting ready—I hadn't forgotten that Ian asked me to marry him in our post-coital ecstasy. Was he serious? I wondered if he was going to do it properly tonight and what I would say.

Do I want to marry him? I look in the mirror and roll my eyes. Oh, for God's sake, who am I kidding? Of course I do. I love the man and I'm only truly happy when we're together. The positives far outweigh the negatives when it comes to Ian and I think I can make him happy, too. He just needs to ease up a bit on the dominance—*but not in bed*. That I like. If he's willing to compromise, so am I.

Okay, make-up: I reach for the mineral foundation powder and puff on the barest amount. A little eyeliner and mascara, lip pencil and tinted gloss. That's it.

Then I add a double diamond stud to each ear and pull my hair back in a loose knot. Perfect. See, Mariah? I can clean up pretty nicely. The specter of Mariah as fashion police reminds me I have to call her and let her know I'm back in Portland. We need some face time together.

I pull on a tight navy cashmere vee-neck sweater over a very short navy skirt. The sweater covers almost all of the skirt so it kind of looks like I have nothing on underneath. Going for the monochromatic look, I pull on navy tights and black leather ankle boot that have straps with big pewter buckles. I stand back and examine myself in the mirror.

No. I look like a coed on the first day of the fall semester, not a woman going out for dinner with her rich, gorgeous boyfriend who may or may not propose marriage to her. I quickly strip off the clothes I just put on and begin again.

First I don a black satin shelf bra that pushes me up so my cleavage is way more impressive—with the added advantage of ventilation for my nips. Going to Ian's closet, I scan the side where I've left some of my clothes. This time I select a slinky vee-neck Merlot-red dress; it hugs my body as if it were tailor-made for it. I choose the diamond pendant Ian gave to me—it looks perfect showcased in the plunging vee of the neckline, dangling right at the start of said cleavage, and I slip on sheer stockings and four-inch black heels. The shoes are Ian's favorites as they are not only stilettos, but they show just the barest hint of toe cleavage, which he finds sexy. I wrap a black pashmina scarf around my throat three times and tie it, and don a black coat the exact length of the dress, which I leave hanging open so the dress plays peekaboo. Now when I check the mirror, I nod in satisfaction. Perfect.

When I walk into the living room, Ian is on his laptop

looking grim but he glances up at me as I enter and his eyes begin to shine.

"Beautiful, Ella." Closing the computer, he stands and takes my hand, kisses it, and leads me to the hall where he grabs his coat from the closet. We go into the entrance hall to wait for the elevator.

The restaurant is housed in what used to be a crumbling old mansion, Ian informs me. Rather than knock down walls to make a large dining room on each floor, the owners of *Oscar's* took that approach with the main floor only. On the upper floors, they left all the bedrooms intact and instead created private dining rooms, each decorated with a different Academy Award-winning film in mind. There is a room dedicated to *The Sting*, a *Gone with the Wind* room, my favorite and the one I want is the *Casablanca* room. They have *West Side Story*, *Mutiny on the Bounty*, *Amadeus*, *Lord of the Rings*, *Titanic*, and more. There are fifteen theme dining rooms, all told.

Somehow Ian managed to anticipate the room I'd want and he reserved it earlier in the day so we get the one designed to look like *Rick's Café Américain*.

The maître d' shows us to our room and then quietly exits, while our waiter enters to take our drink orders. Ian orders a bottle of white—a *Pinot Grigio*—to be served with dinner and a bottle of champagne to be chilled for afterward. Surely that means what I think it means.

Scanning the menu, I'm completely undecided as to what to order. I'm vacillating between three dishes and when I look up, Ian is watching me, amused.

"Shall I order for both of us, Ella?"

"Yes, thank you, Ian."

The meal he orders is superb: a cold cucumber and dill soup, halibut with potato pave, and sautéed spinach. For dessert we have fresh berries with *crème fraîche* and... *Perrier Jouet*, chilled to perfection.

"Oh my God, if I ate like this every day I'd never fit

into any of my clothes."

Smiling, Ian feeds me a strawberry. "I like to see you eat well, Ella."

"Mmm. Thank you for the delicious dinner and the sparkling company, most of all. I'm sorry if I upset you earlier. I just want to resolve this whole thing in my mind so I can put it behind me. Since Lucien was magically there in front of me, I figured it was a safe way to do it."

Ian scoffs "Magically? He was stalking you, Ella." He sighs, pushing his unruly hair out of his eyes.

He needs a haircut, I notice, and then try to give him my full attention. There's something on his mind.

Clearing his throat, he finally says, "I have something to share with you, too, Ella. I'm just not quite ready to do so. Will you be patient with me? I promise that soon I'll explain everything to you, what's been going on at Excalibur... and why I've been in frequent bad tempers of late." His hand reaches across the table to cover mine and he squeezes. "Will you bear with me for a little while?"

"You mean you're not always this grouchy? Well, that's a relief," I say, wiping my brow with the back of my hand. He smiles but just for a nanosecond so I know he wants me to be serious.

"Of course I will bear with you, Ian, but I definitely would like you to share with me. If I learned anything from my awful experience at Lucien's, it's that it's far better to be honest with the people you care about... because you never know when you're going to run out of time."

He kisses my hand. "Hopefully we both have lots of time ahead of us... but you're absolutely correct. I'm... working on it, Ella, on sharing, but it doesn't come so easily to me."

"Okay." I pat his hand. "I'll wait... if you promise to keep me occupied in the interim." I flash him a leer.

He doesn't take the bait, though. Instead, he rises off his chair and walks to mine, and without further preamble, drops to one knee and kisses my hand.

Inwardly, I gasp loudly, nerves jangling like silver bangles on a hyperactive wrist. Outwardly I'm as serene as a mountain lake. He's really going to do it and so traditionally too.

"I asked you to marry me earlier today but you resented my timing and told me to do it again when I was fully dressed and on bended knee. So here I am, Ariel. Will you do me the great honor of becoming my wife and partner forever? I'll settle for nothing less."

I brush that recalcitrant lock of hair off his adored face and then run my fingers down, lightly tracing his perfectly symmetrical features. "Yes, Ian. I will. Forever. I love you."

From behind his back he produces a small cardboard box in the distinctive turquoise color of Tiffany's, adorned with a white ribbon. We open it together, and inside is a small, black velvet case. He removes it, tosses the blue box onto the table, and flips open the hinge on the velvet case. Nestled inside in a bed of satin and velvet is the most magnificent diamond ring I've ever seen. The stone is large but tasteful and the setting so unique: it's fringed by sapphires that form an inverted vee, showcasing the large diamond in the center. The ring itself is platinum. When he slips it on my finger, it somehow fits perfectly. I lean over and kiss him softly. "It is the most beautiful ring I've ever seen and I'm thrilled to wear it, Ian. Thrilled."

In response, he offers me a smile that can light the night sky, and we kiss, a beautiful chaste kiss full of the promises to come. After we toast our engagement with hastily sipped champagne, Ian signals for the bill so we can go home and seal the deal in the way we like best. We take the bottle of bubbly and the rest of the strawberries with us at my insistence. I have plans of my own.

So, as of tonight, we are engaged to be married and life is just fine. It's time I start moving my things back from Los Angeles.

The next morning I make three phone calls upon

waking: the first to the lab to get my results. The results are unsurprising: yes, there was residual trace evidence of a drug, similar to Rohypnol, called ketamine present in my blood sample.

"Does that drug cause hallucinations, do you know?" I ask the lab tech.

"It can. Ketamine is a dissociative anesthetic and it's called that because it tends to distort sights and sounds, and causes one to feel a detachment from reality. Hallucinations are one side effect of this drug."

"I appreciate the information. I understand the full lab report was already mailed to me?"

"Yes, that's correct. You should receive it in the next day or so. If you have any questions, please feel free to call again."

"Thank you very much. Good day."

I disconnect the call and spend the next five minutes staring into space. Lucien's tale is starting to gain more traction with me. What I really want to know now is whether he's really as innocent about BDSM as he made himself out to be—that would also bolster his story. I need to add Mo Jackson to my call list to find out how she knows LP but I'll leave that enticing task to another day and time. Baby steps.

The second call is to Mariah and we make plans to have lunch the following day. I refrain from sharing my massively life-changing news because I want to tell her in person: from Archipelago salesgirl to Mrs. Ian Blackmon in five easy steps. Not too shabby.

The third and final call I place is to Maya St. Sauveur. I know I should just let it go but I cannot. I want to know if Lucien's kidnapping saga is true. Why it matters anyway, I just don't know.

She answers on the first ring. "Yes?"

"Ms. St. Sauveur?"

"Yes, speaking. Who's calling please?"

"It's Ariel Strong, Ms. Sauveur. Do you remember me?"

"Yes, Ella. Please call me Maya. How are you?"

"I'm doing well, Maya. I'm calling you on something of a personal matter... I hope you don't find it too intrusive but circumstances have necessitated me verifying information Lucien provided to me by way of an explanation." Okay, I sound like a blithering idiot. Just ask the woman, Ella, in plain English.

"Lucien told me a story and I wondered if you could... would... offer any clarification regarding it?"

"What story?"

"About his being kidnapped at age five?"

A long pause ensues and I wait patiently. "Yes, it's true. Did you doubt him? Because if you did, I completely understand. He is a pathological liar, you know."

"No, I didn't know, as a matter of fact. Lucien told me that two men, Lithuanian brothers, saved him and his father rewarded them with lifetime jobs."

"Yes, well. My father wasn't always the sharpest knife in the drawer despite his brilliance at making money. My mother always suspected those men were themselves behind the kidnapping. They were never exactly upstanding citizens of the world. My father, however, believed their story lock, stock, and barrel, as they say. He made them out to be heroes."

"Lucien takes after his father in that way, living in his own little house of cards, Ella. He believes what suits him to believe and dismisses whatever doesn't fit into his narrative." There's a pause on her end. "What exactly did he tell you and why?"

"Just what I've told you."

"Yes, it's all true... except that he wasn't held for days but hours. He likes to believe he was emotionally scarred for life but he only remembers what family members have told him. His memories are totally false." She pauses.

"What I'm not clear on is why he shared the story with you? I thought you were merely colleagues. Has that changed since last I saw you?"

"No," I hurry to reassure her. "I had a... um... difficult night... with Lucien and he told me why he has those men in his employ. That's the only reason."

"Difficult? What happened?"

"I'm not exactly sure… mainly because I was drugged apparently. The drug had an extremely… deleterious effect on me. In short, I don't know what actually happened and what I imagined to have happened.

"I see. Inasmuch as his story is true, I still would caution you about believing anything Lucien says. He prevaricates just because he can, for no other reason. He can be extremely self-centered and he doesn't seem to care how his actions affect other people."

Again, she pauses. For a moment or two, I think the call dropped but then she speaks up again.

"Have you spoken to his former girlfriend, Ella?"

"No, I haven't."

"They were together for quite some time. She might shed some light on the situation for you."

"Was their break-up acrimonious?"

She laughs coldly. "Only if you think your lover cheating on you is acrimonious. Lucien had met another woman and began two-timing the girl… Eliza, I believe her name is. I don't know what happened with the new one but he was apparently head over heels for her."

"Do you know what her name was?"

"I can't remember offhand. It was something exotic, as I recall. Ah, it's at the fringes of my memory but I can't pin it down. It will come to me as soon as we disconnect, no doubt."

I laugh in commiseration. "Yes, that's usually how it works. Well, thank you so much for the information, Maya. I do so appreciate it."

"Not at all, Ella. I liked you immediately and I knew my darling half-brother would be bad news for you one way or another. He usually is."

"Yes, well, live and learn. Take care, Maya."

"You, too, Ella. Goodbye."

I hang up the phone, chewing my lip. After speaking with Maya St. Sauveur, I'm left with more questions than I started with and wondering if I should indeed call Eliza.

Would Lara have any information about her? I'll start with her. Scrolling through my address book in my phone, I find Lara's number and am about to punch in the call when I get a chime alerting me to a text. I switch to the message screen.

It's from Maya. It reads: I remembered her name! It's Natasha.

Chapter 37

Abandon All Hope Ye That Enter Here:

He wakes up at two, then three-thirty, and then again at 4:20. He just cannot get any rest; the stress mounts in his bloodstream like a cyanide drip, as the hippocampus in his brain secretes hormones triggering a fight or flight response.

This time it will be fight.

It is his looming four o'clock appointment that is the culprit. He hadn't cancelled it. Instead, he'd decided to meet with the turncoat bitch and find out for once and for all what the hell it was all about.

Too early to go into the office, he tries to reach Daniel Butler—it's later in New York. Shortly after first meeting Butler, he began to suspect the man has... *unique*... abilities, so why not make use of them, since Butler had made the offer? Of course, he could be entirely mistaken. Perhaps the sharp businessman is merely intuitive?

Butler answers on the third ring. "Yes?"

"Ian Blackmon here. Can you spare a minute?"

"I can. What's going on?"

He tells him about Natasha as briefly as possible, ending with the appointment scheduled for later today. "Any thoughts?"

There's a slight pause on the other end. "The fact that this is so personal explains a lot, Ian. My advice is to go ahead and meet with her. Can't hurt and can only help. Just make sure you don't lose it and kill her." He says it jokingly but both men know it's a distinct possibility at this point in the game.

"Any news on the other front?"

Ian snorts, disgustedly. "The bastard showed up in Portland to talk to Ella."

"I'm not surprised. He has motives that you haven't identified yet, Ian. A man like Phillips doesn't go chasing a woman around the country except for a good reason. I say that with all respect for Ella."

"Yes. I agree. I just don't know what more I can do to ferret out the information—short of water boarding."

"Remind me how Ella met him?"

"Through a college friend. I can't remember her name."

"Remember her name, Ian. Start with her. She probably holds the missing slice of information, knowingly or not."

Ian sighs; he's tired of it all and wants to take a vacation with Ella. "Yes, I will. How was your trip, by the way?"

"Perfect. I recommend getting away for a long weekend, Ian, does wonders for perspective, not to mention disposition. Oh, by the way, we received the lovely gift from you and Ella. Thank you. I believe Olivia sent a note of appreciation."

"Yes. She did. I look forward to meeting her in the near future."

"Absolutely. Perhaps you might make it to New York for our wedding."

"I can do that... if you can get to Portland for ours."

"Oh? I suppose congratulations are in order, then. I'm very glad to hear it but I'm sure you'll be breaking hearts all over the great state of Oregon."

Ian laughs. "Thanks for the minute, Daniel. Have a good day."

As the clock strikes 3:55, he swivels his chair away from the large window behind his desk to face the doors of the office head-on. Ian has been glancing at the damn clock all fucking day—he might just have to get rid of it after today. Is she actually going to show? He hasn't set eyes on Natasha in over five years. The last time he saw her was the day he realized she'd betrayed him... utterly. At that minute, her sensual beauty began to take on sinister proportions.

He had loved her since high school. Since the moment he'd set eyes on her. It was the first time in his young life that he'd felt such a passion for another human being outside of his own family. Perhaps pathetically, he'd believed his feelings were fully requited... but he'd been wrong, dead wrong. Instead of love, she'd set her sights on ruining him.

But she hadn't and still could not. And now? Well, it took a long time, over five years, long, lonely ones to be sure, but now he found he could feel again. He loved Ella with everything he had to give, so Natasha didn't win on any count and he would make sure she knew it, if he did nothing else today.

Just after noon, Janine had buzzed him. "Mr. Blackmon. Ms. Yenin is on the line. She wants to know if she can reschedule her appointment for tomorrow instead?"

What? The bitch is just jerking my chain, he thought. "Where's Claudia?"

"She took an early lunch today; I think she had a doctor's appointment."

"Listen to me, Janine, very carefully. Tell Ms. Yenin that tomorrow is not possible. As far as I'm concerned, it's either today or never. But don't tell her that. Just say no to any other time or day she suggests. She'll get the message rather quickly. Then get back to me with her answer."

"Very good, sir."

He sat there, tapping his fingers against the desk, marshaling all of his resources to remain serene, a near impossible task. Finally, he acceded to his inner rage and sent a heavy crystal paperweight sailing across the room. It blasted into the far wall, gouging a crater into the formerly pristine white of the painted sheetrock. Calmly, he rose to his feet, and walked to a small watercolor painting to the left of the hole. Removing the painting, he pulled its hook out, rammed it just above the cratered hole, and hung the painting to obscure his very recently acquired wall adornment.

All of her options denied, Natasha Yenin relented, deciding to keep the appointment today after all. He knew she would because she had a reason for coming to see him and if he'd learned one thing about Natasha— and learned it the hard way—it was that if she sets her sights on something or someone, she would not back down until it was finished.

At ten to four, the receptionist in the lobby calls to inform him that Ms. Yenin is on her way up. Ian rises to his feet, stretches, rolls his neck, and strides to the other side of the office to get a bottle of water, which he downs in one long pull. He's trying to distract himself from the feelings threatening to swallow him whole: agitation, anger, even confusion. He never did find out why Natasha turned on him so viciously. Perhaps today would deliver the moment of truth?

The buzzer rings as Claudia's echoing voice fills the room a few moments later. "Dragon lady just got off the elevator. How would you like me to proceed?"

"Seat her in reception and make her wait, like everyone else. I'll buzz you when I'm ready. Thanks, Claudia."

"You're welcome, Ian. I'll await your call."

Pacing the room, he tries to work off some of the manic energy coursing through his veins, knowing it's stress-induced. Calm is what he needs more than anything else. Calm will allow him to control the situation and that's exactly what he needs to do. He cannot allow his anger—or any other emotion to get in his way.

Toward that end, he makes her wait over ten minutes, figuring with each passing minute he's ratcheting up her stress level exponentially. He'll be calm; she'll be tense and angry, giving him the advantage over her in their "discussion." Finally, at six minutes after four he buzzes Claudia. "Okay. Send her in."

The door is pushed open with purpose and the tall, blond woman strides through it, walking right to his desk, as if she owns the place. The moment she comes into view, Ian feels his body instantly respond to her physical presence: his heart begins to race erratically and he gets an instant hard-on—and it annoys the hell out of him. He can't help it though: he was sexually attracted to the woman from the second he set his teenaged eyes on her.

Natasha appears not to have aged a day since the last time he saw her. Perhaps her hair is now a lighter blond but her face still holds all the youthful animation it always had and her eyes sparkle with her misspent plans. Her long lean figure sheathed in a body-hugging navy suit, she's wearing a low-cut white camisole under the jacket. Around her throat are multiple strands of pearls, from the last of which dangles a large white-gold Russian Orthodox cross. On her feet are navy stilettos, with five-inch heels, worn with flair despite her tall height. With the shoes, she easily breaches six feet.

Ian stands and slowly comes around his desk to meet her head on. Since she refused to sit, he wasn't about to look up to her from his own seated position. By standing opposite her, he still manages to tower over her by a couple of inches.

Ice-blue eyes unabashedly examine him up and down, appraising him as an adversary. "What? No hug and kiss?" she asks, her voice deep and throaty as she smiles, revealing her toothpaste-ad row of teeth.

Ignoring her comment, he instead asks a question of his own. "To what do I owe this unparalleled *pleasure*, Ms. Yenin?"

"I'm not here to verbally spar with you, Blackmon. I've come to talk business: first about TES. Then... other, shall we say more personal, business."

"Personal?"

Waving her hand in dismissal, she retorts, "Table it

for now. Shall we discuss our competition for TES and Alt-En?"

Ian shrugs, his attention on his fingernails. "Nothing to discuss," he says airily. "As far as Alt-En is concerned, have at it. Excalibur is no longer interested and has withdrawn its offer. As for TES, you may or may not know, the sale of the company to a corporation based in Tokyo is already well underway. Is that all?"

The blond woman retains her cool, eyeing him with no apparent emotion. Though Ian finds her inscrutable expression unnerving, he doesn't allow it show. It's a stare down at this point. Finally, she ruptures the silent impasse.

"You've proven to be a most unworthy opponent, Blackmon. You've had so much time and yet you haven't even begun to figure it out. I suppose I should have left a trail of breadcrumbs... or in your case perhaps just a chorus line of whores. Here, let me take your hand and guide you to it, like leading the blind, deaf, and dumb." She cocks her head, pausing for a short moment. "On second thought: I'll give you a hint and it will be up to you to figure out the story. How's that?" She didn't wait for his comment. "Look to your grandfather."

"My grandfather?" He crosses his arms. "What can my grandfather possibly have to do with this matter? Further, I happen to have two of them. To whom do you refer? My paternal grandfather, who was a judge, or my mother's father, the oncologist?" He leans his hip against the desk, barely breathing and never taking his eyes off the shapely opponent in front of him. He treats her like the snake in the grass she is.

Tapping her foot in a staccato beat, she spits out her next question. "What kind of judge, Blackmon?

"Immigration."

"Bingo. Ever notice that I speak with traces of an accent? I'm a Russian national, as are my parents... as are my grandparents." She looks at him pointedly, as if that's supposed to mean something.

He snickers. "Good for you. Now get to the fucking

point. I have no time for chitchat about family history, fascinating though it may be."

She finally deigns to take a seat, and he follows suit. Ian tries not to look but fails miserably as her skirt, already fairly short at several inches above the knee, rides up her shapely thighs as she crosses her legs. He suspects she's not wearing anything underneath since that was a penchant of hers. If she does have on an undergarment, it is probably a skimpy thong. He musters everything he has at his disposal to banish the image that rides on the coattails of that thought.

Natasha grins, knowing exactly what's running through his mind. He could never resist her physically and that gave her enormous power over him. She believed he'd mastered it by now but a few minutes in his presence and she could tell he's still susceptible. If necessary, she'll use it to her advantage. "You know what, Ian Blackmon? I'm not going to make this too easy for you. Perhaps I'll merely provide you with the impetus to solve the puzzle. You know what they say: incentive is the mother of invention?"

"I believe the word is necessity not incentive, my dear. But please," he gestures widely with his arm, "go on. The floor is yours—in more ways than one."

"I had my plan all mapped out: I was going to obliterate your business bit by bit until you had nothing left. All the players and pieces were in place and poised, ready to play their parts. The initial act was executed— and brilliantly at that.

"And then what happens? You dismantle the fucking company yourself! Why would any sane businessperson do something so drastic? Tell me, Ian. Why?"

He shrugs. "I was no longer interested in capitalizing on the misfortune of others. Call it an ethical epiphany, if you will."

"Ethical? I'd call it weakness. You're weak, Ian, disappointingly so. I thought if there were anything I could count on, it would be your ruthless pursuit of success and profit. Yet, you proved yourself feeble, susceptible to pathetic human emotions, just as you're beholden to your emotions in your personal life now." She sneers with contempt.

"Yes, it's a problem among us humans. But you wouldn't know, would you? Someone like you wouldn't be able to grasp my motivations because I was not propelled by self-profit nor aggrandizement. I think those two motivations and some ridiculous blood vendetta are all you're capable of understanding. You are a psychopathic cunt, Yenin, and I have no purpose for you. Get out of my office and don't darken my doorway again. You do not deserve to draw your next breath of oxygen."

"How dare you call me that word?"

He laughs. "Trust me, I never use it lightly or even at all. In this case, it is richly deserved." He leans in closer, making every word count. "You are a cunt, of the highest order. Moreover, I never want to be forced to look upon your evil again. It's ironic that your twisted ugliness is encased in such a glossy veneer; however, now that I can see beneath it, I can easily identify the monster within… and it's so irretrievably hideous."

Pushing herself to her feet and spinning around, she begins to stalk to the door. "I do hope your bravado holds out when your precious Ariel goes missing, Ian. Perhaps then you'll have the time and *necessity* to figure out why I detest you so much."

The fires of Hades are ablaze in his eyes and his voice crackles with fury as he tears into her. "If you harm one hair on my Ella's head, I'm going to take you apart piece by piece and I mean that in the literal not figurative sense, Yenin. That is a solemn vow."

"Oh, please. I've already had her in my grips. Of course, Lucien disappointed me, big time. One would think a sophisticated, one might even say continental, man such as he could take on a silly little schoolgirl like your Ariel. Lucien blamed you for making it impossible."

"So it was you who enlisted Lucien? I should have known: the man gave me the creeps from the first moment I met him... just as you do."

"Your mouth can lie, Ian, but your eyes confess the whole truth." She drops her voice to a low, husky register. "If I were to stand here in front of you and remove my clothing, I'd have you on your knees in seconds."

He shakes his head in disgust. "Keep deluding yourself, Natasha. I wouldn't spit on you if you were on fire, I assure you."

"Yes, the clever Ian Blackmon... and yet again you couldn't figure it out—any of it. It was so obvious. I mean, why would a man like Lucien go out of his way for a mousy little thing like your Ariel? That fact in and of itself should have alerted you.

"Lucien is *mine*: he fell hard for my charm so I tried to utilize his devotion to my advantage. Since he left his long-time girlfriend for me, I wanted to make it worth his while. Your cute young fluff, so apparently innocent, seemed like she might provide my darling with a few hours of fun and, silly me, I truly thought he was up to the challenge. He wasn't though, not up to outplaying you, Blackmon. Complicating matters, I do believe he began to develop feelings for the girl somewhere along his road to perdition, which was funny because he swears he's madly in love with me. Itty-bitty Ella foiled that part of our plan."

"Good for her. Yenin, you're not fit to lick my Ella's boots, quite frankly. Don't bring her into this conversation again. I won't have her name sullied by coming off your dirty lips."

Natasha could easily see and identify the blistering rage in his eyes when she mentioned his woman—intense emotion, love or hate, darkens the light blue-gray to slate, but they remain lighter around the edges. She remembers that about her old friend, her first lover—that and other things. For example, his beautiful face aglow with triumph when they scored a big deal, the way his eyes glistened like late-afternoon sunshine on water when he was amused and gleamed when he looked upon her in admiration, the way his dark locks of hair floated on the wind as the two of them tooled around in his pale blue convertible—the one he swore he bought because the color matched her eyes.

But the memory she adored the most and perhaps caused her the most regret was without doubt the expression on his face when they made love, as if he'd attained Nirvana, the way his eyes fell dark not with anger but with unbridled passion, the iris all but disappearing within the murky depths just before they rolled up into his head when he hit his orgasm. Yes, that was her favorite memory of all. Perhaps she'd see it again one day.

Surprising herself, she also feels a bolt of hot jealousy streak through her, scorching her blood. Ian belongs to her, not that little American snot; Natasha just chooses not to accept him currently. How dare that college girl think she could take on Ian Blackmon? Natasha decides Ariel needs another comeuppance. Maybe this time she'd give the green light to her uncles to have their way with her.

Shaking off her extreme reaction, she tosses her blond head back and laughs throatily at Ian's last comment—every move she makes is calculated to be alluring to him. She's rehearsed it all, leaving nothing to chance and she anticipates his every response. Her responses are the wild cards here: she must temper her emotions to succeed. Ian remains sitting in his chair watching her closely, a strange little smile dancing on his lips. What happened to the fury of a moment ago?

Ah, the master has resumed his poker face: outwardly, he is impervious, like a chess player carefully contemplating his next move. Inwardly, all hell is breaking loose and his sincerest desire is to wrap his long fingers around her elegant throat and squeeze every last bit of life out of her treacherous person.

"So," he begins again, his fingers playing with his bottom lip, "something to do with my grandfather, you say?"

"I've already told you I won't reveal anything more. It's up to you to figure it out. I promise to give you motivation."

"Are you threatening Ella again?"

"Lucien failed miserably but I can assure you my uncles will not."

Ian grabs for his cell and calls Ella—it goes directly to voice mail. Trying Mason next, his heart revs into overdrive.

"Mr. Blackmon?"

"Where's Ella?"

"I'm waiting for her in the car. She's in a department store right now."

"Get in there, Mason, and find her. She's been threatened. Now!"

"Yes, sir."

"Call me as soon as she's with you again." He disconnects. Placing the phone down, feeling as if there's a lump of lead in his belly, he avoids looking into the devil's eyes. "You better hope he calls back with a positive report or your very life is at stake. I promise you."

"So dramatic, Ian. I'm not threatening, per se. Just providing you with a little incentive."

He shoots up and storms over to her; she rises to meet his onslaught. Only stopping within inches of her face, he is poised for attack. Natasha Yenin stands her ground but actually flinches this time at the big man glowering at her. She can nearly match him for height, but certainly not weight or muscle mass.

"If you touch me, you'll live to regret it, Ian."

"Touch you?" He sneers. "Not with a ten-foot-pole, Natasha."

"Is that what you're promising your women these days? Seems a bit of an exaggeration... Though from what I recall, not too much of one." Her voice drops volume with the last remark and she parts her lips, eager to kiss him after all this time. Another thing she remembers about him is that he is quite practiced at the art.

He gifts her with a purely malevolent smile. "I believe my memory is returning to me. I recall my grandfather being involved in getting rid of some unsavory elements, members of the Russian mob, if I'm not mistaken."

Natasha shrugs, not breaking eye contact though the two remain inches apart. "You say mobster, we say businessmen. It's just a question of semantics."

"Semantics, eh? True, why should something so pesky as federal law be taken into account?"

"Purely arbitrary lines drawn in the sand by self-important cogs in the wheel. We choose to ignore them."

"Yes, arbitrary, because money is money and heroin is heroin... not to mention guns and human trafficking, or anything else resulting in the propagation of human misery."

"Fine. You want me to explain and save you the detective work and I find I still can't resist you." She spins on her heel and walks toward the far wall, her agitation now on display.

"Simply put, Ian, your grandfather was responsible for deporting mine, an act that led to his destruction in a very short period of time. He had enemies in Russia: sending him back was condemning him to death. As soon as he stepped foot on Russian soil, he lived for exactly 28 days before meeting with a mysterious accident, lapsing into a persistent vegetative state. It not only destroyed him but also our family in the process. To this day my grandmother has not recovered. My aim was to exact revenge on your family since the first day I met the tall, gangly Ian Blackmon in Mr. Parson's English lit class."

"So it was never real then? Between us?"

Now she sees she's wounded him. Strangely it gives her little satisfaction. "I wouldn't say that. I knew revenge was best served cold so I took advantage of the lead time and was able to enjoy you for a while." She walks to him and grabs his tie, pulling him closer, the action reminding him of Ella instantly, with her pretty face focused in the lens of his mind. "And it was most enjoyable, Ian. I often miss it... and you."

Ripping her hand off his tie, he throws it back at her. "I have nothing but contempt for you. Revenge is stupid and wasteful... and in the end, most unfulfilling. You should turn your attentions to doing something good in the world to make up for your disgusting criminal of a grandfather. What he did to better himself hurt others very badly."

"Since when are you on a moralistic crusade? Where's the Ian I knew who made money by exploiting the mistakes of others? Who called employees redundancies and eliminated them without a thought or regret? As I remember, euphemisms were spilling out of your mouth left and right: collateral damage, surplus human capital, personnel reduction... and the list goes on."

"I'm proud to say that that man doesn't exist anymore. I'm a new man, one who cares about the fate of others... and you know what? I still make buckets of money without hurting others. In fact, I often *help* others keep their jobs. I finally can sleep at night. I suggest you give it a try—I highly recommend it.

"Now, before I toss you out of my office on your pretty little ass I want to make sure you understand something very clearly: I don't give a damn about your vendetta or whatever it is that's compelling you to do nasty things to others. However, you had better keep Ariel out of it because if you involve her in any way, however peripherally, I cannot guarantee that you'll survive the experience. Are we clear?"

"My, my, it appears you do have feelings for this girl. I'm a bit jealous, Ian."

The look of incredulity on his face makes her laugh. "Do you not know how fine is the dividing line between love and hate?" She steps closer. "I miss you."

At the same time he pushes her away, she reaches her hands up, weaving them through his dark hair so there's a push-pull. Ian manages to shove her away and she stumbles backward before reclaiming her balance. Her ice-blue eyes flash, whether it's lust or anger he can't tell.

"Okay, I'll take that as a no but do tell me what that bulge in your pants is all about, Ian?" She laughs loudly and coarsely as she exits the office, followed by a crashing sound as another large crater is blasted into existence on the opposite wall of the office.

Chapter 38

Right in the middle of a personal one-woman celebration in Macy's dressing room, my phone chimes. Grabbing for my cell while trying to pull a shirt over my head makes for a comedy of errors and I almost fall right on my undie-clad ass. "Ow!" I screech, as my elbow slams into the side of the dressing room in my clumsy attempt to arrest my plunge down to the low-pile commercial carpet. The women around me must think someone's getting viciously assaulted or something in the adjacent stall, but, no, it's just me, my iPhone, and my size 4 jeans. The most critical part of that sentence is of course *my size 4 jeans*! When I don't recognize the number right away I elect to answer anyway mainly because I almost killed myself to get the damn call and it seems wasteful to screen after all that. "Hello?"

Mason's voice is urgent. "Ms. Strong, Mr. Blackmon wants me to pick you up right now. He claims the matter is of the utmost importance. Where exactly are you currently?"

"Uh, I'm on the second floor, women's department. Right now I'm in the dressing room."

"Please stay there in the dressing room. Do not move until I get there. Are we clear?"

I roll my eyes, sorry he can't see my disrespectful annoyance. "Yes, Mason, we're clear. Despite how Mr. Blackmon treats me, I'm not mentally deficient."

"Of course, Ms. Strong. I believe Mr. Blackmon will explain it all to you when he sees you. Until then I'm not to leave your side. I'm on my way up the escalator as we speak. I'm going to ask you to stay on the line with me."

"It will prove difficult to stay on the line and get dressed at the same time, Mason. I'll keep the line open but I'll place the phone down on the chair. Will that be okay?"

"Yes, that's fine."

Sighing, I realize my shopping celebration is over. Still, it was spectacular while it lasted. I fit into a size 4 pair of jeans for the first time since my freshman year of college. Since then I've been consistently a size 6 with one brief foray into the land of eights. That was right after a broken heart caused me to subsist on a steady diet of *Häagen-Dazs* and straight-up scotch—all scored by depressive *Radiohead* songs. Now that the broken heart is only a memory, I look back with fondness on that diet.

In less than sixty seconds, I hear Mason's voice at the entrance to the dressing room. "Ella? Can you come out now?"

Grabbing my newfound jeans and a couple of sweaters I'd managed to try on before I got the royal summons, I make my way out to my bodyguard. "Here I am. I just have to pay for my purchases."

Mason sticks to me like *Crazy Glue*, not letting me out of his sight until he's delivered me to Ian's house with the stern admonition not to leave until Ian gets home. I'm wondering what it's all about but in less than half an hour, I hear Ian's deep voice in the hall, speaking to Mason and then the man himself strides in.

It doesn't matter how long I know him—or how well I know him: he still makes my body rev into sexual overdrive when he enters my sphere. The sight, sound, and scent of this powerful man send things spinning, tightening, and shaking inside me. Right now I drink him in and assess: his eyes are alive with emotion and his whole body language is tense. Even his perfect suit looks a bit wrinkled, an unusual state of affairs for him. Something's wrong, I can easily tell. I just watch and wait for his cues.

"Ella," he says with relief, rushing over to me and

sweeping me into his arms.

"Ian, you're choking me. Ease up a little."

"I'm sorry, Ella. I was so worried about you."

"Can you tell me why?"

He doesn't answer. Instead he calls for Mason and the man enters the room in seconds. "Mason, have a seat. I'm about to explain the situation to Ella. You might as well hear, too." He looks at me and grasps my hands in his. "Ella. Remember when I told you I had something to tell you?"

I nod, saying nothing.

"This whole situation has to do with that history. Mason, you only need to hear the first part. I mentioned on the phone that Ella was threatened but I didn't want to go into detail until I could explain it. The same people who were behind your ordeal with Lucien Phillips have threatened you again, Ella."

My eyes widen at that tidbit of information. Why? "How do you know, Ian?"

"I'll get to that, Ella. Mason, what you need to know is that Ella requires a bodyguard 24/7 until the danger passes. After I speak to Ella, I'll meet with you and your staff in my office in," he glances at his watch, "let's say an hour and a half and we'll review the procedures I want in place. Is that acceptable?"

"Yes, sir."

"Good. Right now, I'd like to speak with Ariel alone. Thank you for your quick work today, Mason. It won't go unrecognized."

"Yes, sir."

After Mason leaves the room, Ian sits for a moment looking into my eyes. He looks so tired, almost defeated even. I've never seen him look this way and it bothers me so much. In my estimation, Ian Blackmon is invincible: I don't like thinking someone out there can take him down, even if it's just a peg or two.

"Ella, what I have to tell you is disturbing," he begins, rubbing my hands and refusing to meet my eyes. My heartbeat is reacting to his demeanor—I can feel it accelerate: is this something that will impact our relationship? He's not going to split from me, is he? Is there another woman? I'm now making myself sick so I ask him to have pity on me.

"Please, Ian, just spit it out. The suspense is starting to hurt."

Nodding grimly, he begins. "I met a girl in high school..."

By the time he finishes with the story of Natasha, I sit there flabbergasted. So this horrible woman not only arranged my miserable night with Lucien but my whole employment with the motherfucker? I feel as used as a dirty dishtowel and could probably take the bitch on myself right at this minute, not to mention her boy toy, Lucien.

"So what happens now?"

He looks surprised. "What do you mean, what happens? We ignore her as best we can and you have continuous protection around the clock."

"How long will she be a threat? Ian, it is against the law to stalk and harass other people, you know. Do I now have to live my life looking over my shoulder?"

"She'll go away after a while. If she doesn't we'll have to look into more... proactive measures."

I literally stomp my foot. "I say we look into more proactive measures right now. I'll be damned if I'm going to live my life in fear of some insane woman."

Shooting up off the sofa, he begins to pace in front of me, his hand rifling through his hair, which now suffers unduly from his anxiety. "Ian, your hair makes you look like a madman. How long have you been messing with it?"

Levity doesn't seem to perforate his armor of stress—he's in full-out war mode. I can see it in his comportment: his entire body stands ramrod straight, stiff as an oaken board, and there's an inferno raging in his eyes.

"I'm not sure how to proceed. I need to speak to my grandfather about the case involving hers. But this is revenge, pure and simple. If her grandfather is in a vegetative state, there's no remedy we can provide. Anyway, my instincts tell me he got what he had coming. My grandfather was an advocate for immigrants and tried his best to prevent their deportation unless they were involved in crime. As I recall, during the nineties, there was a huge exodus out of Russia, mobsters coming to our shores to run drugs and guns. I as much as said that to Natasha. It's a little hard for me to believe she's been nursing this vendetta since we were kids but there it is. I'm very sorry that you became involved in this sordid affair, Ariel.

I shake my head at his thickness. "Ian," I get up and walk to him, "I am your fiancée; we are getting married, for better or for worse. Don't apologize for getting me involved because you had no fault here. But I'd like to ask you one question and I want an honest answer."

He nods nervously, I think. I continue. "What exactly are your feelings for Natasha?"

And he sits down again. Feeling like a yo-yo, I seat myself next to him, our legs touching. His body is throwing off so much heat, I start to have carnal thoughts about him but I need his answer first.

Hesitantly, he starts to explain. "I used to love her, Ella. I fell hard for her in high school and we made long-range plans to be together. It was all a lie for her but not for me: I planned our future to be together and I worked toward it. When I learned of her betrayal, it cut me—deeply. I spent the next five years keeping myself from forming any emotional attachment." He stares me in the eye. "Until you. Somehow you broke through the barriers I had carefully constructed."

"How do you feel about Natasha right now? Are your feelings conflicted?" I'm so afraid of his answer that my voice is barely audible.

His face shows no hesitation. "No, not at all. I have no love for her, Ella. Zero. I intensely dislike her, hate her even, especially for what she was responsible for doing to you."

I accept his answer but there's something he's not telling me—I can sense it in the furtive glances he's throwing at me, as if he's guilty about something. I decide to give it one more try.

"Is there something else you have to tell me, Ian?"

Is it my worry reflecting back at me in his eyes or is it his own, generated by my probing question? "Why do you ask?"

"I sense you're holding something back, something you feel guilt over. Am I right?" I never take my eyes off him lest I miss any of his nonverbal cues.

Completely shocking me, he nods and hangs his head, refusing to look at me. That punch of nausea assaults my stomach again as I fight the urge to vomit. "Let's have it, then. Get it all on the table, please."

He looks up again and there's actually amusement in his eyes. Now I'm truly flummoxed but I wait as patiently as I can, my rocking knee the only evidence of my anxiety.

"It's embarrassing and stupid but I do need to tell you, Ella. It's just that when the woman came into my office, I actually became physically aroused. It infuriated me."

Well.

I sit back to consider his confession. I look at his face: he's openly wearing his guilt. It's not as bad as I had been imagining but it certainly doesn't elate me. Still, I could understand it since his relationship with Natasha was predicated on sexual attraction... and in the final analysis, sex was really all it was other than bad blood. It's not out of character for him, either, since it doesn't take much for him to get, ahem, *engaged*. People can't help who they are physically attracted to, can they? Even if a person is deeply in love, that person can still be physically attracted to another. I recall my uncontrollable reaction to the luscious male morsel that is Daniel Butler. It's biology. Or chemistry. Or is it physics? Whatever.

My eyes volley back to his anxious ones. He's barely

breathing as he watches me digest his confession. I choose to take the high road and give him a break... *this time*. Reaching for his hand, I squeeze it and scoot closer to him. "It's okay, Ian. I understand that these things happen."

Genuine shock is etched on his face. "You do?"

"Of course." My curious hand travels from his hand to his thigh... to his crotch. "But," I whisper in his ear, "I'll need for you to demonstrate exactly how you became excited."

Before he can reply, I begin to kiss and lick his neck, working my way down to his collar. Pushing it open, I bite his neck. In one fluid motion, he stands and sweeps me up into his arms, proceeding to rush us up to the bedroom. The rooms flash by my eyes in a blur and in our wake is an echo of my giggles. My boy is so damn predictable.

Chapter 39

"Hello Sarah? This is Ian Blackmon. Is my grandfather home?"

The genteel voice on the line sounds pleasantly surprised. "Ian! So nice to hear from you. I know your grandfather will be pleased but I'll let you be the one to surprise him. Hold the line for a moment."

A minute of muffled static buzzes in his ear and then a booming voice travels across the miles of fiber optics. "Hello?"

"Hello, Edward? It's Ian. Ian Blackmon."

"How many Ians do you think I know, young man? For God's sake, I'm your grandpa. Out of all my grandchildren, you're the only one who calls me by my given name. Why, pray tell?"

Ian laughs spontaneously, overjoyed to hear his grandfather sounding hale. "Because I'm a freak, as my sister is so fond of reminding me."

Thunderous laughter is his response. "No, it's because you're what used to be known as a stuffed shirt. Means too conservative—you have to loosen up. What did they used to say in Hawaii? Hang loose. So why do I merit a phone call? Miss my scintillating presence?"

"Always. How are you feeling, Grandpa?"

"Uh, can't complain. Since the accident my back aches all the time but other than that, things are pretty fine. Sarah takes good care of me."

"Marry her already, Grandpa. Grandma would have wanted you to be happy. You know Sarah's always had a hankering for you—probably her only flaw."

More deep-throated chuckles follow. "Indeed? I don't

know about all that. What's on your mind, son?"

"Do you remember the woman I used to date years ago? Natasha Yenin?"

"Blond, right? And very tall, or the more polite way to say it is statuesque?"

"Yes, that's right. I met her in high school and then later went into business with her. We had a falling out— essentially she tried to destroy my holdings and I never knew why."

The jovial quality of the older man's voice disappears and the stern judge emerges from his sudden absence. Even the down-home idiom vanishes; it's as if another man gets on the phone. "I see. Have you subsequently learned her reasons for doing so?"

"Only partially." He sighs. "She directed me to you."

"To me? Does it pertain to one of my cases?"

"Apparently. Her grandfather. According to Natasha, you deported him and thereby ruined his life. I'm trying to learn more about it and I have a private investigator on the trail now. I just wondered if you had any recall..."

"Do you perchance know the name?"

"No. Not yet. Her name is Yenin but I highly doubt they kept the same name if they shared one. She told me there were people back in the mother country who were only too glad to welcome him home. She claims now, after they seriously injured him, he's left in a persistent vegetative state."

"Well, I had a multitude of cases involving some nasty pieces of work from the Russian mob element, I can tell you. It could be any one of them. Can you get me the name and I'll do a bit of research?"

"Sure. I'll have my investigator poke around and see what he can come up with. Then I'll get back to you. Did they ever catch the guy who ran your car off the road?"

"No. One would think with all the camera surveillance everywhere one goes these days, it would be easy to find anyone. The price we pay for safety is not buying us all that much of it. The police continually inform me they have leads but I don't believe them.

Why? Do you think it could be connected to your Natasha?"

The possibility strikes him like a left hook, a sudden revelation that causes his guts to seize up. "God, Grandpa, it didn't even cross my mind. I truly hope not." Silence drops over the phone line on both ends as each man contemplates the possibility. Ian is the first to speak again. "Just to err on the side of safety, you should be extra cautious at least until I get more information."

"I'm always cautious, Ian, but I will bear it in mind. Please get me the name as soon as you have it."

"I will, Grandpa. Please take care of yourself and Sarah."

After the conversation with his grandfather, Ian understands his dire necessity for more information—and lightning fast. He also needs Ella to remain safe. Knowing how stubborn she can be, he realizes that he must impress upon her the gravity of the situation: the Russian mob is not something with which to tangle and walk away whole. He'll have to be truthful with her... *again*. This candor rests uneasily with a man used to keeping things extremely close to the vest but he'll just have to breathe through the discomfort. He laughs to himself as he recalls telling his sexual partners the very same every time he'd deliver erotic pain to them during the course of their play. *Breathe through it.* Well, he'd do well to take his own advice.

He picks up the phone. "Scott, Blackmon. I'll need the plane for a trip to New York. We leave in the morning for two days. Any problems? Very good; I'll see you in the a.m." He buzzes his assistant next. "Claudia, I want you to pull the report we ran on Lucien Phillips. Copy it and leave the original in the file. Bring me the copy as soon as you have it. Thank you." He doesn't wait for a reply before he disconnects.

"Ella," he snuggles up to her back, sweeping her long hair away from her neck so he could nuzzle it.

"Mmm. Stop that," she mutters into her pillow, "or

I'm not going to let you go to work on time."

He coos, as he relentlessly kisses and sucks the sensitive areas of her neck and throat. "Promise?"

She whips around, encircling his neck with both arms and hitches one leg around his waist. "Promise. Now what?"

Reluctant to share his news, he distracts her by leaning in closer to kiss her. He'd rather stay in bed with Ella all day, only getting up for necessities. But Scott was already at the hangar, readying the plane for the trip. "I have to make a quick trip to New York."

Ella unravels herself from him and sits up in a flash, a thousand questions flashing across her face in milliseconds. "Why?"

Frowning, he internally debates the wisdom of telling her too much truth. She'll worry herself sick and she may try to accompany him. Wouldn't it be better to prevaricate this one time? Or perhaps lie by omission? "I have to meet with someone, Ella. I'll be back by no later than tomorrow evening."

"With whom are you meeting, if I may be so bold to ask?"

His eyes flare with amusement. "Tsk, tsk, so suspicious, aren't we? It's not a woman, I assure you. Now...what about that delaying tactic you promised?" He yanks her back down; she lands with a thud onto his chest and his fast hands begin to roam.

"Oh, no you don't, Blackmon. First tell me whom you're meeting with and then you can distract me."

Ian cradles her face in his large hands. Can she possibly know how much he loves her? Pushing her hair away, he looks—really looks—at every inch of her beautiful face. Her forehead, neither too high nor too low, that gently slopes toward elegantly arched brows. Almond-shaped eyes, large and china blue, watch the world with a clarity that always robs him of breath when they're trained on him intently, her straight nose, the size in harmony with the rest of her face, and finally her luscious, luscious lips, so full and red, the most kissable he's ever seen.

Holding her in his embrace, he knows unequivocally that he no longer could live without her. If something happened to Ella, he'd shrivel and die: she is that precious. He leans in and kisses those lips over and over, barely allowing her a breath in between. He slides his mouth across her jaw to her neck, running his tongue down to the nape and on to her shoulder. Between the two points, he clamps down his mouth—so she feels the warm and wet... and then the sharpness of teeth as he bites down. Whereas she used to protest such pain, she now welcomes it from him—her thready gasp confirms he's stirring her passion.

He doesn't want to talk right now.

Ella's response is primal. She throws her head back to allow him full access to her throat, while straddling his legs. Flexing her hips, she can feel the swelling bulge through his thin drawstring pants and it serves to stoke her passion higher. She begins moving her body against his more aggressively—she has no panties on and the friction and heat he's releasing is sending her body into a frenzied impatience.

Growling in response, he reaches down to pull up her nightgown and slide down his pants. She's so wet that his cock is bathed in her, seeping right through his clothing. With a moan rumbling from deep in his chest, his arms reach up to hold her shoulders in place as he thrusts up into her. Normally there are no words between them, just rhythmic motion and punctuating sounds. This time he speaks to her, whispering in her ear, dirty things that make her control slip away faster until she shrieks, high and loud, and all her muscles clamp down on him. He tries to fight it, marshaling every resource accessible to him, but to no avail: her body forces him into the whirling vortex with her and they both reach the end of it as one, exhausted.

After a few moments their panting winds down, and Ian accepts the obligation he has to come clean with her; he doesn't want to undermine the new currency of their relationship. Inhaling a bolstering breath of oxygen, he prepares himself for the argument.

"Ella, sweet, I have to go have a heart to heart with Phillips. It's critically important that I do so, and I need to know you'll respect my wishes and stay here, guarded by Mason at all times. Can you allow me that one less worry? Please?"

The information shocks her. "Lucien? I don't want you going there alone, Ian. Remember what you did to his face. I'm sure he'd like nothing better than to pay you back, despite what he said about being a pacifist."

"He's not the one I'm worried about—it's his two protectors who concern me. But I'm not going alone, Ella. I promise. I'll either take Daniel Butler with me or some of his back-up. I swear to it." He bends down to peer into her eyes, his gaze penetrating any barrier. "Do I have your word, Ella?"

Ella knows she can't fight him on this front: Natasha is too dangerous. "Okay." Her thoughts run to her conversation with Maya St. Sauveur. She sharply sucks in her breath. "You know, if you had told me about Natasha sooner, I could have told you about her connection with Lucien. I just remembered that Maya told me that someone named Natasha took Lucien away from his longtime girlfriend."

"Really." His comment wasn't an interrogative, but merely a punctuating statement.

"Yes. You might try speaking to his ex. Her name is Eliza, I believe, but I don't know her surname."

"I believe it's in the initial report I had run on Mr. Phillips when you first began your employment with him. I wonder if you might consider starting the conversation with her while I'm in New York?"

She reaches up to stroke his face, stubbled from a five o'clock shadow. "I can do that."

"Good. I'll have Claudia contact you with her telephone number. Thank you, Ella. To know you're safe is one less thing on my mind."

She reaches her hand down and begins to stroke

him. "We work better as a team, don't we?"

His voice drops to a deeper register as his hands begin to reciprocate, "We certainly do, Ms. Strong."

Meanwhile, Scott waits at the hangar, the Gulfstream ready to go.

Natasha Yenin is rarely conflicted: once she makes up her mind to do something, she sees it through. The whole idea began with Ian's grandfather, Edward Blackmon, the man who ruined her family by domino effect. He deported her grandfather back to Russia where the men he double-crossed waited to taste the sweet nectar of vengeance.

Two years before the Yenin clan emigrated to the States, a gang of ten criminals banded together, pooled their financial resources, and entrusted the money to her grandfather. He was the only one who was clean enough to obtain a visa to the States. Once there he was to broker deals for their cache of stolen Soviet-era weapons they had stockpiled in a warehouse outside of St. Petersburg. The money was to be used to grease palms and to acquire drugs to sell—diversification was always a smart move for any kind of criminal, be it a Wall Street type or a Russian mobster.

Instead, Gregori Greshenko pocketed all the money and made a life in the U.S. for his wife and children. They took his mother's maiden name of Yenin and proceeded to prosper using the stolen cash as seed money to finance more lucrative operations stateside. He knew if he ever got sent back to Russia, he'd be in very deep shit.

Judge Blackmon knew a wormy apple when he saw one and Greshenko was the worst kind of bad. Not only did he allow the deportation, he also expedited it. The criminal element surging into the U.S. from the former Soviet Union was overwhelming the streets and the courts, dumping more heroin and guns on the streets of big cities than ever before.

Even though the U.S. would not allow a DNA

database, Natasha knew the CIA covertly maintained one on foreign nationals; in fact, now U.S. citizens would enjoy the same right to violation since the Supreme Court just recently gave the police the right to take DNA sampling of arrested citizens. But back then it was only the foreigners who were infringed upon in this indelible manner. Natasha knew that if any of her family were caught doing anything against the law, their DNA would be captured through nefarious methods and added to the growing secret database. She could not risk being among that data for it would follow her forever, marking her as a criminal element and preventing her legal residency in the U.S.

Going after the judge was too risky although they ultimately tried it, hoping to make it appear to be an ordinary automobile accident. The old iron bastard survived with some serious but not life-threatening injuries. But the whole DNA thing Natasha feared so much gave her the idea about her uncles. They were her mother's brothers, born in Lithuania, twins born a week apart. What Natasha found of particular interest was their dedication to one Lucien Phillips, of French and Danish extraction, but reared primarily in the United States and Paris, France. The record indicated his father was a French national, an exceedingly wealthy financier, and his mother was a member of the Danish royal family.

She knew her uncles were behind his kidnapping: they used the ransom money to help finance their sister's life in the U.S. But why did they bear such lifelong devotion to a child of strangers? Natasha suspected she knew the answer and set out to prove it through DNA analysis.

Tests confirmed her suspicions: Leo was Lucien's biological father but Natasha discovered that the brothers were both fucking Lucien's mother and the two agreed to accept the boy as belonging to both, never getting tested. So Lucien, for all intents and purposes, was both men's son—and such a beautiful one at that. The brothers were proud of their spawn. When they saw his face after Ian Blackmon got through with him, they were ready to wipe the streets with him. It was only through Natasha's persuasion that they relented. She promised them she would take Blackmon down. Killing him could end up getting one of them life and the rest deported, permanently banned from U.S. soil.

Did Lucien know one of her uncles was his biological father? Natasha didn't think so, since he frequently spoke of the French financier as his forebear. The mother never said anything, probably due to the fact that she was not a willing participant in the sex games the brothers forced upon her. Natasha guessed it was closer to rape than anything else. She did pass off her child on her husband for many different reasons, all of them practical.

So in the end, Natasha and her parents decided to make the judge pay for his sins through his son or grandson. After all, isn't it true that the sins of the father are almost always visited upon the son?

Chapter 40

While Ian's in the shower getting ready for his trip to New York, I snatch up his iPad to make a playlist for his flight. I begin with *Seven Nation Army*, a song that I could imagine Ian loving. Then I add songs to the mix that I doubt he's ever heard. Finally, for whimsy's sake, I throw in *El Scorcho* and for irony, *Tainted Love*. When I'm done, his new playlist has twelve songs.

Okay, so that will kill at least a half-hour of his six-hour flight. Now what? Should I write him a letter?

I decide to do just that but I have to be quick about it for his shower has to be winding down right about now. I can't open a word file on his iPad but I can write it in an email text and send it to him. So I do.

I title my letter *Things I Love About You* and in it I tell him all the things I love about him, duh: the silvery color of his eyes first thing in the morning when bright daylight irradiates them, the way his silky dark hair fans across his forehead when we're riding in his new convertible Jag, making him look so young and sweet, and the look on his face when he has an orgasm—his eyes glaze over, then close, and his expression is one of pure ecstasy.

I lie back on the pillow and cast my mind over the days of our nascent relationship. More things to love drift into my head like feathers on the wind: the rakish way he looked dressed all in black that night at his naughty club, his sexy moans that made me physically ache for him when he kissed me that same night, his expression when he first showed me his new houseboat, which we shortly thereafter christened...

Ah, there's just so much I love about Ian Blackmon. The shower is off now but I hear the sink faucet running so he's still busy—I have a few more minutes. Closing my eyes, I see him behind the wheel of his new Jaguar F-Type. Oh, yes, his intense pleasure whenever he slides into the driver's seat of one of his fast cars: his eyes gleam with an unholy light and a focused concentration grips him, as if the sexy car requires all of his attention to operate.

Then there's the beautiful businessman side of him: the suits he wears are not ordinary ones by any stretch of the imagination: they are lovers woven of fabric, that hang just perfectly off his muscled frame, wrapping sensuously around him, in a lush dance with his body in motion. Yes, I wax poetic about stupid fucking *suits* when it comes to Ian. Conservative at work, he favors dark suits and muted shirts with solid ties. But it doesn't matter: they're well cut and expensively made, and with that body he would look good in anything or nothing. Certainly nothing.

I write all of this down, knowing there's so much more that I could be writing this list for days on end. Alas, the limited reasons I've listed will have to do for now. He's emerging from the bathroom and it's time for the *Let's Watch Naked Ian Get Dressed* show. It's my second favorite pastime. I sit up straighter in the bed and wait impatiently for the damn towel to drop.

"What are you up to?" His tone is teasing as he unexpectedly turns to catch me gaping, his left eyebrow lifted in an amused query.

"What are *you* up to, is the better question," I ask breezily, noting a favorite part of him standing at attention. Do we have time for one more go-round? "I was just sending you an email to read on the flight to New York."

"Oh?"

"Yes, plus I compiled a playlist on your iPad," I say proudly. "That should eat up a whole forty-five minutes. Then if you have a three-hour nap and a leisurely two-hour meal, that will get you all the way to New York."

Ian grins and swaggers over, sitting on the edge of the bed. His hand reaches over and he gently brushes back the hair in my face, then grasps my hand. "Promise me you'll keep Mason by your side every single minute when you're not in this condo."

"Should he sleep with me, too? For protection, I mean?" His responding glower is answer enough. "Okay, I promise, Ian. I understand the danger involved. Promise *me* you won't go to Lucien's alone... in fact, you shouldn't go there at all. Perhaps you might meet him at a public place?"

"I promise I won't go alone. The problem with meeting him, Ella, is that the man isn't just going to pick up the phone and joyfully arrange to meet me at the place of my choosing. I don't even know if he's in town for certain but I couldn't exactly phone him for his schedule." He peers closely into my eyes. "Claudia is going to call you with the girlfriend's contact number. Don't forget to call. Okay?"

I nod. "What should I say, do you think?"

"Explain who you are and then, if you think it necessary to loosen her tongue, tell her about what happened to you and how Lucien feared the two men were behind it. Segue from there to ask if she knows anything about them. You may not want to mention Natasha's name upfront because according to your friend Maya, the evil one broke up their long-term relationship."

Again, I nod in assent, now troubled. I never met this Natasha person but I hate her already. She wants to hurt Ian through whatever means she can, and that includes me. I hope we can hurt her first, though I have no idea if it's even possible.

"Ian, do you have a plan of attack or are you just doing reconnaissance?"

"I have a tentative plan, but it's entirely subject to change as needed. Come here," he holds out his arms. "I don't want you worrying. As long as you stick close to

Mason, you'll be fine, Ella. I promise."

"What about you?" I choke out, upset now "will you be fine?"

Ian bends down to so our eyes are level. "I will be fine. I'm going in with protection and extreme caution. Plus, I can defend myself quite well."

"Not against a gun or a knife. These people can be ruthless—you don't know what they're capable of, do you?"

"I suspect I do know but I'd rather not share it with you right now." He smiles. "I'll keep in touch, baby. Just make that phone call and get back to me with whatever info you manage to ferret out of her. Okay? I've got to go: Scott's been waiting on me for nearly two hours."

"Okay, go."

He turns to grab his bag and head to the door. "Ian!"

His face shifts toward me. "Yes?"

I zip over to him and throw my arms around his neck. "I love you."

"Ella, I love you, too. I'll be back soon and we'll spend some time together doing happy things for a change. No business dinners, no corporate events, no fights with ex-lovers or—employers. Just you, me, and some serious fun. Yes?"

Smiling broadly, I nod my head vigorously. "I'll start planning right away. How does roller blading grab you?"

The look of horror that descends over his face leaves me giggling even after the door closes. Five minutes later, I miss him already—desperately.

Claudia phones me at ten-thirty with the contact info for one Eliza McQueen. The hand that is holding the paper on which I've written the number is shaking as if with palsy: obviously, I don't want to do this but I promised Ian. I figure I'll just bite the bullet and get it over with so I pick up the damn phone, deciding if she doesn't pick up, I won't leave a message. Or should I? How will I ever get in touch with her if she screens calls? Okay, maybe I will leave a message. While this internal debate is underway, a woman's voice answers the phone.

"Hello?"

"Er… yes," I stammer. "Is this Eliza McQueen?"

"It is. Who's calling?"

"Um, Ms. McQueen, my name is Ella Strong and I used to work with Lucien Phillips. I wanted—"

"Let me stop you right there. Lucien and I are no longer together."

"Please don't disconnect," I say hurriedly, because I think she's about to. "I know you're not together anymore. I worked for him very recently, Eliza, and I had an experience… a rather terrible one that left me with many questions. Just recently, my fiancé learned that one of his exes was involved with Lucien and asked if I might speak with you about it. Perhaps you might be able to shed some light on the matter. Maya also referred me to you. Will you speak to me?"

"Ella, did you say your name was?"

"Yes. Ella Strong."

"Where are you calling from, Ella?"

Puzzled, I'm not sure what she's asking. "Um, I'm calling from my home in Portland, Oregon."

"I'm in Santa Barbara… in California. This is a conversation we really shouldn't have over the phone. Since you're the one requesting information, you should be the one to travel to me, don't you think?"

"Yes, well, normally that wouldn't be a problem but I've been threatened by Lucien's friend so my fiancé won't let me leave the house for the foreseeable future… at least not without my bodyguard."

"Bring your bodyguard then."

"Is it possible we can just talk over the phone? Initially?"

I hear Eliza sigh through the miles. "What do you want to know?"

What *do* I want to know? I'm just not sure but Ian advised me not to open with Natasha. I opt for vagueness. "Is there anything out of the ordinary you can tell me about Lucien or his… friends?"

There is a small sound of outrage from her. I immediately realize I need to give Eliza more information before I ask any questions."

"Eliza, allow me to first explain what happened to me." With that I give her the whole rundown, beginning with the call from Lara that hooked me up with Lucien in the first place and ending with Lucien's explanation in Starbucks.

There's a dense silence over there in Santa Barbara. I wait patiently for something from her, whatever she deigns to toss my way. "I can't say I'm surprised by any of it, I'm sorry to say. You're still missing some big pieces of the puzzle though. One huge piece, anyway."

"Does that huge piece have a name?" I don't wait for her to reply. "A name that begins with an N, perchance?"

"You got it. So you know about her, then?"

"Yes. My fiancé used to..." How do I explain it? "They used to be a couple, since high school, and then went into business together. She's been systematically trying to sabotage him ever since. He's attempting to find out why. We thought you might have some insight into it."

"I can tell you the woman is insane, for one thing— and a total grade-A bitch, for another. I would even hazard to say she's a C-word but I've got too much class to use such language. If anyone ever deserved the characterization, it would be Natasha."

"What about the goons who work for him, the brothers?"

"They're bottom feeders but as far as I can tell, fairly harmless. They certainly look capable of serious criminality but in the years that I was with Lucien, I'd never seen them do anything untoward at all. In fact, they were downright respectful of me. I never was sure why because I saw them being very antagonistic and even overtly rude with other women."

"I'm pretty sure they were the ones responsible for drugging me."

"God, that must have been awful for you. I wouldn't put it past the Lithuanians but I've never seen them do anything that bad. At their worst, I saw them chase a guy who stole a parking spot from them but, hey, in New York anyone would do that. Parking spots are like the most precious gold in that city."

"Do you know anything about Natasha that might help?"

"Not really. You know the brothers are her uncles, right?

I murmured an assent.

"She initially came around to see them but once Lucien got an eyeful of her, he was always hanging around like some pathetic puppy whenever she was over. She stayed in New York for a long while *visiting* them. It didn't take long for me to realize he was cheating; I think they started up about two or three weeks after she first arrived. I left shortly thereafter."

"I'm so sorry to hear that she ruined your relationship. And now she doesn't even see him, I don't think."

"Oh, it was apparent even then that the attraction was mainly one-sided but Lucien didn't seem to care one way or the other. He was fixated on her. We were engaged to be married, you know. He threw away a four-year relationship for a few weeks with her. Good riddance. I will say, though, that it pains me to learn how she's using him to hurt other people. Lucien can be such a fool."

"Yes. But I do think he might be the innocent in all of this dirty business. I feel for him, if that's the case."

"Well, Ella, that's about all I can offer you: I really don't know much at all. If I think of anything at all that might help, I'll give you a call."

"Yes, Eliza, I really appreciate your time."

We disconnect and I put my phone down and get up to get a cup of coffee from the kitchen. I'm halfway there when I hear my phone singing. I do an about-face and grab for the phone right before it goes to voice mail. It's Eliza's number displayed on the face.

"Hello?"

"Ella?"

"Yes, Eliza, it's me."

"The second I disconnected from you a memory popped into my mind. I don't want to worry you too much but you need to know. Right before I left Lucien, I was at his place packing and I overheard a conversation between Natasha and Lukas and Leo. I didn't hear too much of it but what I did made me very nervous. They were talking about the man in Portland, that's how they referred to him. Leo was saying something like, "If that doesn't take down the man in Portland, we can always arrange for a little accident." I actually thought they must've been kidding, at the time. It was like dialogue right out of a bad TV movie

Her words suck the oxygen right out of my lungs and I feel my throat begin to close. I can't even speak to respond.

"Ella? Are you there?"

I try to make a sound to let her know I'm still here but I'm paralyzed with fear. These people are out to get Ian and they sound like they'll stop at nothing to do it. Eliza is still talking but I'm only catching every third word or so.

"...sorry to upset... thought it would... best."

"Yes. Thank you, Eliza. You just caught me off-guard. I'll be sure to relay the information to my fiancé. Thanks again."

"Sure thing. Good luck to you."

I can't call Ian to warn him of this latest threat because he's in the air right now. I instead send him a text, advising him to call me ASAP. Taking my coffee, I head into the library to do some research on those stupid Lithuanian brothers, Leo and Lukas Sobel. I'm going gunning for them.

Chapter 41

The plane slowly rolls into the next position in the queue for takeoff at the private airfield. Glancing at his watch, he figures it should only be a few more minutes. He rotates his neck and flexes his arms and legs, trying in various ways to relax but every nerve feels stretched like a taut rope, with zero slack. Daniel, he needs to speak to him. Somehow, over a very short period of time, Ian had begun to rely heavily on the other man's judgment. For the first time perhaps in his life, he feels he has a friend whom he can actually trust.

While the jet sits waiting for clearance, Ian calls Daniel in New York. Though he might be mistaken, he gets the impression that Daniel is always up for a confrontation with a bad guy and Ian seems to have no shortage of them lately.

"Hey, Ian. What's going on?"

"Daniel. I'm on a plane right now, on my way to New York. Are you in town?"

"I am."

"Good. Are you in the mood for some face time with the Russian mob?"

"Always."

Ian laughs. He knew he'd go for it. "I'll call you when I touch down and we'll meet. This matter pertains to our friend Phillips, of course."

"I might have guessed. Call me when you get in and we'll make a plan."

"Good enough. Until then." He disconnects, satisfied he's found a kindred spirit in Mr. Butler.

Ian had told Ella he had a plan; that was a total lie. Truth was, he had no idea what to do, short of multiple murders. If he finagled to get Natasha and the rest of her clan deported, then what? He would give them even more reason to regroup and come at him again. What the hell could he do?

Thank God that Ella had no idea the brothers and Natasha were affiliated with the Russian mob. She was worried enough about him thinking they were just troublemakers. He hoped he didn't let on just how agitated he himself was because he was direly conflicted about how to handle this provocative situation.

He leans back in the comfortable leather seat of his Gulfstream. Something begins to slip off his lap and he jerks up, just catching his iPad before it falls to the floor. Reminded that Ella had written him an email letter and compiled a playlist, he turns on the machine. As soon as he reads her words, his chest constricts with emotion, making him wish he could hold her right this minute. As he scrolls past to head to iTunes for her song compilation, his eye catches the books downloaded on his reader, one book in particular. With a devilish grin, he opens the one that snared his attention: *Three and a Half Weeks*, by Ariel Strong. Almost unbelievably, he never got around to reading it before. Maybe this flight wouldn't be so interminable after all.

It was nine minutes and twenty-eight seconds before I could lock the doors to close the shop for the night when in walks a man in an espresso-brown business suit, the most gorgeous man who'd ever fallen to earth. Thus begins the story of my three and a half weeks with a tall, dark (emphasis on dark), handsome stranger (emphasis on stranger).

She has his full attention now. He continues to read the book she wrote, the "fictional" story about her three and a half weeks with a kinky man and a dungeon full of whips and toys.

He reads the whole book in four hours and by the time he puts the iPad down, he has a vicious hard-on. Damn, he's going to have to either live with it or take care of it on his own. No wonder Ella's book was a bestseller: she has a knack for making a scene come alive with hotness. He laughs, thinking of all the girls and women who got their panties wet while reading about his and Ella's escapades over the course of that time. Three visits to his dungeon, yes, but there were many more nights in beds, his and hers. Yes, they'd made good use of their limited time together.

Limited. He lost her after that last time in the dungeon. For a long while the experience and its cost made him never want to use a whip again. Now, though, it was different. He and Ella were secure, engaged to be married—they were in love. Would she want to venture into deeper waters with him now? He wonders.

Ella had made light of that last scene in her novel: she'd obviously wanted to keep the book from descending into too dark or depressing a realm. Still, reading between the lines, her trauma bleeds through. When Rafe (his alter-ego) whips Gia (Ella's alter-ego), she leaves him, too, but they reunite at the end. Did Ella wish for that conclusion all along? If so, he's been playing by the book unwittingly.

Rafe was in a strange mood that day. Insisting we play, he enthusiastically escorted me to the dungeon and waited impatiently outside while I "situated" myself, as he euphemistically put it. In plainer language, I was to demean myself by stripping naked and kneeling in supplication to await his exalted presence. He could take one minute or a half hour to get to me. The suspense, so he told me, was all part of my fun.

It's hard to keep track of time when your knees are aching from being on a cold, hard floor but it was probably only three or four minutes until I heard the door creak open and his footsteps approaching me. Almost from minute one, I realized that this kink was psychological as much as physical, probably in equal measure. The sounds, the silence, the suspense and anticipation—it all mixed and alchemized into intense sexual excitement. This time was so different, though. Instead of leading me to the bench or restraining me from the hooks suspended from the ceiling, he brought me over to what I called the tilted cross. In actuality, it looks like an X and it's called a St. Andrew's cross. Back then, I didn't know what it was but I could certainly guess what it was used for.

Few words were spoken as he lashed my wrists and ankles to each limb of the cross. I bent my face into my left arm, since there was nothing in the middle for me to lean on.

Rafe gave me no details: it wasn't until later that I discovered he was greatly pissed off at me for flirting with another man. I hadn't even realized I was flirting: I called it buying a fucking cup of coffee from some young blond guy who works at Starbucks. Trivial details don't matter, though, when the punishment is a single-tail laid across your bare back, posterior, and thighs in rapid succession. He told me I owed him a thank-you for sparing my calves and ankles. I disagreed: I felt I owed him a bullet in his intestines.

Did he think I would get sexually aroused from a whipping? The answer was apparently yes. Some women—and men—like to be taken to heights so lofty that their bodies can't distinguish between pain and pleasure. Rafe explained it to me by using hot and cold as an example: two extreme temperatures that the body sometimes has trouble differentiating.

I explained to Rafe that he could go fuck himself—not me—and fled the dungeon as soon as I was untethered from the cross. I ran into one of the many bedrooms of his palatial home, knowing it was my last visit. I counted 190 seconds before he came after and found me.

"Don't push me away," he whispered, his voice hoarse, as he lay down beside me. I attempted to ignore him but he was persistent. I could feel the heat radiating off his chest as he pulled me close but I was in pain. I had read sexy stories that included whippings and now I understood firsthand what the descriptions meant by prickly pain. The skin on the back of my body felt tight and hot, with pinpricks of an itchy burn barraging the skin, up and down.

He rolled me onto my stomach and massaged the stripes he inflicted, coating them with some kind of ointment. When he was done, his strong hands kept massaging, areas that weren't whipped, areas that responded to him readily despite my intentions. My body continually betrayed my mind: they were almost mortal enemies at this point.

What happened to mind over matter? My body refused to care about the bridges it was burning. It flipped over and spread its legs, inviting Rafe to come aboard: he did so quickly, before my mind could regain control. We… well, what's the vernacular? Made love? Fucked? Did the nasty? Whatever you call it, we did it for the next hour or two. Sated, I lay in wait for him to fall asleep before slipping out of bed, searching out my clothes, and leaving his ass cold. Oh, I did write him a note. Time has erased my exact words from my memory but it went something like this: "Drop dead, asshole." Yeah. I think that was it.

It took Rafe exactly 17 days, eight hours, and twenty-three minutes to change my mind. That was last year. I'm writing these words on the eve of my wedding day. Rafe, the most gorgeous man who walks the earth, will be my husband by this time tomorrow. He's promised the next whipping will be something more to my liking. I'm holding him to it.

New York in January can be as bleak as the Siberian Peninsula. The magic of all the Christmas lights and greenery, coupled with the joy on strangers' faces, are now firmly part of history. If there's any snow, it's dirty gray and slushy, piled high at the edges of streets and mixed in with all kinds of urban detritus. Usually, though, the air and streets are dry and the cold seeps into the bone, coming off the rivers on all sides of the island of Manhattan. The best part of January arrives with nightfall, when the multitudes of lights illuminate the city: in shadow, the architecture stands tall, stone monuments that are testaments to the hubris of humankind, while the asphalt shimmers in reflected electric glory. At least then one can get the mind off the winter drab and focus on the emerging nightlife.

Location, however, means nothing to Natasha Yenin right now, other than a means to an end. She sits in Lucien's loft, speaking with him. Natasha understands a few things that the pathetic Lucien does not: specifically that first, they cannot be a couple... ever. Second, that Natasha needs Lucien's looks, charm, and money to be utilized to win over Ian's ladylove, something he's been yet unable to accomplish. What will it take? Everyone has a weakness and Natasha knows that well. Ian Blackmon is her own but she will put family first and destroy him. Pity because if not for her critical need to avenge the heinous wrong done to her family, she and Ian would have made an excellent team—at least they would have in the past. Since she began her crusade to destroy him, he's gone soft, weak, and almost unappealing. Almost, she thinks as she remembers his beautiful body and the response he had to seeing her. She would dearly love to fuck him one last time.

Lucien slides closer to Natasha. His left hand begins to caress her long hair as he inches his body ever closer. She can feel the heat he is throwing off and knows it's time to clue him in.

"When did you get to New York, Lady Natasha?"

She chuckles, watching him closely. He certainly looks like a man in love but then she hasn't seen him in months—she almost but not quite forgot how pretty he is.

"Only just got here today and came right over to see you, love."

"Natasha," he breathes, "why can't we be together? You know I care for you so very much. I want to be with you."

"I want you and my uncles to grab Ariel again. This time we're going to make it count."

Standing abruptly, Lucien turns his back to her. "I don't want to hurt Ella. It's not her fault, not any of it, and she does not deserve to pay for Blackmon's sins."

"It's not that she's paying for his sins, per se. It's just a way to hurt him through her. He actually loves the girl."

"So? She's very lovable. I won't hurt her. Now explain to me why, after everything I've done for you, you continue to spurn me. Why? I want to know."

"You really are an idiot, Lucien. Why do you think my uncles are so faithful to you? Hmm? Can you tell me?"

"They've been with me for a long time, since I was a little boy. They're loyal..."

"Pfft." She waves her hand in the air. "Those men are coldhearted opportunists. The only ones they care about are themselves and their sister—my mother. And... their son."

"Son?"

"Yes, Lucien. Their son. You, to be exact."

Unadulterated shock floods his patrician features. "What in fuck are you talking about?" Lucien only uses profanity when he's furious, like right now. Natasha is scheming, thinking nothing about using him as a pawn in her plans.

"I'm answering your question as to why we can't be lovers, my darling. We're first cousins. We cannot legally marry, and having children would be egregiously stupid. It's best we find other partners."

Barely able to move a single part of his body, Lucien flops back down on the couch, leans his head back and his eyelids drift shut. Is nothing what it seems? "How can that be?" His voice is just audible in the quiet room.

She smirks and shakes her head in disgust. "How do you think, dearheart? My uncles both fucked your mother silly; she got pregnant and told the Frenchman it was his child. My uncles decided to consider you a son of both rather than be tested for paternity. That's why they love you so very much: blood of their blood, fruit of their loins, whatever the hell people say. So now that that's out of the way, will you do what I need you to do?"

Lucien somehow summons the energy to stand and begins to walk away and then turns with a newly acquired thought to share. "No, Natasha, I will not. As I said, Ella is a really nice person and I am not going to be party to hurting her. You have a problem with Blackmon? You handle it yourself. Leave me out of it. In fact, get out of my loft and my life. I'm done with you, you heartless bitch."

Daniel Butler's office is located in Soho, in Lower Manhattan. The cab ride from the small airport in Westchester takes a little under an hour and drops him off at the corner of Broadway and Prince: the address he seeks is not far away. Ian appreciates the look of the building housing *White Elephant Design*, one of Daniel's companies. It's an old industrial brick, built during a time when craftsmanship was expected and artisans took pride in their work. Of course, it was renovated and retrofitted to suit modern tastes. WED's executive offices are on the third floor and epitomize a high-end NYC loft.

A pretty assistant sporting purple spiky hair and a suit that looks like Brooks Brothers as interpreted by a punk-rock designer, directs him to the office and Daniel is waiting just inside.

"Ian. Good to see you. Come in."

They shake hands and Daniel invites him to sit. He does so, feeling a little nervous about having to tell his friend how damn dangerous is his situation. He waggles his tie back and forth to loosen it a titch, and then launches into the details of his visit to New York. Daniel listens to every word carefully, scratching his brow with this thumb.

"Any thoughts?"

Daniel smirks, exhaling a deep breath with a laugh.

"Lots."

"What do you recommend?"

Daniel shrugs. "The way I see it you have two options, one more permanent than the other."

"I'd prefer to keep within the law, if possible . How safe is it?"

Another shrug. "Your safety is only as good as the weakest link in the chain. If you want to put your life and the lives of your loved ones into the hands and expertise of every man and woman in ICE security and border patrol, then there's your answer. Me, I'd opt for a more permanent solution but then I've been forced into this kind of thing before. I'd certainly understand it if you're squeamish about such a thing."

"Care to elaborate?"

"Honestly, Ian? I'm not at liberty to divulge certain information about myself and I mean that sincerely—it's not an excuse. But I'll tell you this much: Five years ago I had a snowboarding accident, a bad one. I sustained a severe traumatic brain injury. It was so serious that my doctors were talking up my parents for organ harvest. Obviously, I ultimately recovered. Instead of having lost abilities, I gained additional ones. With those abilities came certain dangers." He looks Ian right in the eye, his expression sober, and says, "I've been forced to defend my life since then, on more than one occasion. Sometimes it requires a fight to the death. I'm prepared to do it if necessary."

The two men stand outside the building. Ian pulls out his phone and punches some buttons. The phone picks up on the third ring. "Lucien? This is your old friend, Ian Blackmon." Without waiting for a response, Ian keeps going. "Listen, I'm downstairs and I'd like for us to have a discussion. Will you come down?"

"Fuck off."

"Before you disconnect, please consider that if you don't come down, I'm coming up. My way, we can go have a cup of coffee and keep our chat... if not pleasant, at least civil."

Daniel holds up his hand and Ian asks Lucien to wait, muting the phone. Ian raises a brow in query.

"I'm thinking perhaps we should go in and engage the Lithuanians. Now."

"They appear to be extremely unsavory characters, Daniel. I'm quite sure they fight dirty. They can have us knifed and gutted before we have a chance to raise our fists."

Daniel shrugs, smiling. "I fight dirtier."

Ian takes a moment to stare into the man's green eyes. They gleam with evil anticipation. "You think we could engage them, as you put it, and give our wonderful men and women of ICE sufficient reason to deport our friends?"

"I was thinking self-defense." Daniel whispers the words so softly but they send an icy chill streaking up Ian's spine as he comprehends Daniel's meaning.

He wants to kill them. In a split second he makes a decision and unmutes the phone. "Lucien? We're coming up."

Chapter 42

As soon as Ian's plane lands, he'll get my text message. I'm not counting on it, though. I'll call him the minute I calculate he'll touch down on terra firma, allowing for fifteen minutes of delays. I won't stop until I reach him.

Ever since I spoke with Eliza, I've been nauseous and stressed. What if Ian is walking into a well-set trap? I'm terrified for him.

Less than ten minutes after I calculate his plane should have touched down, my phone chimes with a text and I almost fall flat on my face in my clumsy haste to grab the damn thing. It's from Ian so I read it hurriedly: *A. Understood but don't worry. Might not even be me they're referring to. I'll explain more when I see you. Don't worry: that's an order. Love you. C.*

Yeah, right, I'm not going to worry: is he insane? I should have gone to New York with him. I could still head there but I promised Ian I would stay put so I'll honor that promise. However, I can put my research skills to good use and get some information on Lucien's henchmen. I remember Lucien calling them the Sobel brothers but I don't know their first names so I'll have to phone Eliza once more. I hate to bother her but I need the names. She answers on the first ring.

"Yes, Ella?"

"I'm sorry to bother you again, Eliza, but I forgot to ask you for the names of the Lithuanian brothers. Can you help me out?"

"Sure. They're Leo—I think it's short for Leopold—

and Lukas Sobel. That's Lukas with a K by the way. Sobel is S-O-B-E-L. Is that all you need?"

"Right now, yes. I need to get more information on these men. I'm afraid for my fiancé's safety."

"I understand. Well, if there's anything else you need, give a holler. I'm in the middle of something right now so I have to go."

"Oh, sure. Thanks again, Eliza. Hopefully someday we can meet and have a coffee or something."

"Sounds good."

Look at me: I'm an anxious wreck. I'm twisting my long hair in my fingers and my leg is bouncing up and down almost of its own volition—both nervous tics I've had since girlhood. Still, if I'm not careful, I'll end up ripping out my hair and have bald spots. I knew a girl in middle school, Ming Lee Chen, who twisted her hair right out of her scalp. She ended up sporting two huge bald circles and was diagnosed with *alopecia areata* when all along she was doing it to herself due to stress over her grades. Her parents wanted to kill her, whether for her bald spots or inferior grades, no one was certain. Okay, focus, Ella, focus on the task at hand. My pep talk is nearly useless for my mind is pulling me in all different directions. I take out my laptop and begin typing key words into search engines. When the entries start popping up, I can't tear my eyes away and don't move for the next two hours and forty-six minutes. By the time I get out of the chair, my back is stiff in protest of my inertia. I make a beeline for the medicine cabinet to swallow some ibuprofen.

The pain is worth it for my research bore fruit: I found arrest records in other countries for the Sobel brothers, as well as various aliases they used. There was even some information about their respective romantic lives: restraining orders against both men for stalking offenses. Reams of data about their connection with Lucien's father followed.

Apparently Lucien's father, French investment banker Jean-Luc Phillips, was very dependent on both men and trusted them with his wife and son. But why? Lucien said his father was grateful that they saved him. But why would they? They don't seem like the compassionate type at all. My instincts tell me there's more to this story than meets the eye but the only one who might have more information and be willing to impart it to me is Maya St. Sauveur. I put in a call to her, pronto.

Maya doesn't answer her phone so I leave a voice mail for her and take the phone into the bathroom with me so I can hear it sing while I shower. Once I'm finished rinsing off, I rub some eucalyptus oil into my back and neck, throwing on my favorite ripped tee shirt and cut-off denims. Hot water, ibuprofen, and topical ointment join forces to make me a new woman—the favorite clothes are the cherry on the cake of my day. I quickly dry my hair and just as I'm putting the hair dryer away, Aretha starts singing: perfect timing.

It's Maya. "Hello?"

"Ella? I just received your message. You need to talk to me?"

"Yes, Maya. That woman you told me about? Natasha? It turns out she's my fiancé's ex-business partner and she's making all kinds of trouble for us. We learned the brothers who work for Lucien are her uncles. I just wondered if you had any other information about those two… or Natasha, for that matter."

"Well, I think I mentioned that my mother was always positive they were involved in Lucien's kidnapping but my father didn't believe it, not for a minute. For whatever reason, he trusted those thugs and kept them around."

"How did he meet them? Was it through the kidnapping episode?"

"Supposedly, yes, although my mother suspected he knew them beforehand. The whole thing was all very mysterious. All my father cared about was getting his only son back in one piece. The Sobels produced Lucien unharmed and earned a friend for life in my father."

"Do you know anything else about their background?"

There was a long pause but I waited to give her room to think. "I should speak to my mother and then get back to you. Are you in New York?"

"No, but my fiancé is there now. Would it be more helpful for you to meet with him in person?"

"Only if I get more information that he might find helpful. Why don't you give me his number and I'll get in touch directly if I learn anything?"

I consider her request; will Ian get angry if I give her his number? I have to make a decision on the fly so I go for it. "Okay, his name is Ian Blackmon and here's his number…"

Once I disconnect from Maya, I try Ian again and once more it goes to voice mail. I hope he's okay and though I received his text, I'd feel a hell of a lot better to actually speak to him. My research has served to only make me worry more: the Sobels are scary, Natasha is scary, and they're both after Ian now. How can I help?

I'm engrossed in what I'm reading on my laptop when Mason raps his knuckles softly on the frame of the open door.

"Ms. Strong? Mariah is here to see you."

"Oh, thanks Mason. Send her right in."

Before the words finish leaving my lips, my friend comes striding energetically through the doorway. "My God, Ella, you look positively ghoulish, sitting in the reflected glow of that damn computer. Come on. We're going outside for fresh air."

"Mariah, I can't," I nearly whine—I'd really love to go out. "I promised Ian I wouldn't leave the apartment. If I do, Mason has to shadow me."

"Why in God's name?" A look of horror washes over Mariah's heavily made-up features.

"I've been threatened by one of Ian's foes." I deliberately chose the word foe over enemy because it doesn't sound as ominous: I don't want her to worry over me, too.

"Threatened?" she thunders. "In what manner?"

"Just forget it. How about I order take-out and we watch a movie together? I haven't seen you in a dog's age."

"Ella, what the hell is going on? I need to know."

I'm exhausted by it all myself. I relay to Mariah the facts as I know them, finishing with Ian's trip to New York.

"How long is this threat going to continue? I mean, this crazy bitch can hold it over you for years, can't she?"

"No," I shake my head. "I'm hopeful that Ian and Daniel will figure out a way to stop it somehow. I'm not sure I want to even know how."

"Who's Daniel?"

Now I grin. "Oh, how I wish you could meet Daniel. He is a new friend of Ian's and words are not fit to describe him: you have to see him to believe him."

"Is he single?"

"'Fraid not, Mariah. But he's still worth a gander, trust me. When he and Ian are in a room together, a girl doesn't know where to put her eyes. It's the kind of dilemma that's the stuff of dreams—wet dreams, of course." I laugh.

"Mmm, why are all the best ones taken?"

"Ah, the single girl's lament. I know it well."

"Oh, shut up, Ella. Look at the one you snagged. When does he get back anyway?"

I frown when I think about his open-ended itinerary. "I don't know—I don't think he knows either. I desperately want to join him but he says I'm better off here."

Seeing me start to sink miserably into the couch, Mariah slaps my hand. "In that case, let's get rip-roaring drunk and watch a comedy. How about the Marx Brothers?"

Mustering a grin, I nod my head in agreement. "Let's do it."

We fill a large crystal pitcher with *piña coladas*—

heavy on the dark rum—with pineapple chunks and coconut milk that I found in the pantry. I find a movie in Ian's library—he has a whole set of Marx Bros. films—and we hunker down to cheer ourselves up. During the middle of the movie, Mason comes into the room. "Ms. Strong, may I speak with you privately for a moment?"

"Sure, Mason," I answer, as I hit the pause button on the television and hop up off the couch. Luckily, I stopped at my second drink so while I'm buzzed, I'm still in complete control. "What's up?" I ask when we get into the hall.

"Mr. Blackmon asked me to inform you that the threat against you has been escalated. Apparently the woman involved asked Lucien Phillips to kidnap you and when he refused to cooperate, she informed him she'd enlist the Lithuanians. Mr. Blackmon said you'd understand. He's very concerned about your wellbeing and he wants you to appreciate the level of threat against you right now. Trust me, Ms. Strong, you don't want to mess around with the Russian mob."

"The what?" I ask, my voice reaching into the octave of an insect drone.

Mason's face goes bloodless: I've never seen anyone so pale before, as if he's been exsanguinated.

"I see," I say. "You assumed I knew and now realize I did not. Okay, Mason, I won't let on but Ian should have told me. I know he didn't because he doesn't want me to worry but I need to know these things, especially when I'm so directly involved."

"I don't disagree."

"Is he safe, Mason? In your professional estimation?"

"I just don't know, Ms. Strong, but I wish I were with him in New York right about now."

"That makes two of us." I glumly rejoin Mariah but my enjoyment of *Duck Soup* has been severely compromised.

Mariah leaves at nine and I settle in for the night. I'm lying in bed, trying hard not to cry because I miss Ian so stupidly much, so I instead focus on the night before last.

I've noticed that when Ian gets stressed out, his dominance emerges big time. That night, he'd come home from work in a stressed-out mood and an hour later asked me to go into the dungeon with him. Fact is, he hasn't asked me to go in there since the bad, terrible, awful time when he whipped me with a single tail and I left the damn country in response. Naturally, I was on full alert and my heart was pounding so hard it was battering my chest wall, but I acquiesced, wanting to give him a good night because I was worried about *his* heart stewing in all that toxic soup triggered by stress.

We'd just finished dinner and were enjoying a tumbler of Drambuie when he brought up the subject.

"Come, Ella. I'd like to visit my dungeon with you. Are you game?"

I just looked at him quizzically. Really? I said nothing.

He smiled reassuringly. "You can ask any questions you like."

"About your weapons?"

"About the *implements*, yes. I don't consider them weapons, Ella, or I wouldn't have them."

As he led me by the hand, we walked upstairs to the locked room, and he began a guided tour of his wee dungeon. I slowly circuited the space, saying nothing, but pointing out each *implement*, as he prefers to call them. Ian is the master of euphemisms, after all—he should probably work for the government. I gestured at one that intrigued me.

"Riding crop."

I pointed to another.

"Flogger."

Yet another.

His voice dropped to a nearly inaudible decibel. "Single-tail."

Just the name forced ice up my spine. I quickly moved on, fingering a pretty one: it was long and almost tortoise-shell in color.

"That's a cane, one of my favorites. She handles

well."

I arched a brow at his gender characterization but said not a word, keeping my emotions close to the vest. I did, after all, learn from a master. I realized it's the second time I'd characterized him as such in less than a minute. *My* master. In the very beginning, he instructed me to address him as such when in this room and I looked at him as if he'd shape-shifted into *Mephisto*—he is my own personal devil, isn't he? I stopped at a chest and opened it, picking up a colorful rope-type of thing with black hooks on each end. What the hell?

"That's a bungee cord. It's for suspension but it makes a good implement of punishment, so I've learned," he said, chuckling. "But then again, so do rulers, large spoons, small pans, or the belt I have on. It's always fun to improvise."

I peeked into his eyes and the heat I saw in them made everything inside me twist and turn. I'm sorry, but this man of mine is fucking hot.

Aiming for strong and confident, the voice that projected from my throat was all breathy and feeble. Pathetic. "It all begs the question, why? Why, Ian? Why is it necessary?"

Without breaking his intense gaze, he responded softly. "Before I met you, the answer would be to keep my sexual partners at an emotional remove."

"And now?"

He didn't look at me as he answered; instead, he ran his hand almost lovingly over a cane hanging on the wall. "Now I haven't done it in some time... but I think I'd still enjoy doing it." Then his eyes traveled to mine and he grinned wickedly. "With you. The moment I saw you, I wanted you in here, baby, naked and entirely at my mercy. I'd enjoy that very much, even now."

"Enjoy inflicting pain?"

His face sobered. "I would think that by now you'd know me better than that, Ella. No, enjoy driving you crazy with sexual arousal. Watching your lovely pale skin flush with heat until it's bright pink. Seeing you gasp from the heights of physical pleasure. My little version of Nirvana, my pretty Ella."

I accepted what he said as gospel but in my bones I knew he'd still like to be able to deliver some pain. Since we've reunited, there's been a bit here and there but nothing with whips of any stripe—ugh, another pun. I'd have to think long and hard before I'd even open a dialogue with him about his using a whip on me again. Frankly, I doubt I'll ever go down that road again... but one thing I've learned is that you should never say never.

So I'd let him tie me down to a bench of a sort and use things on me: a flogger, some vibrating toys, and a blindfold. Now that I felt comfortable with him and knew he'd have reasonable limits to how far he'd go, I felt much more at ease with these things and could actually allow myself to enjoy the experience. When he finally removed the black satin blindfold from my eyes, I realized all over again how extraordinarily handsome a man he is. It seemed revelatory that night, as if I'd never quite seen him clearly before, *really seen him*. That's when I understood that his sexual proclivities are part and parcel of who he is and I'd better learn to enjoy them, for his sake. *Yes*, I thought, *I can do that*.

Thinking about the things we did is now making me want Ian all the more. I've grown accustomed to daily orgasms and he's been gone a good sixteen hours. I close my eyes remembering how, after he tied my wrists and thighs down around the narrow bench, he used the flogger all over my body, sensitizing the skin to the point where I was ready to scream for him to touch me.

But he didn't, not right away. He teased me with feathers and chains, cold and hot, soft and hard, brushing each one ever so lightly over my skin. In addition to lying on my stomach, I wore a blindfold so I couldn't see a thing, not a single thing. The music playing in the background had harps and violins and the staccato beat was unnerving in this environment— precisely why he chose it, I'm sure. When I was so relaxed that I felt boneless, well, that's when he took out the clamps.

My breasts were dangling from the bench. Standing, he straddled me, leaning on me lightly as he reached down and grasped them. I gasped at the contact of his warm hands and enjoyed him playing with my nips but when he started twisting and tugging, I whimpered.

"Don't worry, baby. I'm just getting them ready for some jewelry. You like jewelry, don't you, Ella?" he whispered into my ear, his warm breath sending fire right through my core.

I nodded—I *do* like jewelry—though I yet whined internally at my sore nipples when I felt the bite of sharp metal teeth on one. "Eek!" I screamed.

"Too tight?" he asked gently, but I heard laughter in his tone, as if he were enjoying my discomfort.

"Yes, too tight," I spat out the words in a torrent but he didn't loosen it. He just waited, rubbing my back until the pain faded. Then he took up the other one. I realized it must be almost an art form to know just how tight to make the clamp: too tight and a person could be injured; too loose and there's no point to using it. It must be adjusted to produce just enough erotic pain to contribute to the sum total. Ian knew exactly how to gauge it.

What I was not expecting at all was the clit clamp. When he asked, "Ready for the next one?" and pinched me there, I tried to buck and evade his fingers but he'd tied me down too well—I could barely move an inch. He readied it the same way as my breasts and that, I'll admit, was okay... fun even. Okay, it was fucking hot. But not when the clamp bit down. I squeeze my eyes shut even now as I recall the sharp sting.

The real pain was yet to come, though, for I discovered taking off the clamps is when you get the most punch. Once he'd entered me, his rhythm pushed me all the way up, up, up, and I was about to come. That's when he reached down between us and released the lower clamp. I even scared myself with the scream I produced when I climaxed: I'd never experienced an orgasm like that before. A few beats later, he removed the breast clamps, and I came again, right on top of the first one. When the rolling waves finally subsided enough for me to regain my hearing, I heard him laugh like Satan, and then he picked up a frenzied pace again until he couldn't take any more and let loose. Afterward, we both just lay limp on the narrow little bench, his thighs on mine, resting on a small leather support on either side of the sawhorse.

As he locked the room's door and we headed back to his bedroom, he looked at me with heavy lidded eyes and I took note that he looked so much more relaxed now. "We need to visit that room more often, Ella, don't you think?" His voice was smooth again, the hoarseness ironed out by sexual release. I felt a twinge of pride at accomplishing my mission.

"Mmm, maybe so," I replied truthfully, for I also felt good, as if I'd just received a massage instead of rough sex. I wrapped my arms around his waist and hugged him tightly. I didn't want to ever let him go.

Finally, tonight, with a picture of Ian in my mind's eye, in his blue jeans and white tee shirt, barefoot with disheveled hair, tucking me into bed, I fall asleep hugging my pillow and pretending it's his warm and comforting body. That night I dream of New York, two men, and a blond woman with long, red nails that morph into talons before my very eyes.

Chapter 43

The door to Phillips' loft is sitting ajar as the two men warily approach it. On the way up, they discussed the various options in front of them.

"If they were all Russian, deportation would be a much more attractive path to pursue," Ian pointed out. "With our collective clout, we could facilitate an expedited deportation order and have Natasha's grandpa's friends providing the welcome home. Live or die, they'd no longer be my problem."

"True," Daniel said, "but the brothers are Lithuanian nationals, which complicates the situation. It's also not an ideal solution for other reasons. Even if we succeed in expediting the process, it can still drag on for months—months that could allow them time to put back-up plans into place. Moreover, you can never be sure of their individual fates. For example, even if the Russian welcome wagon took out the men, would they necessarily eliminate the women as well? Natasha is your biggest problem, or so it appears right now."

Ian nodded. "I need more intel on the entire family before I commit to any course of action. I suppose we'll see how today plays out. If the brothers engage us, to use your word, then we'll see to them here and now, and worry about the others later."

Daniel had smirked and agreed wholeheartedly. "I've got your back, friend. Let's do this."

About five feet away, Daniel extends his arm to halt Ian's progress and they stand still while Daniel concentrates. Thirty seconds later, he opens his eyes, gives a curt nod, and lowers the barrier of his arm. They proceed further and step through the threshold of the apartment. Lucien is right there in the room, not ten feet away from them, waiting patiently for their arrival.

"Hello, Lucifer," Daniel says, smiling. "How goes it?"

Lucien sneers when he catches sight of Daniel. Obviously he remembers him from his last visit. Ian stands adjacent, broadly grinning at his adversary and enjoying Daniel's moniker for him.

"So? Where are your henchman protectors, Phillips?"

"They're not here. They're busy conspiring against you with your number-one female fan."

"Ah. I assume you mean the poisonous Natasha Yenin?"

Lucien nods. "What do you want? I will caution you that it's really not safe for you to be here. My henchman protectors, as you so quaintly label them, are dangerous men with little to lose—the very worst kind."

"Oh, I disagree," Ian counters. "Everyone has something valuable to lose, regardless of what he tells himself."

Daniel, meantime, is pacing slowly throughout the room, arms behind his back. At a pause in the conversation, he glances up. "Is there anything you'd care to share with us, Lucifer?"

Glaring at Daniel, Lucien spits out his words. "First, if you expect me to converse politely with you, you'll stop calling me by that name."

Smiling, Daniel replies, "True, you're way too much of a pussy to be equated with the prince of darkness... " He cocks his head in a speculative stance. "Still, I like it on you."

Lucien scowls and mutters at Daniel. "Asshole."

Ian chimes in. "Now that's funny... You see, we think you're the asshole, Phillips, and we'd like the pleasure of never having to see your sniveling face again. But, alas, your friends keep getting in our faces so we're here to lose them. Understand?"

Without answering, Lucien sits on the couch, loosely

gesturing to them to join him. Daniel complies but Ian remains standing.

"Where are they now?" Ian prods.

Lucien shrugs his shoulders. "No idea. I told Natasha to leave and she took them with her."

Daniel now interjects. "You told Natasha to leave? Why?"

"She asked me to go after Ella. I refused and told her to get out."

"You'd better watch your back in that case, Phillips. Those brothers might be fond of you but blood is thicker than water."

Lucien smirks. "Thanks for your concern, Blackmon. Anything else?"

"What did she ask you to do to Ella?" Daniel's face is now devoid of humor.

"She wanted me to grab Ella and hold her as a means to get to you, Blackmon. I think she planned to let her uncles have their way with her, as well."

Ian gets a sick look on his face at hearing that information. "Do they have anyone else working with them?"

"Not to my knowledge," Lucien answers, "but I'm not privy to everything, either. I suggest you watch Ella carefully. If I hear anything else, I'll inform you of it. Give me your cell number."

Hating to do it, Ian nonetheless pulls out his cell, scrolls through his phone book, and calls Lucien's phone, unblocking his private number. The three men listen to the phone buzz twice before Ian disconnects. "Okay, you have my number. Is there any other information you can share with us? Anything at all?"

"Nothing comes to mind."

Daniel stands. "Do the Lithuanians have any other family, other than Natasha's mother?"

Shaking his head, Lucien says, "I've never heard them speak of anyone. Then again, they're not the forthcoming type either... but as far as I know, Natasha's family is their only blood."

Daniel looks sharply at the blond man. "No children for either man?"

Lucien flushes at the penetrating gaze Daniel is training on him. "Not that I'm aware of."

Daniel continues to stare at Lucien for a long minute, green eyes blazing with light. Finally, he smiles and turns away. "Let's go, Ian. Can't wring blood out of a stone." With his back to Lucien, he tosses a farewell over his shoulder, "*Au revoir, Monsieur Phillips, j'espère que nous n'atteindrons pas encore,*" in flawless French, taking Lucien by surprise.

Ian, also fluent in French, knew Daniel told Lucien that hopefully they wouldn't meet again. He hadn't known Daniel was multilingual, however. The man never ceased to amaze him.

Once they get outside, Ian turns to Daniel. "Now what?"

Flashing him a beaming smile, Daniel says, "Our friend is a terrible liar, Ian. He just found out, via Natasha, that one of the brothers is his biological father."

Ian's mouth drops open in astonishment. He starts to ask Daniel how he knows but thinks better of it just in time. "Are you certain?"

"Yes. Did you not see his face when I asked if they had children? It was written all over it. I got the sense he just found out or he'd be more comfortable with the knowledge. He's probably worried, too, that if the truth comes out, he could lose his fortune to his French father's genuine blood heirs, if any exist. I don't know about French law but in the U.S. he'd be protected since a legal father is the one who raises the child... but where so many millions are involved, you never know."

At that moment, Ian's ringtone blares loudly from his pocket. He looks at it. "Ella," he tells Daniel. "Hey there," he answers.

"Ian, thank God! I've been trying to reach you all day. I was worried about you. Are you okay?"

"I'm fine, Ella. I was planning to call you once we finished with Lucien. We've only just now left him."

There's a pause as she digests this information. "I hope you don't mind but I gave Maya your cell number."

"Maya?"

"Yes. Maya St. Sauveur? Lucien's half-sister."

"May I ask why?"

"I called her to see if she knew anything more about the Sobels. She promised to ask her mother for any more info and get back to you. Since she's in New York and so are you, I thought it might be worth it to get together with her."

"I see. Where are you now?"

"Home, where I promised I'd be. Where exactly are you?"

"As I said, Daniel and I just left Lucien's loft. He was alone and didn't know where the men were but said they were with Natasha. Ella, I've another call I need to take. I'll call you a little later, okay?"

"Okay. I love you, Ian."

"Love you, too. Talk soon." He clicked on the next call.

"Yes," his answered tersely.

The voice on the other end was loud enough for Daniel to hear both sides of the conversation. "Mr. Blackmon. I have that name you asked me to obtain. It's Greshenko, Gregori Greshenko."

"Very good," he replies brusquely, a man of few words, and disconnects without so much as a goodbye. Ian's employees and business colleagues are used to his ways and no longer take offense at the lack of civility.

Quickly, he punches in his grandfather's Phoenix number. "Grandpa," he says as the man answers on the second ring. "It's Ian. I have the name you asked for, our Russian friend? It's Gregori Greshenko. Ring any bells?"

The call lasts a little less than three minutes but it is enough: Ian's face looks grim when he disconnects. He turns to Daniel. "This whole thing began with a case of my grandfather's. He asked me to get him Natasha's grandfather's name. I just checked with him: he says Greshenko was bad news from A to Z. Not only was he supplying high-tech assault weaponry to terrorists and other enemies of state, he was also moving large quantities of heroin and synthetic drugs throughout suburban America. I just happened to read a New York Times article about the latter drugs: they cause severe psychosis and astonishingly are largely legal. Once the government acts to ban one, the chemists change a single molecule of the formula, a single fucking molecule, and voila! It's a new drug and it's legal again. The majority of proceeds from selling this shit generally fund terrorism against western countries. On the ground, the tainted drugs cause numerous deaths and other problems associated with them.

"At the time of his arrest and internment, Greshenko was also being accused of getting into human trafficking—actually helping to bring slaves into the United States from other areas of the world, channeling them through counterparts in Saudi Arabia. A real charmer all around.

"My grandfather said that by the time he was deported, Greshenko had both the Colombians and Mexicans after him for turf incursion with regard to the heroin, and the synthetic drugs were cutting into cartel profits on more traditional drugs. Greshenko was trying to move out of drugs—hence the human trafficking—to get the cartels off his back. The Feds should have let them have a go instead and that would have been the end of it—at least for the Blackmon family.

"Did he make any suggestions as to how to deal with them? Legal suggestions, that is?"

Ian shakes his head. "How could he? There are too many of them to get deported right away anyway. There are these three plus her mother and brother. Who knows? There may be even more—my security peeps are looking into that as we speak."

"Good. We don't want to leave any stone unturned, Ian. You have decisions you have to make, the biggest one being whether or not we get our hands dirty."

Ian nods. "I need to make phone calls."

"Come on. I'll take you to my house—I can work from there."

To the casual observer, they are a couple of executive-types sharing a conversation, not friends with brilliant minds deciding the most effective way to eliminate their enemies. Others know differently, however. As the men in suits start down the block, two swarthy brothers and a shifty-eyed blond turn the corner and are coming right at them. Daniel looks at Ian, "Not here, out in the open, in broad daylight. We need some kind of cover."

Both men begin to cross the street to avoid confrontation but down the block, the three stalkers follow suit.

Ian and Daniel continue strolling casually while the brothers and Natasha travel directly into their path. About fifteen feet away, the Lithuanians slow down, take a long look at Ian and veer off in another direction, leaving Natasha alone, smiling as she closes in. Daniel whispers quickly to Ian.

"You've just been made, Ian. They wanted to see what you look like. From here on in, you need to watch your back very carefully."

His expression grave, Ian nods as they reach the blond woman. She wears a smile that looks joyously triumphant, making Ian's guts seize up in hot fury. Hatred is not strong enough a label for what he now feels for this treacherous conniver.

She very obviously trails her eyes up and down Daniel, clearly appreciating the cut of his dark coffee-colored suit. "Well, now, Ian. Please introduce: I'm always looking for a new pretty boy with whom to play."

Sneering his contempt, Ian responds. "Does he look desperate to you?"

Flipping her head back to toss her long hair off to one side, she sneers. "Oh, now you're just trying to hurt my feelings. Are you jealous perchance?"

He doesn't dignify her comment with a response,

even a nonverbal one. Over the years Ian has honed the practice of ignoring nuisances to an art form. The men continue to walk right past her.

She calls back. "I think you're a sore loser, Ian… and make no mistake: in any competition with me, you will be the loser. That Alexis woman wasn't up to the task but I surely am. And my uncles will be a lot more persuasive with your Ella than Lucien ever was, the pathetic creature."

Spinning around, Ian is about to vent his spleen when Daniel grabs him by the shoulder and whips him back around, using his momentum to advance their progress. "Stop it," he hisses. "You're playing right into her hands with your anger. She already knows Ella is your Achilles' heel—if you really want to piss her off, do not react."

"Fuck me, I know! But let's see you do it if someone threatens Olivia."

"I'd expect the same sage counsel from you if the situation were reversed. I hope I can depend on it if the occasion ever arises."

Taking a deep breath, Ian manages a small smile for his friend. "You can."

When they reach Broadway, Daniel hails a cab, tersely gives the driver his address and in eight minutes the taxi pulls in front of the stately brownstone.

As soon as they're seated in the ground floor office, they begin to confer in hushed tones. "I think I have an idea as to how this thing can go with no blood on our side," Daniel says.

"That would be good." Ian pinches the bridge of his nose; he's really tired of dealing with this crap. Leaving Ella alone and vulnerable is weighing heavily on him, and after reading her book, he wants to play with her more than ever, maybe even again venture into his little dungeon. Instead he's sitting in a room in New York planning the annihilation of his enemies—enemies he'd done nothing, absolutely nothing to cultivate. What a ridiculous clusterfuck.

Daniel runs his hand through his hair, a sign of his own agitation, and begins to explain. "You need to see this out and get back to your life—you have a wedding to plan and business matters to see to. You don't need this BS... and don't deserve it. I imagine you also want to protect your grandfather from further harm, assuming Natasha and company were responsible for his car accident."

Ian snorts in derision at the circumstances. "And I imagine you'd like to focus on your own upcoming nuptials and not my travails with Russian criminals."

Making a dismissive gesture, Daniel smiles wanly. "My in-laws are taking care of everything for us."

"You mean your future in-laws. Don't claim them until you absolutely have to."

"No," a weighty sigh escapes Daniel's lips as he rolls his eyes in mock despair and holds up his left hand to display the wedding band, "I'm afraid they're already very much mine. Olivia and I were married at City Hall two weeks ago."

Hesitant to elaborate, Daniel nonetheless continues in answer to Ian's wordless query. "We were feeling insecure about each other's level of commitment so we decided the only fix was to swear to a lifetime of one—no biggie." He smiles broadly, thinking of how he's understating the situation. "It's made a surprising difference, a highly positive one. Plus, my father-in-law is making a huge effort to put our checkered past behind us, and bond with me, as well. That, of course, followed on the heels of a horrific confrontation between he and I, but we'll skip the gory details of that unfortunate incident." He looks Ian in the eye. "So you see, I've been busy, too."

Chuckling in response, Ian reaches over to pat Daniel on the back. "I'm happy for you. Congratulations on your marriage. By the way, you do know it's almost impossible to put one's hands on a Girardi sculpture? The man's work is untouchable."

"Yes, I'm aware of his popularity. I'll introduce you to

him at my wedding celebration—if you're able to make it—and you might bring it up then. He holds back some of his pieces to rework, so I know he has a few smaller ones in his UK studio."

Ian leans back in the padded swivel chair and tries to unwind from the tension of the day. "Okay, so let's have it. Your idea?"

Daniel makes the suggestion unemotionally—he might as well be discussing the weather. "You don't want their blood on your hands—"

Ian interrupts, "Nor to break the law…"

Daniel shakes his head. "Provoking them to attack by merely standing up to them and then defending ourselves with mortal force is not against the law. Still, we don't walk away with our hands clean. Here's a better way: you mentioned the grandfather had both the Colombian and Mexican cartels after him. He had to be moving a great deal of product to get in their crosshairs. Let's get in touch with both of those groups if we can and give them a few names of Grandpa's friends eager to take over his business. They'll take them all out—even the woman." He holds up his finger to make his next point. "We must ensure, however, that Lucien is protected: annoyance that he is, he's an innocent in this whole scenario. I wouldn't want him injured or worse."

Fingers pulling at his bottom lip, Ian contemplates the suggestion. "Go on. How do you propose contacting the appropriate people? I assume you don't travel in the same circles as drug kingpins nor do I."

"I was hoping your grandfather might point us in the right direction. After all, he must have dealt with unsavory types like that all the time. Even the lowly foot soldiers could be of massive assistance. We keep ourselves anonymous, make the suggestion attractive, provide the intel, and give a little push. It's the best way all around." He leans in closer to make his next point. "They want to kill you; they're not content to hurt you financially, especially after you gave their son a beating. I want you to be very clear on that point."

"Clear as glass. Fuck." Ian rubs his eyes, frustrated that every option available to him will keep him awake at night. "Okay, I'll call my grandfather. Let's put this baby in motion."

Nodding with grave satisfaction, Daniel rises. "I need to get some work done. You can use this office—I have another one off my bedroom suite. I'll let our staff know you're here. Please make yourself comfortable, Ian. Olivia will be home soon so you'll get to meet my beautiful girl."

"Good, I'd like to finally thank her in person for her hospitality... and I miss my own, so seeing yours will help. I especially miss Ella after reading her novel on the flight here." He winks, grinning mischievously.

"So she *is* the same Ella Strong who wrote *Three and a Half Weeks*?"

"The same. She wrote it as a joke for her friends but it went wide without her knowledge or approval and before she knew it, it was a bestseller. They're actually making a film of it." He tosses his head back and laughs, knowing Daniel will see the truth behind the book.

Daniel didn't disappoint. "I assume the antagonist is modeled after you then?"

"Naturally."

Now it's Daniel's turn to laugh; Ian can't remember ever seeing Daniel really laugh spontaneously. "Well, I suppose we have even more in common then. I had a girlfriend once upon a time who used to drag me to these private parties, a club of sorts. Very interesting activities, I have to say, and I did enjoy myself."

"Aha. We'll have to discuss it further someday."

"Indeed. Now we have something else to look forward to. I'll be upstairs if you need anything."

That night, as he lay in bed in Daniel's guest suite, Ian reflected on the day's events. A few hours after he and Daniel parted to work, they had dinner together, with Daniel's wife, Olivia. All three of them were seated on one end of a vast stone table in the dining room, and Daniel had introduced Ian to his wife. They'd exchanged small talk about her father's work, and her studies to be an architect.

Olivia was a beautiful young woman but Ian expected no less: Daniel had the looks and money—if not the winning personality—to ensnare any woman so why would he aim low? Olivia Girardi had beauty, charisma, and the smarts to keep a man like Daniel on a tight string. They seemed very well matched and happy to be with one another. Seeing them together made Ian yearn all the more for Ella.

It was just after they'd finished dinner that an awkward moment arose. Daniel reached over and grasped his wife's hand. "Olivia, sweet... Micah told me you have Joseph's number in Bangkok. True?"

The look on her face revealed a story: startled, embarrassed, and even a bit angry. She stuttered out a reply. "I have his new cell number, not a land line, but I haven't spoken to him."

Though his green eyes held fire, Daniel's voice was as soft as melted butter. "That's not why I'm asking, love. I need to speak with him. May I have the number?"

Seeing her hesitation, he was quick to reassure her. "I require information from him. If you prefer, you may place the call yourself. Okay?" He was still holding her hand and now he began to stroke it with his thumb.

She glanced nervously at Ian who only smiled warmly in response. "Um, okay. May I ask what this is about?"

"Nothing big. I'm just hoping he can put me in touch with people I need to contact." It wasn't exactly a lie, just a smooth understatement of his real purpose. "I'd like to place the call now," he prodded, checking his watch. "It's just about seven a.m. there and I can more than likely catch him before he becomes inaccessible. Make the call. Now."

He left no room for argument. Olivia retrieved her phone from her bag, and in seconds, handed her husband the phone. As soon as the connection went through, Daniel stood and waved Ian into the office off the main parlor. He began to speak into the phone even before they reached the room.

"Sorry to disappoint, Joseph, but it's her husband... Yes, that's what I said. We're married. Just so you know, she placed the call so I'm not in possession of your number... but I don't need to tell you that I don't appreciate her having it. However, that's not why I called... I need information. May I put you on speaker? I'm with a friend whose interests are at stake. Very good."

Ian hears a deep voice resonating throughout the office as Daniel gestures for him to sit while easing himself down into a chair.

"Okay. Let's have the details." Terse, cold, deadly: those are the adjectives that spring to mind upon hearing the bloodless voice on the other end of the line.

Daniel launches into a succinct explanation of the events. "I need to be put in touch with both cartels in as anonymous a way as possible. I'd like to hand them some of their potential enemies on a silver platter..."

A pause follows, filling the small room with a tense silence. "Why would either cartel desire such information?"

Daniel shrugged. "Why not? These men had a predecessor who was pissing off both groups. I figure they may want to nip it in the bud before it gets off the ground."

"Small potatoes. These kinds of nuisances aren't worth the lead to kill them. You'll have to come up with something better."

"We're trying to avoid getting the red stuff on our hands, Joseph. My friend is not comfortable with it going that way," he looks over at Ian as he communicates this information to Joseph.

"No one ever really is, except the psychos... but sometimes it's what has to happen. It's going to be an uphill battle to get the cartels interested in a few two-bit drug dealers moving in on their turf. Now, if the operation gets large, then it's another story entirely.

Right now, your best bet is to give me names and I can see to it for you at fifty per. Sending them to jail holds no guarantees nor does deportation. If these individuals are that hot to get your friend, then you have no choice but to get them first. It's self-defense, pure and simple. That's my best advice, Daniel. Barring that option, I can put you in touch with someone who can get you face time with the Colombians—I don't know how far up the ladder. The Mexicans are more difficult to work with."

The room went horribly silent when Joseph stopped talking. It was almost as if the air itself was weighted down by the grim prospects confronting Ian.

Joseph's impatient voice cut through the quiet. "Call me back when you make your decision. I've got somewhere to be."

The call disconnected and Daniel leaned his weight on his knees, hanging his head down. He didn't want to look in Ian's eyes right now. Velvet-soft, he whispered, "How much time do you need to make your decision?"

Ian's sigh reverberated through the room. "First, I need to speak with Lucien again. Then I'll call it." He pulled out his cell phone.

The small office was so quiet that Daniel could hear the phone ringing on the other end of the line, and then the terse greeting. "Yes?"

"Phillips, Blackmon."

"What do you need? I have no additional information for you as yet."

"Phillips, I'm going to be very candid with you and I'd appreciate your returning the courtesy. Right now I need you to answer a few questions, the first one concerns your Lithuanian friends. Are they killers?"

There is no immediate response and then Lucien begins to speak, his voice tired. "To my knowledge, no; however, I cannot state unequivocally that that's the case."

"Fair enough. Second, a threat has been made against Ella. How likely is it they will carry it out even if I make it difficult?"

"Very likely."

"You do realize the three of them have squeezed me into a tight corner?"

"Yes."

"Alright then. They've been warned through you."

"Yes. Blackmon?"

Ian waits, saying nothing.

Lucien continues. "Don't assume they are the ones needing the warning. These men have been associated with some very tough characters and survived. Bear that in mind."

"Duly noted. Stay safe, Lucien."

It was not lost on the French man that Ian had addressed him by his given name for the first time since they met. Lucien realized the implication: Ian didn't want him to get hurt in whatever was coming down. He'd return the goodwill. "Good luck, Ian."

Ian disconnected and looked Daniel in the eye. "Call Joseph. Tell him we're on at fifty per with a twenty percent bonus if it can be concluded within 48 hours. I'm sick to death of this shit and I'm not imperiling Ella a moment longer than absolutely necessary. So be it."

Now he lay in bed, wanting Ella in his arms desperately, needing her in his arms desperately... and knowing he'd just condemned three people to death. Condemned? Hell, he took out a hit on them. True, they left him with little choice but he still would have to live with the burden of guilt for the rest of his days. He fervently wished for another way ... but there was none he could see, none at all.

Sitting up in bed, he checked the small alarm clock next to the bed: one a.m. That meant it was only ten in Portland. He could call, hear Ella's voice; he was supposed to have called her back anyway. Pulling out his phone he hit the speed dial: she answered on the first ring.

"Ian! I've been waiting all day to hear from you. Is everything okay?"

"No. I miss you something terrible, Ella."

There was a protracted moment of delay between his remark and her reply: his words had taken her by surprise. "Oh, God, I miss you too, Ian. When are you coming home?"

"I'm hoping I can leave tomorrow but I'm not one hundred percent certain. Listen, Ella, I texted Mason earlier and asked him to ensure you understood what we are up against right now. Please, I'm begging you, stay inside and next to Mason until I get back. I am taking care of the problem but until it's resolved, I need to know you're safe. Are we clear on this point?"

"Yes, Ian, very clear. I promise I'll do as you ask... but please come home as soon as you can, please."

"I will, baby, promise. Right now I'd give up my whole bank account to be in the same bed as you, Ella: I miss you and I love you and I can't wait to marry you. When I get home, we'll start planning our wedding. Okay, baby?"

"Yes."

"Next month is Daniel and Olivia's wedding and we'll be coming to New York to attend. That should be fun. So you have a lot of shopping to do for weddings plus our honeymoon. Think you're up to the task?"

"Hmmm, I don't know but I'll give it the old college try."

He laughs. "Okay, my girl, I'm going to try to get some sleep. I'll call you in the morning. Ella?"

"Yes?"

"Remember how you were teasing me the other day about Mason sleeping in your bed for protection?"

"Yes." She laughs.

"I'm going to ask him to sleep in your room, just for tonight... and not in the bed with you, Ella, but on a cot next to you. I'm probably overreacting but I need to know you're safe. Okay?"

"Are you nuts, Ian? That's insane."

"No. It's not. In fact, I might have him take you to a hotel. Listen to me: the threat is at an extremely high level right now. It will be removed within the next 48 hours but until then, Ella, you are not safe. Do you hear me?"

Whispering now, she answers in a small voice. "Yes, Ian."

"Good. I'm going to phone Mason now. He'll let you know what we decide. Good night, baby. I love you very much."

"Me, too. Hurry home."

Chapter 44

Today marks the third day Ian is gone and I'm getting more than antsy stuck in Ian's home: I desperately need to get out into the fresh air, or should I say fresh rain? The damn wet stuff is always coming down in Portland. I gave Mason a heads-up last night while we were lying in bed (that sounds so wrong)— albeit, he on his army cot and I on the king-size mattress—that I needed to leave these walls today and he said he'd check with Ian. If Ian says no, I don't know what I'll do but I'm going batshit stir crazy in this place already.

I don't know what's holding up Ian in New York and I'm not sure I want to know, but he swears that he'll be home by tomorrow afternoon. I'm keeping my fingers *and* toes crossed—not easy or comfortable, frankly— that he keeps his word. I've come to realize that I can face just about anything as long as I'm holding his big, capable hand when it comes. I should add that I am fully cognizant of the fact that I'm beginning to spout the kind of purple prose of those awful romance novels whenever I speak of (or wax poetic about) Ian. Hey, maybe there's an idea for my next novel: Mo has been badgering me for months to start writing it.

In fact, Mariah and I had once upon a time even developed a game utilizing the purple prose of romance books. We were especially tickled by these authors' attempts to use adjectives and verbs in new and exciting ways. We gave each other challenges straight from the novels. For example, she'd ask me to "purse my lips in a straight line in a show of blatant annoyance."

It was impossible to pull off. I would try my hardest to accomplish it but, looking in the mirror, would quickly dissolve into hysterical giggles, the expression on my face ridiculous.

I'd give her a challenge: "His face radiates fiery anger, unabridged lust, and unbridled pride in having gotten her into his bedroom." Mariah gives it a go and I snap her picture. "Well?" she asks.

"Um, you look homicidal... but also a bit constipated."

Cackling in delight, we then would post the photos on Facebook under the banner of "Faces of Romance." It was a fun way to pass the time for two pathetic women who found themselves dateless on a Saturday evening.

When Mariah calls and says she's downstairs, my first thought is, why didn't she phone me before she left her house? I absolutely hate when people just unexpectedly drop by just because they feel like it, and Mariah has to know that about me by now. Tailgating that thought, however, are the possibilities that begin to seep into my sluggish brain: we can go out and do stuff! 'Course we'll have to take Mason along, like a big, ole German Shepherd, but it's all good. It might even be fun having him around like one of the girls, a girl with massive biceps and a stern looking crew cut. Imagining him in drag, complete with five o'clock shadow, starts me giggling as I pad over barefoot to the door and swing it open to let Mariah in.

Fuck. It takes a few seconds for my brain to make sense of the two-person tableau arranged in front of me: Mariah stands there, terror etched into her face. A blond woman next to her has one arm around Mariah's shoulders, and with her other she holds something against Mariah's ribs. As my brain kicks into gear, I comprehend that the blond woman is Natasha and she's responsible for Mariah's unexpected visit. I step back to allow them entrance into the apartment.

I don't have to say a word to Mason when he sees us

enter the room. His face pales but he shows no other reaction whatsoever, a well-trained special ops dude to his core.

Natasha looks at him and says two words, and two words only: "Call Ian."

He silently gestures for us to sit as he pulls his cellphone out of his jacket pocket.

In seconds the calls connects to Ian and Mason puts the phone on speaker. As soon as Ian's voice fills the room, Mason speaks up.

"Mr. Blackmon, I need to inform you that you're on speaker right now."

"Is there a reason?"

"Yes, Mr. Blackmon. Some bad news, I'm afraid."

"Is there any other kind these days? Tell me."

"Ms. Strong and I are sitting here in the great room with her friend Mariah and Natasha Yenin, sir."

As before a storm when the barometric pressure plummets, the air in the room feels dense. Nothing comes through from Ian's end of the line, not even static or a whisper of breath. *Nothing*. After a seeming eternity of probably ten seconds, Ian speaks, his voice harsh in the quiet room. "Give me details, Mason."

"Yes, sir. Ms. Yenin coerced Mariah into coming here so that Ella would allow security to send her up and she'd open the front door. She is armed, sir."

"Where is her placement in the room?"

"Next to Ms. Strong, Mr. Blackmon."

"So the gun is trained on Ella?"

His voice is deadly calm and it's scaring me even more than if he were raging—but not as much as the revolver currently poking into my ribs. Making me ever more anxious, the stupid woman has her other hand in my hair, twisting strands of it around her fingers as a lover might.

"Yes, sir... and the intruder is touching Ms. Strong, sir. Her hair."

"What?" the word is barely audible. Then it grows stronger. "Ella? Are you okay, Ella?"

I try to project my voice so it reassures him. ""I'm fine, Ian. Truly. Just speak to her so she'll get the hell out. Now she's dragged Mariah into her little game."

"Yes. Yenin, talk."

"I want you to call off the hit, Ian. Now."

As soon as I hear her say that word, my amplified gasp fills the entire cavernous room, and I know Ian can hear me. Could he really have taken out a hit on her? I just can't believe he'd ever go that far, even to protect me.

He sounds more annoyed than angry: his voice is terse, his words clipped. "I haven't a clue as to what you're talking about. There is no hit."

Natasha's eyes widen, glowing with anger and/or indignation. "Bullshit. My uncles are alive today because they have the skills to detect this kind of threat: their ears are always to the ground. How could you, Ian? After all we've meant to each other, you're actually going to have me killed?"

"First of all, I'm not having you killed. And, second, look who's talking. You set out to destroy my family and I. Are you really in a position to judge anything I do?"

"I would never hurt you physically, Ian. I was just going after your money."

"You're a liar, Yenin. What about my grandfather's *accident*?"

"What about it? I had nothing to do with it. Nothing."

"What a strange coincidence that the man who deported your grandfather gets run off the road around the same time that you go after my company. Odd."

"Yes, it is odd. Nevertheless, it's true. I want you to get on the phone while I listen, and call it off. Now. Before something irrevocable occurs."

"May I ask what gave you the outlandish idea that I took out a hit on you?"

"Word came down the pike: my uncles are connected. Because of it, they had to leave the country and they'll have a very difficult time getting back in."

"My heart bleeds for them."

"I don't want to leave the U.S. so call them off. The ones you hired are professionals: they'll get the job done on the first try. Please, Ian. Now."

"And if I do, what will you do for me?"

"I'll back off both you and your girlfriend. I was actually losing taste for the game anyway. The fact that you would even consider taking me out, Ian injures me greatly. We were in love, for God's sake. You were my first lover!"

"Mason, please switch off speaker and put the woman on the line with me. Ella shouldn't have to listen to this pathetic conversation."

"Yes, sir." Instantly the room plunged into a more innocent silence. Natasha reached for the phone with her free hand but didn't budge the gun an inch. Ian must have been yelling quite loudly because we could all hear him, not in specific words but in tone. Tears in her eyes, Natasha listens to his diatribe, nodding her head at intervals. "Yes, fine, yes. I will. Can I meet with you?"

It might be hard to believe but I forgot about the nasty looking gun shoved into my ribs because my mind was transfixed on the idea of Ian hiring someone to kill Natasha. Could it be true? Nah, I dismiss the possibility. But... if not, why does she believe it so fervently? Perhaps he's playing with her, pretending to take out a hit to frighten her. That must be it. Right? Or could he actually have the stomach for such extreme violence? I'm just not sure about any of it but I know one thing: Ian and I need to have a heart to heart, and very soon.

When I return my full attention to Natasha, I see she's fully blubbering now. Everything's running on her face: eyes, nose, mascara... Nodding her head in agreement, as if Ian could see her, she appears amenable to all he says. I'm suspicious, though: if these people really are connected with the Russian mob, no way are they just going to slink off into the night... nor would they be leery of killing. So I watch our nemesis closely but I can't detect any artifice: she really seems afraid and contrite. Finally, she moves the gun away from me and stands. I hear her say thank you to Ian and then without a word to any of us in the room, she tosses the phone onto the sofa and takes herself right out the door. I grab for the phone at the same time as Mason but I get there first.

"She just walked out, Ian. Now, tell me: did you really do what she accused you of doing?"

"Of course not, Ella. But I still used it to my advantage and pretended to call off a hit so she'd leave you alone. I'm flying back home late tonight or early a.m., so I'll be home soon. I'll see you sometime tomorrow, definitely." He pauses. "I'm really sorry about what just happened. Please relay my apologies to Mariah for what she endured. I had no idea Natasha was back on the West Coast."

"It's not your fault, Ian... and I'll make your apologies to Mariah. Is it okay if I leave the apartment if I take Mason along?"

"I'd rather you didn't. I understand you must have cabin fever but it's only a few more days until I have the situation under control, Ella. Can you wait?"

"I don't think so, Ian. Can't I just go out for lunch?"

He sighs. "Let me speak to Mason, please."

Wordlessly I hand Mason the phone and wait, trying to make sense of only one side of the conversation. I can't, but soon enough, Mason puts the phone back into his breast pocket and looks directly at me.

"Mr. Blackmon said you and Mariah may have lunch out, provided I stay close to you at all times. That means I'll be joining you for lunch."

"Only if you lighten up a bit, old man," Mariah says, winking at him.

Mason's face remains stoic but his lips twitch ever so slightly as if he really wants to let loose, go completely crazy and... *smile.* Instead he responds to her simply: "I'll do my best."

"Mariah," I grasp her hand and gaze directly into her eyes, "I hope you don't believe that Ian would actually have someone killed. He's not a murderer."

Mariah holds up her free hand. "Don't give it another second's thought, Ella; I do not think poorly of your man. Frankly, I wouldn't blame him if he did order a hit on her. For God's sake, did you see her shoes? Anyone who wears shoes like that is just asking to be killed. Talk about tawdry." She shudders in mock horror.

I laugh at her comment and finally Mason breaks down and grins. Oh, he has pretty teeth, I think, since I've never seen them before today. What's more, I suspect that if he hangs around Mariah, he'll be smiling more often. Hmmm.

"Mason, can you entertain Mariah while I go take a quick shower and get dressed? Maybe she'd like some coffee or tea?"

"Go ahead, Ella. We'll figure it out. Just get ready before he changes his mind."

While I shower I wonder what Ian is doing right this minute: having an early dinner? Chatting with Daniel? Calling off a hit? What? I'd really like is to be there, to see him, be with him, interrogate him, and, later on, do other things to him. This whole episode has me also wondering about Daniel Butler. It seems as if anything and everything Ian's thrown at him since they met has been received with support, regardless of how dark and ugly it might be. What kind of man is Daniel? Ian mentioned we'd be going to Daniel's wedding next month and I am truly looking forward to that affair.

Though anticlimactic after the drama of Natasha's visit. Mariah and I have a lot of fun and laughs over lunch, seemingly tormenting Mason with our gossipy conversation. It was quite hilarious to watch him trying to keep up, especially after Mariah told him to pay attention, that he'd be quizzed about who was dating whom on the way back to the condo. And she did quiz him, too, and Mason, with no small degree of pride, managed to answer all but one of Mariah's ten questions on what was discussed at lunch. It went something like this:

"Okay, Mason, who is Hannah Cravitch dating now?"

Mason looks smug so he must know this one. "Hannah," he says, yanking up his starched collar, "is currently dating Tomás, but started only recently. Before that she was with Rick in a long-term relationship."

Mariah and I clap. "Very good," we praise in chorus. And so it went. Truth to tell, I think Mason had the best time ever. Maybe, just maybe, there's a future for these two, judging from the way Mariah's been behaving around him.

After, we went for ice cream cones and sat in the park to eat them while Mason was on high alert. Watching him angst over my safety, I finally gave in and told Mariah I had to get back. Being the good sport that she is, she offered to come back and watch movies with me, and the two of us ended up making a Mexican dinner for Mason and one of his assistants.

Just as I am dozing off for the night, my phone buzzes. Attempting to move nothing save for my arm, an exercise in supreme laziness, I grasp the phone, dragging it to my ear. "Hey."

"Hey, yourself. I'm leaving New York tomorrow at 6 a.m. and should be back in Portland around nine or ten."

"Will you go straight to the office?"

"Probably. But I wanted you to know I'll be with you in the evening, without a doubt, baby. Everything else okay? Nobody else threatening you at gunpoint, I hope?"

"Not today."

"Ella, I'm sorry, so sorry. I had no idea she was back on the West Coast. I had seen her yesterday in New York."

"Everything turned out fine, Ian... but we'll need to have a long talk when you get home."

His sigh seems to come from a place of utter exhaustion, a confluence of physical, emotional, and psychological depletion. "Yes. On a happier note, have you begun shopping for a wedding gown?"

"Not yet. Well, I've surfed through some sites but not a serious hunt as of yet. Why?"

"Because I thought it would be nice to have a late spring or early summer wedding and it's almost March now."

"I suppose I should let the mothers know, huh?"

"I suppose so. We'll do it together. We'll phone yours tomorrow evening and we'll visit mine over the weekend to share the news. How does that sound?"

"Perfect. I can't wait to see you—I've missed you, Ian."

"And I you." His voice drops into a lower register. "I expect to be greeted accordingly."

I giggle because I know he has dirty things on his mind. "Yes, sir."

"Ooh, Ella, you know what that does to me. You'll pay up tomorrow."

"I'm counting on it. Goodnight, my love."

"Good night."

Afterward, I lay in bed, chasing sleep that continues to elude me. Finally, I give up trying and slip out of bed to get a glass of water, maybe make myself a cup of tea. That's it: a cup of tea and a mystery will help lull me to slumberland. On the way back to the bedroom with my tea and a book under my arm, a mystery about a medieval tome that holds unsolved codes, my eyes alight on a framed photo of Ian. I snapped it on the deck of his houseboat. He's standing at the railing, his hair windblown, his endlessly long legs wrapped in dark blue jeans. What I love most about this photo? He's shirtless, and he has a chest to die for. Every muscle in his chest and abdomen is sharply delineated, a human map, a symphony of sinew, muscle, tissue, and bone. Not many people ever get the opportunity to see Ian without a shirt and that's a damn shame for the world. A damn shame.

I bring the photo back to bed with me and look at him long and hard: he's young, gorgeous, stupidly rich, brilliant, sexy... *and he's my fiancé*. How lucky am I? And tomorrow we'll be together again. My body begins to rev as I imagine him without the jeans, his bitable tight, slightly plump butt cheeks, perfectly proportioned legs, trim waist, wide shoulders, masculine feet... and there's the part of him I happen to be extra fond of, the part that salutes me at attention when he smiles deviously, lowers his head, and swaggers over to me. A rush of heat sweeps through my body as I envision him that way: this is going to be a long, possibly wet night since I'm now counting the minutes until I see my lover again.

Smiling, my eyes flutter closed, and I'm down for the count almost instantly. My darling lulls me to sleep from thousands of miles away. I never even had a sip of my tea or read a single word of the book. Tomorrow. Tomorrow holds such promise.

Chapter 45

"What the fuck happened, Joseph? Your so-called professionals were made before they even got to the city of their damn targets. This screw-up could have been costly for my friend—and I'm not talking about money, either."

The voice on the other end of the line is cold enough to freeze water into ice. "You might have mentioned that the targets were professional assassins themselves. That would have proved a helpful nugget of information, Butler."

"You might have asked about their background. You're the expert, after all. Moreover, I had no idea as to their professional pursuits. Isn't ferreting out that information all part of the job description of hired killer?"

"Whatever. The result you got may have been better anyway. They're both out of the U.S. and aren't likely to be returning anytime soon and it didn't cost your friend a penny yet. Plus, the hit is still live."

"If they're so connected why did they have to run?"

"The ones I assigned to the task were not their friends. In fact, they would have gladly done it free of charge except there's an unspoken ethic among killers for hire: only hit those you've been paid to hit. Period."

"There's still the matter of the woman..."

"You said your friend canceled it, right?"

"For now. He wants an additional twenty-four hours. If you don't hear back from him, it goes live again. Has that information been disseminated to the correct parties? We don't want another mistake."

"The monies were returned to the account, weren't they? Trust me: without an advance, nothing gets done. You're fine."

"Okay. I want you to know I'm not ungrateful for your assist. It's just that the woman went after my friend's fiancée and he had a few tense moments."

"Is everyone alright now?"

"Yes. Thank you."

An uncomfortable pause ensues as both men abruptly stop speaking and then they both begin to say something simultaneously:

"Well, I'll—"

"How's Oli—"

Daniel expels a long breath. "You first."

"How's Olivia?"

"She's fine, doing well in school and our wedding celebration is upcoming. Olivia is happy."

"And?"

"I was just going to say goodbye. Thanks again. Take care."

The line goes dead and Daniel looks up at Ian. "I hate the bastard."

Ian snorts. "Really? I never would have suspected from the affectionate way you two speak to one another."

"Yes, well... our relationship is fraught... I'm relieved he's across the planet right now."

"Daniel, considering how much you don't care for the man, I appreciate it all the more that you contacted him for me. I don't know what the hell I would have done here without your help. I hope you know you can always count on me to have your back should you need it."

Daniel smiles, stretching his long legs out in front of him. "I've been treated kindly by the universe of late so I consider it a pay-it-forward type of thing. However, you're very welcome. I truly hope you and your Ella will be able to attend our wedding at the end of the month and we can have some fun together for a change."

"Count on it."

"So now what? You told Natasha you'd hunt down

and painfully kill every member of her family if she didn't keep her distance. Will she?"

Ian's laugh is bitter. "I highly doubt it but if I can avoid putting a permanent end to her, I'd prefer doing so. However, at least now she knows I'm serious."

Running both hands through his too-long hair, Daniel is lost in thought. When he snaps back to attention, he glances sharply at Ian. "You might want to reconsider, Ian. While it's true the brothers are outside our borders for now, Natasha is not going to play nice. I can guarantee it."

"I'm going to meet with her tomorrow when I return to Portland. I'll make the final call then."

"Be very cautious at that meeting. Make it a public place and scope it out before you let her see you. She just might come at you in a way you're not expecting."

"Can you elaborate?"

"It's never a good idea to have the target of a hit you ordered know about it in advance. Now that she knows you're a serious player in this game, she might try to flip the table on you. I can't say for sure and I don't think she'll go for your throat, but what I can guarantee is that you haven't seen the last of her. Frankly, Ian, I think you should just leave the order in place. I promise, you'll get over it."

Ian just stares back at the man, his eyes inscrutable. If the eyes are the window into the soul, his window is currently firmly closed.

Daniel knows Ian doesn't want Natasha's death on his conscience but he feels obliged to give his friend the unvarnished truth, no matter how unpalatable. "If you prefer, you can go home, forget all about it, and I'll see to it on this end." Daniel's voice is petal-soft but his meaning is lethal.

"I'm going for a run—I'll do some thinking while I'm at it."

Daniel nods. "Okay, I have some calls to make and," he checks his watch, "a Web conference in forty-five minutes. I should prepare."

"I'll let you get to it, then." Ian turns to head upstairs to his room to change clothes.

"Oh, Ian? I thought we'd go out for dinner tonight since Olivia will be downtown and I'm going to pick her up. Would you care to join us?"

"Thanks for the invite but I think I'll grab something while I'm out and retire early tonight. My pilot filed an early flight plan and I do need my beauty sleep."

"Don't we all?" Daniel grins. "Let me know what you decide, post-run."

"Will do."

As Ian sits in his jet the next morning, waiting for clearance for takeoff, he tries to get some work done, answering emails, and sending texts. Since it is still too early for business in Portland, his responses won't be received right away but it will be out of the way on his end. After he finishes, with still two planes ahead of his in the queue, he reclines back and mulls over this whole sorry affair. Is it really over? He wonders.

Natasha seemed so horrified that he'd even consider so drastic a measure. He shakes his head. She has to be insane by any standard. She threatened his business, hell, she sabotaged it for years, planned revenge on his family for over a decade, threatened Ella with kidnapping and rape... and was surprised he wanted her dead?

Now a dilemma is in front of him: should he tell Ella the truth and risk her rejection? Or should he lie to her and have that hanging between them forever? In one stroke, Natasha managed to fuck him but good without even trying.

Last night, after it happened, he'd decided to come clean with Ella, tell her everything as it occurred. This morning he wasn't so sure. What if she decided she couldn't marry a man who could make a decision like that? In trying to protect her from harm, he may have pushed her away permanently. He rubs his face with both hands, wishing he knew which path was the right one.

What would Ella do in his position? She would never have ordered the hit in the first place. But what if his life hung in the balance and that was the only surefire way to save him? Would she do it then? Assuming she would and she found herself in the same position in which he currently sat, then what? His heart knew the answer even before his mind recognized it: she would tell him the truth. Ella might be many things, but deceitful is not one of them. His mind made up, he tries to relax enough to take a nap.

The Gulfstream lands at 9:37 at the private airfield just outside the city. At the sound of the metallic groan of the landing gear's descent, he checks his watch, adjusts the time to Pacific, and shoves his electronics and paperwork into his briefcase. Picking up the iPad, he smiles, thinking about Ella's novel. He'd really missed her when he was reading it, *really* missed her.

His mind begins to drift away from all the ugliness with the Russians and back to important things... like his dungeon. Would Ella consider going in there again? If she did, how far would she agree to go? He doesn't think he'll ever try using a whip on her again, but there are plenty of other milder implements. As for the heavier ones, the whips and canes, he knows how to use them so as not to break skin or cause any scars. Still, if she doesn't want to play with them, then he doesn't either. He would never force anything on her again, never. Honestly, he wasn't sure he had it in him to ever pick up a whip again, after losing her the way he did. Saying goodbye to the whips really wasn't much of a loss. The dungeon, however, well, that was a different story.

We'll have to play it by ear, he thinks, grinning wickedly to himself as he imagines Ella tautly stretched out on the St. Andrew's cross. If we get past today, that subject will be next up. He looks down at his pants and shakes his head. Hopeless.

His next thought sours his good mood: he has to meet with Natasha this afternoon, after spending a few hours catching up at the office. What he'd really like to do is to go straight home to Ella, but her safety must be ensured first and foremost. As for work, he'd been away too much lately and his absence caused problems. He needed to meet with his staff, sign a few documents and stock transfers, have Claudia catch him up on details and then he'd meet with the viper. Afterward, he'd race back to his pretty woman.

His eyes glowing in anticipation at the mere thought of ravishing that pretty woman, he drums his fingers impatiently on the armrest, waiting for the pilot to bring the plane to a stop.

Sipping her *Venti* latte, Natasha Yenin sits in the overstuffed chair and considers her current situation, her demeanor clear-eyed and calm. She has to admit she was stunned by the option Ian took. Never in a million years would she have thought him capable of such a coldblooded solution. Even her uncles were surprised by his bold move... and angry as a hornet's nest poked with a stick. They dearly wanted to pay him a visit before they jumped ship but didn't have the luxury of time so they opted to stay alive to fight another day. Before they learned of the order, they were planning to beat hell out of Ian in payback for what he did to their precious Lucien.

Her uncles were not the forgiving type but they were loyal as the day is long. Wondering if she'll ever see them again, she makes a mental note to check on Lucien; her uncles made her promise to watch over him. For some unknowable reason, they consider Lucien as helpless as Natasha is capable. Why, she'll never know, but one thing both uncles know for sure is that under all her long, blond hair, tight dresses, and red lipstick beats the heart of a coldblooded killer. Not so with Lucien.

Killer or not, she told Ian the truth: she'd never have harmed a hair on his pretty head. She'd wanted to make him suffer for his family's sins, oh, yes, but never have him pay in blood. Of course, she had no qualms about hurting his little twit of a girlfriend... but never her Ian. If it were possible for her to love anyone, she loved him. Still, now that she knew he was capable of ordering her death, she might just be able to return the favor... but she wasn't certain of it. They were meeting today, probably each with the same agenda. Natasha didn't believe he'd cancelled the hit order so she might very well be breathing on borrowed time.

Ian had said some hideous things to her on the phone. She wished his little Ella could hear what her gentleman was capable of. Too late she realized she should have switched it back to speaker without his knowledge. The bastard promised to search out and annihilate every person who shared her DNA, no matter how long or far the mission took him. He'd vowed the name and bloodline of Yenin would be permanently obliterated from the face of the earth for eternity. The thing that made her lose her composure was what he said last: he swore he never cared for her in the least, that she was just a convenient lay, and he'd have no qualms about ripping her cold, black heart out of her chest with his own two hands. That was the first really cruel thing he'd ever said to her. Even calling her a cunt was something she considered more of a compliment—it showed he considered her a worthy adversary. But swearing he never loved her? Even though she knew it was a total lie, it still hurt. Well, the first cut is always the deepest, right? From here on in, she'd wear a tougher skin... and it was her turn to cut into him.

Eying the people around her, the tall, blond woman is seated at a corner table in the café, never letting her guard drop an inch. She is following Ian's orders to a tee. He'd been very specific about the table location: away from windows, as far from other diners as possible, and far removed from the kitchen or restrooms. His meticulous instructions included one about her rising from the table as soon as she spotted him and standing approximately two feet away from it until he reached her. That, she supposes, is to ensure against her holding a weapon under the table.

Two minutes after the hour, there at the entrance to the café is the man himself. She allows herself a moment to drink in his fine looks. It didn't matter how long she knew him: every time she sees Ian again, it's as potent a moment as the very first time she set eyes on him. She knew that day, all those years ago, when he loped into the classroom with the goods to back up the attitude, that he had to be her target and it made her heart lurch in regret. Sometimes life can be rottenly unfair.

Now that he had the upper hand for a few minutes, she allowed herself to ponder her commitment to her family's revenge. Was it truly that important? The end result would be the same, her grandfather too far gone to ever return to them. Nothing she could do could ever remedy that outcome. The family's finances were much better these days, thanks to her mother's brothers and her own efforts, plus the windfall from her swindle of Blackmon Enterprises five, nearly six years ago. They all enjoyed a high standard of living. Shouldn't she just forget the vendetta and walk away? She'd never be able to salvage her relationship with Ian, obviously, but it would permit them both to get on with their lives without fear of retaliation. She decided then and there that if Ian were amenable, she'd be willing to lay this whole thing to rest right now.

Rising gracefully from the table, she steps away to the required distance and smiles at the man approaching her.

As soon as he is within her hearing distance, he begins to bark orders in a hushed tone of voice. "Turn around slowly." She complies.

Pointing to the chair she just vacated, he says nothing else so she takes a seat and watches as he joins her at the table. He leaves his chair about a foot away from the table. Obviously, he doesn't trust her. Tsk tsk.

Calmly unbuttoning his suit jacket, Ian focuses piercing eyes on his shapely adversary across the table.

He's not here to mince words, obviously. She sits patiently, waiting for his cue.

"The order for which you expressed concern yesterday afternoon was not cancelled—"

As her lips part to voice her objection, he holds up his hand to prevent it. "Allow me to speak, please, or we'll get nothing accomplished here— I don't have a wealth of time. The order was put on hold for twenty-four hours so..." he glances at his watch, "by my calculations, you have approximately three hours, give or take a few minutes on either side until it goes back into effect. Should you wish for me to rescind it entirely, you must follow my instructions to the letter. I should also add that the operative who accepted the assignment is already stateside. Have I made myself crystal clear?"

She nods, waiting to hear his demands. This meeting was not going as it did in her imagination.

"Fine. This is how we'll proceed: first, before we leave this restaurant, I will administer to you a strong sedative. The medication will take about a half-hour to begin to have effect and will probably last about four hours, at which time you will be dosed again. We will leave the café, drive directly to your home and pick up your passport and a few changes of clothing. From there I'll take you to my private plane, which you will board, along with an escort of my choosing. Your escort will ensure that you remain unconscious until the flight concludes in Moscow. Once there, you will surrender your passport to said escort and he will phone me. I will then cancel the order."

She tried to disguise her horror at his demands. "That will take considerably longer than three hours, Ian."

"Yes, it will. You, however, will be safe and sound on a plane in the sky. No one can reach you there. This, my dear, is my best offer. Take it or leave it." He leans in closer to whisper his last words. "I want your answer now."

She smirks. "You do realize that I can place a similar

order upon your head, right? What makes you think you hold all the power?"

He shrugs casually. "I have my reasons."

"I'm not leaving the U.S. This is my home, Ian."

"Not anymore. You forfeited your right to stay here when you began your blood vendetta against my family, Yenin. Either you leave... or you take your chances."

He sits back into his chair, his eyes traveling in a circuit, scanning the surroundings. When he directs his attention back to the woman and sees her glaring at him, without making any moves, he places his hands on the edge of the table and begins to get up. In rising, he says, "I'll interpret your silence as a refusal then. As I said, I have no time to waste on the likes of you. Good luck."

"Ian, wait! Please," she whispers hurriedly, "sit back down for a moment."

Turning back, he sits slowly, never taking his eyes from her face. "I'm waiting."

"I'll do it, Ian; I'll go. But may I just tell you that I'd decided to stop all of this animosity between us while I was waiting for you?"

"How nice." In his hand he holds out two small yellow pills. "Here you go. Bottoms up."

Something about his breezy fucking attitude pushes her buttons—hard—and instantly her blood pressure rockets into the stratosphere. Her heart is pounding so fiercely that the swollen river of blood rushes through her ears as her anger escalates ever higher. Who the hell does he think he is? Abruptly she bolts up from the table and stands directly in front of him, swinging her hair back, battle-ready. "You know what? Fuck you, Ian. I'll take my damn chances. But make no mistake, there will be a price on your head, too, whether I live or die. I can be just as nasty as you."

His only reaction is a smirk and a raised brow. "Oh, you can be far nastier, trust me. The difference is I subscribe to the belief that actions speak much louder than words. And I never waste valuable time on empty threats."

Her face now tomato-red, she glares at him with venom, spins on her heel, and flounces out of the restaurant, her high heels tapping out an angry staccato beat on the terracotta floor tile.

Ian looks at his watch: plenty of time for Jarvis's team to be in position. Nearing noon, he'd taken care of all of his most pressing business. Now it was time for his reward. His eyes glint in anticipation at the prospect of his reunion with Ella. He pulls out his iPhone.

Chapter 46

The text message from Ian comes in at 12:02 P.M. and reads: meet me on the top-floor restaurant of the Knickerbocker Club-Portland. Give them my name to gain entrance. Wear a simple dress with no undergarments and definitely wear high heels. Be there by 12:45; if you don't see me upon entering, wait for me in the lounge off the bar. Ian.

Perhaps I'm neurotic but I'd rather hear his voice to ensure the message is truly from him. All of this Russian mob crap has me on pins and needles. Since I've showered already, I just have to select a dress and put on some make-up. No underwear? What the hell is he planning?

I ask Mason to confirm the message is from Ian in case there's a reason he didn't call. Before Mason can even put his hand on his phone, Aretha starts singing and it's Ian.

"Ella, I realized after I sent the text that you'd probably rather hear my voice than read a text. It's from me and I want you to follow the instructions. *Comprende?*"

Relief makes me giddy at hearing his voice and knowing he's close. "Si, senor. Hasta la vista, baby, at 12:45." I hear a chuckle before I disconnect and begin a hunt for a killer dress.

Fourteen minutes later, I'm in the elevator with Mason. He insisted on escorting me to the club entrance. I'm mortified because my dress barely hits mid thigh and I'm sans panties. Feeling cool air on those parts—out in public especially —is unnerving.

The dress I chose is a gunmetal-colored chiffon draped dress. The built-in silk shift clings to the body but the outer chiffon swishes enough to conceal what I'm hiding—or what I hope I'm hiding anyway. I added light gray strappy sandals with five-inch heels. My hair is worn loose but I braided some of it last night so it has kinks in it, and I wore very spare make-up since it's the afternoon: a bit of bronzer, pink lip-gloss and a titch of eyeliner. The only jewelry I slapped on is a large silver cuff on one wrist and a watch on the other, plus my rings that I wear daily. Ready or not, here I come, Ian.

Turns out he's ready, of course. Mason leaves me at the entrance of the sedate limestone building and I'm whisked up to the top floor in a whisper-quiet elevator. It's so silent and so smooth that I can't tell when it stops until the doors swish open. Right there, in perfect view, is the most gorgeous man in all of Portland... and possibly North America... and possibly Planet Earth, sitting on a plush settee in a crisp navy-blue suit, snowy silk shirt, and copper tie, smiling at me. How does he manage to look so flawless when he got dressed out of a suitcase early this morning? I always look like I've recently slept on a park bench or in a cardboard box when I travel, unless I take the time to utilize those ridiculous hotel room irons that never get hot enough to cause a sunburn.

Attempting to keep my cool when what I really want to do is hurl myself at him, I sashay over to where he sits, bend straight so as not to embarrass myself while entertaining others, and give him a quick kiss on the lips. "I would have preferred your homecoming to be a bit more private, Ian."

Unapologetically eyeballing me up and down, he grins, obviously approving of my outfit. "Ah, you'll have fun, trust me, Ella." He stands up and extends his hand to me. When I place my hand in his, he brings it to his lips and gently brushes it with a kiss, keeping his smoldering eyes trained on mine. It makes my legs a bit wobbly and that's never a good thing in concert with stiletto heels.

"Come. Our table is ready."

We're seated at a corner window table with four place settings. "Are we expecting company?"

"After lunch, guests will be joining us for dessert and coffee."

"Aha. And may I enquire as to whom those guests will be?"

"Yes, you may."

I wait and he says nothing. Rolling my eyes to annoy him in return for his annoying me, I ask, "Who are our guests, Ian?"

"Our guests are Lissette Simmons, wedding planner extraordinaire, and her assistant Mykonos will be accompanying her."

I drop my voice to a low but harsh whisper. "So why, pray tell, am I not wearing any underwear? I thought I was coming here for sex!" Being deprived for three days has made me testy.

He laughs. *Laughs!* And then reaches for my hand, squeezing it. "Baby, you're not advanced enough for clandestine public sex. But someday..."

I narrow my eyes. "What do you mean, I'm not advanced enough?"

"Ella, I have to bind and gag you to keep you quiet when you climax. You have to learn how to do it with no one noticing before we can try something as advanced as that which you are suggesting."

"Then why?" I tap my fingers impatiently. He knows what my question is.

Amusement still gleaming in his pretty eyes, he shrugs, "Just because you're not there yet doesn't mean we can't start training you. We'll begin slowly. Now, let's order lunch and enjoy being together again, *mon chéri.*"

"Sweet-talking me in French? So obvious, it's gauche."

Chuckling, he says, "I got used to it around Daniel. Since we're both fluent, we conversed in French when out and about, thereby decreasing anyone eavesdropping. Came in handy."

I sip my mineral water as the waiter brings the wine over. Since it's lunchtime, Ian ordered a Merlot by the glass rather than bottle. Watching him take a small taste, swish it in his mouth, and close his eyes, makes me feel needy. I squeeze my thighs together. Judging from his expression, I take it he likes the wine selection. I want him to taste me the same way.

I continue to eye him suspiciously, wondering what exactly he has running through that Machiavellian mind. He must be a great poker player for his face gives nothing away... ever. Finally I can't bear the suspense any longer. "Tell me, Ian, did you do things like this, what we're doing whatever that is, with your previous girlfriends... submissives... whatever?"

He gently shakes his head. "Ariel, is it ever a good idea to discuss previous lovers with current ones? I think not."

"Well, fortunately, I'm not your current lover but your fiancée and I would like to know more about you, sexually and otherwise."

"And you won't find it upsetting?"

"I'm pretty sure I can handle it." I huff, deciding that no matter what he says, I won't react. Visibly.

"All right then, you're on. Yes, I've been fond of these little... adventures for some time now. One of my favorites involved a submissive who had a job interview via Skype. I was under the desk... *supporting and encouraging* her the whole time."

I gasp; I can't help it, damn it. "Why would you do that? That's just horrible."

"She had self-control issues. We were attempting to address that deficiency."

"Did she get the job?"

His lips twitch. "Unfortunately, no. The interview did not go very well. She came across as distracted... scattered, even." He makes a stab at a sympathetic expression but gives in to the blackness in his soul and grins devilishly.

"I'm not surprised. Any other adventures you'd care

to share?"

"There was the one in the crowded elevator—I wouldn't mind trying that one with you sometime."

"Oh?"

"Yes. We traveled from the 75th floor to the lobby. I believe she reached orgasm by floor 10… but it might have been even closer."

"And no one knew?"

There was one young guy who was watching her out of the corner of his eye. He might possibly have known. Otherwise, no. She took her punishment very quietly and gamely."

"Punishment?"

"Yes, she had displeased me. I felt she should be embarrassed."

"Displeased you how?" I ask breathlessly.

"By asking too many questions about previous lovers. What would you like to eat?"

I kick his shin under the table, forgetting I'm wearing sandals. "Ouch!"

Tossing his head, he just lets loose with a howl of laughter at my expense. His laugh is so contagious that I can't help but join in. I've really missed him a lot.

All through lunch I'm aware of my underwear-less status but he acts as if I'm fully dressed. What can he be planning? It's driving me crazy but I wait, wishing I'd brought my panties in my purse. That would fix him. It may seem like not a big deal but it really makes one feel naked without that reassuring strip of fabric covering that so private of places. Then there's the whole bra-less thing going on at the top. The silk shift is rubbing up against my nips and keeping the girls in a near constant state of arousal. Add that to the equation and it makes for one uncomfortable Ella.

Ian doesn't appear to even remember how he had me dress. Fine! I'll just keep my legs crossed and I'll forget, too. I manage to do just that and enjoy the lunch immensely. The fish is cooked to perfection, the salad crisp, the vegetables fresh. Almost as soon as the plates are whisked away by a very efficient waiter, two people present themselves at our table. Ah, the wedding planners.

Introductions are made as I size them up. The woman is attractive but all business: her dark blond hair is pulled back in a severe knot and she wears a no-nonsense suit and black pumps. The man, Mykonos, is quite handsome—Greek, perhaps? Just call me psychic. He's tall and dark but thin to the point of famine-chic, and thoroughly androgynous. By his demeanor and gestures, I'm certain he's gay—and that probably means he's really good at wedding planning, though I know I shouldn't generalize.

Ian and I stand to greet them. "Lissette, this is Ariel, my fiancée. Mykonos, I presume?" he asks the young man who nods effusively, making goo-goo eyes at Ian and confirming my suspicion. "It's a pleasure to meet you. I'm Ian Blackmon and this is my fiancée, Ella Strong." We all shake hands and sit down. Lissette sits to Ian's immediate right, pulling her chair close to his, so we can all look at pictures. Mykonos sits to her right, across from me. Opening a black leather portfolio, she begins showing us photos of her previous weddings.

I'm craning my neck to see the various themes of the receptions and exclaim about the Roman one, complete with ruins. It's so beautiful, I have to give her credit for a fantastic job. Ian sees the delight on my face and his hand reaches over to squeeze my thigh. I grin at him, thinking our wedding is going to be absolutely perfect. That's when his hand starts traveling... from my lower thigh to my upper thigh to my naked vajayjay. I swallow my gasp of horror just in time and it ends up sounding like a strange hiccup. My hand flies to my mouth, face scarlet, as I mutter, "Excuse me," to the planners. I'm going to kill him tonight so wedding plans are truly redundant at this point.

But my reaction does not deter him: he keeps his hand in place and continues to explore, his finger now inside me and he's doing other things with the palm of his hand. Closing my eyes in utter shame, I inhale deeply, and finally work up the nerve to look up: Mykonos is staring directly into my face with an expression that could only be described as smug. Oh yeah? What kind of a name is Mykonos anyway? Isn't it a Greek island, for God's sake?

Surreptitiously, I slide my left hand over Ian's at the exact same time as I lean over to point at something in her book with my right, commenting on the flowers in the photo as I simultaneously dig my nails into Ian's hand in an attempt to arrest his motion. Without any visible reaction whatsoever to what has to amount to vicious pain, he continues his ministrations as he asks Lissette a question. I have to give credit where credit is due: the motherfucker is a professional.

I snap my legs as tightly together as humanly possible but still he continues without interruption and now, though I despise admitting it, I am swamping. I'm so turned on that I must accept the reality that I am a wanton exhibitionist and yet somehow pick up and go on with my life. I stop resisting and just relax into it but as I feel an orgasm approaching, I break out in a cold sweat even though my body is so hot it feels feverish.

That's when Mykonos "accidentally" drops his napkin, having conveniently gotten frosting on his upper lip, residue from his hefty slice of German Chocolate cake. So obvious a ploy, it's pathetic. He bends down to retrieve the napkin and I know Ian will stop now.

But he doesn't stop! At all. In fact, he picks up the pace. Now I know Mykonos must know but Lissette is still clueless. I clear my throat loudly.

"Excuse me." All three turn to look at me. "Please excuse me; I'm just stepping away to the restroom." And as gracefully as I can manage under the untenable circumstances he's put me in, I rise and walk away. I can't wait till I get Ian alone.

The cab pulls up in front of the condo building just before three o'clock. After Ian pays the fare, he opens the door, gets out and then assists me. His arm around me, we walk into the lobby.

Nuzzling his face into my hair, he says, "Ella, it's such a beautiful afternoon. What say you to an evening picnic on the catamaran? We can have our discussion as we watch the sun set."

"Oh, Ian, that sounds so nice, so romantic." I give him a quick kiss and caress his cheek, my love for him almost overwhelming me.

Yes, I've forgiven him for his earlier behavior but only because he finished what he started. When I returned from the restroom, I discovered that he'd thanked Lissette and Mykonos for their time and advised them that we would need to think about exactly what we'd like and talk to our parents to determine the number of guests to be invited. As soon as we had that information, we'd contact them for a follow-up. I got back to the table just in time to thank them myself and offer my goodbyes. As they exited, Ian took my hand and led me to the rear of the restaurant.

"What about paying?"

"I run a monthly tab and they bill me."

"Where are we going?"

He says nothing, just pulls me along with some urgency. When we get to the back, I see a bathroom marked for families rather than gender. He leads me inside, where there's a water closet in a small separate room and a larger lounge, complete with diaper station and a small sofa. He locks the door.

"Come here, Ella, I've missed you too fucking much." He yanks me to the couch but we never make it onto it; he draws me in to kiss me the way I wanted to be kissed by him the second I saw him through the elevator doors. My hands slide into his silky hair as his tongue invades my mouth.

"You taste good, baby," he whispers as he drops to his knees, pushing my dress up and latching on with his mouth. The orgasm I'd succeeded in pushing away before comes rushing back and I can't hold it off, not for a second. Before I squeeze my eyes shut, the room seems to shiver with heat waves. I writhe frantically on his mouth but he never misses a beat and by the time I start to coast down from the pinnacle, I'm panting as if I've run a fifty-mile marathon. When he lifts his head up, his hands slide up and down my legs. "Mmm, you taste good all over."

I pull him up by his collar and kiss him again but I only taste myself; instead, I sink to my knees, sucking him into my mouth so I can taste him. Letting him swing his hips toward me in urgent rhythm, I swallow back my gag reflex to give him the best ride possible. I've barely hit my stride before he lifts me up in one swift motion and propels me into the nearest wall. Lifting me higher, he impales me on his huge erection: I've waited three whole days to feel him here and I want to savor every second of it.

"I've missed you so much, Ian," I nearly weep, my hands clutching huge hanks of his hair.

"Baby, I've missed you, too. I've been literally dreaming about you." A moan escapes, deep from his chest. "Fuck, you're so tight, Ella, you're threatening my control." He pauses for a moment, grimacing, then bends his knees to use the full force of his legs and hammers into me for what seems an eternity. In a couple of minutes, we're both slathered in sweat, my dress is down; my dress is up: it's bunched up in the middle so he could have access to both ends. His mouth closes over my breast and teeth sink into skin, mostly gently. It feels indescribably good.

I decide to bring him down, then and there, in punishment for his earlier torture. I tighten my legs around his waist, push up using my arms on his shoulders as leverage and tighten everything on the way down, milking him with my muscles and allowing him little control over my actions. I do that a total of four times and he finally reaches critical mass and detonates inside me. In a wrinkled heap, we collapse down to the floor to recuperate and regroup.

Chapter 47

The rhythm of the tiny waves lulls every worry away, leaving a puddle of Ella on the polished deck. Ian smiles as he drops down to give her a kiss.

"Relaxed much?"

One blue eye opens, casting him a suspicious look and then she returns his smile. "Mmm. I could get used to this." Her arm rises up to touch his face, stubbled now; he obviously neglected to shave for a day or two.

He lies down beside her. "Yeah, I loved that about sleeping on the houseboat. No matter how tense you are when you go to bed, in less than an hour the boat is rocking you to sleep. Maybe when all of this is over and done with, we can move there again."

"Yes," she sighs. " I suppose it's time to discuss *all of this*, isn't it?"

"Let's get it out of the way. I worried myself sick for hours before I finally accepted the fact that you need to hear the truth. Ella, please don't reject me when you do."

Her whole body tensed when he said the word *truth*. That clued her in right away to what was coming. Now he has to follow through; his choice is gone.

"So you did do what she accused you of doing, Ian?"

Closing his eyes, he says softly, "Let me just take you through it, moment by moment, decision by decision, so you can follow my rationale. Okay?"

She nods. He inhales deeply and begins. She's lying on her back on the bow of the sailboat; he is sitting beside her, cross-legged, staring at the distant horizon. Gazing into the blue depths of her eyes is too difficult when speaking of such dark things. He does not attempt to justify or ameliorate through explanation: he simply recounts history as it occurred. If she were of a mind to judge him, he'd be on the losing end regardless. His best hope remained her comprehension of what it felt like to stand in his shoes.

When he'd brought her up to this morning's events, he went silent and waited. The ball was in her court, and his heartbeat thudded, heavy with how much lay at stake.

"The order in in effect again now?"

He nods. "I have my people watching her every move, listening to her every phone call. Do you remember what I told you about Daniel?"

"About his extra sensory perception, you mean?"

"Yes. He was trying to warn me about Natasha continuing with this vendetta thing without telling me outright that he has this ability. If he doesn't feel comfortable with my knowing about it, I don't want to force the issue. I knew he was telling me she wouldn't stop. This morning I offered her a way out and she declined it. Refused it angrily would be a more accurate characterization. At first, it seemed as if she would take it but then her fury took over and she threatened me and stormed out."

"Threatened you how?"

"She said she'd put money on my head, too. She's pushing my back against the wall. You have to also understand that my grandfather's life is in jeopardy, as is your life, Ella. I'm trying to protect my loved ones."

"I see that, Ian... and I don't fault you your decision and I couldn't care less what befalls that horrible woman. But I care about you and so I'd ask you to think on this: how will you feel afterward, knowing you were responsible for her life being taken? Despite what she's done to you in the years hence, she was once very important to you. That, I think, would make it even worse. Will you be able to live with yourself?"

"Ella, what choice do I really have?"

"She said she would never have physically harmed

you."

"Even if that were true, those reservations wouldn't extend to you or to my grandfather. And I'm quite certain her uncles would have no such qualms: they're ruthless killers, Ella, and I kicked their son's ass."

"Their son?"

"Oh, right. Daniel claims that Lucien is the son of one of the two Lithuanian brothers but they don't know which one nor do they care to find out. They consider him as belonging to both of them and are very protective of—"

"Does Lucien know about this connection?"

"Daniel thinks he may have just recently found out. While I was in New York, the brothers purposely got close, very close to me—Daniel said it was done to be able to identify me for retaliation. He used the word kill."

Shuddering, Ella wraps her arms around herself.

"Are you cold?"

"My father used to say someone walked over his grave when a shudder went through him. But, no, I'm not cold, not on the outside."

"Well? What do you have to say, Ella?"

"What do you expect me to say, Ian?" Her china-blue eyes narrow as she sits up to move closer to him. She's wearing a short white sleeveless shift and it brings out the color in her eyes and highlights her tanned arms and legs—azure and gold, her palette is like water and sand. Ian wants to jump on her, she looks so edible, but now certainly wasn't the time or place. Not yet, anyway.

"You said you were afraid I'd reject you," she continues. "Do you honestly have such little faith in my love for you that you believed I would abandon you for doing what you thought was necessary to protect us and your grandfather?"

"I... I wasn't quite sure. Ella, doing what I did is not only illegal, obviously, but it's highly immoral. I wasn't certain—I'm still not—that you could overlook such a thing. Honestly, if I were in your shoes, I don't know that I could either." He grabs her hand. "Ella, what would you do in my place? I'd really like to know."

Sighing, she shakes her head. "I'd call the police and give them the whole history. I'd take out restraining orders... and try my best to have them all deported—they must have criminal records. I'd hire a lawyer to sue for monetary damages to keep her busy. I'd have a bodyguard, 24/7 and a high-tech alarm system."

"Might I remind you that these are people who don't play by the rules? The police might allow you to take out restraining orders but unless or until an actual crime is committed, they won't do anything else until after the fact. Restraining orders are just pieces of paper, Ella. As for deportation, even if there was legal justification, do you know how lengthy the process can be? By the time ICE straps them into their seats on the plane... well, I'd rather not finish that thought."

"I see your point. If the, uh, *order* is again in effect, why bother having her watched? Is it to prevent her from retaliating?"

"Pretty much. I'm yet hopeful she'll see reason and decide to leave the country. The person who accepted the assignment is on the East Coast. He'll be traveling to Oregon tomorrow. She still has time to change her mind—though she doesn't know it."

"What about the men?"

"They're being watched as well. Word on the criminal grapevine travels faster than the AP. As soon as they got wind of it, they were on the next available flight out of the country—both are smart enough to act first and ask questions later. The problem for them is getting back in: it won't be all that easy. I'm sure they'll accomplish it eventually. The other thing, of course, is that they too can pay someone to get at me; accordingly, my staff hired personnel to bug their living quarters and keep an eye on them. They're too clever to use anything but prepaid cell phones."

He searches her eyes. "I cannot overstate how sorry I am that you got caught up in this stupidity and had a gun to your chest, Ella. You haven't mentioned that at all. Do you want to talk about it?"

As she begins to contemplate how to frame her answer, unexpectedly—shockingly even— she starts to sob, almost hysterically. The tears are raining down and she's weeping uncontrollably, which inevitably brings on the sup-ups. At first Ian just stares at her in shocked surprise, but upon realizing she's experiencing a delayed reaction, he gathers her in his arms and lets her cry it out. When her tears are spent, she becomes very quiet and stays in his arms, her face on his comforting broad chest. The gently rocking sailboat, the definition of poetry in motion, becomes a peaceful oasis for both of them, washing away the stress of the past few days.

They remain serene for the better part of an hour. Ella is the first to move. Reaching her arms around his neck, she hugs him tightly and trails feathery kisses along the side of his head and face. "It's not fair that you have to suffer such vicious hatred when you're an incredibly good and generous man. I'll fully support whatever you choose to do, Ian, and I'll do my best to make things easier for you, anything you need or want." She pulls back to look him in the eye.

Arching his eyebrows, he asks her a question that he's been meaning to broach for a while. "A bodyguard?"

She smiles and nods. "Yes, that's fine. Just make sure he's really hot and he dresses well."

Now he grins. "No fucking way. He'll be balding and in polyester."

Giggling, she nips his neck and he drops down to the deck, pulling her on top of his chest. "I love you, my lovely Ariel. I feel like you took the weight of the world off my shoulders tonight."

Caressing his face that she adores, every plane and angle so familiar now, she understands her love for him is a gift she'll never relinquish no matter what comes their way. "As it happens, I love you, too. Isn't that swell?"

He cradles her face in his large yet elegant hands. "Inordinately swell," he murmurs just before he kisses her.

They make love under the twilight sky. While she's lying on top of him, he unzips the back of her dress, pulling the tab down to the small of her back. Swinging her up, he gets behind her, on his knees, and slips the cotton dress over her shoulders and down her elegant arms. Underneath the shift she wears a skimpy bra and panty set, in white lace. Ian turns her around and lifting her, begins to kiss and suck her breasts through the fabric. She moans and he smiles, knowing that she's complaining that the fabric is preventing a complete connection. He sucks harder, teasing her until she tries pulling the bra down herself. He captures her wrists and holds them behind her back, taking his time to drive her a little crazy.

Slowly, he pushes her on her back and repeats the process with her panties, kissing and gently biting through the lace. Her hips begin to buck somewhat violently, alerting him to her shrinking patience. Ian doesn't let it rush him. He wants to drive her to the very brink of orgasm before he gives in.

Now his lips move back up, tracing her hipbones, navel, breasts again, and up to her neck. He pushes her chin up and wraps both hands around her throat, ever so slightly tightening them as he kisses and licks her lips until she gives him what he wants.

He could kiss Ella all night: her mouth is warm and delicious, and he hardens past endurance when her tongue begins to tango with his. Pushing himself up to a kneeling position, he removes his shirt and unfastens his belt and jeans, shoving them down low enough to serve their purpose. Ella was on birth control now and he'd been screened at his last check-up. It was sublimely wonderful to forego the condoms and feel her warmth directly on his skin.

Unable to resist any longer, he slides off her panties and spreads her legs, leaning in toward her. Tonight will be the missionary position because it's all about love first and sex afterward. Ella would be his wife soon and he wants her to know how much he adores, even reveres her. He can say it with words but tonight he'll also say it with every part of himself.

Chapter 48

As I am preparing for bed, I revisit our twilight boat ride earlier in the evening. Ian once again awed me with his abilities: he could man a sailboat like a pro. Was there anything this guy couldn't do? I should also mention that he's not just competent but he's sexy-competent, that is, he looks mucho hot when he's doing things well—graceful, buff, and just hard all over, mmm.

When he'd gotten us to a place where he wanted to float for a bit, he produced from underneath the helm a beautiful picnic dinner, prepared by our favorite restaurant: wine, cheese, grilled vegetables, and a baguette definitely worth the carbs were all wrapped in a red and white gingham cloth in the basket, along with a Caesar salad and espresso brownies for dessert—the most direct and rewarding way to max out on sugar and caffeine. As we ate, Ian told me what all the parts of the boat were called. I especially liked the jib, because it had a sword in a stone pictured on a purple and gold background in the shape of a shield—the logo for Excalibur.

When we finished our meal, we had the dreaded discussion. After, we watched the sun set, the darkening sky accompanied by a panoply of vibrant colors—it felt as if it were a display for us personally. When dusk fell, we drank wine and made love under the emerging starlight.

I take a moment to indulge in a sigh.

I know I set Ian's mind at ease with my reassurances—and they were true. I trust him enough that I know he won't make decisions lightly. He'll examine them from every possible angle and choose the best path—his is a logical mind. Who am I to judge him anyway? The man carries the weight of the world on his beautiful, muscled shoulders.

I'm still, however, very worried about Natasha. If she manages to survive somehow, she'll try to do very bad things to us; if she dies, Ian will forever have that terrible guilt on his conscience. This is a quandary I cannot help him climb out of. He'll have to do what feels most comfortable for him.

Meantime, I'm going to do something fun for a change. I'm going to shop for the most beautiful wedding dress I can find. For one of the few times in my life, I plan to put looks before comfort and choose the most glorious gown ever, no expense spared. To assuage my conscience at the extravagance, for every dollar I spend on my wedding gown, I will donate the same to UNICEF, to help children in need around the world.

My first order of business is to call Mariah. My second is to make an appointment at an exclusive bridal salon.

So that's what I do, hoping that Mariah could come with me. She is my maid of honor, and I'd like us to pick out her dress together. My mother will probably want to come, too. Ian and I are telling the mothers this weekend. When I finish in the bathroom, I go out to the bedroom to find him already asleep. Poor thing, he's exhausted, probably mentally and physically. Tiptoeing over to his side of the bed, I pull the covers around him, kiss his forehead gently, and slip into the other side of the bed, trying my best not to disturb him. Problem is, he's like a magnet, drawing me ever closer so I give in and cuddle him from behind, falling asleep holding onto him as a drowning person clutches fast to a lifeboat.

"Ella, just tell me what day you want to go and I'll call in sick, for heaven's sake. Your wedding gown is more important than making more money for my greedy boss." Mariah sounds exasperated, her usual reaction to me.

"Okay. I'll make the appointment at the salon and get right back to you. What time do you take lunch?"

"Whatever time I can sneak out of here. Sir Frederick is such a pain in the ass these days that I might just have to find a new job. Can you meet me for lunch?"

"Um… possibly. I may have to take Mason again."

"Please do. I have more gossip for him to memorize." An unholy cackle came echoing across the line, so infectious it gets me laughing even though it's barely ten a.m. and I'm generally cranky in the morning.

"When is this wedding taking place, anyway?"

"Ian wants late spring or early summer. We still need to pick the actual date. Tonight we'll call my mom and tell her the news and then tomorrow, we're headed to Ian's mother to share with her. We should have a date by the end of the weekend if all goes well."

"Why wouldn't it?"

I shrug, though she can't see me, unsure if I want to share my neurotic worries with her. She'll dismiss them as idiotic.

"Ella, why wouldn't it? Is his mother an unpleasant sort?"

"No! I mean, I've never met her but I doubt it. It's just that stupid book I wrote… and those stupid friends who spread it the world over."

"Let's not forget the stupid millions it earned you. Yeah, my heart bleeds, darling. Look: Ian's mother, and father for that matter, will love you as much as I do, book or no book."

"Now you have me really worried," I laugh.

"No, really, Ella. You're very lovable and they won't hold the book against you. Just don't let them read it, whatever you do, or they'll worry about their son's virtue."

"Ha. As if he had any left."

"Oh? Do you two try some of the shenanigans you wrote about in your dirty novel?"

Okay, now she's getting into dangerous territory. I

have to change the subject quickly. Mariah's smart; it's almost a miracle she hasn't figured out the truth already. Thank God for *big* favors.

"Oops, I have to go, Mariah. I'll let you know when I have a date for our first appointment. Talk soon." I disconnect.

What happens when she figures it out and she will? I know now the CA was not really to keep the kinky sex private; it was to protect his company's intellectual assets... despite the fact it is naïve to think that someone who is intent on stealing will worry over violating a contract. Ian wasn't thinking clearly when he crafted the legal protection.

Would Ian freak if Mariah or someone else figured it out? What if it did get out in public? What would be his reaction?

I'd like to believe that our love is much more important than anything else. As far as money goes, between Ian's assets and my literary windfall, we have enough to live our entire lives in comfort, so there's that. Who cares if people know we're kinky?

I do.

And Ian no doubt does too. So we have to tread lightly where the book is concerned.

The next morning before we call my mother to tell her the news, we realize we need to set the date first. Ian has a beautiful calendar on the wall of his home office so we head there with our brimming mugs of coffee to look it over.

"How about the second Saturday in June?"

"Fine with me," I reply. "One Saturday is as good an another. What date will we have for our anniversary?"

"June twelfth?"

"Hmm. So, that's 6-12-14? The tenth would work better numerically but that would put us on a Thursday. Not good, is it? Okay, the twelfth it is. Let's call my mom."

I place my coffee down on his desk and go in search of my phone, finding it in my bag in the entrance hall closet. Making my way back to Ian, I see he's on his laptop and whatever he's reading has his complete interest. I clear my throat loudly and he looks up.

"What's so interesting?"

"Not too much, just reading through my emails."

"Any news you want to share?"

"No, nothing yet." He looks up, bright-eyed. "Let's call your mom."

So I punch in her number and wait. It rings five times before she finally answers then promptly drops the phone. There's a bunch of noises that follow that sound like chairs scraping across the floor and then her chipper voice again. "Sorry. Hello?"

"Mom? It's Ella."

"Ella! My love, it's so nice to hear your voice."

"Mom, I'm here with Ian and I'm putting you on speaker phone so we can both talk to you. Okay?"

"Okay, honey."

I switch it to speaker. "Okay, here we are. Mom, Ian has something to tell you."

I look at him with a gleeful expression and his mouth drops open but his face is filled with amusement. "Brat!" he whispers. "Hello, Ella's mom, Ian here."

"Hello, Ian. Ella has told her father and I all about you and we're both very anxious to meet you."

"The feeling is mutual. As it happens, we have a perfect occasion for that to occur since Ella has agreed to marry me."

"Marry? Already? Isn't that awfully fast?"

I jump in. "Mom, we've been dating for well over a year," I lie. It's sort of true if you count when we met and discount the year we were apart.

"Really." She says it like an emphatic statement, not an interrogative. I know she knows I'm bullshitting her. Takes one to know one.

"Mom, it's true. We did have a period when we took a break to evaluate our relationship but now here we are, back together, and we're getting married on the twelfth of June. I'd love for you to help me pull it together."

"Of course I will, Ella. You two just took me by surprise. Hold on while I get your father on the phone. Mark!!!!!!" she screams in our ears. "Ella's on the phone."

We hear footsteps and then his voice speaking to her. "She has her phone on speaker because she's with Ian. "Okay. Hi, honey."

"Hi, Dad! So Ian and I called to let you and Mom know that we're getting married in June. I want to be sure that you'll be able to travel to Portland to attend."

"Married? Wow. That's a surprise. Of course we'll attend, sweetheart; I'll mark it on the calendar right now. What's the date?"

"The twelfth, Dad."

"Mr. Strong?" Ian pipes up.

"Ian?"

"Yes, sir. I just wanted to let you know that I would have called you first to ask for her hand but she wouldn't give me the number."

"It's true, Dad. He can be ridiculously old-fashioned at times."

"Well, I like that about Ian. You have my blessing, young man, but I hope you two aren't rushing things... or do you need to?"

"Dad! Of course not. Sheesh, it's a sad day when a girl can't even call her parents with good news without them thinking something terrible."

"Hey, a shotgun wedding ain't so terrible," my father says happily. He's referring, of course, to his own wedding since my mom was already pregnant with me when they married.

"Okay, well, glad your calendar is marked. If Mom can come out earlier to help plan it, I would be ever so grateful."

"Have you two told Ian's parents yet?"

Ian answers, "We're heading over there today to deliver the good news in person."

"Oh? Good. Ella, I'll put your mother back on now. All my love, sweetheart, and congratulations on your engagement."

"Thanks, Dad."

"Ella? Dad just handed me back the phone. So... I'll try to come to Portland next month. That will give us two months to have everything in place. Will you wait for me to shop for your dress?"

"Mariah and I are going to start this week but if you'd like, I won't make any decisions until you get here, Mom."

"If you find the right dress, you can snap it up, Ella. There's always the other dresses I can help you select."

"True. Okay, Mom. We'll talk soon. Love you."

"We love you, too, baby. Have fun and give your Ian a big hug from us. I can't wait to meet him."

I smile, hoping it goes through the line. "Bye, Mom."

From behind me, Ian starts kissing me up and down my neck, and tickling me all over. "Haven't I ever mentioned that I hate to be tickled?" I shout between bouts of hysterical laughter.

"I'm sorry but I can't hear you over all the din. Noisy fiancée, you know. What did you say?"

I'm laughing so hard I begin to choke. "Stop right this minute or I won't marry you, Ian."

He spins me around and we kiss, long and deep. "Mmm, want to have a tryst in the bedroom?"

I look into his smoldering eyes, wondering if mine are as easy to read as his silvery beauties are. "A tryst sounds perfect. Should we shower first?"

"How about we have a tryst in the shower? Multitask, you know."

"I love multitasking," I breathe, barely audible. "When will you call your parents?"

"Afterward. I'm big on priorities, you should know."

"Oh. Thank you for the edification: information is always helpful."

As we conduct this silly conversation, he is propelling me backward toward the bedroom. When we get inside, he kicks the door closed and pushes me down onto the bed. "Straight or kinky?" he asks, a devious gleam in his eyes now.

"Let's see, last time it was pretty straight... so I do believe it's time for kinky."

He disappears into the closet for a few moments and comes swaggering out with cuffs. "Let's try something new, shall we?"

"In here? Or in the dungeon?

"Are you ready to go back in there again?"

I shrug nonchalantly. "Last time it was fun."

His eyes spark as he sweeps his arm open and says, "Then, by all means, lead the way."

When we enter the room, he turns around to lock the doors and barks a command at me: "Strip."

It's only one little word but it does insane things to my body because of the promise it holds. I instantly begin to obey him, removing my clothes but I take my time. He shouldn't have everything so easy, should he?

Once the clothes are gone, he has me kneel and he leaves the room. I'm supposed to keep my eyes down when in this position but I don't, of course. I've never been completely obedient in my whole life—why start now? I watch for him to return. It seems to take forever but it's probably about four minutes before the door opens again and my eyes dart down to the floor.

Footsteps. Then I see his shoes in front of me. He lifts me from under my arms and places me under a big hook hanging down from the ceiling on a chain.

Cuffing my wrists with padded leather cuffs, he attaches an O-ring to one cuff and clips it to the other. Then he suspends the O-ring to the hook. I dangle with my feet just barely touching the ground. Either I have to stand on my tiptoes or put pressure on my arms and shoulders. It's not painful but it's slightly uncomfortable. Ian explains that it's a position designed to increase nervous anticipation but that I should tell him if it gets painful. "Okay," I whisper, deciding the position is doing an admirable job of making me nervous.

"I'm going to take away your sight and sound, Ella, so

all you'll have left of your senses is to feel and taste. Okay?"

"Taste?" I ask, breathless now.

"Yes, taste. And here I thought my enunciation was superb."

"I'm just not used to taste being something we... explore... in this room."

"Oh, Ella, there's so much you're not used to doing in here, but we have lots and lots of time ahead of us, hopefully."

"Can you promise that I won't be, uh, *tasting* anything disgusting?"

He laughs. "Promise. Now close your eyes; the blindfold is going on."

He wraps a black satin blindfold around my head. His voice is suddenly in my ear, whispering loudly, "Now your ears," and I feel earphones descend over my head, covering my ears so fully that I cannot hear a thing. In the past we used earphones once, but there was music playing.

It's amazing how being sensory-deprived makes you feel so differently, so quickly. The moment he takes away my hearing, I feel bereft—so lonely and so vulnerable that I almost begin to cry. But Ian doesn't allow me time to sink; he immediately starts the tactile sensations.

Things touch my bare skin: soft, hard, cold, hot. He rubs something against my lips, urging me to open them. The level of trust this entails is titanic but I now have deep wells of it for him so I part my lips and he inserts something for me to bite. The texture is bumpy and cool and when I bite into it, I immediately identify the food: a fresh strawberry. I can feel the juice running down my chin but instead of feeling messy, it feels decadent because I'm naked. I feel his tongue licking the juice off my chin; the sensation makes me very hot.

He must know that for the next thing I feel is cool, something soft and cool right on my breasts. It doesn't stay on long for his tongue once again begins to lap it off. Then I feel his lips on mine and when I open to him, his tongue invades and I get a mouthful of... whipped cream. Mmm.

Back to tactile, he uses feathers, silk, a rough fabric, an ice cube, something hot, perhaps a heating pad, something akin to long fingernails skates down my back, down my legs, and then up the front of my body. When it reaches my breasts, his mouth closes over one and he bites down softly. I can feel the vibrations of my moan, I can hear it echo inside my head, but I can't judge the volume—these earphones are impenetrable.

Back to the food: a chilled cucumber, a salty almond, a kiwi, a piece of dark chocolate and... suddenly something ice cold and wet runs down the front of my body. He begins to lick it off. Is he going to use his tongue on my entire body? Well, the short answer is yes.

He begins to lick then stops and kisses me. I taste the sharp tang of lime and tequila. Damn, was it a margarita? I would much rather guzzle it than have it poured over my body. He gives me a sip from the glass and I could taste the salt around the rim.

He licks more off... and then gives me another sip. And so on. When he's through, he takes out the toys: something sharp and vibrating crosses over my breasts and stomach. A slippery dildo slides into me and then a smaller one goes up the other way. Both are vibrating erratically. First slow then fast then slow again. I can't sink into a rhythm and I'm sure that's his intention. My shoulders and calves are beginning to ache because I've been alternating between them, trying to shift my weight back and forth.

He must sense my fatigue for I'm suddenly lowered to the floor and he scoops up my ankles so I keep going down. When the chain stops, I'm sitting on the floor, and he presses himself against my mouth. I open for him and when he slides his erection in I taste chocolate: melted chocolate. Mmm. I lick every drop of it.

After a few minutes, he pulls out of me, unhooks my cuffs and I feel myself go weightless: he's carrying me. He places me on a padded bench, stomach resting on it but my head and upper body dangle over the other side. He gets behind me and slowly removes the dildo, replacing it with himself. I can feel the vibrations from the other one and I know he can too. He slips something under my front and it begins to vibrate too, a maddeningly staccato rhythm that begins to drive me crazy. When I let myself whine, he changes the rhythm to a steady one and it doesn't take me long to reach the top.

Boom! My orgasm is like an explosion that I can't hear. I try to bear down my muscles hard to take him with me but I fail and he keeps going. And going. He flips me over and I wrap my legs around him and he starts up again—the man has staying power! I'm not going to be able to walk tomorrow. He's waiting for me to come again, and despite my exhaustion, I feel the pressure building. He must see it too because just as I think that, his fingers touch the vibrator on my clit and it goes into overdrive. He rips off the blindfold and earphones and I see his face, slick with sweat, eyes on fire, and... his hotness pushes me over, bringing him with me. We both moan in unison and I collapse back, feeling as boneless as any filet.

"Ella?" his voice is hoarse, even a bit raspy.

"Mmm?"

"We have to go to my mother's now."

"Now? Shouldn't we get dressed first?"

He grasps my thigh and, turning it, slaps my butt hard.

"Ow!"

"Let's go. We'll shower and dress quickly. My parents are expecting us in an hour." He grins. "We might be a little late."

Chapter 49

What is taking Ella so long? They'd showered together and then he left her in the bathroom to do her hair and make-up and he'd dressed and gone into the office to get some work done.

He looks at his watch. Almost an hour had passed since he left her in there and they were due at his parents' house in less than a half hour. He gets up to check on her.

The bedroom door is closed so he eases it open, finding her sprawled on the bed, tears running down her face.

"Ella, what's wrong?"

She glances up at him. Kohl is smeared all around her eyes, and runs down her cheeks in tiny black rivers. From his vantage point, she looks like a frightened raccoon.

"Ella?" he repeats.

Her response is a high-pitched wail, "I have nothing to wear!"

His eyes circuit the room. All around her are discarded outfits that she pulled from the closet and then tossed. He steps over those garments that made it to the floor and peeks in her closet. It is lined wall to wall with clothes, her own and those he purchased to augment her wardrobe with clothes that pleased him.

"Ella, I think you have something to wear. What is the real issue here?"

"I have nothing *appropriate* to wear."

"What does that mean? You have so many different clothes; how can it be that there's nothing appropriate?"

She shrugs her shoulders, tears still trickling down her face. "There just isn't."

"Ella, would you like me to choose an outfit for you?"

"No. I think you may have to go without me, Ian. Just this once; I promise I'll go next time." She presses her hands together in supplication.

"Do you not think it a little strange for me to show up alone to announce my engagement?"

Sniffling, she wipes some of the running mascara from under her eyes. "It is what it is."

"No," he sits beside her on the bed and pulls her close to him, "it's not. What's the real problem? Are you nervous about meeting my parents?"

Dissolving into tears again, she nods her head against his chest. "Oh, Ella, my parents will love you; I guarantee it. What's not to love?"

"I wrote a filthy sex book, Ian. Did you forget that minor detail?"

"It's not filthy; it's risqué, ribald maybe. Moreover, I'm fairly certain that genre of novel is not on my parents' reading list so I think we'll be safe on that front. My father spends most of his time reading science journals and my mother art books when she's not elbow deep in oils. It's all good, Ella. Really."

"What about your siblings?"

"My brothers live out of state so there's just Zoe, my sister. She will absolutely adore you, baby."

He didn't dare tell her that Zoe had read her novel. She'd find out, though, very soon, because Zoe has the biggest mouth this side of the Mississippi. "Come on: let's go. Throw on a simple dress or maybe pants, if you prefer, and don't give it another thought. Just don't wear fuck-me stilettos and we'll be fine."

She shoots him a dirty look. "Give me a little credit, Ian, for God's sake. Okay, fine. If you're going to force me into this den of lions, then..."

Rolling his eyes, he gets up muttering about dens of lions, and gives her a kiss on the tip of her nose. "Did you know you sneeze like a kitten?"

"Say what?"

His eyes brim with amusement. "*Say what*? Are you from the 'hood? Last night, you began to sneeze in your sleep and your sneezes were so small and soft, it sounded like a kitten sneezing, not a human. I almost starting scouring around for a tiny cat."

She gets up and starts pushing him toward the door. "Shoo. I have to get dressed. Now I'm not going to be just inappropriately dressed, but late, too."

He rolls his eyes again and leaves the room.

Ten minutes later, Ella emerges, her make-up repaired, no evidence of her meltdown. Wearing navy tights, a blue and green tartan kilt-style skirt held in place with a giant brass safety pin, a white cotton button-down shirt with three-quarter sleeves, knee-high black boots, and her hair tied back in a loose ponytail, she is ready to go.

Ian's eyes light up when he sees her. "I love the way you look, Ella, and so will my parents." He holds out his hand. "Let's go, baby."

When they turn into the circular drive of the estate, Ian glances over to the passenger seat: Ella looks pale. "Butterflies?" he asks, smiling reassuringly.

"A whole swarm."

He pats her hand. "Do not worry. I promise all will be fine."

Faith is at the door to greet them. Ian's mother is fairly tall, at 5'9" or thereabouts. She has auburn hair cut chin length and is very slender. Her eyes reflect a warm, fun personality. "Finally I get to meet Ella!" She rushes to them and pulls Ella into an effusive hug. "Ella, welcome to our home! I'm so thrilled... *we're all* so thrilled to meet you. We've heard so much about you, all great things, naturally."

"Thank you... and likewise." Ella smiles brightly as Faith hugs her son, holding his face affectionately with both of her hands. "You look very happy, my beautiful boy."

He smiles. "I am, Mom. Truly."

Eyes lingering on his, Faith nods slowly. "Yes, you certainly look it. Come on in, you two."

Trevor and Zoe sit in a small parlor just past the entrance hall. Ian's father rises to greet them. He's tall, about the same height as his youngest son, and his dark hair is liberally peppered with silvery gray. He casts friendly yet discerning eyes at the girl on his son's arm.

"Ella, I presume?"

"Yes, not Dr. Livingstone."

He smiles at her joke and extends his hand. "Charmed to meet you. Ian has told us much about you."

Ella takes his hand in her icy one, trying and failing to quickly warm it first. "So I hear," she says with a beaming smile. "Hello, Mr. Blackmon. It's nice to meet you, too."

Ian can tell both of his parents seem genuinely glad to meet his Ella. So far, so good. Now only Zoe is left.

Ian remembered Zoe's reaction to his news when they met for lunch the day before. She'd already been seated at a center table when he arrived or he would never have been given accorded a public table. As soon as he greeted her, he'd spilled the beans. Her reaction was not terribly surprising, considering that his sister does everything in a big way.

"You're marrying the author of a dirty book?" Zoe practically screamed the question.

Ian rolled his eyes. "You know, I was concerned that Ella's book sales in this neighborhood weren't adequate; thanks for seeing to that for me, Zoe."

She had the good grace to instantly flush, looking around at all the other diners who were now gaping at them. "I'm sorry, Ian, but you took me by surprise. For God's sake, when did this all happen?"

"This all being...?"

"Meeting, dating, asking to marry... you know, that kind of trivial detail."

"I believe I told you that I knew the author way back when you were drooling over the novel. We became *reacquainted* a while ago, and it escalated from there. Wait until you meet her: you'll love Ella and so will the rest of our family."

"If you do, then I'm sure we all will." She took a sip of her Chardonnay. "When will that meeting happen?"

"This weekend. We're announcing our engagement and imminent wedding."

Eyes narrowed. "How imminent?"

"June."

"What? That gives us no time to prepare. We have to book a venue, a band, a wedding planner..."

"We? Actually *we* don't. Ella and I would like to have the ceremony and reception at Mom and Dad's estate. In June the weather will be nice and we'll pitch a big tent in case of rain. I've already spoken with a few wedding planners and they all promise to squeeze us in—great publicity for them since the press release will make it to all the right places. The only thing *you* have to worry about is your dress."

"Oh, you always take every last drop of fun out of everything, Ian." She stuck out her tongue.

"Promise me you won't do or say anything to embarrass Ella. Especially about her book."

Sullen-faced, she nodded and raised her right hand, as if swearing an oath. "Promise."

Now it was up to her to keep her word. She gracefully unfolds her long body from the chenille-upholstered chair she is curled up in, swinging her shoulder-length, chestnut hair behind her. "Ella! I'm so excited to meet you. I'm Ian's sister, Zoe. Welcome to our home."

At that moment, the doorbell chimes.

"Oh, Ian," Faith interjects, "I hope you and Ella don't mind but I've invited a few people to lunch."

"Oh?"

"Yes, Jeff Benson—he and Dad have been working together on a new high-blood-pressure medication—and Jeff's wife, Diana. I also asked Miriam James and her husband Antonio. Miriam curated my last exhibit at the Hackley Gallery. Zoe also invited a couple of her girlfriends, Sarah Nesmith and Kaylie Ayres. You probably remember them, Ian?"

Ian's eyes narrow when he hears the guest list. If he had been told earlier, it would have been helpful but hearing it now for the first time, his knee-jerk reaction gives him away.

He hasn't seen Kaylie in eons but they used to sneak away together whenever Zoe wasn't around. Kaylie was Ian's first and vice versa, and she wasn't happy when he finally cut the cord, leaving her for Natasha Yenin.

But the real shocker is Diana Benson. He'd met her several years ago at one of those infernal fundraisers that he'd been impelled to attend while he built his reputation as a philanthropist, and he had no idea of the connection she had to his father, nor did he know she was married. He'd just pegged her as a hungry cougar... and he was only too happy to accommodate her. It was during the time Natasha was fucking him over and he'd yet to make the decision of swearing off relationships, confining himself to Dom/sub situations.

He had considered the affair to be one that was purely physical but she had not been of the same mindset. She began to make demands on him and he didn't care for the tenor of the relationship. He tried to walk away numerous times but she kept pulling him back. Finally, he made a clean break of it... only to discover her one night, ensconced at his parents' dinner table, with her husband—her husband whom he'd known since he was a child, being his father's friend and colleague since the elder Mr. Blackmon earned his medical degree.

Now he's in an unenviable position: introducing his wife-to-be to his first girlfriend and to his former mistress of a sort.

Kaylie is the first hurdle. Following on the tails of the butler who answers the door, the young blond woman comes strolling into the house as if she owns it. "Zoe!"

she exclaims as Ian's sister rushes over to greet her friend. "I'm so glad to see you. It's been too long!"

Zoe smiles and embraces her high school friend. "Definitely too long." The two women go back to sophomore year of high school. "How are you, Kaylie? I'm glad you're back from Denver."

"Oh, so am I. Denver is a total yawn." Her bright green eyes scan the room, settling on Ian. She smiles broadly and gives a little wave. "Hey there, big bro. I've actually been reading the WSJ to check for updates on you. How are you, Ian?"

He smiles politely but is saved from further comment as the other guests arrive. When the introductions are completed, Ian decides that now is the time to make his announcement. While everyone is milling about, he asks for their attention and the room goes quiet. Grasping Ella's hand, he looks at his parents. "Ella and I are planning to marry in June and we thought it was time to let everyone know. The date we selected is the twelfth so keep it open, please. Mom? We'd like to hold the wedding here on the estate, if that's okay?"

Faith claps her hands together. "I would be thrilled to have the wedding here, Ian and Ella! Of course. June is not far away: we should start planning immediately."

Nodding Ian smiles as his family and friends offer their congratulations.

It is fairly apparent to everyone in the room what Kaylie thinks about Ian's news since her startled reaction is conspicuous: her eyes widen, her mouth drops open, and her face darkens to a vibrant shade of crimson, which on her fair skin is notable. Faith notices tension in the room and jumps in before things become even more awkward.

"Why don't we all move to the patio and Susie will serve drinks? It's such a lovely afternoon."

"Great idea," Trevor adds.

Kaylie is still gaping at Ella but now there's emotion shading her green eyes though it's not clear exactly what kind.

Once everyone is seated outside, Kaylie turns to Ella. "Ella, please tell me about yourself. What do you do?"

"I'm trying to establish a career as an art historian. I've most recently worked with a documentary filmmaker but I'm toying with the idea of going into academia."

"How interesting."

Zoe pipes in "Ella is also a—"

"Zoe," Ian interrupts, "may I speak to you privately for a moment?"

Confused, Zoe rises. "Yes, Ian. Excuse us for a moment please."

Ian gets up out of his chair and propels his sister into the house, leaving Ella to fend for herself in the den of lions. Shortly thereafter, Diana Benson makes her way over to Ella, as Ian and Zoe return to the terrace.

Ella nods politely and says hello. Diana Benson is much more polished and therefore more discreet than Kaylie and easily hides her reaction to the unwelcome news of Ian's engagement. Her smile seemingly genuine, she offers her congratulations. Only Ian can see the fireworks behind her social facade as she digests the new information. It's in the way her back straightens, her eyes slightly narrow, and lines form around her mouth indicating tension.

The conversation shifts to current events, Trevor's new project, Faith's news from the art world, and Kaylie's new career in public relations. Zoe's other friend, Sarah, having recently been married, returns the conversation to Ian's engagement.

"So, Ella, have you considered wedding planners yet?"

Sensing an ally in Sarah, Ella smiles with relief. "Yes, we just met with one yesterday. Lissette Simmons? She seems competent."

"Oh my God, snagging Lissette is like hitting the lottery. How did you manage that one? She's booked for years in advance."

Surprised, Ella turns to Ian. "How did you swing that,

Ian?"

"My assistant arranged the meeting for me. I'm sure Lissette appreciates the fact that planning our wedding is a coup for her in terms of publicity. The advertising capital alone will be worth it, since mention of our wedding and the attendant details will make all of the social media."

Noticing that Kaylie looks about ready to spit bullets, Faith moves the party inside for lunch, sorely regretting her guest list.

Kaylie manages to slide in next to Ian, with Ella on his other side. Diana Benson sits directly across from him. The late thirtyish woman is wearing a very tight white sleeveless shift with a bright green geometric design. Her white sandals sport four-inch heels and show off her tanned legs and manicured toenails.

Thus caged by former love interests, uncomfortable is the only adjective that keeps popping into Ian's head but his top priority is keeping Ella from feeling the slings and arrows directed her way from both spurned women. It's not an enviable task but he's prepared to take on anything for Ella.

The kitchen staff had just served the salad course when Kaylie launches her attack. "So, tell me Ella, how did you and our Ian meet?"

Ella must sense the enmity in Kaylie for Ian could see her face slide into the mask that she uses for people she doesn't particularly like. Her posture becomes rigid and her smile slight and forced. She answers politely. "Ian came into the boutique where I worked part-time while still attending undergraduate school. He was shopping for a birthday gift for his favorite sister," she smiles genuinely at Zoe.

Zoe rolls her eyes and grins. "I'm his only sister, Ella. So, to clarify, I'm responsible for bringing you two together?"

Kaylie is not to be deterred. "So when Ian met you, you were a salesgirl? How utterly *Cinderella*-ish."

Ella responds with the most meager of smiles and

quickly starts up a conversation with Sarah, who is seated on her other side. Sarah asks her which boutique and when Ella tells her, she becomes excited.

"Oh, that's one of my favorite shops. You know, I actually remember you! You were always so nice and helpful. It's so great that you met your future husband while working at Archipelago. You know, all of Zoe's girlfriends were after Ian when we were growing up, but none of us were able to snag him."

Snickering, Kaylie says, "Speak for yourself, Sarah, dear. I did just fine with him, didn't I," she looks at Ian and winks.

Ian clutches Ella's hand and turns to the other end of the table where his father is seated. "I hear your patent was finally approved, Dad. Do you think it will be clear sailing from here on in?"

Trevor laughs, joined by Jeff Benson. "It never is," Jeff adds, "just one hurdle after another."

"Well, securing the patent must be more than half the battle, correct?"

"Half... maybe."

Miriam begins telling them about the financial and critical success of Faith's recent exhibit and after Faith whispers something to the head waitperson, the courses are served swiftly, one after the other. On the surface, things seem to settle down.

After the meal concludes, Ella finds herself chatting about wedding details with Faith when Ian steps away with his father for a couple of minutes. Diana Benson chooses that moment to pounce, joining their conversation with a smile.

"Ella, dear, what designer will you choose for your wedding dress?"

Smiling in a friendly manner, Ella answers truthfully, "I haven't given it any thought just yet. In fact, my best friend and I are going dress shopping for the first time next week."

"Oh? Will you be wearing white?"

Ella blushes. "Yes, I think so. Ivory, perhaps, but we'll

be going traditional pretty much all the way."

"How nice. I'm sure it will be lovely. You might want to look at the dresses that J. Crew offers. They're fantastic and the prices are good if you're on a budget."

"Oh, but I'm not," Ella replies airily, her intuition putting her on bitch alert, "and I plan to splurge on a dress. I have to spend my money on something, after all."

Diana plasters a smile on her tanned face as Faith pats Ella's shoulder. "I'd love to help, if you need any advice. I especially love choosing bridal gowns." Her hint is weighted with iron and drops down on Ella with a thud.

"Of course you're welcome to tag along, Mrs. Blackmon, if you'd like."

"Oh, I'd love to! And please call me Faith. When are we going?"

Fortuitously, Ian returns to rescue her. He comes up behind her and wraps both of his arms around her small waist. "Is my mother torturing you about wedding details yet?"

"Ian!" Faith admonishes her son, "I do not torture people. I was just offering my soon to be daughter-in-law my assistance if it's desired."

Chuckling, Ian takes one arm from Ella to swing around his mother's shoulder. "Only kidding, Mom. I'm sure Ella will appreciate all the help she can get."

"Yes, that's true, Faith. My mother lives out of state so her help will be limited thus, I'd be thrilled to have you around. Thank you for offering."

"Shall we head home, Ella? We can draw up a guest list tonight and our parents can do theirs and then we'll put them together so we can get an idea of the number of guests."

Eager to get away from all these women who covet Ian, Ella quickly agrees. "I'm just going to visit the bathroom. I'll be right back."

On her way back from the bathroom, she passes what looks like a study, in a décor dominated by masculine tones. Inside the open door are Zoe, Kaylie, and Sarah. Kaylie is speaking in a loud whisper and Ella can hear almost everything she's saying.

"... kidding? Why is Ian doing this... marrying her? Do you think she's pregnant? I mean, since when is Ian the marrying kind anyway? He wouldn't marry me and we were very much in love."

"Just because Ian wouldn't marry you doesn't mean he's not the marrying kind, Kaylie. He must love Ella." That was Zoe; Ella could hug her right about now. "And exactly when were you and my brother very much in love? I somehow missed that relationship."

"Ella is charming. I can totally see why Ian would fall for her." This time it's Sarah sticking up for her.

"Some friends you two are." Kaylie sniffs dramatically. "Personally, I don't think she's nearly good enough for our Ian."

Zoe snorts. "*Our* Ian? Since when does he belong to all of us?"

"Oh, pish posh, he's always been ours. He's your brother, for God's sake, Zoe. Don't you feel proprietary over him?"

"No, I hate him, as every normal girl hates her brothers. He tortured me when I was young. Let me tell you, I won't forget..."

Ella steps quietly away before she gets caught eavesdropping and goes to rejoin Ian. He's in the middle of what looks like a heated conversation with Diana Benson. As soon as he spots his fiancée, he smiles and steps away from Mrs. Benson.

"Ready?"

"Yes. Let's say our goodbyes to your parents."

"Oh," Faith cries, "you're leaving already? Ella, please call me this week and let me know details about your shopping trip. Okay?" She pulls Ella into an embrace.

"Absolutely. And thank you for a wonderful lunch and even better company. It was lovely meeting Ian's family."

"Ditto," Trevor says, joining their little group. "We're very happy you're joining our family, Ella. Welcome."

"Thank you, Mr. Blackmon."

"You don't need to be so formal. You can just call me Your Royal Highness." He winks and grins, one side of his mouth going up in a crooked smile.

Ella smiles back. "Are you sure we shouldn't just use the salutation of King?"

"You know, maybe that would be best," Trevor replies with a twinkle in his eye. "After all, I am king of my castle, aren't I?"

"Don't be too sure, Dad. This house has a strong queen; I don't think there's room for a king." Ian winks at his mom.

On the way home, the interior of the fast sports car is quiet. Neither of them want to discuss the day or more specifically the two women who obviously held some claim on Ian in the past. What Ella couldn't understand is why Faith invited them if she knew they were involved at one time? Sooner or later, they'd have to broach the subject but right now she wasn't feeling up to it—her feelings of resentment were too fresh.

When they get to the house, by mutual agreement, they decide to take a nap and end up sleeping until nine that night, which left little time to do much else so they decide to actually do their guest list. When they're done, there are nearly two hundred people who absolutely must be invited.

Ian looks at Ella: "This is going to be a big wedding. You know that right?"

"Unless we elope?"

"Our parents would kill us."

"Not necessarily. By the way, am I still required to have a bodyguard?"

"For now, yes. Until I resolve the Natasha thing... Okay?"

Wearily she nods. "If you say so."

Monday. The day is dragging on interminably: meeting after meeting. It's an endless cycle but no one seems capable of making an independent decision; they all need bloody handholding. Rushing from one fire to the next, he didn't even have any time to dwell on the big news of the day: the information his surveillance team relayed to him this morning.

Ian sighs, running his hand through his disheveled hair. He needs to get a haircut soon. Over the weekend, he and Ella called her parents and then went to Laurel Hill to tell his parents about their engagement and upcoming nuptials. That was a fiasco. How his mother unknowingly managed to invite not one but two of his former lovers, he doesn't know. Ella was nervous enough about meeting his parents—she'd called it the den of lions. She'd really come close since she'd actually stepped into one with Diana Benson being present, not to mention the whining Kaylie. Now the circus will begin: he knows that once his mother sinks her teeth into it, there'll be no stopping her. Poor Ella, he thinks. She doesn't know what's coming. The wheels very much in motion, they were going to be busy for the foreseeable future.

"Mr. Blackmon?" Janine's voice comes through clearly over the speaker.

"What is it, Janine?"

"I have a call from Daniel Butler on line three, sir."

He smiles. Janine using the term of respect reminds him of the first night he met Ella; when she called him sir, life as he knew it was all over. Of course, coming from Janine, it was merely annoying. "Put it through, please. Daniel?"

"Ian."

"Any news?"

"Confirm that you're alone and we're not on speaker."

"Confirmed."

"Are your people still watching the subject?"

"Yes, but as I told you, she was grabbed earlier today and there's been nothing since. Do we know who snatched her and why? It wasn't the operative: he just arrived in Portland about an hour ago."

"I do know. Now I'm going to ask you a question and I want you to think very hard before you answer. Do you really want to know her fate?"

Ian takes a moment to think about it, as Daniel advised. If he didn't know, wouldn't it be better? If she were dead, he'd feel guilt over it; there was no doubt about that. If she were alive, he might still have cause to worry or continue the op.

However, not knowing was unacceptable to a logical mind. He needed to know, despite the consequences. Taking a fortifying breath, he answered his friend. "Yes, Daniel, I want to know."

"Okay, then, Ian. Here it is: Natasha Yenin is on her way to Saudi Arabia to become the sixth wife of an important sheik. Well, technically not a wife—more of a concubine, so I understand. He happens to like tall blonds. She will not have access to travel, means of communication, or any autonomy at all for a very long time, until, as he phrased it, she's fully 'reconciled' to her new situation." He promises she will not be harmed to any extent that will endanger her life or scar her body. He merely wants her to be trained to provide him pleasures that his Arab wives cannot be asked to provide due to religious strictures.

"Her uncles continue to lie low. Right now, they are living in Chechnya. There is no price on your head, anywhere that we could find. You are free to live your life and have some fun for a change. How's that for an update?"

Ian is stunned into silence, trying to process his feelings about what Daniel just described to him. "Were you behind this new venture for Natasha?"

"The concept did not originate with me, no. I was enlisted to assist in the execution, so in that respect it was a joint effort and one I'm hoping my wife never hears about. The whole idea made me squeamish but I thought it might be the best outcome for Natasha while keeping you and your family safe."

"Joint between you and...?"

"Can't you guess?"

"Phillips?"

"That's the one. Surprised me with how fiendishly clever he actually is. He's relieved he lost the brothers, too, and plans to remain in the U.S. as much as possible so they can't reconnect with him anytime soon. Turns out he's actually a nice guy who was being influenced by rotten people." He pauses for a second. "He genuinely cares about Ella and wants her to be safe and happy."

"Good, as long as he keeps his distance."

Daniel laughs. "If anyone understands your position, it's me, Ian. Before I met Olivia, I couldn't understand what jealousy was all about, never felt it myself. Ever. Now, I find I cannot even approach reasonable, rational thought and behavior where my girl is concerned. I know I drive her crazy on occasion... but it is what it is."

"Ditto. By the way, we received your wedding invite and we will be there. I believe Ella already sent in the RSVP."

"Great. We'll share a toast together in honor of Ms. Yenin's new marriage."

"Make it DP: that's her favorite bubbly."

"We'll have to drink her share since she won't be imbibing anytime soon. Saudi Arabia is a dry country, of course. There's always opium, however."

"There you go."

"Glad this is worked out, for now. I'll see you in a few weeks."

"Before you go, Daniel, tell me how this arrangement went down. How would our boy Lucien know the kind of people who would... facilitate this type of thing?"

"Lucien's neighbor in his Paris flat arranged it, a man by the name of Michel Rimbaud, like the poet. I'm quite sure it's not even close to his actual name. Lucien said he specializes in this specific transaction and does not appreciate being labeled a human trafficker. Claims he prefers the title of *marriage broker*. Anyway, he handled the entire matter, including the delicate matter of transportation, and from what I hear, almost all of the parties involved are extremely satisfied. All but one, so he tells me."

"Yes, I can take a wild guess as to who that one party might be. All right then. I need time to acclimate myself to this resolution. Thanks, Daniel, for everything. I'll be in touch."

Ian disconnects the call and returns the phone to his jacket pocket. Leaning all the way back in his ergonomic chair, he groans and covers his face with both hands. "Fuck, what am I going to tell Ella? What will she think of this turn of events?

Contemplation, however, is not to be his lot this afternoon. No sooner did he ask the room that question, did his buzzer tear into the quiet of his office. "Yes?"

"Mr. Haddad on line two, Mr. Blackmon."

"Haddad?"

"Yes, from Saudi Arabia. He mentioned a recent purchase he made through one of your subsidiaries?"

Ian's heart begins to accelerate as his brain connects the dots. "I'll take the call, Janine."

"Yes, sir."

"Hello?"

"Mr. Blackmon?" Ian Blackmon?" The voice is urbane with just the barest trace of an accent.

"Yes, this is Ian Blackmon. How may I help you?"

"Mr. Blackmon, my name is Khahil Haddad and I am the man who made a purchase through one of your subsidiaries in the past week. I wanted to contact you to inform you that the product arrived in perfect condition and I am most pleased."

"Were you asked to contact me when the shipment was received?"

"No, but names of involved parties are exchanged to ensure that everyone adheres to the stipulations of the agreement. I was also informed of some of the possible downsides to the product at the time of purchase. I wanted to at least provide you with a small measure of peace of mind, sir. You may not be aware, but you and I actually have done business together in the recent past."

"Can you elucidate?"

"I purchased an energy company through one of my Japanese firms. I was given a most handsome price and I hold your business ethics in high esteem accordingly. The firm was in very good standing and all the books were in order. I appreciate honest businessmen, sir."

"Thank you for calling. I just learned about the... *sale* and I wasn't sure exactly how I felt about it. You may or may not know but I was not directly involved in either the decision to sell nor the execution of the resulting transaction."

"Trust me, Mr. Blackmon: this is a win-win transaction. Normally, I wouldn't consider Russian-made products but this one is exceptional. I suspect that all parties will eventually be satisfied, bar none, if you understand my meaning."

"Yes. I believe I do and sincerely hope that is the case. I am not a vindictive man; however, I would like to pursue my life without... complications."

"Please do not concern yourself on that point. I have everything well contained. I wish you a good day, Mr. Blackmon."

"And I you, Mr. Haddad. Thank you."

"It is I who should thank you. Goodbye, sir."

Chapter 50

In a sumptuously appointed room devoid of any vibrant color, the oversized ebony-framed cheval mirror reflects an astonishing image: my face on a slender body with a waistline too tiny to be real... yet it is real and it is mine, squeezed into nothingness by a white satin corset, which is part of the dress. I chew my lip, trying to decide if I could bear the pain of the garment for hours on end. It always comes down to the same thing: how much pain I'm willing to bear for the sake of one man. I would chuckle if I weren't in such a cantankerous mood.

"Oh, Ella, that is magnificent, so Jane Austen-ish," Mariah exclaims.

"Stop using words like magnificent so early in the game or the decision will be far worse than it would be otherwise," I snap at poor Mariah, and then look over to my future mother-in-law. "What do you think, Faith?"

The older woman claps her hands together, apparently delighted just to be in the bridal salon with us. "Vera Wang is my absolute favorite wedding gown designer but I do like this one. It's very demure. And it looks marvelous on you, Ella. A British designer, you say?"

I nod. The designer is up and coming, so says Madame Xavier who runs the salon. Like Faith, I much prefer Vera Wang's designs, too. In the first group of five gowns I've selected to try on, two are Ms. Wang's creations.

"Ella, I've taken a photo of this one. Bring on the next," my forgiving friend says. I'll make up my snarkiness to her for sure. I'm still working on pairing her up with the brawny Mason. All that muscle to manhandle has to be worth some bitchiness from her best friend.

"Okay," I mumble, pivoting around to return to the dressing room. Because the salon was almost completely booked for the next six weeks, I had to take whatever opening Madame Xavier had available, and it fell on a day of the month when I'm bloated, uncomfortable, and massively cranky. Yes, I could have used Ian's name to throw my weight around... or even mention that I'm a bestselling author, but I generally choose not to exercise that kind of obnoxious clout.

Contributing to my overall dissatisfaction is the fact that Ian is in DC on a business trip. He wanted me to come and I wanted to accompany him but I had this freaking appointment. Something is going on with Ian and it's causing problems between us. It reminds me of the beginning of our relationship, the second beginning, I should clarify, when we held back and kept secrets from one another. Since we began to be brutally honest—the day I returned from my drugged ordeal with Lucien— our relationship has fared so much better. There's less tension and far less domination tendencies by Ian. I hope we're not regressing.

Ian wants me to continue life with a bodyguard and I don't want to have that yoke around my neck. He claims that the thing with Natasha is over but he won't tell me exactly how. I don't understand what he's keeping from me nor why. A showdown between us is imminent.

After trying on all five of the first batch and being wowed by none, I select a second group of four. The first one she hands me is a dress by a young American designer named Janey Sinclair. The dress is a simple satin shift. It's strapless, hugs the body almost indecently and covers from breast to mid-thigh. Over the satin shift is a gossamer tulle overlay with a taffeta skirt. It is a full gown and flares out from a vee just below the waistline. The bodice is much more demure than the shift though completely see-through: it has a gentle scoop neckline and three-quarter sleeves. It is an ethereal beauty that enhances my figure and yet feels comfortable in motion. As I step out of the dressing room, I see jaws drop and I'm pretty sure I've found my gown.

When the right one comes along, you just know it.

My alarm goes off at eight the next morning. Last night I let Mariah talk me into an all-night drunk. Inside my head were a hundred miniature tap dancers, shuffling off to Buffalo on my vodka-soaked brain. As soon as I got home, I threw myself into bed, eschewing even the basic ministrations of teeth brushing and face washing. Sometime during the night, my phone rang and I missed a call from Ian.

Today I'm supposed to meet an old friend who's visiting Portland for just a few days. I mentioned it to Ian—what I "forgot" to mention was that this old friend happens to be of the male persuasion. Why ruffle his feathers for no good reason?

I sit up, rub my eyes, stand up to stretch, and gasp so loudly I nearly choke on my own spit... for leaning against our bedroom wall is a tall, seething man—mine to be specific. His posture is defensive, slightly slouched with arms folded across his chest, and I can see anger flaming in his gray-blue orbs. That's the thing with his eyes: they're basically clear so they absorb any hue or color of environment or emotion.

I would lick my lips if I had any saliva left in my mouth. It evaporated the moment after it tried to choke me. He's not saying anything, a situation that I always find completely unnerving. It's up to me to defuse the situation.

"Ian! Why didn't you let me know you were coming home early? I expected you tomorrow morning."

"Clearly," he says, not moving a muscle.

"Is there a problem?"

"You tell me, Ella. Do you have a problem?"

"No, I don't. Do you?"

"My only problem of the moment is you."

"Why?" I ask, genuinely confused as to his anger with me. What did I do?

He finally unfurls his arms, stands up straight, and walks over to me, his long legs closing the distance in three strides. "Why? Why." He says the second interrogative rhetorically with a bitter little laugh. "For one thing, your phone was ringing and you weren't answering it. I picked it up the second time and saw there was a text message from someone named Michael. Who is Michael? I didn't want to read your personal messages so I'm left to wonder. My imagination is taking me to unfriendly places, Ella."

"What are the other things?"

"Other things?"

"You said, for one thing, implying there are others. What are the others?"

"You didn't answer your phone when I called last night either, so I've been worried. Also, Mason told me you shook him off when you went out last evening with Mariah. More stress for me. I've been standing here debating the wisdom of dragging you by the hair into the dungeon where I could properly punish you for your multiple transgressions."

I rub my eyes again. "Ian, I didn't mean to lose Mason last night; in fact, I'm trying to get him and Mariah together. But we couldn't find him when we were ready to leave so..." I shrug. "I apologize. And Michael is the old friend I told you I was planning to meet. He's just a friend, nothing more. Dragging me to the dungeon is not a good idea, FYI, unless you're interested in a swift yet crippling kick to the groin along the way. If it's any consolation, you've given me stress, too."

No humor at my remark registers on his face... at all. He is really pissed off. His voice is deadly soft when he asks, "How is that?"

"Whatever you're keeping from me, Ian. And whatever happened with Natasha that you're not telling me. And the fact that you insist I take Mason with me wherever I go when supposedly everything's been resolved."

"Fair enough. Let's go reconcile our differences in the dungeon."

"No. That's not smart. Sex is supposed to be loving and fun, not a way to vent aggression."

"What's wrong with occasionally employing it as an outlet for aggression? No one gets hurt, not really."

"I don't like it, that's why."

He gets closer to me, leans down; he's in my face as he whispers, "Liar. You, Ariel Strong, *love* it. You love it when I tie you up, torment you, tease you, tickle you, and ultimately, fuck you till you scream. How long will you continue to deny it?"

My respiration is speeding up. I haven't even had coffee yet but at this point, I probably don't need any. Is he right? Do I love it? My body is reacting in a way that doesn't please me: it's contradicting my words. I can say I don't like it, but he can tell I do by my body's response. Am I some kind of masochistic pervert?

"What are you going to do?" I ask, voice barely audible.

His eyes bore into me; right now they're the color of a roiling sea. "I never divulge my evil plans, Ella."

When I don't respond, he wraps his hands around my throat and kisses me, squeezing slightly to assert his domination. Should I go for it or tell him no?

"Okay," I finally croak out, "but no dragging by the hair."

He stands straight. "Agreed. You know the drill once we're inside."

"Okay, but first I have to brush my teeth."

As we walk to the room, I contemplate the dynamics of our relationship. When Ian is feeling the need to dominate me, he creates reasons to justify it. He's not really angry with me. He may have been worried but he's had far worse worries of late. It seems to me he's manufactured issues so he could get me into this room and do things to me.

In a moment of penetrating insight, I realize that I

too must need the justification. My sense of self requires that I pretend I'm doing it to satisfy Ian's needs, not my own. For in admitting I like to be dominated sexually, I feel like I'm acknowledging an irrefutable weakness. And that is an admission I find nearly impossible to concede.

The room is early-morning dark and cool, and my skin shrinks in protest when I remove my clothes and kneel. My eyes are cast down so I'm unable to see what he's doing, but my ears tell me that drawers are opening and closing, and his footfalls are heavy across the hardwood floor. After a few moments his shoes—beautiful Italian leather—come into my view. "Stand," he says and helps me up by the arm.

I keep my head down, wondering what he's planning. I don't wonder long, though, for he immediately begins to buckle cuffs on my wrists and ankles. "Come," he says when he's done, and leads me over to a round cushioned piece of furniture. It looks like a hugely oversized ottoman and he tells me to climb onto it on my hands and knees.

Every time I obey a command, I can feel him watching me closely. Is he trying to unnerve me or appraise my mood and level of anxiety? He's left me in this position for at least five minutes without saying or doing anything. At one point, he comes over and using the toe of his shoe pushes my legs open wider without saying a single syllable.

"We've explored this before: I'm going to render you helpless, take away your sight and sound. Any commands will be relayed by touch. It requires a high level of trust but I think we have it by now. Do you trust me completely, Ella?"

Without hesitation, I answer in the affirmative.

"Let's give it a try. First, your sight." He slips the black satin blindfold over my head and tightens it till it's snug. "Now, your hearing," and I feel the cushioned earpieces descend over my ears and the room falls deathly still for me except for the deafening sound of my own respiration. Taking my left wrist, he pulls it back and clips it to my left ankle. My balance is precarious at this point but he gently grasps my shoulders and lowers me to the ottoman thing. I rest my left cheek on the soft fabric as he tethers my right wrist to my other leg.

If losing your sight heightens your other senses, then losing both sight and hearing makes the sense of touch incredibly vital. I feel everything keenly: the warm slightly callused skin of his hands dancing on my backside, the ends of his fingernails, clipped short though they are, skating lightly up my thighs, his satiny lips brushing my skin—everything. I'm practically quivering in anticipation of the hard stuff. One piece of the hard stuff in particular.

From one moment to the next I cannot predict his position. Sometimes it seems he's in front of me but a half-second later, he's behind me. It's as if there are three of him, coming at me from all angles. Though he hasn't touched me in the places that count, I feel an inexorable shift toward an orgasm.

Suddenly, a hundred pings of sensation hit my shoulders, proceeding up my back, and down my rear, my thighs, calves, ankles. A flogger.

The pings get sharper, more painful but in such tiny gradations as to be almost imperceptible. I know it's pain now but I can't tell how we got there. This is the punishment part.

When it gets so sharp I'm about to tell him, it begins to wind down. His hands run over me again, soothing the bite of the flogger. Nice and easy, I drift toward a dreamy trance until his fingers find my nips and pinch—*hard*. I rear back but find I cannot move my body but for an inch or two. It's still too much for him so he knees my legs out wider. Now I have no purchase to move at all.

Pain, pleasure. Pain, pleasure. It continues for a long time, until I'm panting. Tears are running down my face from the extremes and he pushes into me without any advance notice. Empty one second, full to bursting the next. The detail I notice most is his body heat: his body is on fire and it's igniting mine. I come so fast that it takes me unaware.

He rips off the headphones and begins to whisper in my ear. Dirty words he'd never say otherwise—filthy, even. The heat ratchets up again, degree by degree. I want to see him, touch him but he's like a phantom lover. At least I can hear him, his ragged breathing, his sounds of exertion, flesh slapping flesh, my moans layered with his growls.

I'm climbing a mountain, frantically chasing an orgasm that is tantalizingly just out of my reach. Beads of sweat race down my back, slip down my neck toward my head, following the incline of my body. He slaps my backside so hard, I see white and the orgasm comes crashing upon me like a rogue wave. I hear him grunt as he slides into his own satisfaction.

I don't think I can move ever again.

The building is a beautiful example of Art Deco architecture. Daniel told Ian it was constructed shortly after the famed Woolworth building, both in Lower Manhattan, and the design borrowed heavily from it. This one was not a skyscraper, however: it was a five-story limestone building, a former warehouse, now turned into giant lofts. The wedding is being held on the top floor, and includes the roof deck. At 62 degrees, it's chilly for an outdoor event but Ian says it's sure to have heaters, plus I'm wearing a silk wrap.

The cocktail hour is almost at a close when we arrive late due to our delayed flight, so we order drinks first and then look around. Daniel is nowhere to be seen but Ian spots a few people he knows and we gravitate toward them. One of them is Jackson Delacroix, the man who introduced Ian and Daniel.

"Mr. Blackmon, fancy meeting you here," Jackson grins as he walks toward us to close the distance. "And, of course, the lovely Mrs. Blackmon-to-be. Hello, Ella."

"Jackson," I greet him, forcing a smile. Despite everything that's ensued since that first fateful phone call he made to me, I still can't seem to entirely shake the feeling that he's an adversary.

"Glad you two made it in time for the ceremony. It's slated to begin in," he glances at the elegant timepiece on his wrist, "eight minutes. Think Daniel is nervous?"

With a mischievous smile on his face, Ian says nothing in response. I jump in. "I'm sure everyone is nervous when he or she marries. It's the nature of the beast."

"Aha, so you admit marriage is beastly."

I smile sweetly. "It's a revered institution... if you like living in an institution."

"Ha! Ian, you've got a live one here. Yes, Ella, I think you've nailed it. Marriage is an institution. Glad I'm divorced."

Tastefully suited ushers come to guide and escort the guests into the room where the ceremony is to be held. As it is nondenominational, a chapel isn't required. The padded antique pews are arranged in a semi-circle so everyone will be afforded a view of the bride and groom and there are white candles and flowers all around the room. While the reverend stands waiting, his back to the gathered guests, everyone is swiftly seated. I watch the rear, anxious for a glimpse of the bride. I've never met Olivia, even when I was staying at her home, but Ian has, and he told me she is exceptionally beautiful—but I expected no less from looking at Daniel.

Speaking of Daniel, he now enters the room and every female eye is on him instantly. He looks so tall, his carriage perfectly erect, and his face devoid of any emotion. Come to think of it, I've never seen any emotion on Daniel's face. He is wearing a tuxedo that I wouldn't mind seeing on Ian at our wedding: it's silk, cut with narrow lapels, and fitted to accent his long legs and broad shoulders. In a word, or maybe two, Daniel looks spectacular.

Just behind Daniel is a tall, bearded redheaded guy who is likely his best man, followed by an elegant, middle-aged couple—I think they're Daniel's parents. A moment or two behind them come yet another pair: I almost can't unglue my eyes from them to look for the bride. The man is tall and darkly gorgeous—black hair, tanned complexion, and light eyes—and the woman shines in contrast, blond and athletically beautiful. Ian leans over to whisper in my ear.

"That's Derek Girardi, the sculptor and Olivia's father. The woman next to him must be Olivia's mother."

I tear my eyes away to look at Ian. "Isn't she his wife?"

He shakes his head. "They're divorced. His current wife is an Ethiopian model..." he gestures with his chin, "that's her over there, seated in the first row. Daniel tells me Girardi's splitting with her and going back to Olivia's mother. Interesting, eh?"

"Like a soap opera." I look again. The man guides his companion to her seat in the front row and exits. Now everyone is seated, the room is hushed, and the strains of music waft through the room, floating on the air currents. I feel as if I'm in a dream. Everyone is beautiful here: the parents, the guests, the room itself... I want my wedding to have a similar feel.

The music picks up volume and tempo as the bride appears. She's holding onto her father's arm, almost leaning into him and her nervousness is palpable. Olivia is so young, but Ian didn't lie: she is simply stunning. Against the white dress, her complexion is golden and her light blue eyes emerge prominently in contrast. My eyes are drawn immediately to her gown. Is it nicer than mine? I think it's a Vera Wang and the design suits her age, figure, and coloring perfectly—sexy yet demure.

As they pass by us, I get a closer look. Damn, her father is hot. What must it be like to have a father who is as young and good-looking as your boyfriend or husband? Must be beyond bizarre.

Now I realize what's different: the reverend has his back to us and Daniel is facing the guests. Brilliant. We can watch the bride and groom instead of the officiating reverend. Why don't all weddings do that?

Derek Girardi escorts his daughter up the aisle and

then around the reverend, placing her at Daniel's side. He takes Olivia's hand in one of his and reaches for Daniel's hand with the other. About to place her hand in her new husband's, her father first kisses Olivia's fingers, and then kisses them again. At the fourth or fifth kiss, he says in a voice loud enough for many to hear, "I don't want to give you away," and a titter of laughter snakes through the front rows. Then he finally does, putting the couple's hands together and saying something inaudible to Daniel. Daniel merely nods solemnly in response.

Ten minutes later, the ceremony is over. It was a beautiful wedding, short and sweet, and I adored it. Now, finally, I can see emotion in Daniel's visage: he is beaming the most radiant smile I've ever seen—it could electrify the city of Manhattan. I suppose he truly loves his new wife.

We have a total blast, helped along by copious amounts of top-shelf alcohol. Jackson and his date prove to be more than entertaining and Ian chats with another man he knows through business dealings. Daniel and Olivia come over to greet us when we separate from the others. Seeing them up close and personal doesn't at all diminish their beauty.

"Ian," Daniel says, then signals a waiter holding a tray with glasses of champagne and the man rushes to accommodate him.

"Daniel, congratulations. Beautiful wedding, by the way."

"Thank you. Hello, Ella. I'd like you to meet my wife, Olivia. Olivia, this is Ella, Ian's fiancée."

"Oh, hello. It's so nice to meet you finally, Ella. I'm sorry I kept missing you when you were in New York. Thank you for coming so far to share the day with us. We very much appreciate it."

I give her my biggest and best smile. ""Hopefully, you'll be able to attend ours, too. And I'm so glad we were able to make it here because this wedding is magnificent and I wouldn't want to have missed it.

One by one, Daniel takes the crystal flutes of

champagne from the tray, handing a glass to each of us and thanking the waiter.

"Ian, I believe we agreed to toast a glass of champagne to yet another coupling?"

There's the Ian smirk as he lifts his glass. "Yes, I recall. To happy endings."

The four of us tilt our glasses to the center and sip the champagne. It is an excellent vintage.

"What kind of champagne are we drinking?" I ask, after swallowing that first silken sip.

Daniel and Ian look at each other, smile, and say in perfect unison, "*Dom Perignon.*"

I'm confused as to how Ian knew it was DP with one sip, but it seems to be an inside joke between the men.

Daniel cranes his neck to catch a glance at someone passing by. "Oh, lest I forget. Ian, I promised to introduce you to Derek. Hang on." He signals his father-in-law as he's passing by. "Derek? May I introduce you to a friend?"

The man smiles and joins us. Damn, I'm surrounded by startlingly handsome men. I must have done something to please the gods recently. The past year or so I've been lucky beyond measure in that regard.

"Derek, this is Ian Blackmon. Ian, Derek Girardi. The lovely young lady next to him is Ella Strong, his fiancée."

Derek bestows upon us a smile that would make most women drop their panties at his first request, and everyone exchanges handshakes and pleasantries.

"Derek, Ian has been diligently trying to acquire one of your smaller pieces to no avail."

"Oh? Thank you for supporting my work, Ian."

Ian nods, smiling while Daniel continues, "I was hoping you might help him procure one of the pieces that you hold back, Derek."

The older man nods his head. "I happen to have some earlier, more diminutive works in my studio. If you and Ella have time during your stay in New York, you're more than welcome to drop by and see if there's anything to your liking."

"Thank you very much, Mr. Girardi. I will certainly

do so."

"Good. My NYC studio is in Chelsea. Daniel can give you my number and we'll discuss it further tomorrow. Is that suitable?"

"Very much so. Thank you. It's a real pleasure to meet you, Mr. Girardi. I've been an admirer of your work for some time now."

"I appreciate it. And, please, call me Derek." He gifts us with another pretty smile and continues on his way, after blowing a kiss to his daughter.

The next day we spend doing touristy things in NYC, going to Central Park, dining at a little dive in the East Village, browsing the South Street Seaport. Monday, we visit museums, both MOMA and the Met. We were planning to hit the Natural History museum or the planetarium on Tuesday. Instead, we go to Derek's studio where Ian attempts to purchase one of the smaller sculptures but Derek insists on gifting it to him. The Girardis are such nice people and I'm thrilled that Daniel and Olivia will be coming to Portland in June to attend our wedding. I feel as if we've made lifelong friends.

Chapter 51

Walking down a densely populous Broadway at midday on Thursday, Ian kicks an empty soda can in his path, watching the satisfying arc it makes as it takes flight and lands with a tinny plop in the gutter, with nary a casualty. A few feet away are two men wearing bright orange vests; they're picking up litter from the curb, so his can-kicking has done them a small favor. Walking in New York City is akin to highway driving: there are multiple lanes of pedestrians, and some walk fast and some painfully leisurely. It's always the tourists who do the ambling, savoring each bite of the Big Apple (and sometimes it bites back), while New Yorkers do everything just short of shoving them viciously into the gutter to get around them faster. Everything would work just fine if the slow-movers would just get out of the fast lane... just as on the highway. Individuals who clog up the fast lane with slow-moving objects, whether cars or bodies, cause traffic jams. Period. Why don't some people understand the simplest things?

Right now what is taxing Ian's brain is not a simple thing. Decisions as pointy as rapiers poke at his peace as his mind muddles through the past few weeks. He hasn't yet told Ella what has become of Natasha: only to himself will he admit that he's afraid of her reaction. Granted, the fate Natasha is suffering is better than being hunted down and killed by a professional sniper... but from a woman's perspective, probably not all that much better. Since four is the maximum number of wives a man may take under Islamic law, Haddad couldn't legally marry Natasha so she's more of a concubine to him. *For* him.

Not that Haddad is a devout Muslim, anyway, not in the least, but he puts on a façade of being pious in order to prosper in his world.

Essentially, he wants Natasha for dirty sex and that's about all. He surely has enough children running around, considering he has four wives already. In a way, it's the perfect payback for the conniving bitch who's been out for his blood for God knows how long. Besides, knowing Natasha and her devious ways, Ian figures she'll probably manage to turn the situation around to her advantage before too long.

What is gnawing at him the most is the text he received shortly after the operation went down: it originated from a Saudi telephone number. He hadn't recognized the telephone number or caller name and when he looked up the country code prefix, he'd seen it was from Saudi Arabia and his blood streamed cold.

The person who'd sent the message had apparently been interrupted during the transmission. The entire message read, "Please h."

Please help me? Was that it? It had to be from Natasha and it bothered the hell out of him. She sent it to him because she must have figured he was the only one who knew where she was, other than the people who took her. It made him feel horrible.

What he truly worried about was what Ella would think of him after he tells her. Will she see him in a different light? Will she think that a man who can consign a woman to such a miserable fate is one who cannot be redeemed?

Since then, he's been trying to banish it from his mind with varying success. Daniel's wedding helped enormously: he and Ella truly enjoyed themselves. Moreover, it was incredibly relaxing to see his friend not only at ease, but also happy. Since he and Daniel met, they'd been in one tense situation after another. Watching Daniel with his Olivia was a wonderful respite from all that darkness. He could plainly see—as could everyone with eyes—how much Daniel adored his new wife and how his devotion was fully reciprocated. That caliber of love is highly infectious, making everyone around the couple feel elated or at least more optimistic about life in general.

A few days later, Daniel's father-in-law insisted on making a gift of the small sculpture he and Ella had selected from his studio. Ian knew the piece had to be worth, at a minimum, thirty thousand dollars. How could he possibly say thank you to the man?

Girardi is a rare kind of guy. His wedding gift to his daughter and her new husband deserved the label of spectacular. And their father-daughter dance together that followed was so poignant, there wasn't a dry eye in the room. It was clear that he adores his daughter, sometimes to Daniel's detriment.

So, the thank-you is on his mind. Scouring his brain for details about Derek Girardi, he recalls Daniel mentioning that Derek shared his son-in-law's obsession with vintage cars and motorcycles and that's when Ian came upon the perfect way to show his gratitude. An old friend from high school owned a shop and occasionally came across the rare vintage bikes. He'd give Lars a call, see what he had currently, and send Derek a wheeled surprise to show his appreciation.

That out of the way, the only worrisome thing he had to do before his own wedding was to come clean with Ella about Natasha's fate. Recognizing that he is stalling, he reluctantly heads back in the direction of the hotel. It's time to get it over with.

Ella is furiously tapping on her laptop when he gets back to the room. "And what are you doing so industriously?"

She looks up as if she just this instant noticed him. "Oh, nothing. How was your outing?"

"Very good. And your facial?"

"Excellent. I feel refreshed. So," she pats the seat of the sofa right next to her, "sit. Let's talk."

"About?" He's playing dumb and they both know it.

"Ian," she says in an exasperated tone, her hand

reaching over to his. "Secrets are like cancer: they eat away at a relationship, replacing healthy tissue with rot."

"Yuck. Lovely turn of phrase."

"Exactly."

The week before, Ella had insisted they sit down to talk or she refused to continue with their wedding plans; however, as obstinate as she could be, he'd managed to postpone "the talk" until after Daniel's wedding. Now, he knew there'd be no more deferments.

"Ella, the only thing I haven't shared with you is what happened with Natasha. You know everything else. I hold no secrets from you."

She closes her eyes, as if in frustration. He wants to see the blue again; he hates when her eyes are closed, depriving him of their vibrant depths and whatever emotion she's telegraphing at the time.

Ian carefully measures his defense, sifting through arguments that might sway her. "Ella, once the words are out, I can never retract them, never expunge them from your mind."

Again, she says nothing but her obstinate expression indicates her position is resolute: she wants to know.

Sighing with the unfathomable weight of guilt, he continues, "Daniel asked me if I really wanted to know what happened to Natasha and I thought long and hard before answering. I'm still not sure if I gave him the right answer. I'd like to spare you the ambivalence."

"Is it really that bad?" Her voice is strangled, as if each word is a burden.

"It's not great but it was the lesser of two evils. She's still very much among the living."

Eyes wary, she says, "So far, so good. I'm going to push my luck and continue."

"Allow me to say the idea originated with Lucien Phillips who contacted Daniel for assistance. Daniel gave it to him... uncomfortably."

"It doesn't sit well with Daniel either? He seems impervious to everything."

"Yes, well..."

"Just blurt it out, Ian. I need to know."

Both of his hands rake through his hair several times before he rests them on his knees. "Natasha was taken by force to Saudi Arabia to become a concubine to a wealthy Saudi national."

Her mouth drops open but she quickly closes it, straightening her posture as if that would aid her in digesting the information. "Like a sex slave?" she asks, eyes wide and face paler than chalk.

"Essentially. However, the sheik called me last week to ease my mind. He told me she would not be physically harmed and would live in luxury."

"Still..." She gets up and begins to pace, to and fro, one hand holding the other arm's elbow, both arms behind her back. "Ugh, I see what you mean. There's no doubt it's better than being murdered—but it's just barely better. Will she be liberated after he tires of her?"

He shakes his head. "I don't think so, not willingly. However, I suspect Natasha will succeed in finding the best in the situation and manipulate it to her advantage. I really do, Ella."

Ella stares at her fiancé: his eyes are troubled and his body language suggests he's agitated. Of course, who wouldn't be, given his situation?

"Ian... is there something else, something you're not telling me?"

"Can we do a little at a time, Ella? I'm struggling with this right now."

She flips her hair back and inhales deeply. "Fine. Let's put this aside for a moment. There's something else I'd like to ask you before I forget."

"Yes?" he asks, relieved to move to another topic—any other topic.

"If you can remember back to our first night together—the second time around, when you took me home from the club and we went to your new houseboat—you had mentioned something about my spending a year in the UK. When I asked how you knew, you asked if we could discuss it at another time." She smiles to reassure him that this isn't—quite—an inquisition. "I'm afraid that time has arrived."

"Why is it important?"

"Because I want to know. I want there to be no secrets or lies of omission hanging between us. When we marry, I want to know that I know you, and you know me, and we can join together in harmony. That's why it's important."

"*I knew*, Ella, because I went after you."

"What?" He took her by surprise with his quick capitulation. She had to think about what he'd just said.

"You knew... because you went after me? To Britain?"

Closing his eyes, he scrabbles to find his equilibrium. Those days were dark, dark enough to force his gaze inward, to reflect on what he saw, and ultimately to reinvent himself... yet again. This time around it was a force for positive change but change always comes at a steep price and the price is usually acute pain of one kind or another.

The day it all happened was a Wednesday. He'd had a difficult day at work and was about to leave to go home to shower and change to meet Ella for dinner. They'd just begun to date three or four weeks before but they'd been together nearly every day or night. The word whirlwind sprang to mind.

If he'd only left when he'd planned, things might have gone differently. But as he was exiting his office, the phone on his desk buzzed three times. His staff knew that he expected the phone to be answered by the second ring so they must have left already or were otherwise unavailable. So he answered it...

"Ian?" The feminine voice on the other end was small and weepy.

"Yes, this is Ian Blackmon. Who's calling?"

"It's me, Ian. Kira."

Kira: his girlfriend—if you could call her that—from a couple of years ago. Meeting briefly at the club one night long ago, he saw right away that she fit all of his new requirements, the requirements he'd defensively created after Natasha screwed him so royally: not blond, attractive in an unobtrusive way, quiet personality, few aspirations, and very submissive sexually. Yet despite her satisfying all of his criteria, she didn't work out well for him. They'd ended their relationship slash arrangement after the four-month mark and last he'd heard, she'd taken up with another man, and went home to Nebraska... or one of those N states. North Dakota, maybe? Nevada? He couldn't remember for sure.

"What can I do for you, Kira?" He kept his tone professional.

"Um... I was wondering if you're possibly between relationships right now. If you're single, I mean. I'd like to see you again."

"No, I'm not single, Kira."

"Oh, okay, I figured. It was worth a try." Her volume dropped lower with each word.

She sounded as if she were speaking more to herself than to him. Yet, there was something in her voice: a tiny tinkling of alarm rang in his brain. "Is there some kind of help I might lend you?"

Now he could hear her crying. "No. No, thanks. I'm just lonely and was thinking of you. Sorry to have bothered you." She quickly disconnected.

That phone call niggled at him the entire way home, causing him to puzzle about what exactly it was all about. What was going on with the woman that would prompt her to call him out of the blue like that? They hadn't spoken for nearly two years.

It was almost seven when he got home, and he'd told Ella he'd pick her up at eight so he grabbed a lightning fast shower and dressed. He made it to Ella's place ten minutes early: driving the highway at ninety in his 400 BHP sports car didn't hurt any.

He and Ella had just finished dinner and were on their way to his place when his phone rang, cutting off the stereo in his car.

"Yes?

"Ian? This is Jackson. Are you alone?"

"No. I'm on speaker in my car. Can I call you back in a few minutes?"

"Yes, please call ASAP."

Ian didn't like the tone of his friend and attorney's voice. As soon as he parked in the garage, he pulled out his phone. "Ella, please go ahead into the house. Mason will let you in. I'll be behind you in a minute."

As soon as the front door slid shut, he punched in Delacroix's cell number on speed dial. "It's me. What is it?"

"Do you remember Kira Firestone?"

"Of course I do. Why?"

"I just got word from a mutual friend. She took a dive off a bridge an hour ago."

"What? Is she...?"

"Dead. Yes. Sorry to be the one to tell you, Ian."

"Oh, God. Jackson, she called me earlier this evening, asking if we could see each other again. I told her I was involved with someone. She said she was sorry to bother me and hung up. God, I feel terrible."

"Yes, well, not your fault. How could you possibly know she was in such despair? Anyway, I wanted to let you know in case anyone else contacts you. Your answer is *no comment*. There aren't too many people who know of your connection with her, right?"

"No, but..."

"Shit! The cops will find your number on her phone undoubtedly. I'll try to keep it under wraps to the extent possible. You hadn't seen her recently, had you?"

"No. I was shocked to hear her voice."

"Okay, I'll do damage control. You certainly don't need this type of publicity, Ian. You also don't need me to tell you the obvious."

"No, I've always been ace at detecting the obvious, Jackson. But, thanks." He disconnected.

He rode up in the elevator in silence but his mind was screaming in despair. Kira had been important to him once upon a time, and he hated to think of her in such dire pain. Emotional pain is what frequently led people to crave the physical kind—it hurts less and distracts from the more severe psychological variety. Kira was a true sexual masochist, always wanting the worst anyone could deliver. It was ultimately what led to the dissolution of their relationship. He didn't want to be the one to provide that level of pain anymore.

She didn't take it well but she was so passive that her response was barely noticeable. Considering it one more rejection in a long line of them, she quietly moved on. It felt like a huge relief to him, though at times he did miss her tinkling laugh, the sparkle in her brown eyes when something struck her funny. Or when something struck her.

When he got inside, Ella was waiting for him, worry etched onto her face. "Is everything okay, Ian?"

The words came out of his mouth, unplanned: he was on autopilot. "Do you want to play?"

She nodded her assent but her expression showed ambivalence. Ella wasn't sure she wanted to occupy this niche in his life. She was definitely more of a girlfriend type than a submissive, without a doubt. She did, however, enjoy the sex. And without a doubt, he enjoyed her.

"Come with me." He led her to the locked room and once inside, instructed her to remove her clothes and kneel. He could feel something primal uncoiling inside him, stirred from a deep sleep. At the same time, strong emotion twisted his gut and the pain was becoming untenable—he needed to exorcise it somehow. He looked around, seeking a cure, an outlet, in this room devoted to rough and sensual sex.

And there Ella knelt.

He went to her, lifted her to her feet, and, walking her to the far wall, tethered her to the St. Andrew's cross.

"What's your safe word, Ella?"

"Crimson."

"Crimson." He lowered his face to her, until his lips

were next to her ear. "Remember it: you might need to use it tonight. We're going into advanced territory this evening, Ella. You need to tell me if it becomes too much for you, the moment it becomes too much for you. Do you understand?"

"Yes." Her voice was uncharacteristically shaky.

He didn't let that dissuade him from his course of action. Perhaps in that moment, nothing could have. Rational thought had abandoned him and he was operating on nothing but emotion-charged fuel.

He may have even tried to justify it to himself by acknowledging that Ella was a natural at this kind of play: she took to it immediately. But his mistake was in perception. It wasn't pain that she took to; it was sex— rough or gentle, she liked it both ways. She didn't act like a virgin... ever.

For him, the crisis he was experiencing amounted to a loss of control. He couldn't stop Kira from killing herself—one slip of his ability to regulate everything and everyone. He couldn't stop himself from falling for Ella. Another slip. Emotions were eroding his ironclad control and that he could not accept, could never tolerate. He would reclaim control—consequences be damned.

He stepped over to the wall and selected an implement. He knew it should be the flogger—Ella was far from ready for the heavy stuff. Even a flogger might be pushing it. But despite knowing it was a very bad idea, his hand reached for the single-tail—his favorite whip and the one he used to use on Kira.

The first lash caught her unaware and she shrieked loudly. "No screaming, Ella. Just counting. I expect you to take it with grace. If you cannot do so, then use your safe word. Those are your two options." He struck her again.

She never counted but she attempted to take more than she should have. Well before he got to ten, her knees gave out and she would have fallen to the ground if she weren't tied to the crossbars. She managed to spit out her safe word, from a throat parched and running on shallow respiration, both caused by panting. The shock of hearing her safe word catapulted him back into his right mind and he threw down the whip, rushing to untie her from the cross.

Even as he carried her to the bedroom, he knew it was all over: she'd leave him for certain. His initial reaction was a quiet acceptance; he believed it was probably a good thing in the long term. No emotional attachments, he reminded himself... and Ella was starting to wiggle her way under his skin—with her alabaster complexion, her perfectly curvy ass, and her sharp wit, she was invading his thoughts during the day and his dreams at night.

But as he gazed down at her china-doll perfection, he felt crushed at the mere thought of never seeing her again... and he felt like weeping. He was overcome with grief—grief at Kira's premature death and grief at how he'd just killed a young, tender relationship that was increasingly important to him.

Did it ever matter what kind? Grief was grief. And it hurt like fucking hell.

He gently laid her on the bed, soothed the red welts on her skin with a numbing salve, cooed to her, and brought her a shot of brandy and some ibuprofen.

"Ella, I'm sorry," he whispered into her neck, wet from her tears. He could hear the anguish in his own voice.

She ignored him, turning away from him.

"Please don't hate me; I made a mistake. It won't happen again."

"No, it won't. You may need this lifestyle, Ian... but I don't. I can't."

Despite everything, she still allowed him to touch her. He made love to her very gently, trying to show her how deeply his feelings for her ran. Afterward, well...

She got up with obvious difficulty, hissing when the movement pulled on her back. His whip had left one stripe across her shoulder blades and several on her backside and upper thighs. Seeing his whip marks on his women usually made him hard; now, they just made him sick.

"I'd like you to avoid making any decisions until you've had time to calm down. Please, Ella?"

"I'm oh so calm, Ian." She was standing with her back to the floor-length mirror, head turned to survey the damage. "Will these leave scars?"

"Of course not! I would never mark you like that." He was truly affronted.

"Oh, silly me. Are these small signs of affection then?"

He stopped talking at that point. Her snide remarks told him he would get nowhere with her tonight. The shy salesgirl who entranced him was gone; in her place was a strong, pissed-off woman.

Her wits about her again, she grabbed for her clothes and dressed hurriedly, occasionally grimacing when it hurt. She had to go, she told him; she had an early morning tomorrow. He was adamant about driving her home. She was vehement in her refusal. They ultimately compromised: his driver would take her home. When Ian said goodnight to Ella, he knew in his gut it was really goodbye. She merely nodded grimly, turned on her heel, and walked out of his life.

He nearly cried himself to sleep that night, like a child. His emotions were all over the place and he didn't know what to do about it. He began to feel her absence the moment she strode out the door, taking with her his happiness, his contentment, even his pride.

For three days he forced himself not to call her, not to show up on her doorstep. He allowed himself to send flowers once and that was all. Giving her time to think—and hopefully miss him as he missed her—was his intention. He never expected her to disappear.

On the fourth day, he called her cell phone and received his first shock: it was disconnected. A half hour later, he stood on the steps of her condo's front entrance. When he knocked on the apartment door, he had an awful premonition but he refused to allow it into the light of day. It forced itself through anyway: something told him he wouldn't see Ella again.

Mariah answered the door. "Yes?"

Relief. He cleared his throat. "Hello. I'm Ian Blackmon. I'm here to see Ella?"

"I'm sorry but Ella's gone."

What? "Gone?"

"Yes. Forgive my lack of manners. I'm Mariah, Ella's friend and roommate—former roommate now, I guess. Ella left the country two days ago."

"Left the country? How could that be? She never mentioned any plans to that effect when I saw her four days ago."

Mariah shrugged. "I didn't see it coming either but she packed her bags in a rush, handed me her share of next month's rent and said *adios*, promising to keep in touch. I'm sorry, but that's all I know."

"Thank you," he said, and turned away. Whether it was true or her friend was lying was immaterial; he had to be gracious about it until he knew for certain. On his way home, as his heart thundered in his chest in a cold-sweat panic, he outlined in his mind how he'd find her. *Be logical and proactive,* he reminded himself. Hopefully she was using plastic since her cell phone was disconnected. Credit cards and cell phones leave a trail of breadcrumbs.

Two weeks passed, and after zero luck in scouting out her location, he called his security expert to recommend an investigator. He needed to run somebody to ground.

Forty-eight hours later, he had her new address in front of him, courtesy of Allen Larson, the PI he'd hired. Still, he wasn't sure of his next step. Knowing where she was now was comforting enough to allow him some time for reflection and perhaps time to try to resist the inevitable. He didn't want to give in to the weakness of love. Emotion was debilitating; detachment was empowering. For a little while, that became his new mantra. Kickboxing became his new obsession.

Exactly two weeks after receiving the information on Ella's location, he stepped off a Virgin Air jet at Heathrow, a piece of paper with an address written on it in his hand. Would she be happy to see him or horrified he found her? He just didn't know, so he took a cautious approach: he waited outside her flat, sitting on a park bench for several hours at a stretch. When he first spotted her coming out of the brick building, his heartbeat seemed to falter for a moment, then thrummed strongly like a motor revving while his whole chest tightened painfully. It was so good to see her beautiful face. He'd missed it so much.

That was the moment when he had to confront reality: despite his best efforts and his diligent attempt to distance himself from all things romantic, he'd fallen in love. And, another slap in the face: chances were rather excellent that his love was unrequited. He was Ian Blackmon, one of the most eligible bachelors in the country, so said Fortune, People, Maxim, and Forbes, and the one girl he loves probably despises him and all of his evil ways.

The very evening he walked into *Archipelago* and saw her for the first time, he probably began his descent into life as a besotted fool. She was exquisitely beautiful but Ian had seen so many gorgeous women—most wealthy men do. Physically beautiful people almost always use their looks to trade up in life, so he always had lots of them fawning around him.

But it was more than mere looks. Ella had something else, a sort of dual persona going on. On the one hand, she was pristine innocence, almost angelic in her purity. Warring with the innocence, however, was a kind of innate *femme-fatale* allure, daring men—with her azure eyes—to come closer so she could destroy them with her charms, a kind of vagina *dentata*, the nightmare of anyone with a penis and a healthy libido. It sucked him in immediately.

On their first date, he'd decided he would mold her to be his next submissive if she were at all amenable. He could easily make it worth her while financially and she was a struggling student. In return, he could feed off some of that innocent charm while nurturing her undiscovered *femme fatale*. He pursued her with a single-minded determination.

Her virginity threw him for a minute or two—he wasn't expecting it and wasn't quite sure what to do with it. What he did know beyond a shadow of a doubt, virgin or no virgin, was that she wasn't leaving his house that night without him fucking her, one way or another. Her virginity merely caused him to reconsider his plans. His planned domination became a seduction and he found it every bit as satisfying as any BDSM scene could be. Maybe even more.

Did some part of him recognize that very night that she was his, or more aptly, that he was hers? Very possibly.

He went back to the States without ever making contact with her. For one thing, he knew he wouldn't be successful. Too much time had already passed and she had made no effort to get in touch with him. She was done with him the moment he picked up the single-tail. His dour conclusion was that he'd have to live without her and so he went home.

But peace was elusive. At first, he tried to banish her from his mind. It didn't work. Then, he thought he should return to the UK and beg her forgiveness, bring her flowers and chocolate. Or fine wine and sincere apologies. Expensive shoes and jewels, for God's sake. Whatever it would take.

But he knew he'd fail. And the one thing above all else that Ian Blackmon couldn't tolerate was failure—he'd almost rather die. Days passed, then weeks, months, eventually accumulating into a tortured year, a celibate year, a year during which he worked longer hours, and made ever more money, and spent his redirected sexual energy on self-improvement, working out constantly to create a tireless machine out of his body. Going without sex conserved quite a bit of energy, he learned, which was why professional boxers weren't supposed to have sex for weeks before a bout.

Another lesson that came his way was that the idea of taking a whip to a woman no longer appealed to him. If anything, it had the opposite effect. A broken heart can change all of one's priorities in a flash. The anniversary of their split was fast approaching and he still was nowhere near over her but he recognized he had to move on, and made plans to go to the club to meet new women and even considered attending one of his sister Zoe's exhausting parties that were always teeming with debutantes.

That was when providence smiled upon him and during lunch with his sister, he learned about Ella's bestselling book… and he knew he'd come across a way to lure her back into his life.

"Answer me, Ian, you followed me to the UK?"

Ella's voice pulled him back from the past, into the conversation they were having in New York. "Yes," he concedes, "I followed you to the UK."

Her pulse began to race as she realized the implications of his admission. He must have loved her… even then… as she loved him. "Why didn't you contact me? I was waiting for you."

"You were? I thought for sure you would reject me, that you despised me."

"Well, I did. But I also loved you and missed you so much. I would have been thrilled to see you, Ian." She's wringing her hands. "When were you there?"

He told her and she squeezed her eyes closed. If only he'd visited her, let her know he was there, they might have avoided so much pain and loneliness. "Oh, I would have been so happy to stay with you instead of in my drafty dorm room. I missed you with every part of me… but the next move had to come from you."

"It did," he said with a smirk.

"Yeah, right. Suing me for breach of contract a year later. Not exactly what I had in mind."

"It sort of worked, didn't it?"

"So you filed the suit to get me back? Not because of the book?"

"Yes to the first question, no to the second."

It's her turn to smirk; she climbs onto his lap and begins to kiss him, every part of him that's accessible. "A normal man would send flowers or jewelry with a heartfelt apology."

"I've never been accused of being normal."

"You wasted time, Mr. Blackmon, precious time. All those months we could have been together. Now it's up to you to make it up to me. But first tell me what's bothering you about Natasha's situation."

"I think she texted me for help," he admits, feeling anew a stab of horror. He tells Ella about the interrupted message.

"Ian," she says after a while, "let's commit to planning and enjoying our wedding. After our honeymoon, we'll investigate Natasha's new life to see if we need to intervene. I think that will make both of us feel better, don't you?"

He nods.

"She doesn't deserve any mercy from us but as a woman, I'm horrified to think of anyone being consigned to a life of sexual slavery. It would be better to die, I think. So maybe we can get someone we trust to do some reconnaissance. Who knows? Perhaps the man will fall in love with her and treat her well. Truth is sometimes stranger than fiction."

His fingers reach out to comb her hair behind her ear and caress her face. "I love you, Ella."

Rather than answer him with words, she answers him with her lips in a different way. A better way. And suddenly, sitting on his lap isn't so comfortable anymore, as things harden and shift beneath her. He smiles wickedly as she squirms.

"I know where we can stow it in a nice, warm place where it won't interfere with your sitting on my lap in comfort."

"Really? Well, then..."

He pulls up her short skirt—God, but he loves short skirts—and yanking her panties out of the way, he unzips and impales her in one fluid motion. Her head tilts back and a low moan vibrates in her throat.

"Yes, much better," she says. "Much... much... better."

Chapter 52

Countdown: T minus 56 hours and 23 minutes.

At *T minus zero*, Ian and I will stand in front of hundreds of witnesses and vow to love one another until death. No biggie.

I picked up my dress today, having had the last fitting three days ago, which called for one very minor adjustment. Mariah's dress was the height of perfection, but Zoe's needed a bit of taking in since she'd shed ten pounds since her last fitting. Call me unreasonable but I would think that a considerate bridesmaid (not to mention new sister-in-law) would be able to maintain her weight for three teensy, weensy months. Zoe is a definite pain in the ass, no doubt about it. Her mother, however, is not. Faith showed me her gown last week and I have to admit it's a brilliant choice—for her coloring, age, figure, and style. Faith and I will definitely get along for we are alike in so many ways—but not too many ways to make it creepy and weird for Ian.

Anyway, I haven't yet seen my mom's gown but she assures me I'll love it. I'm comfortable she's right since she generally displays impeccable taste. As the bride, I got to select Mariah's gown and though it presented an almost irresistible opportunity to exact revenge for years' worth of abuses by putting her in a horribly garish contraption of a frock, in the end I couldn't do it. I selected a drop-dead gorgeous *aubergine* silk strapless—and quite short—cocktail dress. Zoe's is just as short but on a bias cut with cap sleeves. Why should my girls hide their killer gams? Those legs don't come cheap or easy and they need to show them off to find their own husbands, damn it. I'm still holding out for Mason for Mariah. Hope springs eternal.

We compiled the guest list as soon as we returned from New York and Daniel's wedding. My mother sent me a list of her guests and Faith provided me with hers. When we put the three lists together and subtracted the few duplicates, there were still over four hundred names. And a few of them were women who had a history with my darling husband-to-be. Those names had to be weeded out.

The moment had arrived for us to have the long-postponed chat about Diana Benson and Kaylie Ayres.

We had spoken about it already, of course, that night when we got home. The entire car ride back to Ian's place was silent and tense but I was not going to go to sleep stewing over it. When the front door to his home closed behind us, I went on the offensive.

"So what was that little trap all about? Did you mother do it intentionally?"

His eyes blazed. "Of course not! Why would she? My mother likes you very much, Ella."

"You're not going to stand there and deny you had a relationship with both of those women who were there tonight. Are you?"

Rolling his eyes, he exhaled through his nose loudly. "No, I'm not going to deny it. Kaylie was a fling when I was a kid, for God's sake. I just wanted to get laid and I wasn't too choosy. I never took her seriously and I thought she was doing the same. My mistake."

"And the cougar?"

He smirked. "Funny you should call her that—"

"That's what she is," I interrupt. "She's got to have a good ten years or more on you. She was stealing from the cradle."

"Yes, she is actually fifteen years older than I. When I met her, I had no idea she was married to my father's partner. I just saw a sexy, older woman and I took her up on her offer. The shit of it was she knew damn well who I was and of her relation to my family."

"Were you not offended by the age difference?"

He shrugged. "I asked her if it bothered her after we'd been seeing each other for a while..."

"Bothered *her*?" I shook my head at his cluelessness. "It didn't bother *me.*"

"And?"

"Do you really want to know what she said? I warn you it's obnoxious."

I sneered. "I don't think I can dislike her more than I already do."

"She said, and I quote, 'Old enough to pee, old enough for me.'"

"Okay, I was wrong. It was possible to hate her more and I did now. What a disgusting slut."

"Ella," he grabbed my arms, "let's not waste another second talking about either of them. They're both old news. Forget it."

I pursed my lips stubbornly, wanting to cling a little while longer to my self-righteousness.

"Look me in the eyes, Ella. What do you see?"

I blew out my breath loudly in contempt, vibrating my lips in the process. "A very handsome man who did not develop his discriminating taste until very recently."

He laughed. "There you go. But, no. I want you to see the love shining through, love for you and only you. If I hadn't met and had relationships with all those other women, how would I have almost immediately known that you were *the one*? They were merely yardsticks on which to measure how much I love you, and how high a bar you set, baby."

I let it go after that. How could I not when he said such lovely things to me?

Now I dig in again, and like a juicy steak that gives you colon cancer, this discussion was going to be unhealthy for us to have. "They are not coming to our wedding. What is wrong with your mother? Did you not tell her of your history the day of the lunch she gave?"

"I told her, Ella. But here's the thing: Kaylie is one of my sister's very best friends and Diana is my father's partner's wife. How in hell can my mother not invite them?"

I do not want to back down on this one. But I may have to bend because I see his point. "Can you at least ask her if it's possible before the invitations are sent out? I think I should be able to feel comfortable at my own wedding."

"I will. But, Ella, even if they are present, it's not going to make a difference. There will be so many guests there and we'll be busy. Chances are you won't even see them. Kaylie will be with Zoe and Diana will be with her husband."

"Was she good in bed?"

His eyes pop open, wider than the Continental Divide. "Are you seriously asking me that?"

"No, it was a joke. Yes, I'm asking; I want to know. Was she?"

"Yes, she was... proficient. But it was just mechanical sex: there was no affection involved. When that's the case, it can never be too good, now can it?"

"I wouldn't know, Ian, for as you yourself have pointed out on numerous occasions, I hadn't had any sexual experience before you. Perhaps I should rectify that so I can have yardsticks by which to measure you?"

Smoldering eyes zoom in on me. "Do so at great peril: your own, and whoever has the audacity to touch you."

"You're not smiling. You would kill me if I cheated?"

"Kill you? Ella, what's gotten into you? Are you trying to provoke a fight?"

What has gotten into me? It must be nerves. Maybe I am trying to goad him into an argument so I could call off the wedding. I'm nervous about taking this step. Isn't it usually the man who gets cold feet?

So I backed down. "Just ask your mother. Do it for me. Okay?"

Later that week, when I walked through the entrance hall of Ian's house, I heard his and his mother's hushed voices. The fact that they were hushed just made the prospect of eavesdropping that much more appealing. I tiptoed closer and, peeking in, tried to listen.

"… and it wasn't."

"Ian, I don't want to disappoint her."

"Mom, you cannot allow Zoe to invite whomever she desires. I've already told you about her friends. I won't allow Ella to be uncomfortable at her own wedding."

"Okay, agreed. So we'll ditch Kaylie Ayres. What about Diana Benson? Why the no-go on her?"

"Do you really want to know, Mom?"

Faith just looked at her son in consternation. What is it she does or doesn't want to know? "I'm afraid of the answer but you're just going to have to spill, Ian. I *have* to invite them—he's your father's closest colleague."

"Mom, before I knew who she was I had a thing with her."

Faith stared at her son uncomprehendingly. "A thing?"

He had the good grace to blush. "Yes, a thing. Must I spell it out?"

"Ohhhh, a thing." Now she was blushing. "A thing. Really? My God, what's wrong with that woman? She's too old for you."

"Not to mention married, Mom."

"Not to mention. Huh. Well, then, you tell me what to do, since you put me in this position, Ian. How am I to explain to your father? Moreover, how will he explain it to his longstanding friend and colleague? Please guide me on this one."

I watch as Ian tells me in body language exactly how agitated he is. It's time for me to intervene so I walk into the room, clicking my heels on the hardwoods. "There's no need, Faith. Ian, it's fine if Diana Benson attends our wedding. I'm not going to get hung up on insignificant matters." I lean down to give him a kiss and I smile at Faith. The look of relief on both their faces is downright comical so I allow myself a giggle.

"Any other problems we need to address?"

The night before the wedding we have a small party for our friends. It is just us, Ian's sister, Jackson Delacroix, Mariah, and Mason, plus Daniel and Olivia fly in early enough to join us. We are all gathered in the great room when Daniel and Olivia make their entrance.

Mariah turns to me. "Please, Ella, please tell me that mouthwatering beauty who just walked in is single. Please tell me the beautiful girl whose hand he's holding is his sister or first cousin or ridiculously young mother. I'm begging here?"

I grin. "'Fraid not, Mariah. That's his brand-new wife and he's head over heels for her. He doesn't even notice that other women exist." I almost add a rejoinder to Mariah to be careful what she thinks about around him, as Ian's suspicion about Daniel reading minds flashes through mine. Tailgating that thought, I remember the day I met Daniel, at the Russian Tearoom. I'd had salacious thoughts about a three-way with him and Ian. I groan aloud as the connection is made. Oh, no. Oh, please God, no! Please don't let it be true. I remember now that Daniel looked at me strangely when that dirty little thought went traipsing through my brain. Right now I just want the floor to swallow me up. Right the fuck now.

"Ella, are you nervous?"

I look up to see the handsome Daniel smiling at me, his green eyes twinkling, while Olivia is speaking to Zoe. "Uh," I stammer, "not too bad, I guess." I try, really try, to smile but it probably looks like I'm in grimacing in stomach pain.

Daniel continues, "If that's the case, why do you look so pale?"

He is persistent, isn't he? I want to tell him to go away and let me wallow in my shame. How will I ever live this down?

"I'm pale because that's my natural coloring, silly," I say instead. "Tell me, Daniel..." I pause and then gesture him closer with my fingers, "Ian thinks you can read minds," I say, watching his face closely.

All I get is an enigmatic smile. "Hmm, if that's the case, he'd better watch what he thinks about around me."

"I'd better, too, I suppose," I say suggestively, to see if there's any reaction. Nope. Maybe I'm okay? I press my luck. "I would hate for someone to read my mind because sometimes I have naughty thoughts." Again, my eyes are glued to his face.

"We all do at times, Ella, some more than others. I wouldn't worry about it." He gives me a warm and beautiful smile and moves over to where Olivia is now standing.

I think he knows, damn it. What's more, I think he knows that I know and that I know he knows what I was thinking. He's trying to tell me it's okay, that he doesn't hold it against me... which is great, but I'm still utterly mortified. What would Olivia think if she knew about my lascivious thoughts about her husband? And then I think of having a husband who could read your mind all the time. Poor Olivia.

Halfway through our party two things happen. The first is when I duck into the kitchen to get another bottle of white wine I'd chilled earlier and find Mariah and Mason engaged in a hot and heavy liplock. Score.

The second is when Ian's two brothers arrive— separately, of course: one came from San Francisco and the other, Seattle. Quentin lives on a little, crooked block in the Mission district of S.F., and Nathaniel lives in Seattle in a converted warehouse he renovated himself. Our quiet little party rockets into warp speed when the three Blackmon brothers together in one room coalesce into an undeniable force. The music gets louder, the people get drunker, and laughter drowns out conversation. I see more people arriving, as well— people I don't know. By eleven, I say goodnight to the people we invited and sneak away to bed. I don't want to look exhausted tomorrow for my wedding and I need to be up early to meet up in my mother's hotel room where

I'll get ready for the wedding.

I take one last look at myself in the long mirror. Is that really me? The reflection shows a beautiful woman, dressed in silk and taffeta. My make-up is astonishing, done by an expert. It barely looks like I have any on but all my features are accentuated. Zoe is attaching the veil so I try to hold still in my high-heeled satin shoes.

The dress makes me look even more slender than I am. My hair is swept back in a loose chignon and the veil sits just above it. Right before I exit the room, my mom and I discuss the merits of putting the veil over my face.

"It's traditional, Ella," she insists for the third time.

"Don't you think it's a little archaic?"

"No, I don't. I think it's a charming tradition."

"You do know where the tradition comes from, right, Mom? Veils were used in arranged marriages so the husband didn't see what his new wife looked like until after they took the vows and it was too late to back out."

"Oh, Ella, that's just not true. It's a symbol of purity."

"Yeah, well, I'm not pure, for one thing. Plus, I'm right about its origin. You can check it out yourself on the Internet."

She sniffs. "You shouldn't believe everything you read on the Internet, Ella. Okay," she says, apparently dismissing my comments, "so I've loaned you an ankle bracelet, so that's old and borrowed, you have a blue ribbon on your garter belt, your jewelry is all new, courtesy of a generous husband-to-be—all bases are covered. You look absolutely beautiful, Ella."

Uh-oh. The tears are starting already. "Mom, don't start or we'll ruin our make-up and I sat in that chair for almost an hour to have it applied. Stop."

"I'm sorry, sweetie. Pull on the veil—they're about to call us."

We were supposed to get ready in my mom's hotel suite but things were changed at the last minute. Ian's parents wanted me to come down their beautiful sweeping staircase a la Scarlet O'Hara. Since that wouldn't be possible if I arrived by limousine, Faith requested we get ready at the estate.

Four hundred-plus guests could not be squeezed into the entrance foyer so closed-circuit cameras are positioned along my route, with screens mounted outside so the guests can watch my hopefully graceful descent down the staircase. At the foot of it, my father will meet me and escort me outside. Ian won't be able to see the screens from his vantage point so he won't see me in my gown until I reach the white-sheeted aisle.

A low but insistent knock on the door snaps me out of my reverie at the mirror. My mom answers it and I can spot Mason just beyond. He smiles and winks at me. Mom turns around. "It's time to go, Ella."

Time to go? Already? My heart picks up a warp-speed rhythm and I feel my face perspiring. No! I cannot ruin my make-up. I helplessly look over at Mariah but she can't seem to rip her eyes away from Mason to lend some assistance. I'm only the bride, after all.

I glance back at my mother. "Shouldn't I take some Valium or Xanax or something, Mom? I'm terrified."

"No, honey, because then you'll be in a drugged stupor." She looks around. "I know! Hang on for one minute." She goes to the door and calls for Mason. He returns, they confer, and he nods.

"Just hang tight, sweetie," my mom says as Mason disappears again.

About three minutes later, Mason returns with a tray of flutes filled with champagne. "Thank you, kind sir," my mother tells him and accepts the tray. There are four glasses, one for each of us. I should just take Mariah's and have two since she isn't being a very attentive maid of honor.

"Give me that glass," I say, and down it in one swallow.

"Ella, for God's sake!"

"Mom, what part of *I'm terrified* didn't you understand? There are four hundred freaking people down there. What if I trip on my gown and dive down the stairs head first? Then what?"

"Then we make a trip to the ER. You're more likely to do that with the champagne on board," she says wryly."

"Then why on earth did you give it to me?" I snap.

"Oh, God. If you're like this today, I don't want to be around you when you're giving birth, Ella. For crying out loud, you're going to be married, not walking to the electric chair."

"Let's get this over with," I say, feeling seconds away from breaking down. I am seriously stressed.

Mariah leans in to whisper in my ear. "Just chill the fuck out, girlfriend. You're getting crazed and frightening your mother. Take a deep breath and think about who is at the end of this walk, waiting for you." She pulls back to look at me. "Okay?"

I nod. Yes, she's right. I'm freaking out and have to stop.

We all go into the hallway. I'm relieved to feel comfortable walking in the shoes and the gown. *I can do this*, I think. Too soon we reach the staircase and form a line, starting with my mother, followed by Zoe, and then Mariah. Then... it's my turn. I should have had a bigger bridal party—easier to get lost in the crowd.

The music begins as my mother descends the long, winding staircase. The volume is low as we all make our way down, ten seconds apart. It was timed so that one would reach the bottom when the next begins her way down. They wanted me on the stairs alone so I have to count to fifteen.

Now I'm at the top and I watch as Mariah nears the bottom of the staircase. As soon as she's off, my father appears, looking up at me. I take my first step, focusing on nothing but my dad's face. It helps. In my head, I count the steps. I know there are twenty-four steps. I reach my dad and he takes my hand, kisses it, and passes it through the crook of his arm.

As soon as we reach the French doors, the music

picks up volume to trumpet my arrival. Oh, God, this is horrifying. As soon as I spot Ian, I will glue my eyes to him so I can't see all the people. Just him. Just Ian. *I can do this*.

And then my ivory satin shoes are on the white aisle and I can see him. Ian. He's the most gloriously gorgeous groom on the face of the planet. Standing tall in his fashionable tuxedo, his brother Nathaniel beside him, Ian's eyes are trained on mine and, yes, I feel empowered. Now I have a purpose to my walk: I need to get to my husband-to-be in one piece. I pace my steps to the music and head for those mesmerizing eyes. Watching me closely, he smiles and that gives me all the confidence I need.

Chapter 53

She glides into his line of sight, a vision in ivory satin and he almost gasps. *God, Ella, you look stunningly beautiful.* Outwardly, he's a study in coolness—years of practice honed in front of boards of directors, and media cameras and microphones thrust in his face allow him to appear impervious. Inwardly, his heart is blasting a jungle tempo as savage as if Dave Grohl is in there pounding on his drumset.

Ian and his two brothers emerged from the house a few minutes ago to find the guests already seated and waiting in the sea of white grosgrain-beribboned chairs. The lawn looked like a green carpet leading to a magical forest befitting of *A Midsummer Night's Dream,* with pinpoints of white light twinkling in all of the surrounding trees, though the sun had not yet set, and wildflowers sprouting from giant clay pots all around the circumference of the yard, the woods surrounding the property.

Leave it to his mother to create a fairyland out of dirt and grass in just a week or so. The huge awning-covered terrace off the main house was set up as an elegant, candlelit gathering area for cocktails and canapés, while the formal dinner would be served in the big white tent, with tables arranged to encircle the huge dance floor. Right now they were on the long expanse of velvety lawn. The chairs were arranged in a semi-circle (a good idea swiped from Derek Girardi). The three men in black tie waited for Ella, Mariah, and Zoe under an arbor, the lattice of which was entwined with vines of white-flowering Morning Glory, the all-day blooming variety.

He watched as first Zoe came toward him, her face barely disguising her merriment, as if she were ready to burst into laughter at the slightest provocation. When she reached her brothers, she made a silly face at Ian, obviously trying to upset his comportment but, pro that he was, he remained statue-like. Frustrated in her attempt, she took her designated place opposite Quentin. Mariah was next down the aisle, looking properly somber, as if it could have been a funeral as easily as a wedding. The thought almost made Ian laugh. Mariah stood next to Zoe, opposite from Nathaniel, his best man. He looked at the two *aubergine* bridesmaid and maid of honor dresses and thought Ella chose very well. The cut of the dresses suited the women who wore them splendidly.

Ian barely heard the music as Ella came into view. She seemed to float down the aisle toward him, in the most beautiful wedding gown he'd ever seen. His nervousness disappeared with her appearance, and now he was just impatient for her to be officially declared his wife.

His wife.

And then she was there in front of him and he took her hand.

Toward the ceremony's close, they each read a few lines of poetry to each other that help express their feelings. Ian recites his first, a poem by Henry Dumas, entitled *Love Song*.

After a moment of silence, Ella, not as publicly inclined as Ian, begins her recitation in a soft, halting voice. She recites *100 Love Sonnets XVII*, by Pablo Neruda.

After the simple poetic lines, quiet descends for moments as they look into each other's eyes. The moment feels profound to everyone there, as if a spiritual communion is taking place, sealing the vows they just spoke. After a few moments, the reverend takes their hands in his own, looking out at the crowd of onlookers, and says with a smile, "I now pronounce Ian and Ariel husband and wife. Ian, you may kiss your bride."

Ella did opt to wear the small half-veil over her face so when the reverend pronounces them, Ian turns to her with a beaming smile and lifts the veil. She winks at him, knowing that only he could see it and they kiss lightly. The audience applauds with decorum as the bride and groom turn toward their guests, radiant with love or maybe just relief that it's finally over, to walk back up the aisle, this time as a married couple. They stop at the end of the aisle, where they are joined by both sets of parents, forming a line to greet each guest personally as they exit the outdoor chapel. This part will take a while, since over four hundred people are in attendance.

Ian and Ella never did have any particular song they considered their own so they chose to play the standards at the wedding, music that would suit a wide range of ages. Later in the night there would be jazz and some alternative for the younger guests. Selected arrangements were from varied singers such as Sarah Vaughn, Frank Sinatra, Billie Holiday, and Nelson Riddle's last ones, those he created for Linda Ronstadt. For the couple's first dance together, the small orchestra plays *I've Got a Crush on You*, followed by *Isn't it Romantic,* and *Round Midnight.* The female singer Faith hired is exceptional, belting out one song after the other, each one sounding better.

Ella looks up at her gorgeous husband. *Her husband.* It sounds strange to her ears. "It's a very good thing you could dance otherwise we'd have had to take lessons for the wedding."

As he spins her around the dance floor effortlessly, he grins. "My mother insisted we learn at an early age so as not to embarrass her on the rare occasion it would be called into requirement. Today is the first time it came in handy."

"Didn't you go to your senior prom in high school?"

"Yes, but there was very little slow dancing. How are you feeling, Mrs. Blackmon?"

Smiling, Ella begins singing the lyrics. "I've Got a Crush on You, Sweetie Pie," and Ian swoops down to kiss her.

"Now you can't escape me ever, Ariel. You're officially mine."

"Wasn't I always?"

"I don't know. Were you?"

She bats her eyelashes. "I'm afraid so."

"Didn't you think to tell me?"

"Of course not. A girl never gives up her secrets, silly."

"So I chased you to Britain for nothing because you were always going to come back to me?"

"Well, you might have expedited the timetable if you'd shown your ugly mug."

"Hmmm. Well, I could kick myself now. All those months kickboxing out my frustrations. I could have been having my evil way with you."

She looks up and smiles. "Yes. Silly you. But look at the bright side: all that kickboxing did marvelous things for your legs. And you got a much-needed lesson in self-control. Didn't you?"

"I suppose so..." he leans in to whisper in her ear, "but now I have an irresistible urge to spank you for making me suffer for so long."

"I suppose it's lucky for me that I'm wearing this long and hard to remove wedding gown."

"Oh, ye of little faith. Is our song over yet?"

She laughs. "You still have to dance with your mother and mine and I have to dance with our fathers. Remember?"

"Fine. Immediately afterward, we rendezvous at twenty hundred hours, upstairs in my old bedroom. Got it?"

Her cheeks flushed pink, Ella peers up at him, trying to decide if he's kidding. "Twenty hundred hours, upstairs, your old bedroom. Got it."

The rendezvous is not to be, however, since they have hundreds of guests to see to. After the dances, Mariah grabs Ella to scold her.

"Why did you push me at Mason so soon? I mean, there is a virtual *smörgåsbord* of men here, Ella. A cornucopia. Quentin and Nathaniel, for example, are rather stunning specimens of the male human. And that Daniel Butler, *ooh la la.*"

Ella rolls her eyes. "Keep those little purple panties on, Mariah. First off, I told you that Daniel is oh so happily married, newly married at that. And—"

"Pish posh, he might change his mind. Can't a marriage contract have a period of rescission like other legal contracts? Anyway, Ian's brothers aren't married, are they?"

"No, but I don't know them very well. For all I know, one or both might be gay. And what's wrong with Mason, pray tell? He's strong, handsome, buff..."

"True that. It's just that I'm like a hungry girl at an all-you-can-eat buffet. Seems a shame to focus on just one dish, delicious though it may be, you know? That Quentin is smokin', don't you think?"

"He's not bad looking," Ella replies dryly.

"Ha, the queen of understatement. Hey, your dad is adorable by the way, Ella. And I promised him a dance so I'll go make good on that. Ta-ta." She sashays away in her short little dress, men's eyes following her closely as she makes her way.

Gasping, Ella sees why, when Mariah gets ahead a few paces: the little slut is wearing a thong under that slinky dress so one can see every jiggle as she walks.

She feels hands from behind her, wrapping around her waist. "Do I have to guess who?"

"There'd better be only one guess or I'll have to fight in my tuxedo. How are you doing, love? Feet hurt from dancing?"

"Not yet. These glass slippers are way comfortable.

Hey," she spins around, "I noticed that Jeff Benson, your dad's partner, is here solo tonight. How did that happen?"

Ian's eyes are twinkling. "I hear tell his lovely wife is feeling poorly today and couldn't make the festivities. She sends her apologies."

"Oh? And what, pray tell, is ailing her?"

Grinning wickedly, Ian shrugs. "Perchance, she had a visit from a rather large gentleman suggesting she send her regrets?"

"Aha. Of what large gentleman do we speak?"

"I believe his name is Justin Mason, if memory serves me correctly."

"Oh, I'm going to have to give him a big, sloppy kiss for that kindness."

"Better not make it too big or sloppy or I'll have to take him on... and that I wouldn't bet odds on in my favor."

"Okay. A peck on the cheek it is."

"Do you think we can get away soon? The plane is fueled, ready and waiting to whisk us to the Emerald Isle, and Scott's spinning his wheels in the cockpit."

"I think in another half hour we'll be able to slip out."

After saying goodbye to their parents and the wedding party, Ella throws her bouquet—it's caught by one of Ian's young cousins—and they wave goodbye to their guests and take off for the airport. They're spending their honeymoon in Ireland with a foray into Scotland, since neither have ever been there, so they have a long flight ahead of them. Fortunately, there is a small, private bedroom on the Gulfstream where they could celebrate their nuptials in the way they know best.

Chapter 54

My feet are killing me. I feel as if I've been standing in these dainty yet torturous-as-medieval-contraption heels for a week straight. The thing is, whenever I get a glimpse of my bridegroom in his formal attire, I'm willing to have my feet pinched in these heels for another week, just to see him in these clothes, in this *milieu*—out of the corporate rat maze and having fun.

Luckily we are now boarding the Gulfstream to begin our three-week honeymoon. Just the fact that we can take off for three weeks makes me elated. Another thing that makes me elated is that I can take off these shoes in just a few minutes.

Our wedding was storybook perfect, with nothing to mar it. We got lucky with the weather, getting a beautiful late spring day, with crisp, clean air coming off the sound. Our guests were spectacular and didn't happen to include Ian's ex-girlfriends or lovers (that I know of, anyway). I didn't even have to withstand Diana Benson, treacherous cradle robber extraordinaire, since Mason saw to it that she wouldn't attend. I gave him a big (and sloppy) kiss for that kindness and Ian didn't even fight him over it.

"So, Ian, tell me something that I've always wondered about: why were you drawn to me in the first place? You know, at Archipelago?"

We're sitting in the main cabin of the Gulfstream. When we boarded about twenty minutes ago, the crew, headed by Scott, were all at the door awaiting our arrival.

"Congratulations, Mr. Blackmon, and welcome

aboard."

"Thank you, Scott. I think I speak for both myself and my new wife when I say we're relieved and happy to be on the jet and finished with all the festivities." He looked at me and I nodded.

"Yes."

"And congratulations to you too, Mrs. Blackmon. This is Edward Kessler, my co-pilot on this trip, and Nanette McDonald, your attendant. Please make yourselves comfortable; we'll be taking off shortly."

Ian glances at both Edward and Nanette and nods to each, and then guides me over to the deep leather chairs in the cabin. When Nanette comes over to serve us, I check her out. She is a pretty redhead, late twenties, I'd guess. She seems friendly enough, I suppose, but I get jealous whenever any female capable of ovulation gets within ten feet of Ian. I just can't help myself. Not that he's ever given me reason to be jealous. I just am.

Nanette has just served us a bottle of Perrier Jouet chilled to perfection, and a platter of chocolate-dipped strawberries with *crème fraiche*. Can life get any better?

"What about you?" Ian brings me back to my question. "Do you really need to ask me that question?"

I nod. "Yes. Let's examine this scenario objectively: a very wealthy, very eligible young bachelor strolls into a small, pricey boutique one fine evening, needing a birthday gift for his cherished and delightful little sister."

He snorts at my description of Zoe.

Ignoring his audible commentary, I continue. "A young, nondescript sales clerk waits on him and—"

"Are you really describing yourself as nondescript, Ella?"

"Well, I know I'm unique to people who know me, Ian, but back then you didn't know me from a hole in the wall..." I gasp. "Is that expression dirty?"

Ian laughs heartily. "I don't think so but it sure sounds like it right now."

My face heats up so quickly. Of course it's an expression that Mariah favors, enough said. I regroup, swallowing a sip of my champagne. "To you, I was a young salesgirl. Right? I mean, there was nothing dramatically eye-catching about me that night, was there?"

"As a matter of fact, there was, baby. You looked up at me with those impossibly blue eyes and called me sir. That's all the eye-catching I required."

My mouth drops open—I have to work on that habit. "Because I called you sir, you wanted to get to know me?"

Grinning like a fool, he nods. "To some extent, yes. Look, Ella, here's what I saw and now that we're married, I don't have to mince words."

He leans in, a devilish gleam in his eyes. "I saw a hot, young brunette with a beautiful face and eyes to get lost in. I saw an innocent angel who was ripe for defrocking." His voice drops to a deeper register. "I saw a girl with gorgeous fucking tits and a smokin' ass on killer legs with long, silky dark hair, and lips that could inspire dreams so wet you could backstroke out of them.

"And... perhaps most significantly... a woman who called me *sir*. You brought out the Dominant in me, Ella. Big time. You still do."

"A kitten can bring out the Dominant in you," I grumble good-naturedly.

"Exactly. You're my kitten. Now come here and sit on my lap."

We still have on our wedding clothes, since neither of us wanted to wait to start our trip. I would have had to do the whole traditional thing with my mother and Mariah helping me change, and I wanted to avoid all of the sentimental crap as much as possible. I'm not the emotional type who cries at weddings or things of that nature, though my mom assures me that will change after I have children. Mom swears that maternal hormones can ruin a good bitch in no time. Something to look forward to, I guess.

So now I obey my new husband and crawl onto his lap—I'm nothing if not obedient. I can feel the heated steel under my butt and I wiggle around to torture him further. Since he used naughty words, I suppose it's my turn. Let's see if I can up the ante and shock him. I wrap my arms around his neck, leaning in enthusiastically to whisper in his ear, "How's about I trip the trigger on that giant, hard cock you've got locked and loaded in those trousers? I have a special place to do it. Hot... wet... tight..."

Lazily, I rear back to look at his expression and yes, he looks somewhat startled but then he tosses his head back and laughs. And right there, right in the cabin where Nanette can possibly see us, he flips me over his knee, pulls up my wedding dress, and spanks me—hard. As promised.

I'm sputtering and gasping. "Ian, stop this moment or I'll bite your leg!"

"Do it and I'll spank you harder and then gag you once I'm done."

"You wouldn't..."

"Of course I would," he says, his breathing getting labored. He's hitting me damn hard. But now, after every slap, he rubs away the sting... to the extent possible. I'm so horrified that Nanette might come in from the galley or wherever she is and see us that the pain barely registers. Of course, I'll feel it later when I can't sit down.

"Ian, can we go into the bedroom? Pleeeease?"

He laughs again and sets me on my feet. "I've wanted to do that for hours now, Mrs. Blackmon. Your dirty mouth pushed me over the edge, you know. And now I might just have to take out some of the toys I packed for our destination and use them right... this... minute."

"Promises, promises."

Standing up forcefully, he grips me by the wrist and tugging me behind him, leads us to the tiny bedroom... where he has a bed with narrow wood posts of a sort capped by finials, perfect for clipping cuffs to each corner. Ahh, how am I going to suffer this sexual torment on a plane? I can never be quiet, no matter the incentive or how high the ante is. I might just have to *ask* for that gag.

He strips me slowly, taking his time with each piece of clothing. When I'm standing in nothing but my garter belt, stockings, and very skimpy panties, he steps back to appraise me.

"Very nice, Ella. Even nicer," he says, looking around on the floor and picking up my shoes, "would be if you were still wearing these." He hands them to me and though my sore feet silently scream in protest, I force them back into the heels.

"Perfect." He steps back to appraise me, one elbow leaning on his crossed arm, an index finger tapping his lips. His delicious, sultry lips that make me—"

"Math can be fun," he interrupts my carnal musing. "I've been subtracting—now I'll add something." He walks behind me and in a moment I'm gagged with a soft leather strap of sorts. "Or things," he adds in a wicked voice, buckling cuffs on my wrists and links them together behind my back.

"Here's how we're going to play it," he whispers, taking time to nip gently on the outer shell of my ear. "You're going to be entirely quiet while I do whatever I want to do to my spanking-brand-new wife. Or should I say my spanked brand new wife? Any little sound you make, even with the gag, will be heard by at least Nanette, and maybe even by the whole crew." He gently tapped the wall behind the bed. "They're right on the other side of it. Understand, my pretty?"

Oh, he's evil. He knows I can't be quiet, even at risk of intense nipple pain. But others hearing me? The ante is up, the stakes never being higher than now.

"Oh, almost forgot: if you need me to stop, I can still hear you speak through the gag—you just won't be quite as loud or articulate." He pats my cheek. "Now, stand up straight, and widen your stance."

I slide my legs wider by about two inches and he slaps my thigh with something he's holding in his hand. It's soft but it stings. "Legs open, Ella."

What is that? He puts it behind his back so I can't see it. So I open them much wider now... and wait. He circles around me once, and then again, sending my nerves into high alert. *What's he going to do?*

I have my answer in seconds as he drops down to his knees in one fluid motion and buries his face between my legs. I look down and see the straps of my garter trembling with the thighs they're resting on. How am I supposed to stay vertical when his relentless tongue is going at me? My whole world becomes just his tongue and what it's furiously circling right now. But just as I'm moving into my inevitable orgasm, he stops. Cold.

What? Why does he love to torture me? And now he probably feels officially sanctioned by our marriage license. Methinks, perhaps, that I'm in for it.

"Let's add a few more variables, shall we?" He pulls down the gag, leaving it hanging around my throat. "Do you like math, Ella?"

"No. I hate it."

"Tonight you're going to have a change of heart. Close your eyes, baby, and do nothing but feel."

"Hey, not that I was expecting you to go all sappy on me, but this *is* our wedding night. At least for tonight couldn't we be a titch more romantic?"

His mouth drops open in mock surprise. "I am being romantic, Ella. Don't you think?" He can't disguise his mirth.

I roll my eyes and he wags his finger at me and says, "Eh, eh, eh. We'll have none of that or I'll have to spank you again. And I know your pretty little posterior is a bit tender already."

Coming closer until his lips are just barely touching mine, he softly says, "I promise you, Ella, tonight I'm giving it all to you: everything I have to give, I will give, to my beautiful and sexy wife on our wedding night."

Okay, I'll play. After those heartfelt words, I'd jump into an active volcano for him.

He replaces the gag gently and then slips a blindfold over my eyes. "Not being able to see makes everything more intense but it also frees a person of inhibitions for some odd reason. I want you free to feel and revel in it,

Ella."

His voice is silky and deep and makes things shift deep inside me. A sharp contraction of lust nearly doubles me over as I listen intently to my new husband's sexy baritone, instructing me in our sensuous game. My wrists are still cuffed behind my back. My garter belt, panties, and stockings slip away, the shoes replaced on my feet, leaving me only in my heels.

"Ella, be silent... and don't come. Feel everything but control it. Are we clear?"

I nod because I have the gag in my mouth. This moment is intense; his lips are brushing against my ear as he whispers his requirements. I feel as if I can reach orgasm without him even touching me because his dripping-with-sexy voice alone is ripping me apart.

His warm breath leaves my neck and I wonder where he went... until I feel his satin lips gliding up my arm, from wrist to shoulder. Again they disappear only to return, this time on the back of my knee. This touch and go continues for, I don't know, maybe ten minutes? Time feels elastic when you can't watch it pass.

I'm covered in goose bumps when his fingers start skimming delicately over my skin. Fingers give way to a warm, wet tongue. Finally, an implement, I think a tiny flogger... and that can mean only one thing: it's meant to whip tiny places.

As he brushes the fronds across my skin, flicking occasionally so it stings, I feel my mind carried to another plane, a dimension where the sense of touch reigns supreme and other senses retreat. This is what he's aiming for. My only job is to feel, he said. When the stings grow in intensity, it doesn't hurt: it just feels stronger. He moves quickly, expertly, from my shoulders to my ankles, stopping at various points for extra attention. He lingers on my breasts, making them feel tight and swollen. The pressure is inexorably building and I know this is my other task, to not give in to the encroaching orgasm. Though he's asked me to accomplish this feat from the first, let's just say I haven't mastered the art just yet.

Up and down, up and down, my skin is warm and flushed and I'm reaching a point of no return. "Ian," I say, not knowing myself if I'm asking a question or punctuating my experience.

"Shhh," is all I get in response and the fronds start moving faster, the pattern frenzied and erratic. His hand suddenly grabs me between my legs, rubbing and squeezing me into sensations too big to handle. "Ian, I can't..."

And... boom. I fail at my task, alas.

His voice slides through my stupor. "Tsk, tsk, tsk, Mrs. Blackmon. One or two simple instructions and you neglect to heed them. What shall we do as a punishment? Hmm, I think I've got it."

It's not really a punishment; he puts me on my knees and stands in front of me. I love to do this for him but there is one punitive condition: my hands are tied behind my back. That makes it impossible for me to control the situation and it's a little scary. A little scary is good, though. Exciting.

Soft, hard, smooth, jerky, gentle, rough—all adjectives we used. When he hits his climax, I feel as if I've accomplished something important. I love giving my husband pleasure. After, he flings me on the bed and returns the favor.

Later, we lie in bed, entwined and peaceful. Ian's head leaning on mine, he speaks softly. "Would you like to know what else I saw in you, Ella?"

I look up into his face that I adore. "What else?"

"How much time do you have? Your physical beauty attracted me but it was what was underneath that truly ensnared me. I love who you are: your wit, your sense of humor, your taste in music. The way you give just a tiny smirk before you're about to blow up in anger, and the way your hair blows across your face when we drive in the convertible. You flip it back and flaunt a million-dollar smile as the wind caresses your face. I love the way you wear your clothes, the way you chew your lip when deep in thought, the way you straighten your spine when undertaking a challenge. I love your spirit for adventure, especially when it comes to sex, and the way you meet me dare for dare, never giving ground no matter how much I push. I love how your blue, blue eyes light up from within when you see an adorable child or animal, how you giggle when something strikes your funnybone, how you blush when you're embarrassed.

"But maybe most of all, Ella, is that I love how you love me. You make me feel that my love for you is something you cherish and will keep from harm. If I make you feel physically safe, as you've told me I do, you make me feel emotionally safe, something I've never felt before. I will hold that, protected and warm, next to my heart forever and ever, my beautiful wife.

Tears are streaming down my face when he finishes. I never realized how tenderhearted Ian is behind the polished façade he hides behind. My throat hoarse with unshed tears, I can't manage a response. I am so choked up by his beautiful homage to me. A marriage is a legal procedure, a piece of paper that says two people are united in the eyes of the law. The practical ramifications are important, of course: just ask anyone who's been denied the right. But tonight we both begin to realize that it's so much more than practicalities.

A marriage gives mates the emotional security to open up and let another person inside, not just literally, but more importantly, spiritually. Ian and I have been through a lot, not the least of which were two break-ups, one lasting a year, and one just a few hours. Those few hours when I fled to L.A. hurt more, I think, than the whole year apart because I felt betrayed by the man I love. That was when it dawned on me that I'd rather be whipped than abandoned.

While we're on the topic of whipping, I should add that he's not all that interested in it anymore. And, perverse creature that I am, I'm more interested in it precisely because of that. I'm not saying I want it, per se, but I'm not saying I don't, either. Let's just say those whips wielded by a tall, gorgeous Dominant I know have taken on mythical proportions in my mind... to the point where I might just have to try it again. We'll see.

Snapping me out of my reverie, Ian's voice perforates the silence in the small bedroom. "Ella," he gazes into my eyes, his shaded with emotion so profound it's easy to see it in the liquid mercury depths, "I love you, Ella, so much. I know it took me a long time to say it... but I've been here for a while, maybe even from day one."

He's caressing my face, sweetly and gently, his eyes never leaving mine. The emotion of the moment is so intense, I almost can't bear to look into those light and haunting peepers.

He's still speaking softly to me. "I promise to give my absolute best to be a good partner to you. Since you're willing to put up with the... lesser... facets of my personality, I can surely put up with your tiny imperfections."

Trying to lighten the mood just a bit, I screech, going for indignant. "Imperfections? Name one, buster."

"Buster?" He smiles. "Getting yourself into trouble is a big one."

I can't argue with that assessment, though I'm up for a try anyway. Before I can utter another syllable, though, he speaks up again.

"I'll help you out of every hole... even while getting into a few of my own—the nice, warm kind." He winks at me, smiling sweetly and pulls me into his arms, embracing me tightly. "*The difficult I'll do right now; the impossible will take a little while.*"

I smile. He's reciting the words to one of our wedding songs, *Crazy He Calls Me*. So Ian Blackmon, mogul, Dominant, sexually kinky demi-god, is also a romantic deep down where no one but I can see. I can live with that. I finish the lyrics. "*Crazy, he calls me. Sure, I'm crazy. Crazy in love am I.*"

Ireland and Scotland: what can I say? One might

have to be a poet to do them justice but I'll give it a go: green swaths of hill and dale, sun shimmering on azure blue waters so vibrantly it's blinding, friendly pink-cheeked people, astoundingly good ale, and fantastically superb sex—oh wait, we supplied that last part.

Then we decided to go to the beach.

Not just any beach, mind you, but a beach in the South of France. Yes, the beaches of France are rather incomparable and we've been lying in chaises reading and sipping icy cold cocktails for four days straight. Though we planned to end our trip in Scotland, we decided to stay another week and visit Provence. I'm thinking about Lucien, as I usually do whenever France is on my mind.

I realize that at the time, I wanted to put that whole episode with Lucien behind me as fast as I could... and did. But now removed from it by the distance of time and place, I can more easily reflect. I don't think Lucien was as blameless as he claimed to be in that whole tawdry affair. I think he participated to some significant extent, and participated with a measure of zeal. It's my belief that he actually said some of those awful things to me and did touch me inappropriately while I was grossly impaired.

Afterward, he was ashamed and guilty, which is what I'm figuring led him to turn on Natasha and help us out. I suppose we could say he redeemed himself in so doing. Regardless of any redemption, I still want nothing to do with him. He sent us a beautiful piece of art as a wedding gift, a set of four miniature paintings of a street in Paris, each reflecting a different perspective. We discussed what to do and ultimately decided to re-gift the paintings. Neither of us wanted to keep anything from Lucien fucking Phillips. The paintings now hang on the walls of Quentin's San Francisco Victorian. No reason to take it out on the art.

As for Natasha? We ultimately decided to let things be. Lucien promised Daniel she was alive and kicking—boy, was she kicking. But her new man is up to the challenge of subduing her, apparently. Am I thrilled by the outcome? Let's just say the idea is growing on me and it's certainly a damn sight better than it could have been for her. After all, she started this nasty game with Ian and he finished it. If someone throws down a gauntlet to Ian Blackmon, he or she shouldn't be surprised if he picks up the glove and accepts the challenge.

I reach for my sunglasses, blowing a kiss to my husband who is lounging next to me, reading some boring business magazine. So, Mr. and Mrs. Blackmon send their regrets to Ms. Natasha Yenin and sincerely hope she is enjoying the sands of Arabia with her new... oh, we'll just call him husband.

Epilogue

(Loose Ends)

Kiev, Ukraine

In a dreary convalescent hospice room somewhere in Kiev, two brothers sit at a table discussing a patient's progress with his attendants. A vibrating buzz sounds inside the bigger one's jacket pocket, alerting him to an incoming call, and he reaches in to pull out a phone.

"Dah?"

"It's me," the urgent female voice said in English. "Natasha's missing."

"Missing? For how long?"

"Over a week now. I don't know what to do."

"Gabriele, what can we do? We cannot return to the States right now. We're too hot. You have to handle it yourself for now."

"How?" The woman screeched, the pitch of her voice rising with her panic. "My daughter is missing, maybe dead, and I cannot go to the police. What is my next step?"

"Why don't you try enlisting that useless ex-husband of yours? It's only a shame he's not more like his father."

"What is he going to do?" she sneered. "He's only interested in screwing girls young enough to be his daughter and driving fast cars. He's no help at all."

Leo looked at his watch and sighed. "Okay. I'll make some calls. Where was she last seen, do you know?"

"Her neighbor said she saw her a week ago Thursday near the parking lot of her apartment building. The last call I got from her was the night before."

"I suppose it's good that no body has turned up. That

may mean she's still alive. Let's hope our friend in Portland doesn't have the junk to do anything too permanent."

"That's what I'm hoping and praying."

"We should have handled him long ago. Alright, we'll look into it and see what can be done."

He disconnected and tossed the phone on the table, lost in thought. His brother sat patiently across the table from him, watching and waiting. Leo scratched his stubbled chin, his mind across oceans for a swollen minute and then seemed to snap to it, focusing his beady raisin eyes on his brother, shaking his head in disgust. "More crap for us to handle. The first rule of a successful man: never leave unfinished business... and now our pretty little Tasha has gone missing—very likely belly up."

He looked down at his scuffed Doc Martens, noting the heels needed to be replaced, and then his dead eyes shifted from his shoes up to his brother's matching lifeless eyes. "From now on we take a scorched-earth policy with our enemies. As for this particular clusterfuck, as soon as possible, we hit Blackmon and hit him hard. Finish it."

"He's no pussy and he's got resources—it's possible he'll finish us first."

"So be it. Then we crash and burn trying."

"Yeah, well, it will be hard to hit him from across the North Atlantic. We dare show our pretty faces in the States and we're dog food. It's dangerous enough to be here now and you know it. No. We forget Blackmon and focus on what's important: making money."

Leo's fist smashed into the table, splintering the thin wood. "Our son has more money than he'll ever know what to do with. At this point it's no longer revenge but a matter of honor. If Blackmon hurt our Tasha, he's going down, that's for sure." Spittle was flying from his mouth as his anger escalated through his words.

"We can try to find Tasha but we give up on Blackmon." Lukas looked his brother in the eyes. "It's over."

He picked up his phone again and punched in a number. "It's me. Natasha Yenin, last seen in Portland, Oregon, a week ago Thursday. Blond, blue-eyed American, Russian ethnic, 28 years of age, 5'9" and fucking gorgeous. And my niece. Find her: I'll pay whatever. Just find her, alive or dead, preferably alive. I'll be waiting."

Paris, France

Lucien rubbed his red-rimmed eyes with the heels of his hands. He was still on New York time and his body screamed for rest but he had meetings all week, starting with late this afternoon.

He arrived early this morning and as soon as he left the airport, he met with Aziz's people. Michel Rimbaud arranged the meeting and assured him that all was going well in Saudi Arabia and that Aziz was highly satisfied with his purchase. What Lucien really wanted to know was how Natasha felt about being that purchase, but he really couldn't ask.

He'd betrayed her in the most massive way possible. But she had gotten in the first licks, using him as a pawn in her game to get Blackmon. Ella was the one who got hurt the most and Lucien truly liked Ella though he wasn't exactly sure why. But there was something bright and shiny about that woman and it made him feel all the more rotten about his part in her abduction.

He often wondered if he'd been successful in convincing Ella that she hallucinated the whole thing. Soon after he administered the drug to her, he could see she was having problems and most definitely hallucinating. That gave him the idea once he changed his mind about participating and realized he wanted to extricate himself, put distance between himself and the whole sordid affair.

What were the odds that both her boyfriend as well as her employer slash colleague would be involved in BDSM? He'd been intending to do bad things to her—

Natasha had convinced him that Ella wrote her book to publicly humiliate him... but fortunately Lucien had his doubts followed by his attack of conscience before doing anything irrevocable. Blackmon would not have rested until he wiped Lucien from the earth if anything had happened to his Ella. In the end, however, the one who suffered most was the one who should have suffered most: Natasha.

He'd be lying to himself if he said he didn't feel regret. He did. Imagination was often much worse than reality but Lucien knew firsthand what a man could do to a captive woman—his ex-girlfriends could attest to that, even his ex-fiancée Eliza to some extent, although he went easy on her. He wondered what the Arab was doing to the blond beauty. Lucien was madly in love with Natasha not all that long ago and abhorred the thought of her beautiful body being marked up permanently, by a Bedouin no less.

But she belonged to Aziz now... and Lucien had the funds in his bank account to prove it.

Not that he needed the money; he didn't. Lucien had so much money, in fact, that he could never spend it in ten lifetimes. It really didn't buy happiness.

But it bought everything else.

Riyadh, Saudi Arabia

She opened her eyes and saw nothing but profound darkness. Where was she? Her back ached from lying too long in the same position so she tried to shift over to her other side and found her progress impeded.

Why?

Icy cold fingers of panic skimmed down her spine. She put her hands out in front of her in that inky black space and they almost instantly touched something solid. Now the panic swelled thick in her throat, gagging her.

Buried alive?

Calm down, she told herself. If there's limited oxygen, panting and gasping will deplete it faster. She ran her hands down whatever impediment was inches away from her face. It felt relatively soft but not satiny and padded like a coffin. It wasn't hard enough to be a pine box or anything like that. It felt familiar, like... cardboard.

Then she moved her hands to each side and both hit the same solid wall immediately: she was in a box, a cardboard box. She decided to press the sides: if she were buried in the ground, she wouldn't feel any give. Or didn't she want to know? Holding her breath while her heart performed an Olympic meter race, she gently pushed with both hands... and felt the cardboard give a little outward.

Her huge sigh of relief added to the roar of blood rushing past her eardrums. So she was in a cardboard box but it wasn't buried underground, thank God. So... where was she?

The last thing she remembered was leaving her condo in the early morning. She'd been walking to her car... there was a rustle in the bushes that lined the walk... and that's it, that's the last thing. She must have been grabbed and taken somewhere. But where? And by whom?

She prayed to a God she'd long ago scorned, that no matter how unlikely, it would be Ian's handsome, angular face she would see when the box was opened, and not those of dead-eyed professional assassins. He'd warned her and she hadn't listened. She didn't think he had it in him.

Apparently he did.

She had no sense of time: it could have been minutes or hours before she began to hear noises outside her box. Things being moved, metal things, sliding things. Then her box was lifted and she could see the perforations in the cardboard now. For air. In the dark, they were invisible.

She listened carefully to the sounds being made, deciding they were unloading a vehicle of some sort, a truck or even a boat possibly. Where had they taken her?

A door opened and closed. The box stopped moving.

Minutes later, she heard a box cutter, slicing into the box and prayed it wouldn't cut her. When the flaps were finally lifted, she was staring into four pairs of dark eyes.

They were all men, and very mean-looking. Assassins. Shit. She said nothing; they said nothing. Then she heard one of them say words, quickly, furiously. In a foreign language. Something guttural.

Arabic, maybe?

The voice was answered by a calm, commanding baritone, speaking Arabic, too, but making it sound much nicer. As soon as the second voice spoke, the four men put their hands under her, lifting her out of the box and standing her up. Her legs were wobbly. She was wearing the clothes they took her in—a cropped white tee shirt and a short black skirt— but was barefoot. Where were her shoes? She looked up when one yanked on her hair.

He was tall and so dark: hair, skin, eyes. *Black eyes.* His hair was longish and straight, brushed back away from a noble looking face. He wore Western garb, exceedingly upscale; if pressed to guess, she'd wager the suit was Italian. Versace probably. But those eyes.

She couldn't tear hers away from them. They were as black as Satan's soul... but they didn't look mean. No, they looked... fascinated.

His eyes never leaving hers, he said something else and the men began ripping her clothes from her body. She tried resisting but was quickly slapped across the face twice by one of the men who shouted the English word *no* at her. In seconds she stood before the man stark naked, with the others holding her arms down to prevent her from covering her body.

He appraised her up and down for a long time and then spun his finger in a circle and they turned her around for him to check her over completely. When he was done, he simply nodded at the men. They lifted her up, one grabbing her wrists from behind and another her ankles and carried her down a hall to a room, handcuffed her wrists behind her back, and shoved her inside.

She looked around. The room was painted with pale

pink and white and there was a deep garnet red Persian carpet covering most of the wood floor. In one corner were two women staring at her. They were both dark, as everyone else she saw was dark. While she stood there trembling, one of the women walked over to her, grasped her elbow—neither gently nor roughly—and began leading her to a smaller room. Inside was a giant bathtub filled with scented water. The woman pointed to it and she stepped into it.

"Down." The second woman said in English. She obeyed. The water was hot, with steam rising above it, but it felt good to Natasha. The two women proceeded to bathe her and wash her hair. The scented soaps they used smelled like sandalwood and revived her senses somewhat after being sensory deprived in that box. After, they dried her thoroughly, they removed her cuffs, placed her on a table, and proceeded to wax off all of her body hair, every single part of her. When that torture was over, they brushed her teeth and her hair, sprayed her with scented oils, trimmed her fingernails to a very short length and buffed them. They put kohl on her eyes and gloss on her lips. Finally, they clipped soft leather cuffs on her wrists and ankles. Their final attention was to buckle a large leather collar around her throat, a collar attached to a chain leash. Like a dog.

When they were done with her, they led her out of the room and up a wrought iron staircase, the steps made of white marble, icy to her bare feet. The women wore what looked like ballet slippers and had on strange garments, like something out of ancient Rome—toga-like outfits. They took her inside a door, to a luxuriously appointed room. In the center of the room was a huge bed. The bed had four posters; from each of which dangled a chain. Each wrist was clipped to a chain so that she sat in the center of the bed, her arms raised; her legs were left unrestrained. When she tried resisting, the larger woman pinched her viciously on her hip. A blindfold was slipped over her eyes. The last thing she heard before the door closed again was the strains of some kind of strange music beginning in every corner of the room.

Her ears discerned a door open and close gently, followed by the click of his shoes moving across the hardwood floor before landing on the plush carpet. Abruptly, the volume of the music dropped, and a man's deep, smooth voice spoke, directly in front of her.

"Will you willingly obey your new master?" The words were spoken in clear, nearly unaccented English, it was the cultured voice from before, the man in authority.

Hearing a civilized voice lulled her into a false sense of security, and feeling more empowered in the situation than she otherwise might have or should have, she licked her lips and got a mouthful of flavored gloss. "I do not have a master," she responded.

She heard it slice through the air immediately before she felt the lash viciously bite across her thigh. Behind her eyelids she saw a bright flash of white that accompanied the atrocious pain. She couldn't contain the instinctive wail that escaped her throat.

"Let's try it again. Natasha, isn't it?" His voice was so calm, as if he didn't expend an iota of energy wielding the whip. Perhaps someone else was in the room beating her?

He waited for her to respond and finally she nodded.

"Please ensure your responses to my questions are audible. We don't want any miscommunication between us, do we?"

About to shake her head, she replied haltingly. "No... we do not."

"Very good. Now, I'll ask you again, "Will you obey your master?"

"May I ask who my master is? Because up until right this minute, I've never had a master. I'm not a slave."

"Yes, you may ask. I am your new master and it is in your best interests to address me accordingly and with appropriate deference for the disparity in our rank. From one day to the next, your status in the world has plummeted considerably. You are no longer a free and autonomous American woman. You are now my enslaved concubine, here to satisfy my every fancy. Your entire life will be subject to my whim and pleasure: every little detail. I will decide when you eat, sleep, use the bathroom, speak, walk—everything. The sooner you accept that, the better. Until that happens, you will be kept in chains and under lock and key.

"Personally, I don't care for the word slave. It has such negative connotations, don't you think? Instead, we'll just agree that you are here to satisfy my every want and need. If you do that—and I assure you that you will—I will satisfy your every want and need. Ours will be a reciprocal arrangement, if unequal. Do you understand now?"

"Yes, I understand."

The whip slashed through the air right past her ear, and cut across her left hip. Again, she shrieked in pain.

"Either I was unclear in my instruction or you are slow to learn. Allow me to repeat myself: you will ensure that you address me as your master with proper deference for my higher-ranking position. Again, I'll ask, do you understand?"

"Yes, *Master*, I understand." She spat out the term contemptuously, furious that he would subjugate her to such a depth. She could easily take a knife to his throat and make short work of him.

Aziz just as easily could identify the rebellion in her tone. Raising his voice, he barked an order and she heard the door open. The next thing she knew, she was unchained and lifted off the bed, her arms were raised and she was tethered by her wrists to something hanging from the ceiling, in an uncomfortable standing position, her feet barely touching the floor. It pulled on her body, making her shoulders and neck burn and throb unless she stood on her toes, in which case her calves would soon become strained. She knew this position was standard in any kind of physical subjugation.

The voice spoke up again. "Some people need

556

incentive to learn how to behave. I believe you're one of them, Natasha. You display resistance toward accepting your new status quo. It's not that I am unsympathetic, but my priority is in securing your acceptance as quickly as possible so we could begin to enjoy one another's company. If you require incentive to reach that point, I'm more than willing to provide it to you."

She knew a beating was on its way so she attempted damage control. "Yes, Master, I understand. I'm sorry." She used her most contrite tone of voice.

It was too little, too late.

The whip that she couldn't see coming rained down hard and fast on her body: he slashed her stomach and the front of her thighs before walking behind her and loosing a volley of pain on her shoulders, backside, and thighs. Each stroke seemed to bite harder than the last so that when he got to her ankles, the force behind the blows was unspeakably horrific. She twisted and turned in futile attempts to evade the whip but each time it found her, landing squarely on whatever body part he targeted. She had barely any purchase to take evasive action and in any case, she couldn't see where the whip was coming from, being blindfolded. Natasha quickly decided that death might be preferable to enduring this level of pain. Her body was slick with sweat and probably blood, too, and she screamed so much, she'd lost much of her voice.

She tried kicking him twice when she thought she knew his position but each time she raised her leg, bringing her knee to her chest to strike, he struck the sole of her foot with the unerring whip. The pain seemed to short-circuit her respiration: the oxygen she'd inhaled caught in her throat, and saliva aspirated into her airway, choking her. While she was choking, he continued to beat her, mercilessly, relentlessly. Now her feet felt like they were held to fire and she couldn't bear to stand on them but when on her toes, her calves were stretched into unendurable agony. Her entire existence became her pain—no color, or texture, or shape. Only blinding white pain shocking through her brain and the crack of the whip resounding in her ears.

How long it went on, Natasha couldn't say. She was barely conscious when it stopped but within that sliver of her mind that remained cognizant, she felt a colossal relief when it finally ceased and she was still alive. The room fell silent except for her sobbing breaths.

Hands untied her wrists and lifted her again, their gripping fingers causing her welted skin to shrink back in agonizing pain from the contact. She was deposited on the bed, and she quickly rolled on her side to avoid aggravating the lacerated flesh. Wrists and ankles were secured and the blindfold was removed. He was standing at the foot of the bed, the man with the black eyes. His two brawny henchmen who had lifted her, retreated from the room like ghosts. Natasha didn't see the offending whip.

"Who beat me?" She could barely make her voice audible, it was so hoarse from her screaming.

"I am your master; my hand will be the one to beat you. No one else."

For several minutes she eyed him from her unmoving position on the bed, saying nothing. It seemed impossible to unnerve this man. Finally she broke the self-imposed silence.

"You're not even out of breath." It was a question framed as a statement, lest he take offense.

His face was an impervious mask. "I never show weakness."

Above all, Natasha was a survivor and she didn't like showing weakness either. If she were alone in the room, she'd surely be weeping hysterically at the burning, screaming agony of her abused skin and the inescapable consequences of her sins. Instead she lay quietly, choosing her words carefully. "I don't yet understand what is required of me nor if I'm allowed to ask questions."

"I've already informed you of all you need to know. However, I'm a kind master so I shall entertain the notion of satisfying your curiosity. Ask what you will and if you receive an answer, consider yourself fortunate."

She made an effort to clear her throat but it was so raw she aborted the attempt. "Why am I here?"

"You are here as a result of your own actions. However, I will say that the party you probably think is responsible for your situation is not."

"Then who is?"

No answer.

"Does anyone know where I am?"

"No."

"Not even the responsible person?"

Silence.

She tried to lick her lips but her mouth was parched. "May I have some water?"

He nodded and walked into another room, possibly a bathroom, returning with a bottle of chilled spring water. It was a brand she recognized.

"I don't want you becoming ill from drinking the water here so I imported this bottled water from the States for you." He untied her wrists so she could sit up and drink.

"Thank you," she said, wincing from the bed's contact with her ripped skin but still reaching for the water, and saw the annoyed look on his face. "Master," she said hurriedly. "Thank you, Master."

He smiled.

"Where is *here*?"

No answer.

She kept trying. "The... person you mentioned, the one I would think responsible is going to be held to account for my... disappearance... by my family. He is the one they will seek to revenge me. May I call my mother to tell her I'm alive and that he is not responsible?"

"Our friend can take care of himself, Natasha. Though he was not responsible for your new life, he has been made aware of what has occurred. He will understand the ramifications and will take the necessary precautions. Now, having said that, I never want to hear another word from your lips about him or anyone else. I am the only one who matters to you from here on in. I am a very jealous man, Natasha, and you belong to me in every way possible. Am I crystal clear?"

"Yes, Master, you are crystal clear." In her foggy state of mind, Natasha yet found it amazing how easily the term now came to her lips. She was taught from a young age to be adaptable to her circumstances. It proved useful in her current situation.

"Good. I think our first session together went well. I will have the women visit you to see to your comfort and needs. I will be returning in a few hours. Please spend the time thinking about what you can do to please me."

"Yes, Master."

"Until then." He strode out the door and moments later, the two women returned. They gingerly lifted her from the bed and brought her to a bathroom, placing her in the middle of the floor over a drain. It was a wet room with the large rainfall showerhead directly above her head. One of the women reached toward the spigot and turned it on. Tepid water, more cool than warm sprayed out and it both hurt and felt good on Natasha's abraded skin.

"My name is Mena," the bolder one said. "We will make you feel better."

Natasha nodded, exhausted from the beating. After they gently washed her, they left her standing while their hands worked industriously, slathering cream all over the angry red welts. When the cream touched the broken skin, it exacerbated her agony and she whinnied in pain. The quieter one went out and shortly returned with Natasha's half-finished bottle of water and two white pills.

"Master said to give you these for your pain," she said and handed over both.

Natasha swallowed the pills with the water, no longer caring if they were pain relievers or poison. Either way, they'd help.

She couldn't be sure how much time had passed for no visible windows were apparent in the rooms, hence, no daylight. She assumed there were windows behind what looked like heavy velvet and Dupioni silk drapery. Regardless, Natasha had fallen asleep shortly after the women had brought her back to the bed. They cuffed her wrists and ankles together so she had limited movement. Luckily for her, she'd been able to keep to her side and avoid adding more discomfort. The pills she'd been given had dulled the sharpness of the pain to the point where it was tolerable.

He didn't knock: he just opened the door and walked in. She'd awakened about twenty minutes earlier and drank some water left by the bed for her. His black eyes, animated by God knows what, watched her intently. She tried to separate herself from the horror he was connected with and assess him. Physically, he was very handsome: relatively tall, lean, with chiseled features. He did not resemble a man who had to kidnap women for any reason. The opulent room she was in suggested great wealth. Moreover, he seemed polished and educated. It was mystifying... but everyone has his or her reasons. Reasons, good or bad, are what propel people forward to their fates.

He watched her watch him, a measure of amusement in his expression. After a minute or two, he sat down on the edge of the bed, right next to her.

"In future, you will not be given medicine for your pain from beatings. You need to live with the pain to learn from your mistakes. I made an exception today because you are so new, and thus your mistakes were not willful but plainly due to ignorance. That exception will be a kindness you will only experience this one time.

"I want you to get off the bed right now and on your knees. It's time for you to show me how well you plan to please me, my little Russian bitch."

As she moved stiffly, Natasha dropped her face to hide her smirk. This Natasha knew: how to manipulate men through sex. This man might think he'd humiliate and control her through shocking sexual acts but there were things he didn't know, things no one knew, about what Natasha had endured starting from when she was about six years old. Sex in all its forms was familiar territory to her.

She began to see a possible light at the end of this long, dark tunnel. It was a tiny, flickering one, to be sure, but it was there. She could see a way to manipulate this man and in so doing, manipulate her situation. Time and patience were all she needed—and a strong stomach.

She had all three.

Shaky but on her knees in front of him, he unclipped her bound wrists long enough to bind them behind her back rather than in front. Submissively, she opened her mouth as he roughly pushed himself past her lips and down her throat, causing her to gag. The gagging seemed to excite him as he kept doing it. He'd stop for a while and then start up again, pushing her to the brink of choking. She was about to vomit when he ejaculated and she forced herself to swallow it, forced down the urge to regurgitate everything. At least this time, she succeeded.

L.A. Times, June 30, 2014

Casting News: As Variety reported last week and we can now confirm, casting has now been completed for the film version of the bestselling novel *Three and A Half Weeks*. Producers are allowing the book's author to release the actors' names in her blog tomorrow yet author Ariel Strong, contacted while honeymooning in the South of France, would not comment on the actors cast. Ms. Strong recently wed wealthy Portland businessman and philanthropist Ian Blackmon. Her agent issued this press release from Ms. Strong:

"Everyone associated with this film worked tirelessly to find the right actors to bring our wonderful characters to life. I hope my fans will recognize that casting directors have to work with a variety of factors, talent and availability being first and foremost. I ask everyone to reserve comment until the film is completed and released and they can see for themselves how close to the mark we've actually hit. Until then, thank you for your support and please remember to pick up my new book, *From this Day Forward,* upon its release in December."

Associated Press/Entertainment News:

BLOGGING YOUR PARDON
(with apologies to W. Shakespeare)

Brooklyn Hyatt, an up and coming celebrity blogger was the first to break the news that perhaps the novel *Three and a Half Weeks* was not the fictional tale we all were led to believe, and, of course, the way it's been touted and marketed.

In last week's blog entitled *And Thereby Hangs a Single-Tail*, Mr. Hyatt takes issue with author Ariel Strong labeling her racy novel fiction and claims it's actually a true account of her meeting and having an affair with none other than her brand new husband, wealthy financier and philanthropist Ian Blackmon.

We at **Hyatt Blogs the Question** *want to do a scratch and sniff to get at the nitty gritty of the rumor. Is Ian Blackmon the man behind the whip? Is Ariel Strong the girl who fled his domination?*

Let's look at the facts: Ms. Strong was living in Portland while attending undergraduate school. Shortly after graduation, she left the country (or fled?) for an Oxford fellowship, studying under the eminent art historian, Charles Norwood-Finch. One year later, she's back, and again seen out and about with Mr. Blackmon. The facts seem to follow the novel's arc, and the characters Rafe and Gia, including their reunion one year later.

Ms. Strong's new novel, Three and a Half Weeks...

Again, is another supposedly fictional novel with a similar theme and feel to it, but with a whole new raft of characters. Should we believe this one is fictional, too, Ms. Strong?

We reached out to both Mr. Blackmon and Ms. Strong. Their respective publicists provided us with the identical response: no comment; however, a press release was issued the following day by Ms. Strong's literary agent, Mo Jackson, of Authors' Haven Literary Agency. In it Ms. Jackson assures the reading public that both novels are fictional works of art, calling any other claims "nonsensical" and points out the author, not being clairvoyant, "couldn't possibly foretell the book's denouement a year in advance" as the novel does in fact culminate. Jackson then refocuses the press release on the imminent release of the film, reading like a... well, like a press release.

We think the sizzzlingly hot (that extra z is there on purpose) Mr. Ian Blackmon would make one hell of a sexy Dominant. Additionally, Ms. Strong, who happens to be demurely beautiful, would look oh so good in a bit and harness.

Our response to Ms. Jackson's denial? **Hyatt blogs to differ.**

End

Wait! Keep reading!

Want more of the hot, hot, hot Daniel Butler? Pick up the novels about Daniel and his Olivia: *Complements* and *Complements, Book II: A Force of Nature* (available on Amazon, Barnes & Noble, and Smashwords).